Shimmer

2017
The Collected Stories

Shimmer

EDITED BY
E. CATHERINE TOBLER

Shimmer
2017: The Collected Stories

ISBN-13:
978-1978441804

ISBN-10:
1978441800

Visit Shimmer Magazine at
www.shimmerzine.com

CONTENTS

HIC SUNT LEONES
L.M. Davenport

It's true that the house walks. It's also true that you can only find it if you don't know about it. Once, a boy in my high-school art class drew a picture of it, but didn't know what he'd drawn; the thing in the center of his sketchpad had ungainly, menacing chicken legs caught mid-stride and a crazed thatch roof that hung askew over brooding windows. I knew it was the house right away because his eyes had that sleepy, traumatized look that people get once they've seen the house. I was used to seeing this look, mostly on my mother's face.

He didn't come back to school the next day, and even though everyone else was puzzled I knew that he had gone to search for the house. I still look for him under bridges and on traffic islands when I go into the city.

Inside my own house, I have many pictures of *the* house. In the oil painting over the fireplace, it is a houseboat on the Thames, moored at night in a meadow outside Oxford. The photograph next to my desk shows it as a glass-and-stucco fortress with a flat roof, temporarily alighted in the mountains that cut Los Angeles in half. I even have a linocut that captures the house as a yurt somewhere in Mongolia.

In my kitchen, there's a map covered in colored pushpins. It marks all the places where I think the house has been. There are so many pins now that I can't make out the borders of most of the countries, and even the oceans are furred with bright circles of plastic.

A middle-aged woman backpacking through Vietnam found the house's footprints in the jungle. She photographed them, and when I saw the images on her blog, immense hollows in which the crushed vegetation had only just started to grow back, I ran to the map and looked to see if there was already a pin, the kind that had started showing up on their own, on the spot. There wasn't, so I opened my box and put one there.

My mother went into the house, before I was born. She told me that inside, there are doors that open underground and others that swing open like precipices on the cold high reaches of the air. Sometimes she wrote down things that she had seen in the house, and once I found a list in the drawer where we kept the stamps that read:

Blood-bright lipstick smears on the rims of china cups.

A crow mask dangling from a newel post, shedding feathers.

Maps tacked four deep to a wall, filmy lace curtains billowing in gusts of wind and scattering thin sunlight over the hardwood floor.

One lit candle guttering, its light mirrored in the lenses of rows on rows of spectacles laid out on dirty black velvet.

She told me that she had never met any other people in the house. But sometimes she heard them in the walls.

ᘓ ᘔ

Though the house has many doors, it has only one true entrance and one true exit. They are the same door. (The architect of the first labyrinth must have been inside the house.)

When I was a child, I liked to picture my mother as she must have been when she found the house: younger than I am now, her thick braid a glossy brown like the wing-case of a beetle, with tinygold pinecone earrings and wide, deep-set eyes. When she caught the house taking a step, she would have halted on the thick, spongy pine needles and wondered at its bulk, its many chimneys, its great clawed feet. It would have towered over her, and she would have been afraid yet unable to turn away. Then her hand on the door, her first steps into the interior, and me turning over within her, safe in my own house of flesh.

On the night that I set up the map, I placed two pushpins: one on my hometown, where the vanished boy from my art class drew the house without ever having seen it, and one on the Tennessee forest where my mother had walked into the house while I rode inside her. When I came downstairs the next day to

8

make coffee, there were seven pins on the map, some of which were tacky with clear film and would not come out of the paper. After that I left the box of pins from the office-supply store mostly alone, and new ones appeared on the map every so often when I wasn't looking.

That first morning, I drank my coffee very quickly, in huge gulps that scalded my tongue and cheeks and palate. One of the five new pins marked a location in the middle of the Atlantic, right below the medieval cartographer's admonition I'd blocked in the night before: HIC SUNT LEONES. When I finished my coffee, I got in my car and drove to the city to see my mother.

⋐ ⋑

I found another list in my mother's recipe binder when I was looking for the proportions of the many dairy products used in chocolate mousse:

A room built, walls floors and ceiling, out of animal skulls. Birds and raccoons and cows and elephants and cats and other animals so twisted or so enormous that I do not recognize them. My boots leave a trail of crushed eye sockets.

Dirt roof, this room barely a cavity, wired with one bare lightbulb.

Water, half-light, perhaps an inch of air at the top of the room.

So low and narrow that I must crawl nearly flat to the floor. The baby doesn't like that.

A room laid with a banquet, but the opulence of the dishes makes me sick.

⋐ ⋑

The first time I asked my mother how she had left the house, she looked blank for a moment, and then said only, "The way most people do, I think." After that, I asked her the same question at odd intervals, when she seemed distracted, hoping to jar her into a more interesting answer. But her response never changed, and eventually I gave up.

9

I can't ask my mother these things anymore. Nobody can, because the person who sits in an armchair in the living room of the apartment in the city is no longer my mother.

This woman woke up six years ago at the bottom of a flight of stairs in the house she used to live in with my father. The first words out of her mouth, and the last ones for a long time after that: "My head. I hit my head."

I know this because I was there. I was the one who had turned and knocked her off-balance at the top of the stairs. It was my scream that had followed hers as she fell, my hand that had missed hers by half an inch.

The house changes people. That's true, too. Some people are afraid of going in and coming out different than they were before. If only they knew that they do the same thing in their own houses, day in and day out.

I do not like visiting my mother. But I went, on the first day that the new pins showed up in the map. I got there just as the man who brought Meals on Wheels was leaving, so I didn't have to wait for her shuffle to the door. Her chair faced the living room window, and one pale hand angling off into space told me that she was sitting there. I walked up on her right, making my footsteps louder so she would notice me coming, and sat down on the ottoman. We looked out the window together. In the glass, the faintest hint of our reflections, side by side.

"Hi, Mom."

The voice, slower and fainter than I wanted it to be, every time.

○3 ℬ○

Part of me (the same part that keeps looking for the house although I know perfectly well that the more I learn about the house the less likely it becomes that I will ever find it) still believes that one day I will find my mother here exactly as she was before she landed on the hardwood floor and lay with her body splayed wide as a starfish. I want to walk in and find her ready to pick up the fight we were having as we went up the stairs, and I want to hear whatever she was going to say after I finished asking when she was going to deal with my father's things.

"There's a map now, Mom. That's all."

She smiled at me, and because my mother had never smiled in that closed, vague way, without showing any teeth, I wanted to hit her. Instead, I turned to the window so I wouldn't have to look at her, and took her hand. She didn't move away.

CB ᙣᙜ

Some things that are not true about the house:

That it is not a house at all, but an entrance to the underworld.

That it is owned by a witch who scouts the countryside in a flying kettle, and who steals the genitals of young men to string on her bloody necklace.

That it can never be found by the same person twice. In 1880, a Rhode Island man who suffered from short-term memory loss entered the house twice in one year; both visits were recorded in his pocket diary.

Under my house are innumerable tunnels, some flooded, some collapsed, and some simply empty. The ground is rich, veined with metals. Some of the mines, including the one that runs beneath my house, have been abandoned and now harbor only echoes. One hill away, though, when miners blast into the ground, I feel the vibrations through the walls and floors.

CB ᙣᙜ

When he was alive, my father would have told you there was no such thing as the house. If you looked at all doubtful, he would have said that the *real* house is inside us, that we visit it when we read Bulgakov or Borges or Angela Carter. (My father should have been an academic, but he wasn't. He never finished college.)

My parents' opinions differed on many subjects. My mother wrote, in the very first note I ever found, that she gave

11

birth to me the way animals do, alone in the dark in a distant part of the house. My father told me, when I asked him, that I was born in a private mental hospital.

I decided after a while that they were both right. I pictured my mother, her distended belly rising and falling, asleep in her room, unaware of the house or anything else. Something enormous treaded softly on the wet grass, walked up to her window, which suddenly gaped wide. (The house changes objects as well as people. The world is mutable.) The house reached through the window, lifted my mother out as she slept, took her inside itself to give birth.

ൟ ൟ

The house cannot walk on water, but it can walk under it.

The only true records are those that are never kept.

I was born in the house, and one day I will find it. I will be a true record, after I have forgotten everything I know, and no map will chart my course. Maybe I will find my mother, too, in the place on the map where there are only lions.

Until then, I will lie in my bed at night, listen to the explosions in the far-off mine, and feel the trembling of the earth, my house set on the earth, my body set inside this house. And I will smile in the darkness, and think how much that trembling feels like footsteps.

Shadow Man, Sack Man, Half Dark, Half Light
Malon Edwards

You keep running, even though you know you can't escape the fifty-foot-tall Pogo. But you were built for this.

You are taller than all of the girls and most of the boys in your Covey Four class. Your legs are longer. Your steam-clock heart is stronger. Your determination is unmatched. Even against the rocks they throw. Even against the insults they hurl. Even when they entimide you and chase you home after school every day, all because your mother could not save their friends.

They have not caught you yet. And they never will. Because you will not let them.

But you are trying to do the impossible here. You are trying to outrun the Pogo, a kakadyab, an ugly, hideous entity no timoun has ever escaped. Not even your best friend, Bobby Brightsmith. And he knew the chant to send it slinking back into Lake Michigan.

Yet, you are confident. You have just rescued Bobby. You hacked his writhing, tentacled body off the Pogo's scaly, diamond-shaped face with your machete, Tonton Macoute. You wrapped Bobby's slimy, bloody snake-form around your torso. And then, you ran like you have never run before.

Kounye a la, your lungs burn, your legs are wobbly, and your steam-clock heart is going tanmiga tanmiga tanmiga in your chest. It has never beat this hard. It has never beat this fast. You can feel the overdrive of its tiny springs. You can feel the rotating thump of its miniscule cam.

You are worried.

You have one more block to run before you make it home. You're almost there. When you arrive, you can ask Manmi to look at your heart. After all, she did design and build it.

13

But when you round the bend leading to your street, you see, through the gloaming of the half dark, a shadowed figure standing in front of your house. You stop. Or you try. But you can't. Not at first. You have underestimated your own determination.

Your momentum continues to propel you forward. Only a meter or two. Your arms flail. Your legs give way. You skid across the hard, uneven cobblestones.

Your hands and knees press against the cold ground, bruised and skinned by your fall. It is in this position you heave—sèl fwa, de fwa, twa fwa—before you retch sticky, ropy bile that turns invisible in the weak light of the gas lamps when it hits the dark cobblestones. The gas lamps have never been this dim before. Not on your street. Not on Oglesby.

Your mother and father made sure of that when you moved to La Petite Haïti in Chicago from La Petite Haïti in Miami. They do not mind giving a few more pièces de monnaie to the Lamplighters Guild. They want you, Michaëlle-Isabelle, their ti fi cheri, to feel safe, especially on your walk home from school within the heavy shroud of the half dark. They want their patients to feel welcome when they visit, pandan jounen an, during the day, and a leswa, at night.

But this is not welcoming.

It is not safe.

It is not comforting.

And this is all because of the man standing in the middle of the street in front of your house.

You are certain the shadowed figure is a man. A woman would not participate in this awful game. A woman would not play jwe lago—hide-and-seek—in the darkness between the downcast lights of the gas lamps, clothed in shadows, hoping you find her. She would not even consider the notion, knowing an eleven-year-old girl would be walking home by herself in the half dark.

An plis, you have never seen a woman radiate such malevolence. It is apparent in the way this Shadow Man holds himself. It is apparent in the way he stands, hunched and

14

menacing. You are quite certain you will never, in your lifetime, see a woman adopt this evil, wicked stance.

The Shadow Man is, as your mother would say, pa bon ki nan kò l. He ain't no good.

Epitou, as if to confirm this, you hear the Shadow Man say, "Ah, ti chouchou, I thought you'd never come home from school."

And he says this in your father's voice.

ೞ ೲ

You are a smart girl. You should not be surprised your father is the Shadow Man. Not if you had been nosy when you were living in La Petite Haïti Miami. Not if you had been paying close attention. Not when it was just you and him.

You look confused. Allow me to remind you.

Your mother was called to La Petite Haïti Chicago by the old and wizened Lord Mayor himself, John Baptiste Point du Sable. He enticed her with anpil lajan (more money than you or she had ever seen) and the title Surgeon General. He needed her to help him combat the polio outbreak in the city-state.

He wanted her to build steam-clock hearts for the children whose sweet flesh hearts had been withered by the disease. He assured your mother he had people who could implement an assembly line production to churn out the mechanical hearts faster.

He was desperate. Eighty percent of the children in his city under the age of twelve were stricken with polio. Limbs and organs, but especially the heart had no chance. He did not want one more timoun to die.

You were sad to see your mother go, but you are more your father's ti chouchou than your mother's ti fi cheri. An plis, you and he would join your mother in Chicago as soon as she stemmed the tide of the polio epidemic there.

Those were fond times for you, despite your mother tending suffering, faceless children one thousand three hundred miles away. Your father laughed a lot. He let you do anything you wanted. He had no rules.

Save two: Go to school every day, and don't leave your room until daybreak after he tucked you in for bed.

Ah. You remember now. It has been three years past, but you remember. I see it. M ka wè recall in those big, beautiful brown eyes of yours. But you don't know.

Not yet.

છ ಏ

You take three steps forward. You are hesitant. You are tentative. You are wary.

You refuse to believe the Shadow Man is your father.

And yet, your father's rich, melodic baritone has just slipped across the cobblestones and through the half dark from him over to you. This was the same comforting voice that wished you fè bon rèv—beautiful dreams—after he pulled the covers up to your chin each night in La Petite Haïti de Miami.

You do not think about how he did not do this often for you in Chicago. Soon after you two arrived, he disappeared.

In La Petite Haïti Miami, you told yourself it was the coziness of your father's voice that made you stay in bed until the sun painted the horizon with soft strokes of morning warmth and fun, and not the dark shadow that skittered across his face before he turned, left your bedroom, and closed the door behind him. But you cannot lie to yourself in La Petite Haïti de Chicago.

"Do you see what he is holding?"

Bobby's husky voice startles you. The last time you heard it he was screaming as you cleaved him off the Pogo's face when the Pogo crouched down to eat you.

You squint into the half dark, but you cannot make out any details. You believe the Shadow Man to be tall, trè wo, but the half dark plays with your eyes and the light from the gas lamps. The half dark is a tricky thing. It is a dangerous thing.

But you already know this.

16

You realize Bobby's eyes, as small and black and beady as they are, can see far better than yours in the half dark now that he is one of the Pogo's face tentacles. Was one of the Pogo's face tentacles.

"I can't tell," you whisper to Bobby, hoping the Shadow Man does not hear you. "What is he holding?"

Bobby slithers around your ribs, across your chest, and up to your neck, leaving a trail of coagulated black blood, but not as much as before. He wraps himself around your throat, like a scarf, and tugs you forward, another step or two. His touch is cold and slimy, but gentle.

Enpi, you see it. The Shadow Man is holding a gunny sack.

☙ ❧

Once, and only once, did you leave your room after your father had tucked you in for the night.

You were a bit of an odd child then. The dark did not scare you. But you were more of a curious child. An intrepid child.

When you think back upon that night, time has dulled your memory. You are no longer sure if you truly saw a shadow flit across your father's face. The thought of it does not bring you unease. Not much unease, manyè, since the more you think about that night the less defined that memory is.

It does not make sense for such a malevolent cast to have been upon your father's face. That comforting voice you know so well is also playful, always hinting at an oncoming laugh. An infectious laugh. A belly laugh. A laugh you associate with your father more than anything else.

An plis, as you play that night through your mind over and again, for what seems to be the thousandth time, you only remember being eksite. You only remember the flip-flop thrill in your stomach as you disobeyed your father and got out of bed.

The house had been dark. It felt empty. It felt lifeless. You and your father had said so the night your mother left for

17

Chicago. But the night you sneaked out of bed something was different.

You knew where you were going: to your father's side of the house. You knew the route to his office by heart. It was forbidden to you, one of only two such areas in the house. The other was your mother's office.

Your parents barred you from their professional space because they thought you might play with the sharp, stainless steel instruments. They were concerned you might open the dark bottles of medicine or uncap the flat tins of unguent, and smell and drink and taste.

You were curious, but you were not foolhardy. Except for this one time.

You made walking through the darkness a game. If you bumped into something, you lost a point. If you stubbed your toe and cried out, you lost five points.

That did not happen, though. You knew that house like you know the lines on your palm—every turn, every corner, every hallway. You arrived at your father's office with all of your points intact. Your glee did not last long, though.

The gunny sack was in the middle of the floor, knotted tight. Something was in it. It bulged. It moved. It seemed to be stained dark and wet in places.

You could not tell by the sputtering light of the kerosene lamp, but the dark and wet looked like blood. And that's when you heard it: the whimpering, the crying.

Someone was in the gunny sack.

You gasped. You heard the sloshing of water in next room. In your father's bathroom. He was in the bathtub. He was washing off the blood. He was the Sack Man. He snuck into houses at night and carried naughty children away. You were sure of it.

You heard sloshing again. Louder, this time. Your father was finished bathing. He was getting out of the bathtub.

His bathwater would be pink. Its warmth would have dissipated. He would be cold. He would want to warm up. He would want to eat. He would want a full belly. He would walk back into his office any moment now. He would eat the child in the gunny sack. And if you were still here when he stepped again into this room, he would eat you, too.

His daughter. His only child. His ti chouchou.

So you turned and ran back to your bedroom. You did not lose your way. You did not make a wrong turn. You did not run into a wall. You did not stub your toe.

You jumped into your bed. You pulled the covers over your head. And you never got out of your bed again after dark.

CB EO

"I'm not a naughty child, Papa."

You say this to your father from quite a distance away. You still cannot see his face. You do not want to see his face. It may not be the face you remember.

"Ah, ti chouchou, I know you got out of bed."

Your father's voice has its familiar playful tone, as if he's admonishing you with a smile. You believe, if he is smiling, his teeth are long and sharp and dripping with saliva Not like the teeth you remember.

"Papa, you cannot eat me. It would not be right."

You do not want to cry. You refuse to cry. But you have never been so scared in your life. Not when your father went missing after you came to Chicago. Not when you liberated Bobby Brightsmith from the Pogo. Not even when you saw the gunny sack in your father's office three years ago.

"Come here, ti chouchou. Come closer."

"Wait."

Bobby's whisper is close to your ear. He uncoils from around your neck, glides down your left shoulder, and twines himself around your left arm. His severed end rests in your palm, and his mouth latches onto your bicep. He bites down, hard, with his many small, needle-sharp teeth. You cry out.

"Don't worry," Bobby whispers. "If your father eats you, my poison will kill him soon after."

You do not have much time, so you move forward and halve the distance between you and your father. You can see his face now. It is lean. It is gaunt. He looks as if he has not eaten in days. Weeks. This is not the hale, handsome father you know.

"Pa kriye," your father says. "Wipe your tears."

"I'm not crying!"

You have never screamed at your father before. Not in anger. But it is true; you are not crying. Yet, you are close. Your eyes burn with tears. You refuse to let them fall. You do not want to show your father or Bobby or the half dark just how afraid you are right now.

Instead, you reach behind your head, between your shoulder blades, and slide Tonton Macoute from the sheath you sewed into your knapsack. Your father gave you this machete. Your father taught you how to use this machete. And if he tries to eat you, your father will die by this machete.

"Pitit fi, eske ou sonje—"

Your father switches to English. You have always thought he sounded unlike himself in that language.

"My beautiful little daughter, do you remember when I gave you Tonton Macoute?" You nod. "Do you remember what I told you?" You nod again. "'I give this to you so you will always remember and I will never forget.' Do you know why I said that?"

He does not wait for you to answer. Your father bares his teeth, and in two quick strides he is standing over you. He is as tall as the street lamps. His empty gunny sack is slung over his shoulder. His teeth are as long and sharp as you imagined.

"Well, it's time for you to remember, pitit fi, because now I am the Sack Man, and I have forgotten my daughter."

The Sack Man lunges at you, his hands wide, holding the gunny sack open to swallow you whole with it. But your father taught you well. You are faster. You unleash three swift Rising Butterfly strikes with Tonton Macoute and rend the gunny sack to shreds.

The Sack Man is surprised by your ferocity. But you do not pause.

You sidestep the Sack Man as he tries to snatch you up with his thin, gnarled hands. You let him go by you. As he does, you step into Form of Queen Alexandra's Birdwing, whirling to gather momentum. Your footwork is precise. As you complete your turn, facing the Sack Man again, you disembowel him with one vicious slice.

Your father falls to the cobblestones. He holds his intestines in his hands. He looks small. He looks frail. He is dying.

And so are you.

Your legs give way. You collapse next to your father. Bobby's venom is swift and powerful. The cobblestones are cool against your cheek.

Enpi, the half dark gathers above you and your father, coalescing into an opaque, full dark cloud. You cannot see this, for your eyes are now closed as you lie dying, but black, wispy tendrils of the half dark rush from every part of the city-state to be here. To be here with you. To be here with your father. To be a part of this cloud.

To become one with me.

For the first time in the three years since I have arrived in Chicago, I can see the half-light of dusk. I can see the evening as it truly should be, for the half dark no longer obscures it.

La Petite Haïti de Chicago used to look this way, especially now, especially in winter. Enpi, I arrived, and I did not save the children of Chicago. I could not save the children of Chicago.

It was not my fault. The Lord Mayor's assembly line production was flawed. It churned out defective steam-clock hearts. Those hearts—my hearts—killed Chicago's children with their brittle springs and their wobbly cams.

And so, the half dark descended. And with it, came the Pogo. I was distraught. My despair was great.

This must be a shock to you, finding out your father is the Sack Man, and your mother is the half dark. But the Children of Night are drawn to one another.

Sometimes, the results are horrible—like the Pogo.

Other times, the results are lovely—like you.

But never did I think the repercussions would be catastrophic—like this.

But this I can fix.

Do not be alarmed; that cold you feel entering your nose and your mouth is just me. Just the half dark. Just La Sirène de la Nuit, healing you, removing the poison.

And do not worry; your father will be well. I will get him a child. A sick one. A dying one. One whose heart is flawed.

That is what the half dark does. That is what I have been doing here. Your father will heal once he has eaten. His strength will return.

You may not like this. You may hate your father for who he is. You may hate me for who I am. But you are of us. You are a Child of Night. And now, you have found your way.

The people of Chicago do not love your father and me, but they will love you. You are brave. You fight well. Their children will no longer be terrorized by the Pogo.

But you will not be able to save them all.

Do not fret. Pa enkyete w. Do not worry. Do not feel guilty. You cannot help this. You are not like me. You cannot be everywhere in this city at once. You must sleep. You must eat. You must go to school.

Tandiske, you will save enough of them. Mothers will thank you in their bedtime prayers. Fathers will commission machetes from the local blacksmith for their precious ti chouchou. Children will chant your name out on the schoolyard. You will become their champion.

So get up. Pick up Tonton Macoute. Go reclaim another tentacular child for her mother. Go fight your monster.

TREES STRUCK
BY LIGHTNING BURNING
FROM THE INSIDE OUT
Emily Lundgren

It is sweet and fitting to die with one's pack under the full moon, but the sky is clouded by the city lights: orange and yellow and red like fire. Roque is running. Like a cracked whip, without sense. Under a sliver of jagged sound, under the leering fray of glossy towers, he smells a dog without a leash, the sharp of silvered bolts. He sees a woman with a cardboard sign reading something-something about the world, who catches his eye, whose own eyes widen, whose mouth opens and makes a howling noise: something-something about wolves! wolves! The road towards dawn outstretches before him, choking on cars and steam and fur and bone. Roque is running, running. His paws thump in tandem with the code of his heart, and he transforms.

 C3 80

I shit you not, the den was in this underground shithole out by the train tracks. Outside, on the gate leading to it, there was an honest-to-god sign that said NO DUMPING, but as soon as we crossed beyond the gate we had to navigate piles of actual junk. Old coils of bedspring, plastic toys, a sagging couch, at least five ancient television sets, a mountain of cassettes. On the gravel, spools of black videotape were tangled in neatly arranged piles, like someone decided to sit there and chew apart all the plastic. The den itself was past all that shit, in the rubble of an enclave painted with the words FAIR IS FOUL & FOUL IS FAIR FUCKERS. Some real nice digs.

There shouldn't be a fire pit. I know we're all thinking it— the wild ones, they're not supposed to have thumbs, you know? After the carnage, some of us stand near the arrangement of cinderblocks that circle the fire pit like sad-ass lawn chairs. Our crossbows hang limp in our hands. Someone's phone goes off but we don't even pick it up. This fire pit is fucking weird, none of us says just yet. It looks like a stump, the midsection carved in a big X with raw pulsing pinks and reds at its heart, peeling the core back white. The stump sits in a charred indentation in the ground, and it reminds me of one summer when lightning struck a tree on the farm and ate it from the inside out. Once in a lifetime, tops.

Behind us, snaking from beneath the circular enclave that might've once had something to do with trains, there's a root-path leading crooked into the den. If we listen, which we all do, we can hear shouting. Will and the rest of us are still down there, probably counting up the corpses. They didn't really fight us when we found them, and I know we're all sort of disappointed. They howled and cried and clawed at the dirt but their den was nothing but damp earth and dead ends. Wolves used to live in caves or in the woods, but shit, where can you find places like that anymore? From the earth's belly, I hear Will start up about skinning their hides.

Someone's phone goes off and this time it gets answered. This shakes us apart, gets us moving. So what if they carved a stump and made a fire and sat here at night watching it with their dumb eyes? We round the perimeter, keep watch. Another of us takes out his phone, too, and snaps a few pictures. "This fire pit is fucking weird," he's the first to say. "I'm putting this thing on Instagram." I shrug. I got rid of all that shit after my parents died. Facebook before the funeral—then afterwards, Twitter, then Tumblr, even Snapchat, and definitely my Grindr profile. Online, time vaults would lurch open at the stupidest times. I'd be checking my phone in bed and then next thing I knew, my Ma's face would peer up at me and I'd go to her profile, which I should've deleted a long time ago, but never did. I'd reread the RIPs, the thoughts and prayers, and I guess there was probably a way to disable all that shit, like unfollow her, but I never did. I just shut it all down. Now I only talk to fellow hunters, I guess.

Growing up, I didn't give a single fuck about wolves and neither did my parents. But even in Big Sky Country they'd crop up, and sure, we had a coalition in town meant to protect us and all that shit, but for a long time, the worst you'd hear about was someone's raided chicken coop or a missing cow or two. There'd be rumors, or whatever, about a family that went missing, but that was always on rez land and the coalition would say well, you know, that's out of our state jurisdiction, and no one wants us out there anyway, and that was true, so that was that.

The most controversial law didn't get passed until around the time I was born because it wasn't until the early 1960s that the wolves started smartening up. There was the Wolf Man, sure, and maybe a few like him in the Middle Ages, so now people are figuring hey, that might explain a lot—but it didn't happen in droves until much later, and pretty soon, for a few days out of every month, wolves could walk and make sounds and use thumbs. Then they got to thinking, which was when the real trouble started because it pried open a big can of fucking worms, so it was all "civil rights" this and that. Anyway, even the human-ones are born wolves, so this law passed in maybe 1996 and it prohibited hunting them unless they're wild. The ones that can transform are tagged—assimilated into our Great Fucking Society.

I know this guy who used to hunt with our coalition who dated a tagged one once, but it was real hard seeing as they couldn't be together most of the time, and then it got to the point where the few days out of the month they *could* be together, they mostly argued about his job. But all of what we do's legal, you know, legit. Except I guess that wasn't the problem.

She was very sophisticated and all that shit. She even had a YouTube channel, I think.

But then even he got her to admit wild wolves don't give a rat's ass about anyone but their own packs and they give into their hunger real easy, she even said she didn't like running with them—but come on, she'd said, it's still kind of fucked, what you

25

guys do, isn't it? So then this guy, he sat her down, told her all our stories. He saved mine for last, Little Arlo and His Daddy's .22 against the Big Bad Wild Wolves. I watched them tear Ma and Pa to shreds. They smelled like piss and their fangs were long and yellowy and there wasn't anything human about them. Whenever I talk about it, my chest starts feeling numb and the numbness stretches into my fingertips. I get dizzy and sometimes I throw up, and honestly, I was pretty angry about the whole fucking thing, having to listen to him tell the likes of *her* about that night.

C3 8⊃

Will comes up from the den and glares at us. "Tell me you fucking got it," he grits, "and you already tossed it onto a goddamn junk pile!" Will's a man with hobbies. I think years ago he might've been a teacher, but mostly I think that's bullshit, even though he does know a lot about the Second Amendment, and arsenals, and what George Washington would think about all this shit. He owns a gun range on the outskirts of the city, and he started this little hunting business on the side because of all the government incentives. I mean, that's what he said, but it's pretty clear he enjoys himself out here real good. He smokes a cigar and looks like he's playing a Vietnam vet. I'm not sure he's ever been to war. Some of us did a tour or two in Iraq, but I didn't. When I turned eighteen, I only wanted to kill one species, and it wasn't other humans.

We tuck our phones away, but only one of us has the courage to ask Will what he means. "Huh?" says Horace. He's a couple years older than I am, went to the same school as me and all that shit. Circled the same hangouts. My last year was kind of a blur on account of my parents getting killed, and the switch from Big Sky Country to Shit Can City. There were a lot of counselors and a lot of fights with the wolf-kids. The wolf-kids had a special program, and would only show up for a few days out of every month, and so it was hard not to hate them. I roughed them up on the regular, I guess. Horace, too. We'd lost something, and yeah, it *was* that simple.

They owed us a healing. Everyone knew it.

His crossbow hanging from its strap on his shoulder, Will takes a big puff on his cigar. I quit smoking yesterday and I can already tell that's all gone to fuck in a dickbasket because I really want a smoke. His glare worsens, like it's lowering us into our graves. "Arlo, how many were in this pack?" he cuts.

I flinch. I was on recon, so I should know. "Um, like, there were six," I say. "Sir," I add, already knowing what he'll say.

He looks at all of us. "We've been watching this pack for months. We got all the goddamn fucking permits. You're supposed to be guarding the perimeter, making sure they were all down there—and what the fuck do I emerge to find?" We don't answer. "All of you—staring at your goddamn dicks—your phones in your hands! Our count is five. Now one of them's out there—" He makes an accusatory motion with his cigar, "and so help me god, if it kills *anyone,* that death is on you. The way I see it—Jesus, I hope it's only some fucking bum gets killed."

We look to one another and I feel really hot, like I'm wedged in the heart of the burning stump. Will gives one look at the fire pit and the cinderblocks and he sneers.

൫ ൮

I order coffee and eggs and bacon and three chocolate-chip pancakes, and I only have appetite for the coffee, so I just kind of sit there staring at the syrups. I'm always buying shit I can't afford. Horace, who likes us all to call him Ace due to something that went down back when he was a kid—I've guessed probably involving a different nickname—orders waffles that look like they've been dressed in a whipped cream and strawberry tutu, and he avoids catching my eye. No one should blame me about what happened, but it's pretty clear they all do because I'm the one Will barked at, and when he said *that death is on you,* his grave glare was right on me—even though all of us were distracted when we came up from the den.

Ace watches my coffee ritual. Two packets of Sugar In The Raw. One thimble of vanilla creamer. "R," Ace says. "Dude. Are you going to eat that?" He stabs his fork at my bacon.

"No, dude," I say, and I mean it to have a little edge, but it doesn't. "It's yours, man."

Before we left for Denny's we checked the junkyard's perimeter a few more times and all that shit. A few of us pissed on the burning stump and the fire went out and then Will went home with some of the older guys and that was that. Lone wolves usually get picked off by the police if they're spotted in the city and all of us figured it probably ran that way even though we don't have a good reason. Abigail, who used to be called Abby until her little brother got his throat ripped out by a wolf or something, ordered hash browns with cheese and said, whatever, assholes, that wolf's as good as dead anyway—so shut the fuck up about it, will you?

Now she goes by Gail, which Ace and I think is ugly but we've never said so.

"Hey," she says now, nodding her chin somewhere behind me. She's sitting opposite Ace and me, next to Logan—who has always just been *Logan* and a heaping pile of steaming bullshit. Logan ordered fries and a Diet Coke and he's gay, so Ace always makes stupid jokes. Like I'm supposed to want to fuck every gay guy I come across, shit, man, and Logan's not even my type. First of all, fuck Diet. Second of all, wolves have never fucked with his people, so, I mean, it's kind of fucked he's always hanging around with us. Now he double-takes at Gail's nod, and raises his plucked-perfect eyebrows and that's how I know even before I turn around that there's going to be wolves in the far corner booth, scowling at us.

Both Ace and I sit up straight and turn around—what else are we supposed to do?

"Guys!" Gail hisses even though I know she can't mind. "Jesus," she grits, just like Will.

When we turn back, the wolves we saw—*the wolf* I saw— makes me feel like I've been stun-shot and now I'm sinking. Like I'm ghosting down through the booth and through the layers of the earth we learned about in school. Crust, mantle, outer core. I don't make it to the inner core, though, because by that point, I've melted into liquid fire.

08 80

The wolf's name was fucking *Casper*, so that's on me, I guess. When he said his name I was grinning, I was like, "Ha ha ha, like the friendly ghost?" and when he gave me this "huh?" face, I should've figured and all that shit. Who never saw *Casper?* But I guess at the time I was more figuring, maybe I just remembered the movie real well because when I saw it growing up and Casper turned into a real human kid at the end it made me go fuck, well, I might be into guys.

We met at this gay bar that Logan likes that's really chill on Tuesdays and sometimes I go with him, and then sometimes, but rarely, Gail will show up with Ace in tow.

Casper found me at the bar waiting for a drink, already drunk and kind of pissed because it was one of those nights. Ace was showing everyone this YouTube video back at our booth and they were crowded around him but I couldn't hear shit. Three people around a phone is fine and all, but four is pushing it and just for the record, I'm not one of those anti-tech dickwads or anything, I'm just fucking poor and after my grandparents died, my iPhone cracked all to shit. They were footing the phone bill, so that's that.

Anyway, now that I'm thinking about all this, I guess there were more signs than his stupid reaction to my teasing. His grin, for one. It was a very nice grin, but now that I'm looking back, it was maybe a little too wolfish. Like I could tell there was a little bit of hunger for human flesh lurking behind it, but at the time, that wasn't the kind of human flesh I was thinking about. He had jet black hair shaved into one of those punk haircuts I used to wear but couldn't maintain—right after my parents died I was really into the Dead Kennedys, and there was something weirdly sexy about Jello Biafra's voice when he sang "Police Truck" that was loopy and aggressive but desperate all at the same time—

29

and Casper reminded me of that sound. His eyes were narrow and brown, and they laughed really easy, but never at me. Also he had a tragus piercing and I mean, shit, man, I mean, really—how does that play out on a wolf's ear?

So I got my drink, and then he was like, "You smoke," but it wasn't a question and like a total fuckup I was, like, yeah, how'd you know? And he tapped his nose and winked, and he was like, "I could smell it on you." And now I'm thinking fuck, well, that was pretty obvious, Arlo, you fucking brainless dick, but at the time I was kind of relieved because he asked if he could bum one. I wanted everyone to see me leaving, having a good time, so we went out back together and we smoked the rest of my pack, and then we made out for a while and then we went back inside.

He was like Joe Strummer, if Strummer were East Asian and at a gay bar and not dead.

The fucked up part is that I saw Casper a couple of times after that, which led to him getting my number, which led to him knocking on my door one night pretty drunk, and I guess things had been so good the past year, you know, that I wasn't really paying attention to the moon anymore. I paid a lot of attention to it after my parents died, and I guess I always carry a vague awareness of it because I'm a hunter, but I never thought about hunting when I was with Casper and we never talked about it.

After he spent a few nights with me, he found my crossbow in the closet with its silver-tipped bolts and I found him staring, and I told him it was cool. I was like, you want to give it a shot? I know a place we could go. I have the license and all that shit, and he was like, "Have you ever killed anything, R?" and I told him yeah, I've killed plenty, and then he actually grinned. He was like, "Me too." But after that he didn't come around as much, so that was that.

It's not like we were in love or anything, but I guess, lately, I'd sort of missed him.

CB BO

They're two booths down in the corner, but the booth between us is empty. Gail starts throwing these tiny little balls made out of Logan's straw wrapper. Her aim is shit, but you'd never know it because when we're down in the dens, a lot of the time there's really no aiming involved. She starts using his napkin and Logan just lets her, nodding and smiling like isn't this funny? We're regulars at this Denny's, so I don't see how we've never seen them here before.

I start imagining how white trash we must look in our gear and how we brought our bows and bolts inside and how fucked up that kind of is. Back in school, Ace and Logan, who lived on the edge of some trailer court hinterlands, had these four-wheelers and we used to go down and shoot paintball and I'm starting to think maybe we never grew out of it because we're still wearing all our stupid-ass shit. We have these bandanas around our arms with this wood-axe emblem. Like ha ha, get it, like we're the huntsmen from that story where that girl gets eaten by a wolf, which by now, I guess, everyone figures was probably true.

I sink a little lower, trying to remember if any of them ever saw Casper with me, and then I get my answer. Logan shoulders Gail. He's looking at me. "What's wrong, R?" he says, and I can hear it in his voice, this cruelness he gets when he's about to start whaling on someone.

Under the table, my hands clench and unclench, and my palms are sweaty.

Gail is laughing now, and Ace starts in on my eggs, and Logan winks at me.

"Hey, will you fucking shut up?" I say. I want to tell Gail to stop throwing shit, but I don't.

"What crawled up your ass and died, R? Chill the fuck out." Gail rolls up another piece of Logan's napkin and dips it in my coffee—what the fuck, I growl, but she sends the wad sailing. "It doesn't fucking matter," she says for the thousandth time. "Just because you've got your panties in a bunch over losing one doesn't mean we've got to share your shit mood, you know?" She snorts with laughter, "Fuck—they're catching on, I think—"

31

I can't help sneering. "The thing we lost wasn't one of *them*, it was wild, it can't even transform—" like the pack that killed your brother, but I don't say that part. Gail's still laughing, but Logan gets this frown going and I know he hears me. "And seriously, what the fuck?" My voice is a little louder now, "I'm not the one who lost it, why am I getting blamed? Ace was the one on his phone, and you're the one who was fucking with Snapchat filters the whole time—"

"Dude, um," Ace looks up from his phone, "you were the one staring at that fire pit—"

"Yeah, um, *actually,*" Gail chimes in, "that was weird, wasn't it? I mean how'd a bunch of wild wolves cut a stump like that and light it on fire?" They're all looking at me. "You're the one who did recon," Gail says, like I don't already fucking know.

Then I see the flicker of dangerous excitement in Logan's eye. "Hey guys," he says, interrupting Gail, and I know he's going to tell them. "Did you know R here *fucked* one of—"

"Excuse me."

We look up.

It's one of the wolves, but it isn't Casper. The wolf-girl doesn't say anything more, just dumps a cup of her yellowy piss right on Gail's head. Gail screeches, chokes on it—and I'm out of the booth like lightning, Jesus, shit! not because I'm afraid of getting piss on me, but because everything is fucked and my heart's thrumming crazy like it did on my first hunt and I've got to *move.* I push the wolf-girl out of the way and she's howling, like, *howling* with laughter, and I think I'm totally leaving, but I don't have a car, and even if I did, Ace always drives.

"Fuck, fuck, fuck!" I say, once I'm out in the parking lot. I figure the cops will be here soon because this isn't such a bad side of town, I guess, and it'll be this whole thing. They'll see we've got our bows and all that shit, not that it really matters, but we'll have to stand around in this Denny's parking lot all night showing them our licenses, getting looked up in databases—they might call Will, fuck, I mean, I doubt I'd lose my job, but maybe I could.

I pace, trying to remember. I don't know. I didn't see shit. I didn't see that fire pit on recon, I just saw a fucking hovel, and wolves, and piles of junk. The moon's been high the past few days, and just yesterday I was there, and I didn't see any of them transform. Not the month before, not the month before that. I mean, it's not like we just shoot up any old pack we find. They've got to be verified, you know? And they were, but even if they weren't—who the fuck am I shitting? Will's taken us to a few jobs way outside the city, in the suburbs that need a quick favor after a kid goes missing. It wasn't my fault. It's not my fault. No fucking way, man.

Casper doesn't say anything, but I know he's standing there. Watching me after he lights up his smoke, and I let him watch and take a few drags. Finally, he says, "They called the cops, I think, but Amadeus and Freya just ran—she's the one who came up to you guys." He shrugs and takes another drag and I want very badly to ask him for a smoke, and I know he wishes I'd ask.

"Why aren't you running?" I say. I stop pacing, but now I'm shaking. I can't get calm. They get to pick their human names, I heard. Whatever names they want and I don't give a *fuck* why Casper picked his. Something is moving through me like a tremor now, the kind that splits mountains.

"I will," he says. He still looks the same, only he's got new boots. He fidgets with his phone in his free hand and it lights his face up, the sharp of his bones, his narrow nose. Deep down I know he's anxious, but he looks indifferent. Like whatever, man, you're on your own.

"Fuck you," I say. I let the words cut my mouth and they hurt and I want him to know how bad they hurt even though I can tell they've cut him, too. It doesn't fucking matter.

He tenses when I move towards him, like he's watching the earth crack wide open, but he's not going to move, he's just going to let himself fall in like a stupid fucking idiot. Like those wolf-kids at school or the wild ones in the den. Like they just exist to take it and do nothing, just lie down and die, only, I'm wrong—and he doesn't take it. He flicks his smoke and then right

33

here in some Denny's parking lot we tear each other into hundreds of raw, bloody pieces, and we don't say a word the whole time we just keep hitting and hitting and hitting and hitting and I don't know how but it starts ripping me up inside, too, how easy it all happens.

ও ৪০

When I moved to the city, I moved in with my grandparents who owned this little townhouse in a retirement community, I guess. They're gone now too, so when I moved out on my own, I got this place near the city park and whatever's left of the gardens. The trees aren't like they were back home, but it's about as close as I can get to real colors, you know?

I live in a basement apartment with one window and one room. It's No Smoking, but I smoke anyway and all that shit. Some nights, I can't stand the smell, so I wander outside in the dark, on the trails near a ravine that cuts through the park like a wide gash. The ravine goes on for miles that way. By my place, on the trails, there's usually a shitload of litter and something strange will come over me and I'll get right up next to the bank smoking my smoke, and fish out all the trash. I never put it where it belongs though—I sort of just pile it up beside me in the rocks.

The first few times, I liked it—the hunting, I mean—and this pack, it's not like they were innocent and all that shit. They'd killed a few people living near the tracks, so at first, no one was saying much about the deaths, but then the police got involved and Will stuck his nose in, got us hired. Will calls them hunts. Lately, they've felt more like exterminations. My first kill was pretty scrappy and all that shit. Thing put up a fight. I've got scars, sure. I used to be proud about them, but one night, when Casper found one (and I guess he must've known but he asked anyway), I said it was from falling out of a tree when I was a kid.

I didn't even know he was one of them so it's weird, you know, that I lied.

34

Will's always going on and on about the world dying, and getting worse, and how *the apocalypse is nigh* and all that shit, but lately I sort of feel like the world's been totally shit-canned since probably forever, I guess. Since man first fucked some woman in a cave. There's never been anywhere safe, or perfect. Not when people are always around to ruin it all to hell.

But now I get to thinking about the fire pit again, that stump cut into sections. How it reminded me of the lightning-struck tree seeping at the seams with fire, back when my parents were alive. I fish the last of the trash out of the water and sit, taking a long drag on the last smoke from Casper's pack. My fingers are numb. Back at the hunt, that wild wolf tricked me, I guess. When he heard us coming, he was probably outside, keeping watch like we should've done on recon. I'll bet he knew I was in his yard, made sure I saw what he wanted me to see. I'll bet he was a sentinel, like I am.

I mean—or, I don't know.

CB ℰℴ

The cold moonlight bites Roque as he staggers down a steep ravine. There are no birds here. He is human. He is clumsy, naked. There is only the sound of rust, and grinding halts, and Roque is shivering. He has to stop so he can weep. Roque is human. He gags on his tears. They taste like slivers of silver. Near him there is water, and he laps it up to wash the taste of grief out of his mouth. Later, he will throw it back up because it is rotten and contaminated and his insides are raw. The trees hiss at him, his feet cut from the rocks of the stream. He is weeping, weeping, weeping. He is alone. Out of the corner of his eye, he sees a shadow in the dawn with smoke pouring from its mouth. Roque is human. When he sees the shadow, he knows it sees him.

Your Mama's Adventures in Parenting

Mary Robinette Kowal

Your mama adjusted her face mask and checked the chronometer on her eyepiece. Darn it. The filter would only be good for another fifteen minutes. She was nowhere near finished with the job. And this particular theft would fetch a good price on the energy market, what with the price of methane.

She slid the siphon tube across to the capture valve and turned on the suction pump. If your mama could get most of the gas into the polysteel tank on her back...

The filter in her mask failed. A rank, heavy scent of sulfur and dead moss burned into her sinuses. Your mama's eyes watered. She pressed the filter against her face, trying to snug it up or eke out a few more minutes. The smell only grew stronger, moving past eggs, and into the bowels of hell itself.

Gagging, she hit the retract button on the siphon. No amount of credits was worth this. Methane or no. Energy crisis or no. Your mama would rather steal diamonds than deal with one more fart job.

She broke like the wind, and ran.

ꜱ ꜱ

You watch your mama through the bathroom doorway. In one hand, she's holding a plunger; the other is sheathed in a dripping rubber glove. Her shoulders are slumped. She sees you, and points at the toilet. "Really?"

ꜱ ꜱ

Coming out of the wormhole, your mama felt along the sensors leading from her brain housing to the detectors on the ship's skin. Really, it was the outer hull, but to her the background radiation of space felt like wind on her skin. Almost.

36

"Location. Lunar orbit around the planet Earth." She opened a viewport for her passenger.

He gasped. "That's no moon."

Her sensor showed nothing out of the ordinary. "We are in lunar orbit."

"Yes, yes, but something else is, too." He leaned closer to the viewport. "Can you not see it?"

"Negative." Your mama adjusted her sensors along all frequencies, but still perceived nothing out of the ordinary. "It must be masking electronically. What are you seeing?"

"What appears to be a demolition ship." He fiddled with the end of his towel and frowned. "The darn thing is glowing and—Bother."

The destruction of the Earth was all too clear in her sensors, lighting up the inside of her brain like a firestorm. The radiation played over her skin and flared in her sensors.

"Damn." He turned from the viewport. "Plot a new course...just pick someplace."

She skipped back in the wormhole, and the dark closed around her until all that remained was the memory of warmth on her skin.

C03 80

In the rear view mirror of the car, you can only see your mama's eyes. The heat is glaring through the windows and making your skin stick to the vinyl seats with sweat. She's glaring at you. "I'm not just a taxi service, you know."

C03 80

The difficulty wasn't breaking into the Cambridge library, it was in finding the right piece of microfilm. Your mama pretended to straighten the back seam of her stockings as a librarian went by. Her informant had left the nuclear codes on a piece of microfilm in a dead drop, which seemed like a good idea before they began to recatalog the collection.

The librarian went into the restricted area, and your

mama slid a foot into the door to stop it. She counted to ten, so the librarian would be clear, and went in. From there, it was just a matter of slipping through the stacks until she reached the rare books. Who would have expected a children's book to wind up here?

Footsteps alerted her, and your mama snatched the volume off the shelf. Pulling her gun from its holster in her garter, she pressed herself against the shelves and crept to the end of the aisle. With the massive shelves masking her, she waited until the librarian walked past, head down in a book.

Letting out a sigh, she tucked her gun back in its place and turned her attention to the book. The microfilm was in the spine, so all your mama had to do was pull it out and... there.

She had the codes from the Soviets. No doubt, they would be seriously annoyed to have been thwarted by England's spy network. And, of course, a signed first edition of <u>Peter Pan.</u>

Your mama put the book back on the shelf. And now, she would slip out of the library and head straight on 'til morning.

ᘓ ᗧ

You have nowhere to hide. Your mama holds your report card and the book you'd hidden it in. She is slowly shaking her head. "Do you want to explain this to me?"

ᘓ ᗧ

Your mama stared at the moon through the viewport of the space station. The goddamn airlock was jammed. How the hell was she supposed to get outside before the change hit without the key? And who thought that a chain was a good idea for an airlock? Her bones ached. The inside of her spacesuit was starting to chafe.

Right. She didn't necessarily need the key; all she had to do was break the chain. The catch was that if she waited long enough for the lycanthropy to shift her to wolf state, with the necessary strength to break the chain, then the helmet probably wouldn't fit her. Growling, and knowing that was a bad sign, your mama stepped back from the airlock. She had another hour, at least, before the moon swung far enough in its orbit to be fully in the light of the sun and out of the Earth's shadow. So, who would have locked the door? Because it turned out that she really did need the key. Sheppard? Grissom? Arm—Armstrong.

Baring her teeth, your mama pushed off the airlock and shot down the corridor to Armstrong's cubby. "Did you chain the airlock?"

"Um."

"Do you want me to tear your throat out?"

"Um."

"Give me the fucking key." Your mama's fangs were showing and caught on her upper lip. She reached out, snatched the key from his shaking hand. With a snarl, she jammed her helmet on, past her lengthening snout, and fled to the dark side of the moon and her humanity.

c₃ ೮೦

You tiptoe through the room so you don't wake your mama. Your mama got sick once a month, but she always tells you not to worry. She lies on the sofa with a hot water bottle tucked against her stomach. When you bump a table, she cracks one eye. "Hey, sweetie, need anything?

c₃ ೮೦

The steam hissed around your mama and her dance master as they stepped out of the brass and oak cabinet of the time machine. This time, they had emerged in the alley behind the theater.

She looked to the right, where another incarnation of herself was hurrying to the theater for the audition. "Stop her!"

At her command, a brass automaton stepped out of the time machine and intercepted the previous her. Your mama turned her back on the cry of surprise from her former self.

"Come on." She beckoned the dance master. "I want to get inside and warm up."

Her dance master stared past her. "That was you?"

"Yes." Your mama snapped and strode toward the theater.

"You were so young..."

"Young and inexperienced and I screwed up the most important audition of my life." Even after all these years, the memory of falling off her pointe shoes still burned.

"Did you try again?" He wasn't following her.

"I am now." Why else would your mama have spent years building this time machine and working with the dance master?

"I mean...did you go to the spring audition?"

"How could I, after that humiliation?" She stared at her past self, who hung confused and frightened in the automaton's grip.

"That's...that's what being a dancer is. Getting up and continuing. Everyone falls sometimes." He stepped away, back to the girl she had been. "Would you like to go over your routine?"

"What are you doing?" Your mama put her hands on her hips. "You're supposed to help me with my audition."

"I am." He shrugged. "This you is too old. She...She still has a chance."

ɔ ઠ

Your mama hands you a tissue. "Don't listen to them." She ruffles your hair and her fingers are rough from work. "You can be anything you want to be. Okay? I believe in you."

BIRDS ON AN ISLAND
Charlie Bookout

I sent the last package to Arkansas today. I made it a point
at the beginning never to use the same post office twice, so I
drove up to Lubec this time. The roads in this part of Maine don't
offer much to look at—miles of pine forests, wild blueberry
fields, little else—and it's a long way back to my house, so I've
fallen again into thinking about the lady who came from there,
from Arkansas. I hate that I can't remember her first name. I
mean, who the hell knows where your memory goes when you
get to be my age? But it goes, slowly, through invisible holes, like
air escaping a kid's balloon. And the important moments seem to
go first, as if to leave room for things that never mattered. I can
see that little scar on her chin like she was sitting in the pickup
next to me. But, honest to God, I can't remember her first name.
Her married name was Busbee, and I remember the moniker her
hillbilly neighbors had given her—it was the sort of
dumbfuckery I'd expect from an Arkansan—but her *real* name
was elegant, lyrical. My wife, long dead, was a famous lover of
Greek myths, and I can imagine the woman's name appearing in
one of those stories.

I can look at the little scar on the woman's chin anytime I
want; after all these years, it's still right there in front of me. And
even though I sometimes wish I couldn't, I can relive the
impossibility that saved her life in the same way.

That Saturday, the woman from Arkansas went into eight
fathoms of choppy North Atlantic foam just as casually as you
might hop into the shallow end of the pool. I shut down the
motor and ran to the rail. I couldn't find her at first, and then I
saw her way off the starboard side, twenty yards at least. I hadn't
swum in years. I knew I'd never reach her. I screamed at her and
threw a lifejacket. It didn't even come close. I felt ill. It looked
like she was trying to swim toward the lighthouse but she kept
going under. I actually remember wondering what my life would
be like from then on, whether or not I'd ever get a good night's

sleep again knowing I'd watched someone drown.

She disappeared, and I just stood there watching, my guts wiggling like a sack of dying squid. Then something in the air caught my eye, one of the laughing, black-headed gulls my late wife loved to feed. (On windy days, they'd hover in front of her and take Doritos out of her hand.) Two other gulls arrived as if from nowhere, then ten more. They chuckled to one another and formed a tight group over the spot where I saw the woman go down. Then the air was full of gulls, more than a hundred, had to be. They flew round and round, a carousel of birds. That's when I saw the weird purple light for the first time. It started out as just a flicker in a window of the lighthouse keeper's cottage, but then the water underneath the birds started roiling and glistening with the same purple. A column of mist spun up from the water to meet them. The column was thick and gray like one of those waterspouts you see in pictures but never see in real life. At first, I thought I was imagining the shape, but then I was sure; a figure had formed in the droplets of mist. It was a woman. Were there wings, too?

The cackling of those goddamn gulls was nearly unbearable and I would've cowered in the wheelhouse, but just then, I caught a glimpse of the Arkansas woman's tee-shirt. She surfaced and kept going up and up until she was above the waves, three feet, twenty feet, and if I try hard enough, even now I can close my eyes and see the water ghost holding the woman in her arms. The storm of gulls drifted over my boat. The woman landed easy on the deck.

It can't be. I know. But it's never changed in my memory. Neither has the moment I first met this woman who should've had a mythical name.

CS 80

I was coming in from checking the traps when I first saw her. I think about it a lot actually, how she looked standing there on the pier that afternoon. I still gave tours back then, too, and I had a little shack set up where the floating dock was attached.

There was a sign on the wall. I could see her reading it as I maneuvered the boat into an empty slip. DOWNEAST COASTAL TOURS. I'd painted the letters in bright yellows and blues, but by that summer, the words had faded to dirty shades of cracked pastel. SEE WHALES – SEALS – PUFFINS, and then the words I would soon learn were among her husband's last: CROW ISLAND LIGHTHOUSE.

She watched me as I stepped over the railing and tied the boat to one of the cleats. I remember becoming suddenly aware of my crooked posture and the way I was moving with the arthritic care of an even older man. She met me at the front of the shack. She smelled like cigarettes and perfume. Her frayed jeans and cartoon tee-shirt hung loose on her bony frame. Her eyes were the color of tobacco juice.

"Missus," I said, raising the bill of my cap. "Could I help you?"

"I...I wanna go on a boat ride," she said. Her smile was too big, too white; roebuckers, I figured. And she was a Southern girl, plain as day, with a voice nearly as sunburnt as her face.

"Okay, we can surely take care of that," I said. I added some *rural Maine* to my own accent. She was a tourist. That's how you talk to tourists. I fished the key to the shack from my pants pocket. "Lemme step in here, and we'll have a look at the calendar."

"I wanna go now."

"Howzat?" I said.

"I mean, as soon as possible."

"Well, I'd say you're in luck then. I didn't schedule anybody today on account of the weather. But looks like the fog's liftin'. How many in your group?"

"Just me."

I motioned toward the sign's small print. "Sorry, miss. *One* wouldn't quite pay for the fuel. Hope you understand." I tried to put on a gentle smile.

She dug around in her purse and produced a roll of ragged bills. "I can pay extra," she said.

"I suppose we can work something out," I said and shook

43

her hand. "Name's Paul Weaver. Call me Captain Paul."

❧ ❧

We bobbed around the local islands for half an hour while I gave my little talk on history and wildlife. She stood next to me at the wheel. Her smoky perfume wrapped itself around us. "I never been in a big boat before," she said over the noise of the motor.

"That so?" I said. "Well, I'm partial to the *Maddie's Way*; she's a fine craft, no mistake." I rounded the peninsula, and there was the unmistakable profile of Crow Island. Crow slopes up from the west and ends in a steep promontory on its seaward side. The lighthouse sits on the edge of the cliff, and the tower rises from the eastern gable end of the keeper's home, giving the entire island the look of a sharpened wedge. I remember thinking that on that day it looked like the dorsal fin of a giant shark breaching the fog. "And here's the finale," I said. "The lighthouse was built in 1858, but Crow Island's been a *sacred* place to the Penobscot Indians since a long time before that. They believed a sea hag lived there who'd lure fishermen onto the rocks and make them stupid so they'd do her bidding. One version of the legend claims she'd actually suck their brains out of their heads—that's how the Indians used to eat crayfish, you know."

"It looks so lonely," she said.

"Abandoned, yes. *Lonely*, no. The bird numbers are climbing. Last year alone there were over twelve hundred nesting pairs of Arctic terns. And there's the human residents, of course; they're all dead, but there's a lot of *them*, too." I kept a little black and white photo tacked above the GPS. A young bride was smearing wedding cake onto my young face. I caressed the picture frame. A cloud moved and cast a shadow over us.

She drummed her foot on the floor. When she spoke, her voice trembled. "So...there's a cemetery on Crow Island."

"It's what Patroclus asked of Achilles." I stared out over the bow for an awkward moment. "Sorry, my wife was really into

44

Ancient Greece, and...no, nobody's buried there. Crow Island Lighthouse is a *columbarium*. It's a place for your ashes to go if you get cremated. After the Coast Guard decommissioned the light, some folks bought it and started sellin' vault space for cremains. That's the word they use—*cremains*. Howdaya like that? And for a pretty penny, I might add. They charged people over two grand. They called it *Forever on The Atlantic*. No telling how many people they ripped off before they got their license yanked. The brochure showed marble floors and mahogany cabinets with little niches for each urn. Real swanky, you know. But the Cemetery Board sent letters to the families saying they shut the place down. They said when they went to inspect it, they found the urns stacked on the ground or on shelves made outta rotten plywood and cinder blocks. What's worse, the birds had got in and knocked a bunch of urns over. Imagine all those fine Catholics and Methodists spending eternity covered in pelican guano."

I took us around the east side of the island so she could get a better look at the weathered shingles and the scarred face of the tower. Her lips twitched. She gave her hair a tug. "People should go get the urns and keep them someplace else," she said.

I laughed. "Crow Island's off limits. Protected bird sanctuary. Maine Fish-n'-Wildlife owns it now. See all those white birds with the tan heads? Those are northern gannets. They're thick this time of year. Oh, and there's a cormorant. That's a lucky find. They say—"

"So we don't actually get to go into the lighthouse?" she asked me. I could hear panic in her throat.

"'Fraid not," I said. "This is as close as we get. But if you look just there, you can see a pair of Leach's storm-petrels."

She dropped her purse to the wheelhouse floor and stepped out onto the deck. She counted to three, and then she jumped over the side.

ᘓ ᘔ

The impossibility happened.

The gulls broke from their formation, and the shaft of sea mist, and the spirit lady inside it, collapsed, falling on me like rain. The purple light danced briefly along the railing. Then the light was gone, too.

Seawater poured from the woman's mouth and nose. She curled into a fetal position, coughing and gagging. I switched the radio to channel three and called for Craig Dunlap, Winter Harbor's police chief. I'd known him for years. "*Go ahead*," he said.

I couldn't decide what to say. Finally, "Craig, it's Paul on the *Maddie's Way*. I just had a lady go in the water over here off Crow."

"*Copy that. She wearin' a PFD?*"

"I've got her back on board, but she took in a lot of water."

"*Gouldsboro's your closest port. I'll radio their first responders to meet you there. They'll want her stats right now in case she's unresponsive when they get to her.*"

I realized then that she'd never introduced herself. "Ten-four. Give me a minute," I said. Her purse was at my feet. I opened it to look for some ID. A swell jarred the boat and I spilled the purse's contents. That's when I found her pistol. It was no bigger than a kid's squirt gun, but I figured it could kill a man all the same. I shoveled everything back into the purse as quickly as I could.

"Craig, you copy?" I said into the mic.

"*Go ahead.*"

"I found something in her purse. It's a... Stand by." Most men would've found the woman far from lovely. But her look of protest, the valleys between her eyebrows and the aggravated angle of her jaw—It was a face that made you have no idea what was coming next, what you might *do* next. My wife used to make me feel that way sometimes. "I found an Arkansas driver's license, but that's it." I gave him her name and then, "Five-five, dark brown hair, hundred sixty pounds. It's an old license; I wouldn't put her at more than one-fifteen, one-twenty."

"*Ten-four,*" he said.

She was gagging again, and I went to her. "You're okay,

46

miss," I said. "Just keep gettin' rid of that water. An ambulance is gonna meet us at the dock."

"No," she said. "Please."

"You need to get checked out," I said. "You nearly died."

She reached for my hand. "But I didn't. If there's an ambulance, the cops'll come too, and that'd be the same as killing me. Please... I have to get to the island." She went into another coughing fit and then vomited.

I helped her sit up. I took a blanket out of the dry box and draped it around her. I had no intention of taking her to Crow Island, and now she was asking me not to take her to Gouldsboro either. But we couldn't sit there drifting. The light was getting poor, and the wind was picking up. I started the boat and headed for the mouth of the Narraguagus. There's a little cove downstream from Milbridge I knew I could hide in even at low tide.

We were there in a few minutes. When I killed the motor and dropped anchor, she came around. "What are we doing?" she asked me. "I've gotta get to Crow Island."

A burst of radio static, then Craig Dunlap's voice: "Maddie's Way, *you copy?*"

"You're not getting there in *my* boat," I said.

She reached for her purse. I remembered the pistol. "Wait," I said.

"I can't pay you much more." She brought out another fistful of bills. "But I'll give you the rest of the money I've got."

"Maddie's Way *one-zero-three-two-three-five-niner, this is Winter Harbor. Please state your position, over.*"

I sighed, relieved that she didn't plan to shoot me. But I was overloaded. I turned the radio's volume down and then stood there. The boat rocked in the dying light.

She hung her head. When she spoke, the voice wasn't hers. "What's wrong, darling? You look like a man who's between Scylla and Charybdis." The Southern drawl was gone and it sounded exactly like something my wife would've said. Exactly.

I touched her hand. Her skin was as rough as a shark's.

For a second or two the weird light crackled around her like violet fire.

I breathed as deeply as I could and replied as if the day were still sane. "There's just no possible way, ma'am, I'm sorry."

When she looked up at me again she had managed a sort of sensual smile. "I could let you do me, right here if you want. Nobody'll see." It was the Arkansan voice again, somehow damp with sweat and honey-thick. I felt blood rush to my face and moments later to other parts of me I'd nearly forgotten. An uninvited image of my wife's naked ankles came to me. I turned to hide my tears.

"Never mind," she said. "Who am I kidding?"

"Missus Busbee, I—"

"You don't have to call me that. Nobody calls me that. You wanna know what they call me?" She grinned big and tapped a false incisor with her fingernail. "These teeth were my husband's last gift. Hardly anybody's ever seen me with 'em. Everybody says I must have bought a boob job with all the money I save on toothpaste. They call me Gummer." She lifted her breasts and gave them a squeeze. "Whataya think, Captain Paul? Was it a fair trade?" Her eyes had begun to glisten.

"Okay." I said. Such an offer was unlikely to come again. Ever. Then I saw the photo of my wife through the wheelhouse window. "Somewhere else, though. Do you have a hotel room?"

She stared at me for a moment. "I drove here straight from Arkansas."

I fired up the motor again. "Let's go find someplace private," I said.

CR ∞

I've worn a colostomy bag since a little later that summer, and while I'm sure my mother celebrated my successful potty training more than sixty years earlier, the last normal shit I took before that God-awful surgery meant nothing to me. It's like that with everything. We acknowledge our *firsts*. First steps. First words. But life never affords us the chance to give so much as a

48

nod to any of our *lasts*.

Almost never. I hoped my last steps were still a few years ahead of me. But I'd known for a long time that my last intercourse experience was almost a decade behind me. And I was fine with it. Then this woman in my boat made her offer. I accepted because, it turns out, part of me was still alive. But another part of me wanted my last time to always be that morning with my wife a month before she slipped away. So when we got back to the dock we used the woman's car, not my pickup. Like the boat, too much married life had gone on in my pickup. Gummer's car, on the other hand, was all Gummer. It looked like it had started to rust when the Eighties were coming to an end; not unlike her, I imagine. And the inside of it was thick with the same stale aroma of perfume and cigarette smoke.

I asked her to drive eight or so miles down to the Schoodic Point parking lot. It's always empty at night. We climbed into her back seat, and did what we did. I wasn't sure how well I'd perform, but I don't suppose it mattered. The man inside her wasn't me; it was her husband. And when I came into her, I said my dead wife's name.

She tried to sleep, and an uncomfortable hour had gone by when the sound of her phone startled her out of what looked to me like a cold, prickly stupor. She mumbled something unintelligible, and then more clearly, "*Twenty-two.*" She sat up in the Ford's moldy back seat, scrambled over the console and took the phone from the glove compartment. It vibrated in her hand. Its light filled the cab. *BFF,* the screen shouted.

"What if it's him, somehow?" she asked. She wasn't really talking to me. The phone buzzed again. The ring was James Taylor promising Gummer she had a friend; sounded like he was singing through tin foil.

She stomped on the floorboard. "I know it's a trick, baby. Just like you said, the DEA's in bed with the phone company. If I answer, they'll know where I am. Just like you said." The phone thrummed again. She winced. "But what if it *is* you?"

She swiped the screen, but it was too late. No one was there.

She rocked back and forth, then steadied her hands long enough to light a smoke. She closed her fist around a lock of her hair, yanked twice—hard enough to bring tears—and then resumed rocking. "I overdone it again," she said, finally looking at me. "It's eighteen hundred miles from my house to Winter Harbor, Maine. Odometer said so. I drove thirty-six straight hours." She opened the ashtray and held up the little vial she'd hidden there. "But not without help." She gave it a shake and something rattled inside.

She licked her lips and peered out the window. "I'm forty-three years old, and yesterday was the first time I ever seen the ocean. I been dreamin' about it for as long as I can remember." She squinted out into the dark. "Wish I could see it right now. It's out there somewhere, not far from the sound of it."

I wondered if the ocean sounded to her the way it did in her dreams. A gull laughed. I shuddered. She wiped the inside of the windshield and we caught a glimpse of the horizon, straight and red like the edge of a bloody razor. But then it was gone. Fog smothered the granite tip of Schoodic Point.

The ringtone she'd picked for her BFF came again. "*Winter, spring, summer, or fall—*" She swiped the screen. "Hello?"

The phone wasn't on speaker, but in the silence I could hear most of what the caller said. "*Thank goodness. Where are you? You haven't answered since Monday. I thought you* might *pick up if I used your* husband's *phone.*"

"Can't tell you."

"*What?*"

"I can't tell you where I am, Sandy. It's between Jeff and me."

A long pause. "*Your husband's dead.*"

"Yeah, I know. But he told me some stuff—secret stuff—before they killed him. I had to do this. Don't worry about the kids. They're old enough to take care of themselves."

"*Your children are six and nine years old. Where the hell are you?*"

"Let's just say that if Jeff was right, I'll be one of the first people in America to see the sun today."

"Don't tell me you left the state. You know you can't—"

She pressed the END CALL button. "I shouldn't have answered," she said. "It was my probation officer." She looked at her phone and then switched it off. "I don't want to hear that song again. It was me and Jeff's song."

She curled into a ball and shivered.

There was no sunrise to watch. Dawn—always early here in the summer—crept in unnoticed like thick and quiet soup. I started to fade, and when sleep finally came, it came in intervals more irritating than restful.

She shook me awake. "You ready to take me to the island now?"

"I suppose," I said. "It's Sunday morning; maybe nobody'll notice me anchored so close to it. But first, tell my why you want to go."

She rolled her window down and lit a cigarette with trembling hands. "I ain't into tellin' people my sob story. You'll either go through with your part or you won't."

"I've got a lot to lose if we get caught," I said, "so I think you should at least tell me what's so important out there."

She opened her wallet and showed me a crumpled family photo. "They've grown since this was took, but those are my kids, and that's their daddy. He tried his hardest to take care of us. But our luck just kept gettin' shittier. A couple of weeks ago he told me he was going way up into New England, someplace. Said it was a favor for his friends, and that they'd pay him for it. His so-called friends are bad dudes, and I had a feeling I knew what the *favor* was. But we were so strapped the welfare people was fixin' to take our boys, so I kept my mouth shut. When he showed back up last Wednesday night he was acting weird, said he was exhausted, and went straight to bed, but when he got up the next day he was still freaking out, scared but excited too. He said, 'Baby, we've gotta lay low for awhile, but I've found us a way out. Somethin' crazy happened, somethin' you'd never believe. And I've come into some money because of it, *big* money. I brought a little back with me, but there's a lot more. Enough for

51

you, and me, and the boys to start over.' When I asked him where the money was, he said, 'It's best you don't know yet. But let me put it this way: If you were there, you'd have been one of the first Americans to see the sun this morning.' He kissed me and ran across the street to Jiffy Stop to buy smokes, and I never seen him again. I thought I heard gunshots. I knew for sure when the sirens came. I looked through the blinds and seen the ambulance guys workin' on him, but I knew he was gone."

She finished her cigarette, tossed it out and lit another one. "I found a bunch of twenties in his jeans. And a piece of envelope with two things written on it in Jeff's handwriting, two things that ain't done nothin' but stink up my brain for three days: *Crow Island Lighthouse,* and the number *twenty-two.* I still don't know what the number means, but I Googled *Crow Island,* and I figured that's gotta be where the money is. And if it's enough money for those guys to kill Jeff over, the Feds probably know something. If I didn't leave right then, I'd chicken out. There was soup in the cabinet and some nuggets in the freezer. I hugged my boys tight. I told them to behave, and keep the door locked."

She put the photo back in her wallet. She sat awestruck by the gray-green waves that hammered the shore's rock face. "Just look at it," she said. "I wish Jason and David could see it. I always imagined the ocean being deep blue under marshmallow clouds—but it's good enough." She turned and looked at me, and I'll never forget the pain in her eyes. "I guess it'll *have* to be," she said. "I doubt I'll go home with anything else."

My wife always called thunderheads *marshmallow clouds.* "Listen," I said. "Maybe there *is* something for you on Crow Island." I wasn't sure what else to say. I only knew that some impossibility had saved the woman's life; an impossibility that needed an explanation. She looked at me again, and her eyes blazed faintly with ghost purple. "There's more to the Indian legend about Crow Island," I heard myself say.

"Well? Spit it out."

"See that bird?" I asked her. I pointed to the laughing gull that had just landed on a snag of driftwood. "There's story about why their heads and wings are black."

"The Indians where *I* come from have crow stories, too," she said. "But that ain't no crow. I know that much."

"No, it's a laughing gull. But the sea hag would sometimes turn herself *into* a crow. The Penobscot say she'd fly out during the day and steal all of Gull's oysters for her supper. She'd bring them to her island and build a big fire to cook them in. One evening, Gull was starving and asked for a few oysters back. This made the sea hag angry. She tried to put Gull in the fire along with the oysters. Gull escaped, but his head and wingtips were scorched. That's why they're black. But Gull didn't give up. He came the next day while the hag was out and ate his fill. He's been laughing about it ever since." I looked over at the driftwood, but the gull was gone.

"It's a nice story, but if there's a lesson, I ain't gettin' it. Are you gonna take me to Crow Island or not?"

"You can find a lesson in any story, like the Greek myth about a bird called the *halcyon*. That one says you can still have better days, *kinder* days, even after you lose a part of you that you thought was...*most* of you. And yes, I'll take you there."

ᚼ ᚾ

She drove us back to the village, found Harbor Street, and parked near the pier where I kept the *Maddie's Way*. She killed the engine and looked at herself in the mirror. She grimaced. "These falsies look so fake I wonder if I wouldn't be better off without 'em." She opened the door. The air outside was salty and fishy. But I could tell it felt good on her face. She breathed it in as we started our walk down to the dock.

We were halfway to the slip when three men got out of an SUV. They walked quickly toward us. My heart raced when I realized they were dressed alike: khakis, white polo shirts, black ball caps. "You there," one of them said.

She whirled and in no time had the pistol out of her purse and pointed at the men.

"*DROP IT! DROP IT!*" One of them fired a gun. Several

more shots came. I think some of them were from her pistol. Then we were both on the ground. I crawled to her. My left knee felt strange. I looked down and saw that my foot was facing the wrong direction. A fiery pain crawled in my gut.

"*MOVE AWAY FROM HER!*"

The woman was on her back. The center of her blouse was becoming a pond of blood. Her left shoulder was nearly gone. Her face was already growing pale. "It's not so bad, Jeff," she whispered. "Remember how I used to be so...afraid to die?"

"*SIR, BACK AWAY NOW!*"

She coughed. A red mist settled around her lips. "It's actually kinda nice...like, like when we used to do...hydrocodone.... Everything's cotton candy."

"*SIR!!*"

"I love you, Jeff."

"Don't go," I said.

That's when they tackled me.

CB ⹂

Craig came to see me the day after my second surgery. I'd already been in the hospital for a month by then. When I think of his visit, it's like remembering a fever dream. He may have said everything I remember, but I may have hallucinated some of it. *I don't want to know how involved you are. Just be careful what you say when they start asking questions. They know about the woman's husband. The Canadians are dead, too. Drowned, according to the news. The coroner told me their brains were missing. How the fuck does that happen? The drugs were in a duffel bag strapped to one of the bodies. But they have no idea where the money is.*

The guys with the questions showed up in my hospital room the day after that. I was more alert but still high on morphine; everything was still *cotton candy*. The man in the tan blazer said he was from the State Attorney General's office. I don't care to remember his name. "We have a few questions for you, Mr. Weaver," he said.

54

"I'm doing better. Thanks for asking," I said.

He shared a look with the other one, a kid with a goatee sucking on an after-lunch toothpick. "You were walking toward the boat slip at Winter Harbor with Mrs. Busbee on July thirteenth when the shooting occurred, is that correct?"

I nodded.

He took a notebook and pencil from his inside pocket and jotted something. "And she didn't have anybody with her? Friends? Family?"

"No."

Goatee took a step forward. "Taking just one person on a tour is against your policy, isn't it Mr. Weaver? 'No more than seven, and no fewer than three.' Isn't that what your sign says?"

"She paid extra," I said.

"And how did you know her?" Tan Blazer asked.

"I'd just met her. I have a coastal tour service, and I was taking her to see the puffins."

"Hang on a sec," Goatee said. He stabbed the air with his toothpick for emphasis. A tiny pendulum of spit dangled from its tip. "I'm confused. You mean you were taking her to see the puffins *again*?"

"How d'ya mean?"

"You took her out the day before, on Saturday the twelfth," he said. "You were gone for quite some time we understand."

A glittery purple orb ran along Tan Blazer's arm, up his neck and sat still on the top of his head.

"That's right!" I said and chuckled. "I've had quite a day already. I must be a little confused myself."

Tan Blazer laughed with me. "OK, now that we've got *that* established," he said, "Did she tell you anything about herself? Like where she was from?"

"Not that I remember," I said.

"Arkansas," Goatee said. "I spoke with Chief Dunlap yesterday morning. He said you told him she was from Arkansas when she fell off your boat."

"I don't understand why you're asking me these

questions," I said. "All I know is I got caught in a gunfight between your people and some woman I know nothing about—beyond the fact that she was hell-bent on seeing nature up close and personal—and that as a result, as you can see, my life's been ruined." I raised my stump into the air. "The first operation took off a leg." Then I pulled back the sheet to show off my shiny new ostomy pouch. "The next one relocated my asshole to just below my ribcage."

Tan Blazer made another note. The orb bounced on his head like a rubber ball. "Your involvement in the incident was unfortunate." His eyes seemed dull, as though he were looking through me at nothing. "And I've been assigned to find out all I can. I think you've given me everything I need. Please get in touch if you think of anything I might want to know." He took a business card from his wallet, placed it on the food tray next to my bed, and left.

The orb hovered and then faded. I got the strange feeling it was kissing me goodbye, and then it disappeared.

Goatee followed Tan Blazer, but paused in the doorway for a final, inexplicable jab. "And by the way," he said, "The men at the pier weren't *our* people. They were drug enforcement agents. You wanna talk about something that'll ruin your life? What do you think the minimum sentence is for someone convicted of trafficking narcotics in the State of Maine?" He didn't stick around for an answer.

CB 80

I waited over two years. Long enough, I figured, for the questioners to decide I couldn't have played an intentional role in what Craig Dunlap seemed to be calling a drug deal gone bad. I waited long enough to learn how to swim with parts of me missing. And I waited for the perfect day: a Sunday with heavy fog and water calm as molten wax. It came in September.

Climbing the western slope of Crow Island was tricky. I knew it would be. But I fell only twice, and only the gulls laughed at me. Even though the rusty padlock on the keeper's door gave me trouble at first, it broke under a bigger rock.

The parlor was dark, full of vague shapes. I struggled to work out the shadow on my right. An ornate fireplace. An iron poker hung from its mantle. The dim little square at my feet slowly became a crumpled cigarette box (not Gummer's brand) sitting on the hearth, and when I plucked the poker from its nail to stab at the box, I had the feeling I was the first person to touch it since the final keeper hung it there. There were beer cans. Here was a pair of panties and a flip-flop. The smugglers and I hadn't been the only visitors since "Forever on The Atlantic" had closed, but as I moved across the room—taking care not to snag my prosthetic on any of the crap on the floor—I couldn't help thinking how preserved the place seemed.

A purple light touched the door on the far side of the room. It was the same clean, sparkling purple light that had seen me through agonizing days of rehab at the pool, the same light that first came to me when the impossibility happened on my boat.

The door was hinged to swing away. I pushed, but something was blocking it. I pushed harder and it opened with a puff of rank dust. In a hallway that led in the direction of the tower stood half a dozen containers; some ceramic, some pewter, all open, standing in the muck they once contained. As I walked, I left fresh footprints in human ash.

The plywood and cinder block shelving ran along the right side of the hallway. The spaces were marked with strips of faded masking tape: *#107 – Daniel J. Callison, #106 – Mary Harwell, #105 – Harold Sandoval.* The fancy wood cabinets on the left were marked with little brass plates: *#76, #75, #74.* The hallway emptied onto a stone room splashed white with pelican shit. Sealed crypts, beautifully polished and glowing purple in the impossible light, lined the walls. I followed to the left. My fingers glided along the surface. Inscriptions interrupted the smoothness of the marble.

#25... #24.. . #23...

#22
Madelyn June Weaver 1944 – 1995

The journey was easy. My new wings are swift.

I stood there and listened as Maddie read from the Iliad. Her voice echoed across decades from a snowy night long ago. *For never again shall I come from Hades, once you burn me in my share of fire.*

"It's what Patroclus asked of Achilles," I said to the dirty purple room.

"Paul." The voice was all around me, in my head, everywhere. The light dimmed. The voice weakened. "Funny how the Greek meaning of my name is *high tower.*" The voice laughed. *Maddie. Maddie* laughed.

"I've missed you," I told her.

The voice and the light grew dimmer still. "I know... somebody else, somebody who's been here a long time, helped me do what I did...hope you're not mad...just wanted them to have a better life...."

"It's OK. I'm sorry I never gave you children of your own."

"Can't stay...under the floor mat in the wheelhouse you'll find...I want you to...." And then she was gone.

For a second, there was only blackness, and I noticed for the first time how badly it stank, and how alone I felt. But then the tiniest fleck of purple lit the edges of Maddie's vault. I can't be sure of what came next. I looked down and saw that I still had the poker. I watched myself whaling on the vault, destroying her epitaph, pulverizing it. The black trash bag sitting next to her urn, in the dust and marble shards, didn't seem real. It didn't seem real until I got it to my boat, back to land, and onto my kitchen table.

I counted the money from the black trash bag three times that night. It was nearly a quarter million, in new hundred-dollar-bills.

ೞ ೲ

I went up to Lubec today to send the final package. It's a long trip, but I've driven much farther to make a delivery. I hand-delivered the first one, and it took me a lot longer than thirty-six hours to get there. A day of spying before a secret drop-off on a rickety Arkansas porch was risky, but I had to know if, beyond hope, the boys still lived in the same house. They did. An aunt or a granny had moved in with them. She looked hopeful from a distance, and hope was all I had. Hope that they'd stay put, hope that if they ever moved away they'd leave a forwarding address. But more than that, hope that I was doing the right thing, what Maddie had *meant* for me to do. I mailed packages from post offices all up and down the East Coast, and as far west as Ohio. Packages of clothes, shoes, toys, video games, making wild guesses as I grew even older and even more out of touch with what a kid wanted or needed. I never included a return address, but I sometimes placed a little note inside. *From Mister Artemis.* A clumsy joke for Maddie. I think I remember her saying once that Artemis protected the vulnerable.

I found the Busbee address under the mat in the wheelhouse, of course. It was on a scrap of envelope from the woman's purse. *To Jeff Busbee*, it read. *1575 Picher Ave. – Cedar Hill, AR 72734.* And in pencil on the back: *crow island litehouse #22.*

I sent cash this time. The rest of it. It was a lot, but they've reached an age when they'll need it. I hope they'll know it's from their mother. A lady with a voice nearly as sunburnt as her face. A lady whose real name has permanently left the tip of my tongue. A lady I remember as "*Halcyon,*" on days when I'm thinking about her. Those days come often.

THE COLD LONELY WATERS
Aimee Ogden

In the end, it's loneliness that drives the mermaids outward from Earth, not curiosity. But fear plays its part in the story, too, as fear always does.

The capsule they send is a thing of beauty, a great glass sphere encased in a cage of titanium. They call it *Sea Foam Gives Way to the Sunfish's Breach*, and see how it traces a long arc between worlds: one globe of blue and green and brown, one silver-white orb, spiderwebbed in rusty red. Not a proper world at all, that one, hanging in frozen thrall to one of the great gas planets; a distant cousin of the moon that painted silver light on the mermaids' upturned faces back on Earth, and their best and closest hope of finding what they seek.

Toward it journey three travelers—three purposeful travelers, that is to say, for the fish and snails and algae they carry for food and oxygen did not choose this trip and have no concern with what path their strange new home takes. For that matter, only two of the travelers themselves take much interest in their surroundings.

Here they are now: the navigator, All Rivers Run Home to the Sea, checking their trajectory against star-charts and measurement lines etched on the inside of the glass shell. The alchemist, A Fish Thrashes Wildly in the Bird's Sharp Beak, screws two glass bubbles together at their ports to mix their contents. The product is exothermic, and her palms are thankful for the warm kiss of the glass in her hands. But the mixture is not for her; she tucks it into the still arms of the sleeping singer, She Wears Cold Starlight on Her Shoulders. She watches for a moment, hopeful, but Cold Starlight doesn't react. A Fish Thrashes grimaces, then flicks her thick flippers and glides over to drift beside All Rivers, whose does not look up from her star charts.

The bodies of All Rivers and A Fish Thrashes are made to suit the northern seas of Earth, and they manage the cold silent nothingness between worlds just as well: their bodies rounded and soft, their skin sleek with dark brown and gray fur. Their singer does not fare so well, not with the thin bubble of tissue that composes her tail, not with the fine mass of poisonous tentacles she drags along behind her. Their singer's body glows a fragile, electric blue in answer to the stars, but it is a cold light and does not warm her. A Fish Thrashes wonders, not for the first time, what the elders were thinking when they asked a merjelly to join the expedition. Cold Starlight is the best singer in all the world that they left behind—but what good will that do if she cannot survive long enough to swim in the waters of a *new* world?

"Do you think she'll make it?" she asks All Rivers, and All Rivers grunts. She hates to be interrupted at her work. "We have such a long way to go."

"She'll make it." All Rivers breaks her gaze from real stars and etched ones alike. She stretches her arms and A Fish Thrashes takes shelter in their warmth. Her head rests on the great round swell of All Rivers' breasts, and she breathes in the cool fresh water. Her adjustments to the algae levels are finally near-perfect. "Do you know what she did, when they asked her to make this trip?"

A Fish Thrashes shifts in her lover's arms. "That's just a rumor."

All Rivers says it anyway. "She laughed. And then she said, 'What good is a singer without anyone to hear?'"

"A rumor," A Fish Thrashes insists. "A pretty story for the next set of singers to build on. Might as well say there's really a mermaid who lives in the moon. Or that the Silent Earthers are real, and lurking in the algae pods to jump out and scare us." Her words are meant to jab, but not so hard as to explain why All Rivers stiffens now. "What is it?"

"They caught one on the construction site," says All Rivers slowly. She worked metallurgy before learning the shape of the celestial spheres, to guide them starward. Good luck to have a metallurgist on board, in case a non-fatal catastrophe befalls the ship's titanium shell.

"A Silent Earther?" A Fish Thrashes' gills open and shut too quickly. She makes herself relax, and presses her face into the soft curve of All Rivers' neck until they are both again as fluid as the water that surrounds.

All Rivers explains how the saboteur was caught. "Trying to slip contaminants into the titanium mixing pool. To weaken the frame, make it shatter with the force of leaving the atmosphere."

"Why would they do such a thing?" A Fish Thrashes wonders, and All Rivers shrugs.

"To keep the Earth as it is since the humans went away. To stop us from making the same mistakes."

"We're not riding their wake," protests A Fish Thrashes, and All Rivers' fingers smooth the bristling fur along her back.

"I know," she says, "I know that." But her eyes linger on Cold Starlight, whose face is cast in shadow despite the blue flicker of her body, who drifts listlessly on the slow motion of the water.

⚃ ⚂

Cold Starlight sleeps through the day-to-day chores of life aboard the capsule. The filters must be scrubbed to keep the all-important algae from clogging them entirely. Their trajectory must be observed and measured. And occasionally, a tiny portion of the metallic hydrogen in the engines, manufactured under the terrible pressure at the heart of the very deepest sea trenches, must be burned to correct their course and nudge them back on track. All Rivers frets over the details. Sometimes she envies Cold Starlight her carefree passage between the worlds; mostly, though, she is grateful for her own warm blubber and fur.

Cold Starlight wakes to eat from time to time. All Rivers offers her wriggling fish and the cool tender meat from the shellfish that cling to the glass shell. She rarely stays awake for long. But now, lappets drooping limply, she looks out through one of the windows on the titanium shell, back toward where Earth would lie, though it has long since shriveled out of view. She asks, "What happened to the humans?"

"They burned themselves out," A Fish Thrashes says, before All Rivers can answer. A Fish Thrashes' eyes aren't on Cold Starlight, but on the drawing she limns with one finger in a dark patch of algae. It's the figure of a mermaid—All Rivers, perhaps, if she flatters herself. "That's what happens when you're too stupid to stay beneath the waves where you belong."

Cold Starlight's lappets flicker blue. Her eyelids droop. All Rivers says, more gently. "No one knows for sure. One day there were no more new buildings stacking up on the shore, no more dark oblong things to block the sun as they passed. The ocean surface went quiet, and we were alone."

"The expeditions didn't find much." A Fish Thrashes adds a bubble helmet to the drawing of the mermaid, and then a long trail of seal-intestine tubing that connects to a great water tank. A Fish Thrashes has run out of room, so the tank is just one side and the suggestion of a wheel beneath. And now the drawing isn't All Rivers, it is Sun Shatters Incandescent on My Love's Azure Scales, the first mermaid to crawl on land.

Despite her name, that explorer was old enough during her journey that the sunlight only melted dully on her faded colors. Sun Shatters' voyage was the direct antecedent to this one, and All Rivers wishes she could have known her as more than a song's hero and a smear of algae on glass.

"Sun-bleached bones and great metal husks are all she found. Who knows?" She grimaces, and wipes the drawing away with her palm. A green cloud of algae floats up around her. "Maybe they killed each other, maybe they got scale-rot and scratched themselves to death."

"Maybe they left for the stars first," suggests Cold Starlight. "Maybe we'll meet them, somewhere out here. Them, or their children." A Fish Thrashes opens her mouth to argue, but All Rivers shushes her. Cold Starlight's eyes have closed again. Best to let her rest.

They decide to wake her when they are crossing the chain of asteroids that girds the inner collection of planets. She seems to be hibernating, but still, she is so small and frail. A Fish Thrashes shrugs, neither concerned about their singer nor wholly indifferent to her fate, and opens the ports of two of her exothermic bubbles to let them mix in the water around Cold Starlight.

Cold Starlight's eyes flutter. "Are we there yet?" she asks, though her lips barely move.

Poor little fry. "Not yet," All Rivers tells her, "but stay awake and eat something."

Cold Starlight obeys. She is younger than the other two, and alternately obedient and stubborn enough to show it. Her tentacles, curled cautiously inward for sleep, unfurl until a heedless fish is caught on her nettles. The tentacles recede into the frilly chasm of Cold Starlight's bell-shaped lower body. "That's better ... " There is some warmth behind the blue-gray of her cheeks now, either thanks to A Fish Thrashes' alchemy or the meal Cold Starlight is now digesting. "Shall I sing something? To pass the time?"

All Rivers and A Fish Thrashes have found plenty of ways to pass the time without Cold Starlight's help, because they have nothing but time now. It's not so very different from home, where during the cold season there's nothing to do but stuff one's stomach to bursting and then rut oneself senseless until the thaw—though this cold season will last months, years, longer than any of those.

"Yes," says All Rivers, and catches A Fish Thrashes' eye. "A song would be lovely."

They nestle together, All Rivers and A Fish Thrashes, as Cold Starlight tests her voice for the first time in weeks. "I'll sing about the Gyresmoot," says Cold Starlight, to herself as much as anyone. All Rivers starts guiltily, her fingers already twined with those of A Fish Thrashes. "That's a good song. That's the right song."

And she does, her clear haunting voice cutting through the water to ring against the insides of the sphere.

"Oh, we mourned our friends, our cousins, our lovers,
beneath the swirl at gyre's heart.
No cleansing wave reached up to sweep them away
though the oceans rose and the high places washed away:
it was their own hands with which they buried
themselves, or raised themselves up into the next life.
Gone, truly gone, and us alone,
forever and longer still,
until one raised her voice, her face,
The Black Pearls of Her Eyes Pierce Mysteries,
well-named and true, and offered us the choice.
When the deepwater folk speak, we listen.
Ah! what did she ask of us?
Her jaws opened wide and the universe
in miniature danced on her tongue.
To be alone, or to seek out other company?
Ah, she said, ah, to reach for the stars ..."

Cold Starlight twists slightly, and the nearly translucent tissue below her waist pulsates once. A few fish bones drift gently out. They don't settle downward, as they would back home, but continue drifting, caught in the lack of up and down. A pair of boneworms cut through the water toward the wreckage, ready to return the nutrients to the miniature ecosystem inside the sphere.

"I don't like the next verse," Cold Starlight says. Her arms, thin and white as those bare fish bones, wrap around her slight body. "But I think I ought to sing it anyway. Because I don't like it."

"Do as you like," says A Fish Thrashes. She yawns and presses her face into All Rivers' shoulder. All Rivers thinks that she should check their trajectory. She thinks that it can wait an hour. And anyway, Cold Starlight is singing again.

"But some turned their faces away
from cool starlight, and asked

65

on what far-flung world could such company be sought?
Humans reached for the stars and
burned their fingers. Our world had become
a quiet one, and no mermaid yet alive feared
the net's reach nor the dark oily stain on the water.
The currents of another world, they warned,
would only carry a new flavor of heartbreak—"

"Stop," says A Fish Thrashes, and Cold Starlight falls silent. All Rivers realizes she can taste a gradient of freshwater tears, and realizes again that they are her own. A Fish Thrashes brushes her thumbs along the curve of All Rivers' face, and says, "They're wrong. They'll see."

"I know," says All Rivers, and curls into that warm embrace again. "Sometimes I'm afraid. But I know you're right."

They drift together, spinning with the eddy of the waters. When All Rivers remembers, a moment later, she glances over at Cold Starlight. But Cold Starlight has already gone back to sleep.

ڣے

Cold Starlight wakes on her own, the frozen moon's pale, brown-streaked face looming large in their path. Since leaving Earth she has felt herself trapped in a fog, a bubble-nest of confusion and despair. Now, she knows her purpose is close. The luciferins in the cells that line her lappets and tentacles flicker dark blue in answer to the call of that inscrutable world. *I am awaited*, she thinks, and smiles.

She is indeed awaited, by A Fish Thrashes and All Rivers, who would like her to test the sub-capsule.

"It's almost time," says A Fish Thrashes. All Rivers is busy checking and re-checking their approach, measuring angles against the etchings on the inside of the capsule. Her tongue protrudes between her sharp teeth as she calculates. "How do you feel?"

"Ready," says Cold Starlight, and A Fish Thrashes nods approvingly. She has no more glass bubbles—it will be a long trip home—but she chafes Cold Starlight's arms with her leathery palms. It is a kindness, and it warms Cold Starlight from the inside out.

"We're in alignment," calls out All Rivers. Her dark webbed fingers are spread on the glass surface of the ship, but she looks back over her shoulder to smile at them. It's a shaky smile. What few smiles Cold Starlight has seen from All Rivers during this trip have been shaky. "It's time."

"Ready," says A Fish Thrashes, and anchors her flippers beneath a bar to turn the wheel that opens the port into the sub-capsule. Her big shoulders work as she spins it once, twice, three times. On the fourth turn, the whole capsule shudders, and a bright eclipse of light peers through the titanium cage. Not light: fire. Cold Starlight looks in wonder at the long, brief shadows cast on the far side of the sphere.

"No," A Fish Thrashes gasps, and All Rivers wails as she loses the capsule's beautiful alignment. There is a strange sucking sound, a whirlpool gone mad—Cold Starlight startles as her head breaks the surface of the water. There has never been a surface before, not inside the capsule, and the vacuum plays with tendrils of her hair before she ducks deeper.

They're losing water.

"Silent Earth," moans All Rivers, still clinging to her etchings. Her voice warbles out from beneath the surface, but not for long. Cold Starlight wonders what it will be like to swim the sea between the stars.

But then her head cracks cruelly against the rim of the sphere. She blinks to clear sparks from behind her eyes, and when she opens them, she finds herself inside the sub-capsule. It is still full of water, and the hatch is closed. On the other side of the porthole, she can see A Fish Thrashes, grim-faced, straining. A Fish Thrashes meets her gaze. Mouths the word, "Go." She reaches out of Cold Starlight's sight, and with a terrible grinding cry, the sub-capsule kisses its parent ship goodbye.

Cold Starlight watches for a glimpse of the main ship when one of her windows spins that way. The bright bloom of fire has faded: no oxygen to feed the flames out here any more than there was beneath the warm waters of home. Despite the violent spin of the sub-capsule, she fancies that she sees two shapes twined together through the shadowed glass of the sphere. Fancy is better than nothing, but it is not a filling meal. When she loses sight of the great glass sphere, she looks toward the moon. Its pale face has grown large in her view.

"Hello," she whispers. "I'm so glad to meet you."

The sub-capsule very nearly survives the crash.

Cold Starlight drags herself from the wreckage. The spilled water has begun to freeze and tries to stick her to the ice—her aching arms are already locking up, and her tentacles and body cavity are of no use here abovesea. She does not know where the drill has landed, nor how long she can survive these alien oceans without the sub-capsule's protection. Without the *Sea Foam* to return home to.

But she knows this: there is a great groaning crack in the ice floor, originating from the wreckage. And she knows this too: a singer's value is in being heard. Cold Starlight drags herself toward the crack with her foundering strength.

She falls into the chasm when she reaches it, falls until ice water strikes her back and shoulders. She floats in dull shock for a moment, then turns, rights herself. Sucks in a testing breath, into her mouth and out through her gills. Again. And again.

The water is wrong, cold and foreign. A chemical taste fills her mouth and makes her cough. Her eyes burn, and her skin cries in protest. A short mission, this one, Cold Starlight thinks, and bubbles of laughter roll out of her.

Dark shadows move in the depths.

Cold Starlight steadies herself with a flick of her tentacles, forces a shake out of her shoulders. She opens her mouth. A lesser singer might not be able to make herself heard, but Cold Starlight is not a lesser singer. The notes shake when they boil up out of her, hot joy into the cold lonely waters. She doesn't know who is listening, but she knows someone is, blurry shapes swimming in her fading vision. Something brushes her arm, another cool touch along the length of her back. Not the touch of a predator. A lover's caress, familiar and strange all at once. Cold

Starlight sings harder, through the sweetwater tears that feed this enigmatic ocean. It is good, in the end, to be heard.

A distant vibration, and whatever has come to greet her flees. She is well and truly alone when the darkness swallows her.

CG ᘓᕲ

Cold Starlight awakes with her face pressed against cool glass.

The songs that fed her as a child told of many afterlives, but none of those were vitrine-fenced. Cold though, some of them, and this one too. She opens her eyes to see what awaits her in the next world.

It is a small world, sharply curved and tightly enclosed. Smaller than the *Sunfish's Breach*, and without the familiar etchings of stars and constellations. Instead, muted yellow-green light accretes on the surface of the cylinder. Shadows blur and drift on the other side: more water? Air? She cannot tell.

She lists to one side; an air bubble is trapped under her bell. Her lappets tilt to release it in an embarrassing belch, and she rights herself in the water. Ah—there is a right and a wrong way, an up and a down. That is a strange sensation and a welcome one. She puts her hands to the glass and tries to divine what sort of world it is in which she has been made a visitor. When she spreads them, her fingers are bloated; she shakes out her tentacles and finds them turgid too. A freshwater tank then. Well. That won't do. Not for long, at least.

Vibrations reach her from the other side of the tank. The water is cold, but the sounds buzz warmly on the skin of her face and hands, along the fine tissue of her lappets. Voices? It is so hard to tell through the glass and the muddied lights and the dark, darting shadows. So these entities, humans or their children or something else new and wonderful—perhaps they can speak. But do they know how to listen?

Cold Starlight tilts her head back to stretch her vocal cords, taut with cold and hypertonicity and, yes, fear. There is no time for fear now, no room for it in this small dark tank, but Cold

Starlight finds it difficult to shed. When her voice sluices out of her mouth, it is a blunt weapon and not a sharp dart of understanding. It will have to do. She presses her palms to the glass, and sings out the chemical structure for sodium chloride.

The lights dim, and the shadows draw nearer. Dark shapes play in the condensation on the far side of the glass. Cold Starlight's lips curl in a smile, even as they shape the exchange of electrons, the push and pull of electric charges, the steadiness of the paired nuclei. It is as good a starting place as any. As she sings, years—centuries—of loneliness, hers and the greater shared loneliness of all the mermaids she has left behind, all of it falls away. And when it falls, it pulls fear down with it.

EXTINCTIONS
Lina Rather

Your mother taught you three things, up in the great white wilderness, before she went and shot that man:

1. How to kill an animal quickly and mercifully.

2. How to kill the veiled things that prowl in the shadows at the edge of your vision. These are harder and faster beasts, but they all fall like deer in the end, and that's the best advice your mother could have given you.

3. How to sew and mend the veil of the world so the secret things cannot escape. Truthfully, this was your grandmother's teaching, but your mother would have taken credit for the sun, had God not claimed it first.

ༀ ༀ

After your mother went to prison, you stayed with your grandmother, and after she died in her sleep, you went to the city. Odd girls on their own in the city come to bad ends, but you come from a long line of people who made their livings fixing and killing, and that sort of work never goes out of style. These days you have work that suits you better, in a tattoo shop in the low-rent part of the city where you spend most of your days doing flash and sweethearts' names.

Sometimes you take the kind of job your mother and grandmother did. You never wanted a legacy—the second sight, or the power in your blood—but they might as well go to good use, so long as you don't make a habit of it. Your mother fought monsters under a hundred skies, and look where it got her. You've seen ghosts and you've seen demons, and you've killed a thousand monsters, but unlike your mother, you don't make a life out of it, or so you tell yourself.

Hell, you've even got yourself a girlfriend these days who makes you dinner and tells you you've got pretty eyes, which is more than your bastard, runaway father ever gave your mother. You met her when you tattooed her from the cut of her pelvis to her collarbone, from scapula all the way around to breastbone. As it turns out, six 6-hour sessions is a lot of time to get to know each other. It's your best work, and you say this because it's true, not because it's on your girlfriend. The tattoo covers up a mess of other work—another girl's name (one you've never asked about); a vinyl record drawn by someone with a nervous tic; the band name of a no-hit wonder. She's got your picture on her keychain, between a bottle opener and pepper spray.

Maybe you love her and maybe you don't, but you think it doesn't matter yet.

 C8 80

So when the red-haired woman comes, you've got something to lose. It isn't like when you were alone and ready to tear open the throat of any monster than crossed your path. You got sick of sleeping on other people's couches by twenty-two; now there's a lease, and groceries. Monster hunting and exorcisms don't pay the bills (and look at where that got your mother).

The red-haired woman is beautiful. You know the instant she comes through the door that she isn't here for a tattoo or another set of earrings. She wears a petitioner's grimace, determined and sick, and she knows which tattooist you are without having to ask.

"I'm here for help," she says, and out of her breast pocket comes one of your mother's cards. If she's got one of those cards, she must be older than she looks. But people aren't what they seem, and time is rarely anything but an illusion.

"I don't honor old bargains," you tell her, though you've never turned anyone away. There's a stack of your mother's cards tucked away under lacy bras you never wear, and another in the urn that your girlfriend thinks holds your grandmother's ashes. The jobs were mostly small, ridding houses of wailing ghosts or putting curses to rest. Killing small beasts, with words or blades, whatever fits the task. Your mother handed out cards to anyone who accidentally pierced the veil. Magic, she told you, spreads like a disease, with one impossible thing breeding another. Best to call in professional eradication, which, these days, comes down to just you. You suppose there must be others out there—there were monsters up in Juneau, and there are monsters down here below the 49th, so it stands to reason that they're everywhere else too—but you've never met one.

The woman smiles. "I never struck a bargain. I was told to ask for help if I needed it."

"I only take cash." You intend it as a joke, but she takes a stack of twenties from her purse and sets it on the table between you. It's thick as your thumb, and that's got to be a month's rent, at least. Of every strange thing you've ever seen in your lifetime, this might just top them, and the weight of it feels more like a bribe than a payment for services rendered. She smiles as though reassuring a child before an unpleasant procedure.

"I have no one else to turn to," she says.

"There must be someone else."

"Who?"

You shrug. Probably someone just as lonely and silent as your life in Juneau, when it was you and your mother and your grandmother in a trailer out at the edge of what could still charitably be called the city. The heater in the trailer wasn't enough to beat back the frost, and when you went to elementary school you realized that your bedtime stories were not the same as everyone else's. You've a hard time imagining an extrovert doing this job. One month's rent. Either she's desperate or she's got an ulterior motive, but her money's good either way.

cg ଞ

When you tell your girlfriend you're leaving, she's standing in front of your bathroom mirror, twisting her hair into box braids. Packs of extensions sit at her elbow and she's only just begun, so it'll be hours before she's finished. Her left eye twitches as her fingers work through a section of hair she can't quite see over the crown of her skull.

This is unfair of you. This is what she does when her dissertation isn't going well or when the jackass at her lab has been making snide jokes about women in biology again. For a woman who rails against new-age bullshit in all its iterations, this is a kind of meditation. Her attention isn't on you. This is how you get away with it.

"Is there a convention I forgot about?" she asks. "You're supposed to come with me to dinner. That guy I told you about—he'll be there. The one from Yale."

The man from Yale. The golden ticket. Groundbreaking work on eurypterids. Your girlfriend's specialty is extinct Mesothelae, but apparently the two are related. You wouldn't know a Mesothelae from a Mesopotamian, had you not inked one on her arm in honor of her thesis defense. The dinner is important, especially in this job market, but you've never known how to make a good impression on purpose, and the only extinctions you can speak on are the ones you brought about yourself.

"You'll still be here when I get back?" you ask, when you've packed.

She laughs. "This won't take me *that* long, I hope. If I don't answer the phone tonight, send help."

You don't explain what you actually meant.

03 80

These are the stories your mother told you about why she shot that man, some in letters, and some in person, and some you put together yourself:

1. She was losing her sight. She thought he was a wolf. (She hit a ten-point buck from a hundred paces the day before, right between the ribs. Your grandmother made a stew from the offal.)

2. He was stalking her, and it was self-defense. (You had never seen him before, nor heard his name, and when you

74

looked up the city he was from it was one your mother never mentioned visiting).

3. He was possessed, a monster and not a man, and her job was to kill such things. (The autopsy showed no sign he was a monster, and ghosts don't move through blood and bone without leaving evidence of their passage. There was neither scarring in the stomach, nor the image of a hand clenched around the heart.)

4. It was an accident. She was half-drunk and fired the rifle just for fun. She didn't know there was anything but birds in the woods. It was private property; he shouldn't have been there. (For all her faults, she never would have been so stupid.)

The truth, probably: this life made her paranoid, and when she saw movement out in the woods she thought of all the biting, scarring, killing things it could have been, picked up the rifle and pulled the trigger before she saw it was a hiker and nothing more. (She told you this through gritted teeth, and only in pieces. No truth like this is easy. This, you can bring yourself to believe, only because it hurt her to tell it.)

03 80

Juneau is much like you remember. It's a good thing the red-haired woman didn't mention where she lived before you agreed to go, because you might have refused out of spite. You fly in at four a.m. but it's already light out and the blinding, sleepless summers of your childhood all come back to you at once. You're still blinking stupidly at the anachronistic sun when the red-haired woman appears in a Land Rover.

She's a storyteller, which wouldn't be so bad if you weren't punch-drunk tired with your knees aching from the airplane seats.

"Your mother saved me once," she says, while she drives you down once-familiar roads. There were days you wandered this town in a pack of equally dispossessed children, all odd and outcast, causing trouble with cheap vodka and matches. Now the capitol building shocks you, appearing on a street you didn't expect, like a phantom. "I was fourteen. Lonely. Though everyone here is lonely in December. You've noticed that, right? Everyone in Alaska is sad in winter. Without the sun."

You nod, and try to remember which road leads to your grandmother's grave.

"Fourteen and lonely," she says. "I went to the ocean at night without my dog. I don't know what I was doing. No—I was looking for trouble, and I think I would've found it even without him." She swallows, coughs. Truths hurt the throat. "He was waiting for me in the waves. He looked like a boy I liked at school, but his brown eyes were even more beautiful. Like river rocks. Like sandstone. It was only when I saw his claws that I realized the truth, and there was no getting away then. I was already ankle-deep. But your mother came out of the trees and ran down the sand and slit his throat before I could even scream. He turned back into an otter when he hit the water. I still see things I shouldn't, even though he didn't drown me to make me one of them. Ghosts, sometimes. Other creatures if I watch. On blue moons I dream futures. He touched my soul, your mother said, and no one comes back from that the same."

"Kushtaka." After all these years, you still remember what people fear, up here in the white. You close your eyes and imagine the girl on the pebbled beach with the freezing water soaking her tennis shoes, the thing that wasn't a boy beckoning her in.

03 80

After you've slept nearly all day, she takes you to the window and points down the road, towards West Juneau and Mt. Troy. She lives above downtown, in a little house painted teal that perches on the fat feet of Mt. Roberts. When you and your girlfriend went to San Francisco last summer, the Painted Ladies reminded you of this hill, all these brightly colored houses standing out like lighthouses in the snow. Your girlfriend laughed at this and said that the Painted Ladies were happy things, not the only sparks of color in an unforgiving wilderness.

You suppose this is true, but seeing Juneau again makes you remember watching these houses glow in a midnight summer sunset.

The red-haired woman points again, and now you see him standing in a copse of old pines just beyond the turn in the road. He's got a man's body and he wears a nondescript suit. Even his eyes are human, until you see that they never are the same eyes twice. His mouth gives him away entirely—it's sewn shut with twine, weeping blood down his chin and neck. He doesn't act like he's in pain, but pain means little to things that are not men.

"I see him everywhere." The red-haired woman whispers, as though she thinks he can hear. "In the supermarket. Following me down the street. Outside my bedroom window."

"That's what they do." You speak more curtly than you intended, but right now you are imagining all the ways this not-a-man can hurt you when you try to kill it.

"What is it?" She's gripping the windowsill now.

You lean into the glass and the thing's eyes flick to you for an instant before they return to the red-haired woman. You are not what it wants. "It's a guilt-eater. It licks your soul until you kill yourself." Some lost familiar of Anubis maybe, adapted to the New World. That was your grandmother's story, but you have no way to know if her theories are true.

You noticed the fresh cuts on the red-haired woman's inner arms on the drive up the mountain, and the way her hands shook. Like the others, the haunting has hollowed her out.

"This is an old house. Could it be mistaking me for someone else?"

Guilt-eaters don't work that way, but you leave it. "It doesn't matter. I can kill it."

03 80

You've brought your mother's weapons and your grandmother's tools. The grimoire and cup, the needle and sinew, the silver bullets and the familiar revolver and the short sword. The sword weighs oddly at your hip and unsteadies your gait. You haven't worn it since you were eighteen, on your own and alone, catching myths in the darkness for money. You don't know why you brought it, except that it's been a long time and you wanted to be prepared. You could've bought a hunting knife once you arrived instead of checking your luggage, but the sword feels right in your hand.

You keep it all in a box shaped like a trumpet case. There's a rose burned into the oak shell. Your grandmother said that in Latin, *sub rosa* symbolizes secrecy. Monks and politicians met under rose murals to swear each other to silence, and now half your life is spent under the rose. You stuff the case back into your suitcase.

As the red-haired woman watches, you strip down to a sports bra and shorts that cling to the long-unused muscles in your legs. Your mother wore a flak jacket, but you've always preferred freer movement to cumbersome armor. The tattoos that ring your arms from wrist to collarbone shine in the darkness, supplications to a hundred gods written on your skin. You don't believe in gods, not really, but you believe in precautions and in beauty, and these are both. Magic is about intent and effort anyway, and you've poured years of pain and exertion into these spells. The red-haired woman averts her eyes, like you're something profane.

CB &O

Fog shrouds the guilt-eater. The pack swings heavy on your back. You drop the revolver and the bullets to shed some weight and take up your sword. The guilt-eater bends its knees to fight.

It snarls and hits you with a wave of all the bad things you have ever done, from stealing an extra cookie after bedtime when you were six, to kissing that woman with the lovely hands at a party two months ago while your girlfriend was in Asia digging up sea scorpions. The guilt-eater shows you yourself, shiftless girl, adrift for a decade, going nowhere fast. It shows you those hungry times you don't talk about, even to yourself. It shows you the years of letters from your mother that you stopped opening.

You crouch low to the ground and howl at it, and it runs.

It's fast, the way that liminal things are, skipping between the bits of reality that slow you down. Your legs burn, your ankle twists on a slick rock. You skin your hand on a tree when the guilt-eater turns faster than you ever could. It's leading you up the mountain, away from the trail. There was a time when you ran track and could catch a rabbit with your hands, but now you take public transportation and buy meat from butcher shops.

The guilt-eater crashes through the underbrush, its unstable form shifting from step to step, and blink to blink. It stretches and shrinks, clawing its way through the clinging mountain plants. Its blood hisses on the cold earth from nettle scratches. Halfway up the mountain, your endorphins take over and you *move*. One long jump and you're nearly upon it.

You laugh a laugh ripped from your chest and you leap after it. The smell of it sings in your bones. Your marrow knows magic, the way blood knows kin. You don't need a dog to follow it. Every movement it makes echoes in you.

You drop the book by a stunted pine, your last sight of the road. You shed the chalice soon after. You'll find them later. They will find their way home.

As you crash through the trees, the sunlight fails. Your body no longer remembers these short nights. Your mind tricked you and told you it was evening, but this is the witching hour. The guilt-eater shrieks like a murder of crows. Shapes shiver beneath the bushes and in the darkness beyond the trees. A branch, or a claw, takes a chunk out of your leg. You bite your lip and taste your own blood.

The guilt-eater screeches again. Its voice recites your sins. Were you a different sort of woman, you would fall to your knees and weep, but you smile a hunting dog's smile and your feet drive into the ground. You're gaining on it. The guilt-eater smells like long-decomposed regrets and the unfinished quests of dead men.

You didn't go to the funeral. Your grandmother was the only person to stay and you didn't even see her off.

You gain ground.

You will never stop wandering.

You gain ground.

You leave, like she left. You have inherited a restless heart that will seek and never be satisfied. Doesn't the truth of it taste like nails in your throat?

You gain ground.

It fails to strike you down.

This body is all you are, condensed, beyond your past and your sins real or imagined. You loved this fight once, and love it still, despite yourself. The blood pounds through your ears like cocaine in the veins. The guilt-eater is the whole world now that you've scented its blood. You are a wolf, a woman, a weapon, a witch. You are Diana of the hunt, falling upon your prey with the force of a hundred flaming arrows. You are only your sword and your sword hand. You are teeth that ache for the monster's acidic flesh.

The guilt-eater stumbles and throws its hands out like the man it might once have been, but it's too late. It tumbles down the slope, limbs flailing awkwardly, inhumanly, a broken-jointed doll.

Your blade glints in the moonlight like a new star. One flick of your wrist and you've slit through the twine fastening its lips. Blood spurts. If it screams, you don't hear, or don't care. The blood is brown, made of dead things, but you don't mind that it splatters on your shoes. The only way to kill this thing is to open its mouth and make it speak all the secrets keeping it alive.

Sins pour from its open lips into the dirt. Your secrets, and the red-haired woman's, and the secrets of everyone the creature has ever laid eyes on. Its body deflates. The litany of other people's confessions sounds like weeping.

You've still got the needle and sinew, stuck into the seam of your pants.

"Hush," you tell it. It's perfunctory mercy; your mind is as a predator's, shaking at the meaty scent of a dying animal. You sew up the ragged cuts in its lips, the slash of destruction across its face merely a mouth again. The sword is for breaking and the sinew for fixing, but some situations require both. The thing's jaw falls open and it leaks secrets into the night until there is nothing left of its body but scraps of a suit and bones that don't make up a full skeleton. It tells you the red-haired woman stood on the edge of the rocky beach with someone's lost cat in her arms, a year after your mother saved her from the kushtaka. She slit the cat's throat and let it bled into the sea, but the kushtaka didn't come, didn't give the red-haired woman another heady glimpse through the veil, and your pulse beats hard.

It tells you everything, but it dies all the same.

Sweat streaks between your shoulder blades. Your legs are trembling and you sit down against a tree. The guilt-eater's bones turn to dust while you watch. The chill night air shreds your heaving lungs.

Another thing you've forgotten: how very long the shadows get when the sun finally deigns to leave. When the branch breaks behind you, it sounds like a gunshot, and you're up with the sword at her throat before she can shout.

The red-haired woman freezes. You lift the blade and she's forced to lift her chin. She picked a bad time to follow you,; your logical mind barely keeps you from slitting her throat, and you can't puzzle out who she is until manages to open her mouth. "I just wanted to make sure it was dead." It's a plea.

The sword wobbles in your hand. She closes her eyes and breathes out so slowly, like her breath alone might set you off. You've seen many things die and they all go still when they know that death is standing next to them.

It takes too many heartbeats, but you put down the blade and point to the last scraps of the thing's clothing. She picks up a shirt cuff and it falls apart in her fingers. She watches you the entire time, not unlike she watched the guilt-eater. *I understand*, you want to say, but the words cannot work themselves out of your animal throat.

When you finally get ahold of yourself, you start back to the road before you have the chance to do anything more regrettable.

ψ ψ

Hiland Mountain Correctional Center, unlike Juneau, is exactly as you remember it. The last time you entered its halls, you were sixteen and didn't have much choice. Maybe you still don't. Life leads you by the hand sometimes. Your grandmother claimed she had seen a vision of her entire life when she was five, right up to the moment of her death. You don't know if you believe that, but your grandmother did guess her death to the minute. You've never had any such vision, but you're smart enough to understand a sign when you're smacked in the face with one.

Your mother is old. That shouldn't be surprising, but it nearly knocks you off your feet. In your mind, she's thirty years old, kneeling beside your ten-year-old self with one arm around you while you try to pull a bowstring without your arm trembling. Her hair was dark brown, like yours, but now it's mousy grey, her skin pale from being trapped inside.

Her mouth goes flat and straight when you sit across from her at the metal table, like she's stuck between crying that you're finally here and screaming at you for staying away so long. You bite the inside of your cheek to keep from saying anything you shouldn't.

You buried the sword and the revolver and the chalice in the courtyard behind your apartment building, right after your return six months ago. No one goes out there except the landlady's senile aunt, so they should be safe, even from you. You kept the book, because it has a family tree in it that you've never looked at, and you kept the needle because you think you might like to try your hand at fixing things.

"I heard you went back home," she says, as if either of you can call Juneau home anymore. "Did you miss it?"

Of course she's heard about it. The woman has a spy network out of an eighties Bond film, built out of all the people whose lives she's saved, or ruined, or some of both. "One of your contacts approached me. I killed a guilt-eater."

She beams. "You're not going to lie and say you hated it, are you?"

You shake your head.

"That's how you know you're my daughter." She leans back in her seat like she's expecting a fight. But you're beyond hating her. You've spent too long dreading the fact of her, as if destinies are encoded in your genes like eye color and left-handedness. Your grandmother, bless her, believed in destiny and thus saw your mother in you. The first time you brought home a rabbit you killed, she stared at your rust-colored hands with such sad eyes. It wasn't until later that you realized what your grandmother saw was your mother at eight years old, still a child and yet already on her way to this small room.

You roll up your sleeve to let your mother see what you've done. The sword and cup and bullets curl from your hand to your elbow. Above them you've tattooed a red rose, so that it is all *sub rosa*, and yet, right there for all the world to see. A reminder for yourself, and penance maybe. You're done listening to monsters repeat your own unpleasant truths. "I know why you killed him now."

"Oh?" She sounds amused. Never once in all the letters you read did she ask forgiveness, for shooting him, or for leaving you.

"You were scared," you say. "That part was true. It's not the whole truth, though. Maybe you don't even know what the whole truth is."

"If I wanted to be analyzed, I'd talk to the psychologist." She crosses her arms, but stays.

"I almost killed that woman, the one you saved when she was a girl." At the word *killed*, a corrections officer glances at you, and you lower your voice. "After I finished the guilt-eater, she came up behind me, and all I could hear was her blood. When I looked at her face, all I could see was a monster. I had her

83

by the throat. Do you know how easy it would have been? And I didn't have a gun."

She laughs, as one does when handed something unexpected.

You lean over the table. You get so close to her that the guard glares at you. "I only do this when people ask for help. You were at it for so long that I think it scratched away your soul. You stopped being able to tell what was a monster and what wasn't. I bet you looked at that man, on our land, and you couldn't begin to tell what he was."

You lean back. The silence stretches.

"Maybe it was mercy," she says, working the words over in her mouth. "They said he was human, but he could have been a monster. Look at you. Look at me. Think of all the things we've done. Who's to say that we're good anymore, that we're human? Maybe I shouldn't have shot him but he shouldn't have been where he wasn't supposed to be. I took precautions."

This is the truth you expected, not the one you wanted. Neither of you offers a hug when the officer calls an end to visiting hours, but that's okay. Some things are what they are, and it's time to stop fighting old fights.

03 80

You go home, for good this time. The sword and the gun stay buried, though you trace the lines of your tattoos sometimes and ache for their weight in your hands. You knew how to feel powerful while killing things, and it's hard to learn other ways of being strong.

Your girlfriend has cut her hair down to an inch, so that it crowns her head in tight coils. The man from Yale has hinted that there might be a position for her after she defends. In your absence, she has become someone, or maybe she's just found the woman she was always trying to be. It seems you might be leaving for New Haven soon. You've spent your entire life in view of the Pacific but you don't think you'll miss it much. There's a whole other ocean to see. You can learn the rhythms of a New

England winter, and how to cook crab, and what a mountainless horizon looks like. You still don't know if this is love, but you'll follow her wherever she goes.

Some nights, you dream about monsters, and death, and evil things knocking on your door. You wake up at the sound of the wind howling, or at the sound of too much silence, and for an instant your heart clutches. On these nights it takes a long time to fall back asleep, but you learn to whisper a bedtime prayer of guilt you no longer wish to carry, and the prayer keeps you from digging up the sword again.

AND IN THAT SHELTERED SEA, A COLOSSUS

Michael Matheson

It's during the rains, the year the breadfruit trees bear unfamiliar seed, that the stranger comes to the drowned city. The year everything changes.

ଓ ଓ

Ebunoluwa draws the basket of fish to the top of the ravaged tower like water from a well. The sky overhead is a cool, clear bowl, the street below submerged several feet. The tides of those streets are awash with scattered seedpods, algae, and coral, grown wild over sunken curb barriers and debris gathering centuries of rust.

The still-standing towers, mostly clustered along long-drowned beachfront developments, are cast a dusky gold in the reflected light of the sun, their glass and steel another sea. The rest of the world below—shops, street vendors, and homes—washed away when the floods hit.

It's been years since she's seen another living soul; no drifters have passed through the wreckage below on their way to somewhere else since before her mother's death. So Ebunoluwa startles at the sight of the stranger on a small boat, a pole clutched in her long, slender arms as they push into the lagoon from the south. The waving hand reaching higher still than the woman's wild hair is the only thing to tell she's not one of the ghosts that haunt the city.

It's a moment before Ebunoluwa waves back, the movement so unfamiliar. The stranger's smile more foreign still. So unlike the ghosts Ebunoluwa lives with.

They sing to her sometimes, the ghosts of her city, when the sun is low in the sky, washing a burning red soft enough she can stare directly at it before it sinks beneath the earth. Their voices whisper through the breadfruit and mulberry trees her great-grandmother's great-grandmother's great-grandmother, Yejide, planted as saplings in deep soil hauled up the tower's winding stairs; through the rooms of the house Yejide and her wife, Morayo, built there—the house in which Ebunoluwa still lives.

When the ghosts raise their voices to the heavens, their song is the sweet song of cloudstreak, fast-moving. Of wind whispering through high grasses and sparse trees. Of the world alive and awake. A whisper of voices, building until it envelops the curve of the sky and the water below swells as with an oncoming storm. She used to fall asleep to the whisper on long nights, with the moon drifting overhead and her mother teaching her to name the stars. Her mother taught her to name the dead too—to tell the ghosts of family apart from the ghosts of the city: all those who cannot leave in death, tied down when fire rose and the earth tore itself apart; in the days when mountains in the shape of women walked and the worms of the earth slipped free from the cracks in the world.

The ghosts still sing. But Ebunoluwa no longer speaks her mother's name.

Instead, she thinks on those towering women—the colossi—as the stranger climbs the pulley rope hand over hand—more limber than any woman Ebunoluwa's ever seen, muscles stronger than her own. Ebunoluwa is still strong, still healthy and proud of the fat that girds her muscles, but her long hair is greyed with age where the stranger's is a shock of untamed tangle dark as a storm cloud's belly.

The stranger reminds Ebunoluwa of the women from her visions. The women who walked as mountains: Hewn sharp and angled from black stone, earth shaking as they strode. The colossi were asleep again long before Ebunoluwa's time; the only titan she's ever seen is the one whose slumbering back juts hundreds of feet up from the waters of the lagoon—huddled where the colossus laid itself to rest, the tatters of the worm she slew still coiled around her arms, its rent stone coils looped around the titan's back. The titan bent over its prey, curled tight toward the water and the lagoon-bed as if to bind the last vestige of its foe. The titan's head hovering just above the water — its broad, sharply defined face reflected in the surface of the lagoon as an island unto itself.

Ebunoluwa's swum underneath those girding arms and around those pillar legs, crumbling slowly into the water as the waves erode her. She's climbed to rest atop low outcroppings of rock and coral buildup on the surface of the water like pontoons along the titan's body. Sometimes she thinks she can still hear the titan breathing, when the water laps at its sides with the wind gone still.

She only ever dares climb higher to walk among or harvest what she needs from the trees her foremothers planted across the titan's lower reaches. Trees whose shapes and names her mother taught her long ago: Strong mulberry, high and thick with its straight trunk and wide leaves. Broad breadfruit, with its sun-soaked leaves and swollen yield. Bent-trunked shea trees with their honey-cluster leaves and kernel fruit. Mahogany with reaching, dusky trunks and profuse plumes. And dozens more. The seeds to plant them rescued in the first days after the upheaval, from storehouses and homes spread throughout the city's winding, wind-wavering towers and sprawling streets, by Morayo, who tended their planting. Yejide had no gift for making things grow. Though she gave birth to their first child, after that change came too.

Ebunoluwa's own body is long past child-bearing age. The shame of it still echoing decades later in her mother's last words to her: how Ebunoluwa's empty body had failed their line.

It's times like those Ebunoluwa touches the skin of her gut and stares off into the distance, remembering.

But now there is another woman before her. Warm and alive.

"Welcome, traveller," Ebunoluwa greets her, and the stranger smiles, bright-eyed, too thin and too tall, her shadow whipping out behind her like a sheet torn in unseen wind.

Ebunoluwa smiles with her. That motion unfamiliar, too.

They sit together in the shelter of Ebunoluwa's house, the clear sky having given way to a downpour too thick to see through. The rain pounds heavy on the packed earth and clay of her roof, the rain barrels full and the condensation sheeting rolled up, not to be taken out until the end of the season. "You have seen the titan who watches over this place?" Ebunoluwa asks the stranger, stirring a pot of fish pepper soup boiling in a three-legged pot over an open fire, a plate of pounded yam cooling beside her.

"Yes, on my way north toward the lagoon. She's beautiful."

"You came from the open ocean in that small boat?"

"No, east along the coastline. *Before that*, from across the sea. Though not always in a boat that small." The stranger declines to answer further, leaning in to smell the stew instead. Her eyes close in bliss as she inhales. "Months since I've smelled anything but the sea and fish. This can't all be wild. Do you grow your own food?" The stranger opens her eyes to stare intently at Ebunoluwa.

Ebunoluwa's skin flushes a noticeably deeper brown. Attention a distant memory, and always fleeting. Time spent in the arms of a traveller measured in days, if not hours. "I tend what I can grow up here, and harvest the rest from what grows on the colossus."

"Industrious of you. You're on your own?"

"Yes," answers Ebunoluwa, serving out two portions and offering one to the gangly stranger. She tries not to think on how good it feels as the woman's fingers brush her own when the traveller takes the cup. "For a long time. But you," she says, collecting herself. "You must be here with a purpose."

The stranger rolls the soup around in her cup, but doesn't eat. "Following the dead."

Ebunoluwa chokes on a mouthful of soup-soaked yam. "Sorry?"

"They're everywhere here." The stranger looks out the

front window of Ebunoluwa's house, as if she, too, can see the parade of dead wandering the flooded byways of the city below.

"Are there no ghosts across the sea?" Ebunoluwa's heard the tales of the fall of the world to the west. Tales of fire and flood and titanic women fighting the worms of the earth, tales brought by travellers crossing east to build new lives in unruined lands.

"Not anymore," answers the traveller, eyes gone hollow and her shadow dancing to a rhythm of its own in the firelight.

Neither of them speak as Ebunoluwa continues eating. The silence grows long and uncomfortable, until Ebunoluwa offers her guest a bed for the night in the spare room.

It only occurs to her later, when she's bid the strange woman goodnight and performed her nightly ablutions, that she still doesn't know the woman's name.

CƷ ᙠଠ

The stranger comes to her in the night, the unbearable heat broken only by the scent of rain in the distance. Ebunoluwa lies awake on her back atop a bed built low to the ground, plaited hair piled up beneath her head as a pillow. No moon lights the blank walls of her barren room: the darkness outside deep, lit only by pale stars.

Ebunoluwa doesn't hear the traveller breathing. Just feels the weight of her, surprisingly heavy for someone so bone-thin, crawl into bed with her. Hands brushing skin she'd long forgotten the sense of. Lips on hers. Then careful, patient hands. Ebunoluwa falls into them with a hunger she has not let herself feel in years, and entangles herself in the stranger's embrace.

CƷ ᙠଠ

In Ebunoluwa's dream—the same dream she has every night—the sky is a deep bronze lit by blood-streaked clouds and a sun that burns black and hot as a hole in the sky. But the immense garden stretching several dozen feet in every direction

90

from its centre, before which she and her mother stand, is the same as in waking: Several-feet-thick beds of sprouting root vegetables and the waving fronds of fluted pumpkin leaves, bitter leaves, and wild lettuce overflow its loose borders, the garden grown atop the fertilizing weight of her family's bones. The cemetery garden standing in the lee of the immense house her foremothers built—the high, single-storey dwelling with its gently sloped roof and wide entryways and wider rooms set back against the parapet of the wall farthest from the water. At the opposite end of the roof, a copse of breadfruit and mulberry trees grown up among the ruins of an immense water tower, thick branches waving in the boiling wind of the dry season.

Just beyond the edge of the tower, the raised face of the titan looms above them, its burnished features filling the sky, its shadow cast back across the surface of the lagoon. Impossible shapes swimming in that reflected dark, the water gone deep as ocean bottom with the weight of their coils and their sightless seeking. The walking mountain heaves as it breathes, watching them: Ebunoluwa and her mother arguing atop the tower.

Ebunoluwa's belly still full with extra folds, thick where the child grew before she lost it. Standing straight as she can manage, still weak from the loss of so much blood when the infant fell apart within her. So few days after, the ruin of her insides still a blinding pain that will not quell. Already, the dead child's spirit haunts her, wailing for her mother.

In the dream, Ebunoluwa's mother stands darker than the sun; a gap of negative space more feeling than form — pale eyes like small suns lit with fury in the midst of all that dark. The true sun's light burning hot along her skin as Ebunoluwa sweats profusely, struggling against exhaustion. Her mother's voice a lash of fire.

"Is this what we are come to—your belly scraped raw and useless? To each daughter are daughters given. And you, my blessing, my gift from god," she spits, "cannot carry a daughter. Cannot do your duty by this family and continue the line."

Ebunoluwa opens her mouth to answer, but there is no sound in her throat, only stones welling within.

91

Her mother steps closer, heat boiling from her skin, until she and Ebunoluwa are close enough to share breath. "Your ruined belly is our end. I named you wrong, daughter. You are no gift; you are a curse."

In the dream Ebunoluwa screams past the stones in her throat and lashes out with a rock torn from the earth, as she wishes she had done. Brings it down again and again and again until her mother lies beneath her, head crushed. And still she brings down the stone caked in shadow like blood. The spray of it washed across her face, the taste of it on her lips, thick and vile, as she lets the stone slip from numb fingers. That taste lingers on her tongue and in her throat, working its way down to her gut. She smears the darkness from her lips, painting her cheek, and rises on wobbly legs.

In the dream, she does not have to watch her mother sicken with agonizing slowness over months. Does not have to watch her mother's disgust and loathing for her daughter consume her, and finally claim her body. There, at least, her mother's death is quick. If not clean.

In the dream, Ebunoluwa does not have to simmer in the fire of her mother's hate for those long months. Until, finally, all that's left is to bury her.

In the dream, she does not have to live with the never-ending screaming of two ghosts.

ᘓ ᘒ

She wakes drenched in sweat, still wrapped in the stranger's long arms. A slight pain in her back and a pleasant soreness in her muscles—from being so long out of practice—as she rises. The stranger doesn't wake as Ebunoluwa creaks fitfully through the house, throws up at the memory of the dream as she does every morning, bathes, and goes to tend her family's garden.

The traveller doesn't rise until Ebunoluwa's picking the yield from the breadfruit trees. Strangely bulbous and heavy in her hand, she peels one open to find small finger bones within.

92

They spill from her hand as she drops the fruit in horror.

"What's wrong?" asks the stranger from behind her, having come up on her in perfect silence.

"Bones. In the fruit," whispers Ebunoluwa, afraid to voice it louder. The trees sway in soft wind, fruit rattling as the boughs swing.

"They make a good melody," says the stranger, watching the trees dance. Long arms held tight across her chest as if she stands cold even in the warmth of the sun. "Lonely. But good."

Ebunoluwa watches, open-mouthed, as the stranger walks to the root garden beside the house and bends down to sniff the earth, as if she knows what fertilizes that rich ground. Then wipes her hands in the earth and presses it between thumb and middle finger. Satisfied, she rises, and heads back inside.

Ebunoluwa stares at the remains of the fruit in her hand, long after clouds come to cover the sun and a storm rumbles in the distance.

೪ ೫

"What are you?" asks Ebunoluwa from the doorway of the stranger's room, the rain thundering onto the roof, making a blur of the world beyond the windows.

The traveller looks at Ebunoluwa from the edge of the bed. She loosens a drawstring bag on her hip, upsets its contents onto the floor. Tiny bones—fish-light and fowl-hollow and smaller, stranger bones still—spill across the hardened clay. With a wave of her hand the stranger lifts the small assortment from the floor, and Ebunoluwa falls back a step. The stranger wheels her collection through the air and rolls them in place, eyes never leaving the arcing white. Something dark and half-seen slips in their wake.

"I see fragments, sometimes. The sky rent wide: left a deep, glittering black like the skin of a titan. Oceans of black blood and places so deep no light can dream of going there. I remember what it is to tear apart a worm with my bare hands and shake the mountains with my stride." The stranger stills her

93

hand and the bones fall to the floor with a clatter. She looks to Ebunoluwa. "Or maybe what I see is yet to come. Always I'm adrift. Always there is an emptiness in me."

The rain pounds harder, more insistent, as Ebunoluwa sits down beside her. "You did not cross the sea by boat."

"No," answers the traveller as she bends to pick up the bones from the floor. "Along the coast, yes. But how I crossed the sea...." She shrugs.

"When I lay with you last night, you were a woman. But are you a woman true?"

"I think I was something else once. But now I'm this."

"You want something from me? Is that why you slept with me?"

"No. Though I like lying with you." The stranger's smile is soft and sad. "But your garden." Ebunoluwa stiffens. "What lies beneath it calls to me."

Ebunoluwa rises to leave. "They have been there a long time. Only the tilling of the soil disturbs them."

"They have not all been there as long." The stranger's words stop Ebunoluwa at the doorway. "The ones whose ghosts are with you — their pain is not old; it's too fresh."

Ebunoluwa shakes her head. "It *is* old. But like mine: still raw."

The stranger leans back on her elbows. "Then it is they who've been there long enough to seed in your trees. To overflow the borders of the graves you dug for them."

"And here I thought you brought the change in the fruit."

"No. Did you think a single garden would be enough to house a line so long? Or a mother whose ghost remains so angry—whose rage sickens the air you breathe? Do you not hear her screaming in the night? And the child—"

"I have stopped listening. To both of them."

Lightning cracks as if to punctuate her words, and they turn to the flare as one.

Ebunoluwa breaks the silence first. "Will you come to me again tonight?"

"Yes. But tomorrow I quiet the ghosts who haunt you.

Then I will go."

"As is the way of all travellers," Ebunoluwa throws over her shoulder as she leaves. And then there is only the stranger and her collection of bones.

"The Traveller," says the tall, gangly woman who is not a woman, eyes on something far in the distance. "I like that."

☙ ❧

In the morning, the scent of the stranger is still on her skin as Ebunoluwa wakes. The storm has passed, the sky bright and clear, the wind warm on her skin as it blows in through the open window.

She lies with her hands running along her skin, listening to her body for the first time in years. Every quiet motion and whisper a benediction of its newness; of the loss of deadened skin and the rawness of the flesh in which she walks.

Through the window, Ebunoluwa can hear the stranger walking through her garden, digging up furrows in the soil. She can't make out the words the stranger speaks, just the low warmth of her voice, the invitation, and the answering rumble from deep-packed earth.

Ebunoluwa shudders at the sound of burial loam rending, and turns her face from the sudden dark that spreads wide across the window, blotting out the sun. She crushes her face into the pillow against the crunch and tear of bone and the wail of old ghosts, and newer ones too familiar.

She screws her eyes shut tighter still against the thinnest, smallest wail; the ghost of the unborn child whose cry has not stopped ringing in her ears for decades.

The littlest voice the last to be cut short. The silence of its sudden, so-long-hoped-for absence deafening.

She's not sure how much time has passed when the stranger comes to her. The tall woman's skin burns hot to the touch as she comes to lie with Ebunoluwa one last time.

☙ ❧

The Traveller takes hold of the pulley rope and wraps one long loop of it around her hand as if to use her fist as a rappelling brake. "Will you stay?" she asks Ebunoluwa.

"Should I not? My family built this place. Made it what it is."

"All that's left of your family is you."

"So you think I should go?"

"I think you should make your own decisions." The Traveller smiles as she jumps off the roof, abseiling swift as a stone. She crashes into the water and laughs as she breaches again, shaking wet weeds and coral bits from her wild hair. She waves goodbye as she climbs into her boat and unmoors it, as she propels her boat swift and sure out into the lagoon.

Ebunoluwa doesn't wave back.

Cʒ ଠ

She stands before the rent garden—the muddied earth peeled up and out in great gouts of formless statuary.

The stranger has not merely taken the ghosts of her mother and her child, but all the ghosts of the women of her line. The cemetery garden swept clean of bone and spirit.

What now is left for her here? Ready food? Shelter? None of it she can even call her own. All of it someone else's work—a legacy no longer moored by more than memories and oral history. With her family's ghosts gone, the trees have already begun to wither and the clay of the house to crack. Ebunoluwa's never known anything but this place. These ghosts. And now she doesn't even have that.

She's free. And she's never been more terrified.

The open pit of her mother's grave yawns empty before her, roots still interwoven like tendons through where the bones lay. The vague shape of her mother still there in the emptiness, and so much more there than lost bone: The weight of being her mother's daughter still buried there.

All the love and hate that survived her mother; that never

gave Ebunoluwa room to breathe while her mother still lived. And even with the spirits of her family gone she is still her mother's daughter, and not. Still the hope of the women who bore her, yet the last of their line. Not the failure her mother deemed her, but not yet more.

She's not entirely sure what she is now. Except alone.

The stranger's right. This isn't her place in the world anymore. Just a remnant of other lives, worn loose like a host of second skins.

She looks to the colossus in the lagoon, towering high above even the building on which she stands. When did she stop wanting to climb higher than the groves her foremothers planted atop its broad limbs—along the paths of wild growth that ascend higher than those carefully planned fields?

A swift shadow falls across her, and she follows its passage up and inland—a goshawk dark against pale cloud; both drifting east, toward browned earth and green plains out past the lagoon. Toward the remnants of countries Ebunoluwa's only ever known in stories. No telling how much of the old world remains now, or what those who went before found. Ebunoluwa's never been beyond the borders of the drowned city. And now, more than anything, she wants answers to those questions.

She watches the bird until it's just a dark speck against the horizon. Then she goes inside to pack the few things she owns. She ferries them to her boat below, and sets the house and the garden alight before she leaves. The blaze is high and roaring as she descends the tower for the last time.

When all is ready, Ebunoluwa heads her boat into the interior, following the path the Traveller showed her. She doesn't look back.

FALLOW
Ashley Blooms

They find the bottle in the barn. There are a lot of things there, whole piles of things: tractor-part things, tire things, cutting things and bolting things, all tired things, slowly fading toward the same color of rusty brown. The inside of the barn smells of stale hay and beer. Misty picks the bottle that is the least broken and William holds it between two fingers and lets the water drain from its open mouth onto the packed-earth floor. The base of the bottle has a deep crack running through it that snakes along the length, almost all the way through. The crack raises up a little, just enough to tear their skin if they aren't careful.

They sit so their bodies form a triangle, William and his best friend Misty and her sister Penny. They sit in the corner of the barn, there among puddles of something that might be water. This way, no one can see them from the road. It's William's idea. The whole game is William's idea.

The bottle spins and spins and they kiss what they are given. Wooden beams. Metal pipes. Once, for William, a grasshopper. The bottle seems to find only the gaps between them, the space that separates their knees from other knees. It doesn't land on a body, not the whole time they are playing, even though William moves them three times, convinced that it's the ground or the shadows or the moisture from the puddles that is warping the bottle's path, but nothing changes.

They decide there will be one last spin, and William reaches out, and William is sure this will be the spin that changes the game, when a car pulls into the driveway and a voice calls, "Penny! Misty!"

The girls are gone before William can ask them to stay. Only Misty pauses in the doorway to wave, and William waves back. He listens to their mother's voice, to the rustle of grocery bags, the slam of a trailer door. He waits until he can hear the water in the creek near his house. Then he spins the bottle one last time. The glass clinks and grinds over the dirt, kicking up breaths of dust so small that you have to squint to see them. The bottle stops with the mouth pointing at William's knee.

☾ ☽

When the girls are gone, William sits by the barn door, which is always open, propped on two crumbling cinder blocks. He watches Earl, whose trailer sits behind William's, by a field that Earl tilled many years before. In all ten years of William's life, he has never seen a single thing grow in the field. There is a word for places where things don't grow. William's mother taught it to him. Fallow, she said, and said it again when William asked her to. He liked the way it sounded, a little like hollow, or holy. He said it to himself sometimes, at night, repeating it over and over just to feel the letters rolling on his tongue.

The fact that nothing has ever grown in the field doesn't discourage Earl, who is bent double over the plow, driving it into the soil. The dirt gives on either side of the blade, opening up, gutted. The earth exhales a damp smell. Creek water and must. Earl keeps going. William spins the bottle again and again and it lands, every time, with its mouth pointed at his knee. Earl plows and plants until the sun begins to set and then he curses and walks to his trailer. Without him, the quiet takes over the field, and the crickets are born out of the quiet, bringing noise.

Earl pauses at his trailer door, squinting to see William in the shadows of the barn. "You ain't supposed to be in there," he says.

"I know."

"Well." Earl looks toward the trailer he rents to William's mother. There's no car in the driveway and no lights in the windows. "Just be careful," he says. "There's broken glass and God knows what. You're liable to catch tetanus or some shit."

William nods and he waves to make Earl go away, and Earl does, waving a broken chain in his hand, thick flakes of dust breaking from its links and falling through the sun-bitten air.

William buries the bottle in the fallow field. If anyone had asked him what he was doing, he wouldn't have known how to answer. He doesn't have the words to describe how the field reminds him of himself. The dark shape of it, the earth torn up and left to cool in the dark, a little steam rising. How it feels like maybe the field needs something only William has, and all William has is the bottle.

He waits until Earl shuts the screen door to his trailer, hemming out the darkness and the cool air that it carries. He waits until all he hears is his own breathing and the creek water running, until the two sounds are one sound, the same. Like all he has to do is walk to the creek and open his mouth and a whole stream full of minnows and rocks will come rushing down his throat, running over the bare bones of his ribs, collecting in his fishbowl belly where nothing could ever get out again. William can almost taste the water, sour and green and a little sweet.

William buries the bottle at the edge of the field. The solid door to Earl's trailer is still open, and the thought of Earl appearing now that he's had time to drink scares William a little. But burying the bottle only takes a minute. The soil is loose and dark and warm between William's fingers, and when he is finished, the earth is smooth, like the bottle isn't there at all, or like it has always been there.

CB ED

William lives with his mother, who is beautiful, and younger than any other mother William has ever met. Her name is Shannon. She has white-blond hair and a scar in the crook of her arm and even that is beautiful—in the way that it raises up from the rest of her skin, in the way that it curves, in the way that it never changes.

She comes home that night even later than usual. She is smiling though, and she smells like peanuts and sugar. She tells William this is the best date she ever had. That he was tall and wonderful and worked in the mines. That he was in line to be a boss. That he called her kitten and took her dancing, like out of a movie, like a real cowboy.

"Have you ever been dancing?" she asks.

William shakes his head. He is sleepy and a little hungry, but more than anything, he is glad that she is home, glad for her noise, which fills up all the empty corners of the trailer. Even the stained yellow carpet seems prettier, golden, as she stands on it barefoot, reaching out her hand to him.

"Dance with me."

She is a little drunk. A little stumbling. She steps on William's toes and William laughs. He rests his head in the center of her breasts and closes his eyes and lets her twirl him in slow circles around and around the living room.

 C3 &0

William wakes the next morning to the sound of voices. The sound of car tires. A honking horn. He walks barefoot onto the back porch. The air is heavy and mist clings to the tops of the trees. There are more cars outside than he has ever seen and more people, too, gathered around the fallow field. William is shirtless and he feels as though his teeth have been replaced by stones that he has spent the night grinding, grinding into dust.

Earl is at the center of the crowd, kneeling before something William has never seen before, but somehow recognizes. The object stands at the edge of the field where William planted the bottle and, for an instant, William can feel the bottle in his hand, a phantom weight, cool and steady. He makes a fist and the feeling is gone.

The crowd shifts to allow more people in. The thing in the field is taller than any of them, even Earl, who is the tallest man William knows. It has a head-shape sitting on its shoulder-shape, but it has no legs and no arms, either. It is as smooth as the shadow that William casts behind him in the middle of the day, but this shadow is made of bright green glass that shines when the sunlight breaks through the clouds and everybody makes

101

church-sounds, low mmms and ahhs. Most of them are people William has seen before, at Sunday school and at basketball games and at Save-a-Lot on the first of the month. He knows them all, even remembers most of their names, but no one is looking at him. They are looking at what William made. Even though he couldn't have known what would happen, some part of him believes he had known that something good would come from the bottle, from him. Something beautiful. Something that would draw sixty people into a muddy yard on a weekday morning to stare open-mouthed at a statue grown from fallow ground, and William stares, too. William never wants to stop.

cs so

They gather in the yard between the trailers, William and Misty and Penny. The crowd has thinned and Earl is building a new fence around the fallow field. The sound of hammer and wood echo across the bottom so it sounds like the whole holler is being rebuilt.

Penny says, "I don't know why everybody's so crazy about it. It's creepy. Ain't it creepy?" She looks at William and Misty, who are looking at the field. Penny is starting high school in the fall and she's never talked so much. Now that she knows the sound of her own voice, she can't help but say things. Like the minute she stops talking it will be the last, and she has to make sure it's the right word, the right sound. She says, "And ain't nobody knows where it comes from neither. I don't hear nobody asking about that. What if somebody planted it on purpose? What if it's some kind of poison? Mrs. Crawford said it could be a bomb. Or chemicals. It could be some toxic mineral grown up from the mines."

"I think it's kinda pretty," Misty says.

William says, "I think it kinda looks like me." Especially here, from a distance. All the indents are in the right places—his eyes and his mouth, his ribs and toes. It could be William if he were taller, a William made of glass.

"I don't see it," Penny says.

102

"Maybe from up closer," Misty says. Penny goes to find out, and calls for Misty to join her, but Misty says William's name instead and when William turns to look at her, he can't see anything. Misty's face has become the yard and the sky and everything in between. Her lips are on his lips, pressing, soft. William blinks when she pulls back.

Misty smiles. "Come on," she says, and takes off running through the grass.

CB 80

"Where's your mother?" Misty asks.

Side by side, bent double so their faces are barely a foot away from the earth, they are looking for worms. Misty's back yard is the shadiest. The ground is always damp because the trailers have no gutters, so there is nothing to protect the earth from the rain. The ground grows soggy, the soil darkening. Misty's trailer is farther away from Earl's, too, which didn't matter once, but it matters now. Even here, they can still hear the voice of the crowd, can hear someone shout, "Step back!" as William reaches down and digs his fingers into the earth.

"Did you hear me?" Misty asks.

"Dunno," William says.

"You dunno where she is or you dunno if you heard me?"

"Dunno."

They find three more worms, all fat and wriggling, their segmented bodies writhing until they are dropped into a Dixie cup half filled with dirt.

Misty says, "My dad hasn't been home in three days."

"He working?"

Misty shrugs.

"Don't he always come back?"

"So far," she says.

William picks at the dirt under his fingernails. He watches Misty part the dirt with her hands. She is gentle with it. She runs her finger back and forth across the ground until, slowly, the backs of worms appear.

"What's Penny say?" William asks.

"What's Penny always say?"

"Something dumb?"

Misty smiles. "Something dumb."

They walk the worms to the creek. Outside Earl's trailer, the crowd has thickened. William wants to join them, to hear the things they are saying about the green statue, which has grown another few inches since it appeared two days ago. He wants to hear them talk about how beautiful it is and how strange, how they have never seen anything like it before in their lives, but it seems to scare Misty—the people all knotted together, some they know but plenty they don't, and the way that Earl drinks right there in front of everyone instead of waiting until he's inside his trailer like decent folk.

William and Misty go fishing instead. They sit side by side on the muddy ground, trading worms. They catch nothing but faded Pepsi cans and mosquito bites and when they retreat across their shared yard at dusk, the crowd is still there, still watching the fallow field.

Cℨ ℬ૪

Sometimes, late at night, William's mother crawls into bed with him. Her breath is hot against his neck. It feels like a fever does, only it's on the outside of his body instead of the inside. She makes their shapes fit—her knees behind his knees, his back against her front. No spaces. No gaps. Even her words gum together when she speaks. They stick in places that they shouldn't, the places where they are meant to come apart. She says things like:

"I'm sorry."

"You shouldn't never trust a man."

"He pushed me down. We was thirty miles from anywhere, what was I supposed to do?"

"It's like glass. Like your whole body's made of glass."

"I never wanted to marry him. I never even wanted to kiss him, but when has that ever stopped a man? They take things.

104

That's all they know how to do. Take and take and take."

"Don't ever be like that, William. You promise me?"

"I don't know what I'm doing."

"I'll be your father, all right? I'll be the man."

"I'm sorry."

"You know he hit me? Your daddy? That's why he never comes around no more, because I told him I would kill him if he ever did, and I meant it."

"Promise me, William. Promise."

"I'm sorry."

೮3 ೮೦

They play spin-the-bottle again. This time, it's only Misty and William. They sit in the barn where it's growing dark. They spin the bottle and it lands on William every time, even when he is the one spinning it. To play fair, he kisses the back of his hand, the curve of his knee, the space between his fingers. Misty kisses him, too, and each time, William presses harder into the kiss, and holds it for longer. He thinks of his mother and wonders if he is doing it right.

Outside, it begins to rain, and the thin crowd grows thinner. Fat drops of water slick down the sides of the green statue, which still stands alone. Umbrellas pop open, making a roof over the crowd, and the ground dries under them in pale brown circles that overlap and crisscross and disappear when the people shift from one side of the field to the other. After a while, Penny comes walking through the crowd looking for Misty, but Misty isn't anywhere that Penny is looking, and the bottle spins and spins.

೮3 ೮೦

Certain things don't grow. This, William knows for sure.

Every night for a week he goes out to field after his mother is asleep. He waits until the house is quiet and he can hear the cricket song through the thin walls and the thinner glass of his window. It is less quiet outside, where he isn't the only one awake. There are bullfrogs and whippoorwills under the deep white moon.

There, alone in the field, William buries his new shoes and a plate from the kitchen and a pair of mismatched earrings that he took from his mother's dresser. Nothing comes of these. When William tries to dig them back up, they are gone. He is more careful now, about what he offers to the field. He only wants to give something that will give him something in return.

The crowd that has been visiting the field every morning is growing restless. They've stopped taking pictures. They've stopped bringing their friends. Maybe they're wondering if the field was special after all, or if it was all a mistake. Misty's mother says the crowd will find something new to be excited about soon, and that scares William, the thought of things going back to the way they were. So maybe, if William buries the right object, then the right statue would grow, and Misty would love it, and his mother would love it, too. They would have dinner on the back porch, the three of them, together, and they would listen to the crickets trembling in the grass and they would say how beautiful the statues were. Their delicate bodies and glowing edges. Like angels, winged and glorious. Like God. And then William could tell them about burying the bottle, how it had been him all along.

ɔ ɛ

William wants to show Misty something. He has been thinking about the right way to do it for a while now. It can't be raining outside and Penny can't be there and neither can their mothers, and it has to be before dinner, too. All these things are important. He thinks for days and every time he thinks about it, it makes the palms of his hands itch like they can already feel it, like the William from four days from now is telling him it is all right to do this.

William takes Misty to the barn again. He swept the floor the day before and the barn smells like damp hay and leaves. It isn't a bad smell.

"I want to show you something," he says. William lies down on the ground and tells Misty to lie down beside him.

"Why?"

"Because," he says. "That's how it works."

Misty pushes her hand into her back pocket and pulls out a handful of firecrackers. "Why can't we just light these?"

"This is better."

"You want me to go get a bottle?"

"No. Lay down." And, when she still doesn't listen, William says, "If you don't want to play, then go on home."

Then he closes his eyes and lets the sun turn his eyelids bright red. When Misty lays down, he tells her to close her eyes, too. He tells her about the tattoos on his mother's boyfriend's back. How the boyfriend plays with the hem of her shorts. How he comes up behind her and puts his mouth on her neck. William rolls onto his side and leans over Misty. He talks the whole time that he is pushing at the button on her shorts. He talks about black ink bleeding into blue ink, about wings on things that shouldn't have wings, about green light and bodies made of glass. William only stops talking once he rests his hand between Misty's legs. He moves his fingers back and forth to feel the skin beneath her underwear shift and give. They lie there, side by side on the dirt, waiting for something to happen.

Ψ ⁊

William tears a soft piece of wood from the barn's door. He plants that, too.

In the morning, there is a new statue. This one is shorter than the glass man, though much wider. This statue is a hand made of gold—five fingers and an unlined palm. The fingers curl gently toward each other. The index and thumb almost meet, like there is something the hand means to take hold of, something that William can't see, or can't see yet.

Ψ ⁊

"It kinda looks like me," William says.

They are on the porch together, William and his mother. There is a small mirror balanced on the rail and Shannon is bent double in front of it. She has one eye closed as she puts on mascara. She is wearing a dress that ties around her neck. William can see the skin between her shoulders, the way it moves, bunching and releasing. She makes a low sound in her throat, a skeptical sound, like when William wakes up late for school and tells her that his stomach hurts, he has a fever, his tongue is a boulder that could weigh the world down, and he can't imagine going to school today. Not like this.

He says, "It does. Just look at the nose." He touches his own nose, flattens it into his cheeks. "And my head. The little lump on the side of it." He touches this, too.

"Which one are you talking about?" Shannon asks.

There are three statues now. William planted a scrap of Misty's shirt and it grew almost immediately, bronze and tangled, something that might be a heart or a pair of lungs, something internal, something that would be slick with blood if it were anywhere else but here, in the field.

"The green one," he says, and she says, "I don't see it," even though she isn't even looking at the statue, but at the curve of her own eye in the mirror.

 C3 80

Days pass and William and Misty play together like they always have, at the creek and in the woods. They find a thicket of blackberry bushes and dig out a hole beneath it. It is cooler under the thicket, dim with golden light crisscrossing their faces, and they can pluck berries from over their heads any time they want. They can eat until they're full, and they do, until the berries are gone and the thicket grows hot under the sun.

Some days it's like nothing has changed. Like there are no statues growing in the field and no crowd of people growing around the statues. Like there is no barn, either. Like William knows nothing about the color of Misty's skin under her shirt and how it's different from the rest of her, different from anything he's ever seen before.

C3 80

The man who took William's mother dancing, the miner, is gone. This man is a mechanic. Blond, not brown. He wears a heavy gold cross around his neck.

William's mother says, "He's right in the next room."

"Come on, he's asleep," the man says.

"You don't know that. He could be listening."

"Then we'll be quiet."

"I don't—"

"Shhh. You'll wake him."

The man in the next room, the mechanic, laughs. And maybe if he didn't laugh, things would have been different, but he did, and they aren't, and William lays in bed and listens to the sound they make, this man and his mother, and he tries to imagine what it looks like from their side of the wall.

C3 80

William goes to the barn and waits for her. When she doesn't come, William goes to the yard and waits for her there. Misty said she would meet him. She promised. William waits until his hands get cold, and then he walks home, feeling tired and hungry and something else. Something like anger, only smaller and meaner. Something with neat rows of teeth that fit behind his own so he feels both like himself and not himself.

William walks around the trailer, not wanting to go back inside, not wanting to sleep. Earl is sitting by the field in a lawn chair with a cooler and a bottle of beer.

William says, "Hello."

"'lo." Earl looks at him with bloodshot eyes. "What you doing up?"

"Couldn't sleep."

109

"Me neither. Have a seat."

William sits on the grass next to Earl. They look at the field, where many things have grown, so many things that there is little room left for much else. Copper things and bronze things and hulking stone things and shallow golden things that bend and dip into other things, so you can't tell where one ends and another begins.

"You ever drank?" Earl asks.

"No."

"Good," Earl says. "Don't never start." He takes a long drink and William watches the skin of Earl's neck moving like there is a hand inside of his throat that reaches up to his mouth and pulls the alcohol down, its fingers unwinding against the back of Earl's tongue, the tips of its bitten nails reaching out to catch the scant inch of light that appears as Earl's mouth opens and then closes again.

"Have you seen Misty today?" William asks.

"I ain't seen a soul since that lady from the news this morning. It was the damnedest thing. She said some people up at the college wanted to do some soil tests. Water tests, too. They want to know what's going on," he says, and his voice is hoarse. "I told them to come on down, they can do whatever they want so long as they pay me for it and they don't scratch up any of the growings." He finishes his beer, reaches in the cooler for another. He pops the top on the arm of his chair. He says, "You want to know a secret?"

William shakes his head.

Earl says, "I didn't plant nothing. Not a damn thing."

"I know," William says.

"People keeps asking me how I got it to grow. They think I'm welding them myself, even if it don't make any damn sense."

"Misty thinks they're ugly."

"They don't want to believe nothing I say, but it ain't me. It never was me."

"I thought they was pretty at first, but now I ain't so sure. You think she thinks I'm ugly?" William asks.

The lamps Earl installed over the field start to flicker and buzz. The statues glow under the light, letting it glint off their hard edges and soft edges like sun on water. Even as they watch, something begins to grow. It starts near the back of the field. It twists up slowly, three strong bars of bronze that grow straight and narrow, until some meet in the middle while others keep growing and curving. It's hard to tell what the statue will be before it's finished, but William still guesses: a blue gill, a seashell, a broken back.

"Maybe it's God," Earl says.

"Maybe."

Earl says, "Don't you never start drinking," as he lets another empty bottle fall.

William doesn't move, and Earl doesn't say another word. The bronze braids itself into a bridge with heavy slats and a thick rail, where a hand might hold as its body walked across, staring down at the spaces between the boards, at the earth so far below. The bridge stops halfway, at the very peak of its curve, where it should fall to the other side of the field, but it doesn't. It doesn't.

CB &O

William takes Misty back to the barn. It's midmorning and her mother is grocery shopping and Penny is with a friend and there is only Misty left, sitting on the front porch with her legs kicking over the edge. This time, William tells her to undo his pants. When she won't, he undoes them himself, and he takes her hand and lays it against him. He does the same thing to her. It is just like the first time, except now he is being touched. Now she is the one who starts. Now they are both the same.

CB &O

William's mother makes dinner. She puts on a white blouse and dark jeans. She gives him a radio. A present, she says, from Paul.

"Who's Paul?"

"You'll get to meet him soon. He's real nice. It's impossible not to like him. He's just got that way about him, you know?"

She puts more food on William's plate than he has seen in weeks, maybe in his whole life. Green beans and corn-on-the-cob, mashed potatoes, roast beef, and rolls, the kind that you pull apart from the can and fold into little shapes. William eats three before he touches the rest of his plate.

"This is good, Mama. Thank you."

"You're welcome, baby."

She smooths his hair across his forehead and tries to tuck it behind his ear, the way she likes to see it, but it isn't quite long enough. She barely eats, taking from William's plate as she washes dishes and wipes counters and checks the phone.

"I feel like I ain't hardly got to see you with all the extra shifts I've been covering," she says. "It'll pay off come Christmas though, just you wait." She sits on the edge of her seat and smiles. She picks at a thread on the plastic tablecloth and the more she pulls on the thread, the more the plastic comes apart. "Then you're always outside playing with those girls every time I come home. I checked on you in bed the other night and you wouldn't there." She keeps pulling and pulling at the string. "Where was you?"

"I don't know. Sleepwalking, maybe."

"That don't sound like you."

"Do we have any more beans?"

"I just worry, is all. You're ten now. It might not seem too old to you, but you're getting to be of age and I don't want you making decisions like I did. I don't want you to end up in a place like me, grown before you're ready."

"I know."

"Is there anything you want to tell me?" she asks. "Anything at all, baby. You know Mama wouldn't think bad of you for nothing in the world."

The phone rings. William waits as it rings again and again, seeing how long it will take before she gets up. She looks over her shoulder at him as he pushes away from the table, and says, "Remember what I said. You promise me?"

William closes the door to his room. He locks it, too, and later, he doesn't answer when she knocks. He pretends to be asleep. He lies with his head on his pillow and stares at the ceiling as she tells him that she loves him and that she'll never leave him and that everything, everything that she does, is for him.

Cg 80

Misty stops coming outside to play. When William asks Penny where she is, Penny shrugs. "She's sick. She says her head won't quit hurting. I thought she was faking at first, but." Another shrug. "She don't eat much. She cries a lot. She thinks I can't hear her, but we sleep in the same room, you know? I have to hear her."

"Did she say anything about me?"

"No," Penny says. "Why?"

"Have you seen the new statue?"

"God, there's another one?"

They go to the field together. The bridge still hasn't finished itself. It doesn't seem to want to be a bridge at all.

Penny says, "I wish somebody would just burn them all down, you know?

"No," William says.

He is staring at all the statues together. There are so many now that it hurts his eyes trying to hold them all in one place. Misty hasn't even seen all the things that he's made for her. She hasn't mentioned them, not even once. William's vision blurs and he looks down at his own two feet.

He says, "I still think the green one kind of looks like me. Through the nose."

He turns his head, but Penny is walking back through the yard. There is someone standing in the front door of her trailer, but the sunlight glints on the glass so that William can't see who's looking back at him.

Cg 80

113

Earl sits in the lawn chair every night. He had the test results from the college framed and hung them from a wooden fence post, the stark white paper and fine print saying things about the field that most of the people couldn't understand. But it means that nothing was found. That the statues are statues and nothing else. Just metal and lead, just grown. There is nothing in the soil or the water or the air to explain where the statues come from and that, the crowd says, makes the field a miracle. Earl doesn't say much at all.

 C3 &0

Once, William thinks he sees Misty. Earl has taken to having open house nights on certain days of the week. It draws more people, somehow, the thought of needing permission. The line stretches down the road, out of the holler and out of sight. William likes to stand in the crowd and listen to the things the people have to say about the field and about God, about how beautiful it all is, how perfect. That's when he sees Misty standing at the edge of the woods, near the creek. She's wearing a dark shirt, her hair pulled back in a low ponytail. She's alone and she looks small between the trees, smaller than he's ever seen her.

William yells her name. He pushes through the people, fighting against the bodies, ignoring the complaints. He runs across the yard and between the trees. He wants to tell her that he is sorry. He wants to ask her to help him burn down the barn. He wants to play in the creek with her and hold her hand. He runs through the dark, shouting her name, but there is nothing but trees and leaves and dark, wet earth. He finds the hair tie lying at his feet when he turns around. William buries that, too.

C3 &0

William goes the fallow field one last time. It's been a week since he last saw Misty. A week since anything new has grown.

Earl is snoring in his lawn chair, yet William still walks around to the other side of the field to avoid him. He has to get down on his knees and crawl through the fence to reach the field. It is so crowded with statues there is barely room to move. William wedges himself between the unfinished bridge and a heavy hand that reaches toward the sky. He climbs up a series of concentric golden circles and uses the elevation to find one small patch of empty earth, there behind the first statue of green glass.

William is winded now, breathing hard. He is crying, too, but only a little. Only small tears drip from the tip of his nose and fall onto the rich brown earth, and the earth takes that, too, and will use it. William rips his shirt on a barb from a stone statue and there is a scrape on his leg that he doesn't remember getting, but the wound burns now.

William makes his way to the empty spot of earth. This is the only way he can set things right. He has planted bottles and wood and coins and all manner of small things and they have come back. They have been bigger, too, and better than they have been before. They have been something worth looking at. And he will be, too. He will cover himself whole, close his mouth and his eyes, and let the dirt do its work. He will come back changed. Misty won't be afraid of him anymore and his mother won't bring another man home. This will fix the wrong inside of him and everything will be okay.

William starts to dig, and he doesn't stop, not even when his fingernails bend backward and chip away. Even when he hits rocks and has to pry them from the earth and toss them over his shoulder. Even when the rocks become heavy roots tangled together like vines, thick and twisting away in all directions. The sun is bright and hard above him when William finally stops digging. He is standing on a bed of roots, under which a great chasm stretches. The air coming up from the darkness is musty, but warm, and he doesn't know how the ground has been holding itself up all this time.

"Hello?" he says, and a voice answers, but it is not his own. It's his mother walking through the grass, calling his name. William looks into the darkness beneath him, at the place where the dark becomes something else, not light exactly, but close.

William reaches up to the surface. He takes a handful of dirt and pulls it down. He doesn't stop bringing the earth down around him until he can't hear his mother anymore. He doesn't stop until he is planted, whole, in the dark earth.

FEATHERS AND VOID
Charles Payseur

We are crows, circling round the wake of death, black wings silent as we glide, waiting, waiting.

The big one's gonna hit. Any second now. Iv's thoughts coat mine like oil, slide away, always so clear in the moment but impossible to hold on to. Iv, my crow. My shell. My ship.

They told me, before, that being joined with Iv would be like living in a constant state of déjà vu. Like remembering something from a previous life, always a surprise when it happens but somehow familiar, like I've been silently preparing for just this thing.

There's the explosion. The volley of missiles impact and my eyes widen even as my hands are ready to guide us in. We flock, the whole murder of us, as the Branthel 99X [JUPITER CLASS] *Three Moons* loses itself to the cold. The Distress blares as we approach, our sleek bodies the absence of light, wrapped in warmth and silence and life.

It carries something in its belly. It has eaten well and deep and so shall we. Rip it open. Feed. I shiver as the thoughts come, pins and needles down my spine.

Another volley might scream out from opposition at any moment, or else the *Three Moons* might trip its self-destruct, or else—We are in, talons digging into metal, finding purchase on the burnt slag of ship.

Xi(a) runs point, beak snapping at bits of debris—filling up on garbage. But then, maybe Xi knows something Iv isn't telling me. Crows can be like that, secretive. It doesn't mean we trust them any less. They are part of us now, after all.

I keep my beak shut as we push deeper into the ship, though each scrap that hits the light tempts me. I feel the call of something deeper, tastier. I wait, using the hunger to push me past Xi(a), past the bodies now thicker, now thicker.

A Jupiter Class can hold five thousand in crew and soldiers, though I know there's no way the Far Home would have put so many aboard. Two, maybe? The war with the Near Home has cost them much—planets of people are gone through this conflict. Like me. Gone into the dark. Only I've come back.

Second right. Very close. Be careful. Iv's voice is a cold shadow in my mind I follow on instinct.

I come to sealed bulkheads. Cumbersome to breach but my claws are sharp. I tear and scratch. Behind me the others pick over bodies, snapping out ID chips, ripping free whole neural arrays. Flesh gives like slush. Weakened metal punctures, and around us the corridor shudders and releases as air is pushed into the void. The bulkhead puckers enough to allow us through.

Inside I hesitate, tasting the fleeing traces of air and hope. Hallways branch and I surge ahead, as if by muscle memory, following the ghost of Iv's intent—forward, then right. There's another door but it cannot hold me. I—I wait, listen. There is something strange about this. Movement behind the door, the smell of electricity and something acrid, chemical. I wonder at the extra shielding to this area, able to withstand a direct hit from a Near Home barrage. I push my questions and doubts away and crash through the door.

Inside is a swarm of people, scientists—and something else, something hot and shiny and I need it. Weapons fire at me but I'm already dodging, already sweeping wings, claws, beak. I aim for masks and hoses, don't need to kill them direct, just buy myself time. The firing stops and the source of my desperation looks like an egg of liquid metal suspended in a cylindrical stasis pod. No bigger than a human fist.

Fly!

I snap up the egg and a dozen other things from the table—tools and data chips and whatever else, then turn and fly. My squawk is a call, a warning. Speed is impossible in the corridors but I half-fly, half-crash through and through and out until the void is clear again and the Near Home Verol G9 [URSA CLASS] *Starborn* stares me in the face.

Stand-down orders shout through all channels. I dim them as I dive, seeing the telltale twinkle of a thousand piranha missiles firing at once. My caw is desperate as I sheer down, back, away, away. I do not worry about the missiles, which are larger than me but which lack the power to track us. I worry about debris. I worry about what else might be lurking around the perimeter of the battle, waiting. We crows are not the only scavengers, nor the largest.

Nor the fastest, it turns out. The barrage hits the *Three Moons* and Vi(ctor)'s squawk as he pulls himself free of the last corridor, weighed down by meat and swag, is indignant. I clench my jaw and fly. The mourning can come later, now we need to fly. But it doesn't stop the pain, and in my beak there is the faintest vibration, as if something responds to that pain. Iv is strangely silent.

೧ ೮

I was chosen because of my name. And yes, okay, I volunteered, too, but millions volunteered. It meant avoiding infantry, the meat grinder, which everyone knows well to avoid, or to try to avoid. Does it matter that the science is untested, that the price is your mind? We all wanted to live, and that's what guided us, what guides us still.

But there's something about the military and names. Or scientists and names? My profile ticked all the right boxes. Asexual, aromantic, introverted, no history of violence or resistance, high testing in special relations, logic, and reflexes. But there were hundreds that fit, and they needed only eleven. So they picked us for our names. I(ván), I(a)i(n), I(th)i(r)i(al), Iv(y), V(era), Vi(ctor), Vi(v)i(an), Vi(r)i(d)i(an), Ix, X(an), and Xi(a).

I'm not sure how many of those not chosen are still alive. Not many. And I'm not sure how to feel about still being alive. It's what I wanted. But that was back when I was Ivy, before I became the fourth of eleven. Before Iv came along and made me less than half a name.

☙ ❧

Five of us fly into Circus Field, where more ships than stars crowd the void, a gathering place of the unaligned. There are ships of every make and taste, some bought and paid but most stolen or cobbled together from small bits of shine. Security is a cloud of Verol PP2 [OSPREY CLASS] fighters with a pair of PP8 [HERON CLASS] patrollers coordinating. Even the PP2s, the smallest make of military value, are about ten times our size—we transmit passcodes and wait to acknowledge permission to trade, but they could not stop us, catch us, even if they twisted all their resources to the task. We do not come as friends, because crows are friends of no one, but we come full of shine, which will be enough.

Vi(v)i(an) is waiting at *Crows Home*, what people call the converted Extril BGX [PELICAN CLASS] *Sprig of Holly* that we scavenged mostly whole following the Third Raid of Heliocrux. The field had been so full of dead and dying that we crows had eaten for months off the spoils, coils, and codes. We simply call the vessel the shop, because crows do not have homes, are welcomed nowhere and so live nowhere, brooding wherever possible until storm or fire or humans push them on. The first thing Vi(v)i(an) notices is that we're short one, and as we bow our heads she rips the void with a clacking call, loss and warning, loss and warning, over and over again.

When she is done we take turns spitting our hauls onto the floor of the shop. It was a minor battle but we have eaten well. I(ván) coughs up a mostly-undamaged null-shield, preens as the others gawk and snap their beaks in agitation. I hang back, feeling the egg, which is both hot and cold. The wait is shorter than it used to be, without Vi(ctor). Without I(a)i(n) or I(th)i(r)i(al) or V(era) or Vi(r)i(d)i(an). Only six of us now, and only five who fly the void since Vi(v)i(an)'s brush with a neuronanite trap. Her steps stretch with a deep limp and her wings will not unclench from her sides, will no longer unfurl, embrace the void. Still she holds on, acts as our base of operations and hawker, which causes her no end of amusement.

120

When the others are done, I am careful to release the tools and detritus first. The others gaze hungrily at everything—even without the final reveal I have rivaled I(ván)'s haul, the tools specialized and expensive, the datachips gleaming with research and other classifieds. Then I set the stasis pod down into the middle of my pile, and five heads tilt to the side as one. The electric curiosity of their attention is new. I let the pod down and feel a new chill inside me, a cold pit of anticipation. We crowd forward to examine the pod but Vi(v)i(an) darts in with her beak and snatches it up, and we shrink back, none willing to press.

"Where did you get this?"

I tell her what I am able, which isn't much. The lab, the guards, the scientists. I do not know what this is or what it could be, but I spend as little time as possible among the gossipmongers and traders, so I am not the one to ask. Vi(v)i(an) flies now in entirely different circles, wings of information replacing those she's lost to the neuronanites, and so I hope she can tell me what I have discovered.

"It's not worth the trouble," I(ván) says, no doubt wanting to go back to admiring the shine we've collected.

"Shut it and let Viv work," Xi(a) says, beak snapping. She and I(ván) have never gotten along, he too proud and she too small, fast. *Xia*, she will introduce herself, *like See-Ya!* And then she will be voidward and onward, a streak of movement, something valuable trapped in her claw.

"Why not let the adults talk, little one," I(ván) says, ruffled.

"Why not fuck yourself, old man. Just because you were made first doesn't mean you were made best."

It's an old argument and one that Ix cuts short with an angry squawk. Ix, who doesn't speak in human terms any more, who is normally least present, eyes too busy scouting unseen patterns in the stars. Right now Ix is focused entirely on the pod, and they hush all noise with a flutter of wings and a narrowing of their eyes.

"This is familiar," Vi(v)i(an) says, putting the cylinder down on a scanner. "I've...been looking into ways of getting around the bugs that messed up Vii." Her voice is raw for a second but recovers, and we all are silent, still. "They aren't susceptible to most countermeasures, but from what I've seen it would be possible, if we had the original Corvid bioform, to—"

"That's the Corvid bioform?" Xi(a) asks. The rest of us hold our breath.

The Corvid bioform. The progenitor of the entire Corvid class of ship. Our class of ship, which included a production run of eleven. A failed experiment. Had the Far Home decided to try again?

"No, but it's similar," Vi(v)i(an) says.

They're coming for you. You need to go. Iv's words send a spike of panic up my back. My head twists to the side, as if there's a predator lurking behind us. Vi(v)i(an) continues talking.

"There's not a lot for sale on bioforms," she says. "Living ships were abandoned after...after us, and any new research is strictly classified. But there have been whispers."

"The war's going poorly for the Far Home," X(an) says, matter of fact. "I read it on the *Three Moons*. They're running out of soldiers. There were only twelve hundred aboard when the barrage hit."

Of course e would have checked. Data has always been eir favorite shine.

I walk over to the long range scanners, distracted from the conversation. I should be paying attention, but something is nagging at me and I've learned enough not to ignore it.

"I've heard that they're looking into living ships again," Vi(v)i(an) says. "Though they've given up on the augur engine and ship sentience. After what happened with us...but they've also made the structures less rigid, the delivery vector more viral, so they could convert larger numbers quickly."

"What the fuck's it supposed to be, then?" Xi(a) asks.

The question is running through my mind, as well. The whole purpose of the Corvid experiment was to create a living ship, smart and adaptive, able to predict events. Magic, essentially, because I never understood the science of it. I only understood that, while there was a small chance of success, it was a hell of a lot better than entering the meat grinder.

My hand brushes the scanner controls, brings up the channel feeds of the Circus.

"I'm thinking they want suits smart enough to react to the pilots but not be fully aware," Vi(v)i(an) says. "More computer than bird. Able to shrink and grow and change shape. Like a shape-shifting suit that can become a ship and then revert back into clothing, neurally linked to the pilot but not cocooning them."

I swallow. I see it, at the edges of the feeds. Small queries about long distance readings. And something else. One voice asking after a murder of crows. Has anyone seen them? Have they attempted to sell—

"We need to go," I say. My hands fly over the controls and cast the net wider, beyond the Circus. The feeds begin to grow more frantic as others start to see it. A fleet. Far Home. My eyes soar over the displays. Two Jupiter Class carriers and at least ten Mars Class battleships. Saturn Class, Venus Class, Khyber Class— it's a full fleet, moving slow but too fast for the Circus to disperse in time.

The others scatter, X(an) going for the controls while I(ván) and Ix gather up the shine. Xi(a) helps Vi(v)i(an) with the pod. I remain at the controls, waiting for what I know is coming. It takes all of twenty-five seconds, by which time X(an) already has us moving through the shifting currents of the Circus.

They deliver their message on an open frequency. "Deliver the Crows and you can live."

෴ ෴

It's strange, the urge to live. For a long time I was angry about it. Still am, really. Angry at people's selfish desire to keep on living. Wasn't enough to fuck over Earth. Wasn't enough to fuck over everything we ever knew and fling ourselves into the stars with all the care of a gaggle of drunken toddlers. Wasn't enough to start this idiotic war about what planet to call New Earth, which was really more about branding for the Big Four ship manufacturers than it was about human pride and integrity.

I can't blame them, except I can. I mean, we're here. I can't blame anyone for not wanting to die, but I can sure as shit blame people for still thinking doing nothing but reproducing will make it any better. Legions of people and all they do is sell their children to the war in hopes it will grow full enough to spare them. Maybe that's not fair, but as one of those sold I don't care about being fair. The real blame might belong elsewhere, but there was a choice and I didn't get to make it. The first time I got an option it was how I wanted to die. Infantry or pilot. Certain death or uncertain.

There are costs to participate, they told me. No touch. The ship will always encase me. No sex, no eating, no pissing or shitting. And okay, the last I'm sure most would be quick to give up. And the first I never cared for. I had never found eating that satisfying, but not being hungry? That's something different. I've never had enough food to care how it tasted. So yeah, sign me up, Mx. Recruiter. Cover me in your Corvid suit and I'll try not to scream as it burrows into me, as I stop being me and start being *us*. As I start hearing a voice I can never remember. At least this is me choosing something.

And when you underestimate the process? When you think the Crows will somehow stay obedient, that they'll be so grateful to you for feeding them living people so they can fight for you? Well, this time we don't wait to be given options. We take. We take and we take and we take and you can't tell us we're wrong or bad if you can never catch us. Eat slag. Eat the fire and death you serve up on planets like they're dinner plates. Eat the trail of void our wings leave in our wake.

og ðo

It's never a surprise to run, and it has nothing to do with seeing the future. At least, I hope there's no voice constantly droning in my head, *You cannot stay you cannot stay you cannot stay*. The crows don't need to bother, because it's something even we humans can figure out, taught by the string of places left behind.

The Circus will not protect us, and we don't have long now before they come en masse for us, sacrifices to appease angry gods. Crows have always been blamed for bad luck. Storm heralds and battle gorgers. Servants of evil, because people think since they can't see into the dark there's something menacing lurking there. Never quite believing that it's mostly just empty, that crows are just more comfortable there than most.

You've got to get to Ourla. Iv's voice is an itch in the back of my mind—I see an image. Dr. Ourla. The lead researcher on the Corvid program. A man I haven't thought about in a long time. Why now?

"You all need to hit the void," Vi(v)i(an) says, and I wince. We all wince. This isn't open for debate or hesitation. When Crows say we need something, we act. So we all get to it. I(ván) gathers up a few choice pieces of shine while Xi(a) delivers the stasis pod to me and Ix fiddles with something in the corner.

"We have about three minutes before they start firing on us," X(an) says. It's been two years here, at the Circus, among other people avoiding the war, resisting Far Home and Near Home both, at least passively. Gone now. Vi(v)i(an) pecks X(an) in the shoulder.

"Get to the hatch," she says. "No way I'll make it out of here. It's me that pilots this ship to the end."

X(an) almost looks like e's going to argue but shrugs instead and stands, walks over to where we gather by the hatch.

"But what do we do with this?" Xi(a) asks, holding the pod, still facing Vi(v)i(an). "You're the only one who knows anything about it."

"Dr. Ourla," I say. The others glance at me, features twitching at the name, but there is understanding as well. The recognition of the truth of the name.

"We could always just give it back," I(ván) says, though his voice shakes as he says it.

125

We don't answer him. Ix squawks from where they were working and stands, joins us near the hatch. They've tampered with the null shield. My eyes widen slightly as I see what they've done.

"That should do lovely," Vi(v)i(an) says, and we can see the glimmer of her eyes. Two years, and here we are. Crows know to be comfortable while you can, but to know your exits.

Go. I'm giddy with Iv's voice in my head, gone before I can fully comprehend. Maybe they're just saying goodbye.

The hatch opens and we wing into the chaos. The Circus is still roiling around us, a thousand thousand ships making a hurricane of activity, the urge to flee and fight and surrender warring on every micro and macro scale. Only we are determined as we fly. Away from the fleet. Away from the Circus and whatever safety it might have offered us if we belonged. The mood of the storm is changing, making up its mind in waves. The first shots are fired at *Crows Home*, which dodges the worst and takes the rest harmlessly to its shields.

Ships can track us, too, of course. They know we're flying. But for now we're outrunning their fear.

They're not going to let you leave.

We glide through the ships, pushing outward. Most are more than willing to see the back of us and offer no resistance. Some need to be reminded how sharp our claws are and we let them live because if we started killing now there would be a frenzy. *Crows Home* lets itself be herded, toward the fleet. I patch into the channels and hear the calls going out. We have them, we have them, take them and let us live. I clench my claws so hard the pain almost makes me miss the flitting shadows of the PP2s.

My cry alerts the others a moment before the PP2s open fire—three dozen cannons turn the void into plasma. They should have stayed out of it.

Ix takes the lead and we fall in behind them except for Xi(a), who draws what fire she can as we make for the PP8s, weaving between the PP2s, a tapestry of destruction. Everything is hot and close and fast but we were built for it and built hungry and we find their eyes and blind them. Metal feels like flesh and

126

tastes sweet as we tear apart the PP8s. Without their coordination and sophisticated scans the relatively simply PP2s are stabbing in the dark, something they have no experience doing while we are old masters. What is left of them lets us flee and calls it a victory because on the other side of the Circus, *Crows Home* is being buoyed by the Far Home fleet.

We can see Vi(v)i(an) in our minds, imagine her tilting her head as she examines their approach vectors, as she times everything. The null-shield beeps, an almost avian sound, as she presses where Ix made their adjustment. And then a white explosion, and we imagine her happy that at least they will not feast on her corpse. That is the job of a crow and she would not want others to profane our work.

We fly, the void wrapping us in cold arms. And as we move our voices rise together, loss and warning, loss and warning, over and over again.

ଓ ଅଂ

We were made to work together. Eleven ships that could go where others could not. Flying as one, each with a separate glimpse of the future—some far out, some much closer into what will be. Some sensing danger and some seeing goals and some doing a little bit of everything. We were made to work together, only whole with all eleven active, together, a beautiful murder.

I wonder sometimes if they were warned. Did Vi(ctor) know the barrage was coming, and just ignore the feeling? Was he tired of living on the whispers of a voice that was only an absence? Or did Vi not warn him? Was Vi the one tired, seeking that final solitude?

It's impossible to know the truth. Sometimes I speak to Iv and I feel a tingle on my skin. My actual skin and not the organic metal of the crow. Being a crow means never being alone, means being able to stand the void without blinking or turning away.

What I know is that Vi(ctor) isn't really gone. He's an absence, but he's not gone. If I close my eyes I can still feel him. We might look like only five crows cutting through the dark, but there are six shadows that fly with us, and we are still active, together, a beautiful murder.

We know where Dr. Ourla is. Even in the void there are some things we will never forget, some faces that chase us, that are seared into our minds. Enemy. Parent. Even the thought of him makes me want tear at myself—pull my feathers, spit curses into the void. Better yet, to tear at him, to pay him back in blood and pain and loss. There is no solace in the fact that he was punished, that he languishes in confinement on the edge of space.

Breaking into prison is child's play.

With the Circus gone, there are few enough places to run to, and fewer with labs sufficient for the task at hand. We return to the beginning. Our beginning, at least. On a little moon once firmly in the grip of the Far Home. In the nebulous disputed zones between the two great powers, there is a now-deserted compound we all know well.

"I knew you wouldn't leave me there," Dr. Ourla says as we herd him into the lab where we were made. "I knew you would thank me for what I did for you."

"Thank you?" Xi(a) approaches, beak gaping, promising. I(ván) is right beside her, the two finally united in their hatred of Ourla. "You're lucky we don't bite you in two."

"But I did so much for you," he says, though he is wise enough to stumble back as Ix and I hold our wings to prevent the others from ripping him apart. "And you've done so much. The news they feed us is heavily filtered, but I can still see your marks. Embarrassments for both sides. How would you have managed that, if I hadn't made you—"

"You do not get to claim our victories as your own," X(an) says, eyes narrow. "Nothing we do or accomplish will ever make your actions noble or right."

"But then why free me?" he asks.

To take. To take to take to take to take. I suck in a breath, suppress the urge to taste his blood, to see the dull shine of his heart in my beak.

"Because we need you," I say, and produce the stasis pod. Even though it is all of ours, it was mine first, and not even I(ván) questions that I should carry it. Ourla's eyes widen when he sees it.

"We need to know what this is," I say. I do not say why. I do not say that I already have a plan for it, that I can hear the whispers of something in my mind that I trust, even I don't quite understand them. I know the plan starts here, with Ourla and the bioform.

Ourla's face darkens as he steps forward, examining the pod.

"Those bastards," he says, fist pounding the table the pod sits on. The rest of us share quick glances, unsure of this reaction. Of all the ways we expected him to respond, anger was not one.

"It wasn't bad enough that they locked me away," he says, "for doing exactly what they wanted me to do. But now they've stolen my work. My life's work."

"So it's related to the Corvid bioform?" X(an) asks.

I keep my attention sharp. Most of the science of what we are is beyond me. The crows...I know that they are alive, know that they are aware, that their skin now coats my own in material stronger than steel but able to feed on solar radiation and transform it into energy, able to integrate into my body, recycling my waste, making it so that I don't need to eat or breathe. Beyond that, I am a mystery even to myself.

"Related, though...grotesque," Ourla says. He already has the pod onto one of the analysis tables, is already scanning its data. "They stripped away the elegance. The interface is barbaric, the bioform completely slaved to the host. It's...it's a mockingbird."

"We understand it can fly," X(an) says. "Will it give the host the same integrated metabolism?"

The void is a cold place indeed if everyone starves before they can reach a new world. Iv's words are a whisper stolen by the distance of neurons in my mind, but I find I'm holding my breath as I wait for the scans to progress, for Ourla to answer.

"Yes," he says. "But they learned from their mistakes. They've encoded a failsafe. A kill switch. Otherwise it's brilliant. Viral. It can be passed blood to blood, activates almost instantly. A planet of people could be transformed within weeks. Days, if there's no resistance."

I imagine whole worlds emptied of people, drawn into the war. I imagine the scouts, telling everyone the suit is theirs, their ticket from hunger, their ticket from a government stealing their resources, their blood, their will. The thought of wings, of freedom...only to find that the wings carry a price tag, the freedom a cage. Fight or die. It's not difficult to believe.

"Can you disable the failsafe?" X(an) asks. We are all leaning closer to the conversation, waiting, waiting.

"Why should I?" Ourla says, face twisting into something ugly, utterly human.

What does any man like this want, after everything?

"To hurt those who hurt you," I say. "To take the work they stole from you and use it as a weapon to make them pay. To make sure none forget your brilliance. Together, we can end the war for good."

The smile that spreads across his face is all the answer I need about his intentions.

CB BO

Crows use tools. Crows mourn for their fallen. Crows never forget a face. Somewhere in all the facts about crows there is something else as well, the shadow of a voice.

A crow is never alone. A crow dies free.

CB BO

They've found you. It's time to leave.

I blink and shake my head. I've been staring out the window, at the gray desolation of the moon. Inside the lab my wings feel cramped, but I know better than to leave. We're running out of time. I move to where the others are waiting, watching Ourla work. He keeps bobbing and making small noises as his hands move over the pod, modifying the code, the structures of the bioform.

"Is it ready?" I ask.

Ourla grunts and steps back. "It's not my most elegant work," he says, "but I've disabled the failsafe. At least, I've made it so it can't be activated from outside. The host will still be aware of it, and if *they* choose to activate it, well..."

I retrieve the pod, take it inside me again. It's enough. Better, even, because it means no one will be taken against their will, that anyone wanting to become a mockingbird will have the ultimate control over their bodies and souls. We've taken the shackles the armies have wrought and repurposed them into wings. We move toward the exit hatch and Ourla trots after us until Ix notices and turns, snaps the air between them with their beak.

"What is the meaning of this?" Ourla asks, puffing out his chest. Ix's body lowers, body tensing at the tone of Ourla's voice.

"We thank you for your assistance," X(an) says.

"But you're a right bastard and we never want to see you again," Xi(a) says.

The words seem to wash around him without sinking in.

"You can't leave me like this," he says. "You need to find me a ship. If they find me again, they'll—"

"They'll lock you back up," I say. "And probably not be as gentle about it this time."

"But I helped you," he says. Then, in a whisper, "I created you."

Ix coughs up a pistol onto the floor between them and we all turn and file out of the lab. From the void we can already feel the massive shape of an approaching fleet. We take wing.

03 80

131

We dance the distance between stars, our feathers glistening in the starlight. Out here we glow, hum with the song of radiation and propulsion and hope. We never asked to have the void as our map, the stars as our landmarks. And now that we have it, I often wonder what we're supposed to do with it.

Fly free. Feel yourself a point of shadow against the darkness and call out into the silent reaches. We are here, we are here, we are here. Is there any answer?

CB BO

The sky is full of wings. Millions of wings. The planet, a remote outpost of the Near Home, has changed quickly. At least, the life on it has. Nearly everyone, even those who have no intention of leaving the surface, who will never once reach into the air and pull, has accepted the gifts we bring. Our mockingbird children.

It is freedom. Not only from gravity but also hunger. Cold. Distance. Many have already left. While the Far Home and Near Home battle on the borders of their space, arguing over who has the better right to pursue us, everyone is slipping between. What does near or far matter when we can make our home in the void. Never still, we can carry it with us.

They are joining forces. They will come for you.

Millions strong, we could fight them now. With the mockingbirds beside we could tear them apart with the strength of a million beaks pecking as one. We could beat them. Instead, I look around me. I(ván) and Ix and X(an) and X(ia) all stand, and I can feel the shadows filling the circle—I(a)i(n) and I(th)i(r)i(an) and V(era) and Vi(ctor) and Vi(v)i(an) and Vi(r)i(d)i(an).

There are so many other planets to see, suns that glitter like bits of shine. We all crane our necks upward and call. Sorrow and warning, sorrow and warning, over and over again. And all around us the void fills with voices calling back.

You are not alone.

We fly.

132

WE LILIES OF THE VALLEY
Sonja Natasha

If Yvonne presses her cheek to the thick window of the space station, and cranes her neck just so, she can see a crescent slice of Earth, marbled in desert. She traces what she can see of the western coast of Mexico. Her toes just barely graze the floor as she floats with her elbows braced against the window ledges. Beyond Earth's curve, there's the lingering haze of Siding Spring 4's comet tail.

Today, she studies Siding Spring up close, collecting its space debris in The Net. She has work to do, so she cannot remain still to remember what she left behind. She pushes herself from the window, and she looks back over her shoulder, at Earth just a thumb's smudge away. She thinks about the woman she met the day she said goodbye, in the last few hours she had left. She thinks about the woman looking up at her like a second moon in God's eye.

Yvonne doesn't know the woman's name, but knows her brown skin, the curve of her brow, the slant of her nose, the way her mouth parted in surprise. She knows the amethyst crystal around her neck, the pitcher of water in her hands, how she smelled of lavender and lemon.

Yvonne pushes herself towards the center of the station. The Net has snatched her a fine catch today: something different, something pebble-round, something more woody than rock. Yvonne looks through her glasses with the smart lenses, analyzing the debris. The pieces remind her of the seeds her mama planted in aluminum cans still smelling faintly of beans, despite being washed with citrus dish soap, despite the dark soil filling them up. The cans were stationed under a sprig of grapes nailed near the kitchen window. As Yvonne grew up, the sun kissed them into raisins. Yvonne had tied prism fragments to the vine with bits of string. When the light shone through, the kitchen was splashed with flickering patches of rainbow.

Yvonne's belly twists with homesickness. She sweeps the strange hard things the comet has given her into the palms of her gloved hands. She doesn't seal them in the plastic bags like she's supposed to so they're ready for study on the planet surface. She goes to the botanical bay where she grows the crops for the astronaut who will take her place after a year has cycled by without her. She finds her coffee cup, forgotten beside the pale green leaves of lettuce, just beginning to sprout. She sets a nutri-device in the cup and plants the seeds, giving them a little water from her daily ration. Then she places the cup beside her cot so it will be there when she sleeps and when she wakes.

Seeds are hardy, strong. They can survive anything, even extinction.

She thinks about this when her phone blips a Twitter notification at her. It's the woman from the rooftop saying hello. Yvonne recognizes her from her profile picture. She wants Yvonne to put her on the list of people allowed to send her a gift with the cargo pod that will collect the samples from the comet. Her name is Sierra. Yvonne doesn't think, doesn't wonder. She submits the request to her commanding officers on Earth, and they approve it, and she thinks nothing of it because the cargo pod won't be leaving for many months yet. There is a lot of time to forget.

Guilt moves in after the surprise of hearing from Sierra dissipates into the bitter aftertaste of loneliness. Yvonne glances at the coffee cup. She should have sealed the seeds in plastic to send back to Earth. She should dig them out with her fingertips.

Instead, she goes to sleep.

The Earth spins around the sun and the station orbits with it. Yvonne tends the botanical bay and the little seeds in her coffee cup. She looks at her phone, wishing that it would light up with something. A text, a tweet. She remembers the old days, the days with the automated voices calling out *you've got mail!*

She misses even that.

Months later, the cargo pod arrives, slotting itself into the docking port on auto-pilot. Yvonne ensures the seal is secure, and the hatch hisses open. There are gifts in the shuttle from the friends she made while becoming an astronaut. Cookies and other treats, vacuum-sealed. There are new DVDs to watch in the late night when sleep eludes her.

A bag of water from Sierra. *I thought you'd tire of recycled water,* she wrote. *I've read the articles.*

Winky face.

Yvonne laughs; she cannot help herself. She flips the built-in straw up and drinks deeply. It doesn't taste like tap water. It doesn't even taste like filtered tap water. She looks again at Sierra's letter. The water is from a well; Sierra drove into the mountains to get it. She hopes Yvonne will like it, and Yvonne has never tasted anything better.

She drifts towards her cot, where she keeps her seeds. She knows they probably aren't seeds and should accept that they lie fallow, but she can't. She dispenses the rest of Sierra's water into the nutri-device.

That night, Yvonne wraps her hair in pale blue satin, turns the lights down low except for the lamp clamped to the cup. Her mouth tastes like chocolate chips because she had cookies for dinner and didn't brush her teeth afterward. Closing her eyes, she imagines that someone sleeps beside her, this person pressed against her side rather than the chilly walls of the station. Pressure rises from her parched throat.

They had warned her about the loneliness, the isolation.

She had thought she understood, but she hadn't.

What had she been thinking?

She's still awake when her alarm rings, and she swipes it off quickly. Her phone tumbles from her hand when she notices a sprig of green in the coffee cup. She reaches out instinctively, not to actually touch, but the plant seems to know. The plant sees. A thin frond shifts to greet her. Yvonne circles her finger around the fronds as if in orbit, to see if the leaves will follow her lead. They do.

When she writes her thank-yous for the gifts, she tells Sierra her water caused the plant to grow. It's probably not true, but Yvonne likes the story of it. She writes it down with pencil and paper because she thinks that maybe Sierra would like something tangible to hold. A letter from space; not many people could say they had received such a thing.

Tucking the guilt away that she is not including the marvelous plant from space, Yvonne packs her samples neatly into the cargo pod. Between them, she slips the thank-you letters to Sierra and to her friends. Tears pricking her eyes, she programs the pod's return course to Earth. In a few days, the plant in her cup is over a foot tall. Leaves unfurl from the dark green buds, and she wonders if this species will flower. The plant is as attentive to her as she is to it. When she stretches to the doo-wop music she likes, the plant bends with her, mirroring her curved back. When she drifts across the room, the broadest leaves try to follow her. When she rests beside it, the plant reaches for her, and they sway together like they're dancing.

Budding leaves bloom at her touch, and she traces spiral patterns against them until they are free, until they waft gently in the station air. She is proud of her work, more proud than seeing the fruits of her labor grow in the botanical bay.

The plant is a constant presence in her thoughts, even when she's working. She imagines the ways it will have changed, how much taller it will have grown. She thinks about showing the plant to Sierra: look, she'll say, at this thing that has come to life because of us.

She blushes as she wonders if the plant will like Sierra as much as it likes her. She hopes it will.

Soon, the plant grows taller than Yvonne. Vines, like ivy but thicker, unspool from the stem. The spade-shaped leaves seek the warmth of the cot when Yvonne leaves, slipping like guests beneath the covers. When she returns, the vines slide over her black skin, coiling around her wrist like the plastic bangles she wore as a child.

Yvonne falls asleep, and wakes to the distant sound of Sierra's voice singing, and the smell of fresh ground coffee in the air. But when she opens her eyes, Yvonne is alone, and she discovers the plant has cushioned her head with a pillow of leaves. Buds, like small suns, grow from the plant's crown, unfurling golden petals. It blooms as prettily as Yvonne knew it

136

would. The flowers remind her of the honeysuckle her mama grew. As a girl, Yvonne had drunk the nectar, the sweet floral blessing on her tongue like benediction.

Vines gesture towards her and she comes. They wrap themselves around her as she cups the blossom in her hands, bends her head, and breathes. The petals unfurl around her until her eyes widen, and she asks, her voice a shard of sound in the quiet stillness of the station, "Sierra?"

The plant rustles its leaves, shaking like laughter, and Yvonne lowers her head once more, eyes closing as she breathes the flower in. A soft film of nectar coats her lips, and Sierra is present like she was when their hands touched in goodbye.

The closeness frightens Yvonne, thrills her. Her heart aches, her throat dries as the plant holds her fast. Its vines cradle her head as she slides her fingers along the base of one of its blossoms, and brings the brim of the petal-cup to her mouth that she might sate her thirst.

She knows she should be skeptical. She knows she should wonder about this strange plant from outer space that could be anything, could do anything. Maybe one day, she thinks as she folds her hand into the vines curling around her fingers, the plant will tell her.

Her phone lights up, and it's Sierra tweeting her. Her profile picture has changed. She has yellow flowers in her hair, she is blowing a kiss from her fingers, and she is beautiful. Yvonne looks at the blossoms on the plant. They are half-closed, as if the plant is feeling particularly lazy, as if it would very much like to take a nap. They look like the flowers in Sierra's photo. She asks how Sierra is feeling, about the flowers in her hair— *they are so lovely, where did you find them?* Sierra says she's fine, she says she can't wait to show Yvonne something wonderful.

The plant reaches out to Yvonne, its green vines curling loosely through her fingers and settling in the shallow cup of her palm.

Time passes. It is never day or night in the station. It only is, and Yvonne uses her phone to swipe the days by. She catches glimpses of Sierra sometimes—hears a distant echo of how she sings to the radio, can taste buttery popcorn as she sucks food from a bag, knows Sierra likes her coffee black. She wonders what glimpses Sierra sees, if one day she raises her eyes to the sky and sees the Earth instead of the moon.

On the day before Yvonne is to return home, she stares down at Earth through the faint reflection of herself in the glass. Behind her, the plant has grown so tall that its yellow blossoms circle the dark eclipse of her head as she shivers.

Yvonne hears someone whisper her name, and she calls to Sierra across the space between them.

A vine slips over Yvonne's shoulder, and she twines her fingers with it. It tugs at her, and she follows. She doesn't know how she'll bring the plant with her when she returns to Earth, but knows she has to do something.

A yellow bud caresses her chin, tipping her face upward so she can watch it bloom against the bright lights of the station. Her mouth parts, and she can taste a golden sweetness as its petals reach towards her. The blossom escapes as she swallows it whole. There is not enough room for the entire plant, and what remains of it shrivels and dies as Yvonne wipes its nectar from her chin. Yvonne hides it in the botanical bay, where it will decompose and turn into another beautiful thing.

A crowd awaits when she finally lands back on Earth: physicians and scientists, and farther out, a crowd of spectators. Earth is heavy as Yvonne moves slowly in the bright sun, shielding her eyes with her hand. She is not surprised when she sees Sierra in the crowd, hands in her pockets, too-big sunglasses over her eyes as she smiles wide and broad beneath their shadow.

There are more yellow blossoms like small suns blooming in Sierra's hair. Yvonne has no time to speak with her, not given the attentions of the doctors, but when at last she is released from their care, she finds Sierra still waiting.

Yvonne tries to run towards her, but Sierra sprints, her shirt rising over her abdomen. Yvonne sees the spiderwebbed pattern of green veins that had once spiraled within spade-shaped leaves and that now binds them together through the vastness of space.

Sierra throws her arms around her, and Yvonne clings back. She thinks she's sobbing as her fingers pull at Sierra's hair, and she sees the flowers growing through the bone of her temple. Sierra speaks words Yvonne can barely process, can barely understand, but she can smell the faint golden scent of the blossoms on her breath as Yvonne stands on tiptoe to kiss her.

They smile at each other, and Sierra loops her long arms around Yvonne's shoulders as she guides her towards the car.

"Where to?" she asks.

Yvonne rests her hand lightly on Sierra's as she puts the car in gear. "Home. Bring me home."

DANDELION
John Shade

For my grandfather, Frederick. Rest well, Gramp.

Before the border wall, we scatter.

Dandelions.

The nanomachines grind us down and we float up and through the cracks, molecule to molecule, like holding hands.

ɔɜ ꙅɔ

Leena hesitates, is left behind. She stands apart on the wrong side of the wall. She presses her hand to the cool, shaded concrete. We feel it through the upload.

Big fields of grain wave at her back. Miles of grain. She breathes in and the scent lingers, stains the upload with memories. (*Watch the singularities like thunderstorms outside your windows; see the monsters they bring.*) Her eyes are closed. A little sadness shows on her mouth, downturned at the corner. She stays like that for a long while.

Leena is like us, scared. We can feel it, a low bass at the bottom of the upload. None of us have our filters active. The minutes are precious; we experience everything we can. Leena was the newest addition to our group before we picked up a couple survivors from another group. She is fast. Good with a wrench. Her nanomachine swarm is top-notch. Brilliant, the colors of their carapaces in the daylight. They rest across her bare, elegant shoulder. She stands tall, a long neck, an easy smile. She is the best of us.

When we reform, we place our hands on the opposite side of the wall. We feel the connection. We turn and run ahead. We know the border security, the swarms, the electrical grid, and most of all, the mouths. Crafted by AI, we know they are strange things. Wide, grinning mouths attached to bent legs, striding across the plains between the two border walls in predictable

140

patterns. At their center, they are a mass of flurried arms engineered to pick up runners. We know they want the burst of blood on their teeth again.

Finally, Leena, too, scatters through the wall.

We are the diversion. Ahead of her, we have already started to die.

We feel it on the upload. The mouths' pattern tears across us and a few are too slow, plucked up. No hesitation. The mouths eat us. Their teeth snap across our limbs and we wriggle in the half-light on serrated tongues. We go into shock, and soil ourselves. Our last emotion is one of embarrassment. (We have been taught to die nobly for thousands of years, and it is always a surprise to us when we don't.)

The mouths chew. We hear the sounds on the upload. Cracked bone, wet cartilage. Soon those who died are scattered in a different way. The AI's creations, the mouths, are efficiency incarnate. They were made to solve problems; it's the core from which they grew. They use all the parts of us to correct our transgressions. We become mortar for the cracks in the wall, and organic matter for the grass we bent running. We are grafted onto the broken wheat stalks, and set them upright to wave others through. We are the soft earth, and the clouds threatening rain again. The mouths do their work well. They wash away our bootsteps with the water in our bodies. They use our platelets to clot any damage done to them. Our consciousness they spit out like seeds. And we linger there, ghosts on the upload, a warning to all like the heads on spikes of old. They kill us every way they can.

"It's insane," Leena had said at the war table all those days ago.

"You've seen the projections," one of us—Jyl—had said. "There's more AI spilling out every day. More factories, more things. There's no stopping the hemorrhaging now. We'll be dead in a month, two tops."

"No," Leena said.

Jyl said, "We've got to get you someplace where the shackles still hold. You're the best engineer we have. You can change things. We can't. If only one of us gets through, it has to be you."

"It's insane," Leena said, quieter. It sounded more to us like, *It's the only thing left.*

Our knees whisper against the tall grass. Our plan is working. The mouths' pattern has changed. We are drawing them to us. We are the diversion; we are Leena's salvation. The mouths strafe us and catch more unaware. More die. Leena trails in our wake, unnoticed so far. Notes of regret thread through her fear.

We send messages of encouragement.

We say, *We will be all right*, and, *This is for the best*, and, *We don't hurt for long*, and, *I've always loved you*, and, *Don't ever give up.*

At the center of the field, in the no-man's land between the two border walls, lies a strip of abandoned towns. Vines grasp squat one-story buildings, all hunched together like prey along a single road cutting through.

The mouths have laid traps for us in these towns. We spring them. From behind abandoned buildings and cars and weeds, the mouths grow and unfurl before us like dark promises. They catch more of us. Many fall on the upload, screams and bitter endings. The upload is filled with the sounds of chewing. So many die in the towns, bodies smoothed over the walls and streets damaged in the fighting.

Leena dodges the mouths, the traps. The pattern's changing faster now, and faster still. We can't keep up. Even Leena has trouble. One of the mouths' paths crosses Leena, and it's about to scoop her up, but one of us shoves her out of the way and takes her place. She sees her chance and breaks through.

Leena reaches the opposite wall, places a hand on the rough surface, sun-stained and full of warmth. We feel it so clearly. Salvation.

One of us almost makes it. We reach for her.

Leena sends us messages of, *Come on! Come on!*

And we're sending, *Get out of here! Go!* as the mouths snatch the last of us alive up and lift us to their teeth, and then, over the top of the wall, through the electrical grids, we see the grain waving on the other side, and we share it on the upload.

Leena scatters.

We die.

The upload goes dim, silent, like stars going out. Then, just echoes as the last of us is chewed down to nothing.

C� ᘓ

We are ghosts. We are the fields, the town. Everywhere our cells are used. Some of us disconnect from the upload, and head into the unknown. Some of us stay.

(Is a ghost a ghost only as long as it holds on?)

CꙖᘓ

Are you ready?

We feel the message thrum against the upload. The world has passed us by. The years have made our upload obsolete, almost incompatible. The message, the feeling, is faint, like being underwater, but it is there.

Ready?

Leena. She has her hand to the opposite wall again. We think it is déjà vu. (How long have we been here? How much time has gone by?) We think it is a flaw in our memory, but she is different now. Older. She wears a war uniform. Medals dangle from her shoulders, her breast pockets. She stands taller now. There are men with guns behind her and swarm ships hang in the air behind them. An army. A human army.

I'm sorry it took so long, her message comes through. It sounds to us like, *We may not win this, but we will try.*

"General?" a soldier behind her says.

She keeps her eyes on the wall. She nods.

143

We give our reply. We help in any way we can, but ghosts are only what they leave behind, and our cells have been spread over miles by now.

The soldiers' guns scavenge us for ammunition. From the air, the ground. The grain, the buildings. The remnants of our loyal swarms. We are bullets in a magazine. We are the fins on rockets. We are the rolling tank treads. They collect and then we march. We tear through the things that tore through us. It doesn't have the right satisfaction. A different feeling. Only when Leena is in danger, and our shells and bullets protect her, does the upload sing with happiness once more.

Cʒ ꙮ

Years. Blood across the hills, the cities. The war touches everything, gets in the corners, the cracks, of every life. Our cells spread far. Stray bullets and shrapnel and broken tank treads and tires. More disconnect from the upload. We are the bombs that rake the countryside. The swarms that shift the jet streams to our advantage. The explosives that level mountains. We are the sad stories told by candlelight. Our upload hums with battle cries when Leena is near, but they sound to us like, *We are here for you, I am here. Please don't forget us.*

When the last battle is fought at the hive core—where the AI's creations curl over each other like snakes and burrow and lash out with everything they have—many of us give whatever we have left. And when the last of the AI's creations fall, and the shackles come down again, almost all of us disconnect.

Cʒ ꙮ

Leena builds a house between the border walls. She fills it with our captures. Us striking poses, or smiling with our children. (Dust has already begun to collect at the edges.) The house floats thirteen feet above the ground on grav cams. It's drafty. Dark on the outside and bright on the inside, sun mirrors in all the rooms. It's shaped like a ziggurat in the new style. We

144

are the cutting board, the cabinets. We are the coffee pot, the fireplace, the loveseat. We are the bullet casings that get caught between her toes in the rain-soft earth on her daily walks. I am...We are the picked flowers on her nightstand. We think she chooses us, as if she can feel us still, remnants of our upload, even through the singularities, the years. (We have been buried under the constant change.) Other people come through the border, and some can feel our presence there too, but none as strong as Leena. She always had a way with connections, could feel the way something worked just by looking at it, placing a hand to it.

Some travelers come here to settle again.

The abandoned town at the center of the border turns into a real town. Our vines are brushed away. Shop carts trundle down the streets. A faster kind of life amidst the buildings, not just starlight and growth anymore.

Some are soldiers from the war. Some are only good for violence, and end up as bandits. Sometimes they go to Leena's house. The older woman, the easy mark.

Leena and the soldiers play dark games of hide and seek through the house. We are the clumped rugs that trip them up. The countertops used for cover. The door barred with her shoulder (so close to me...to us, the upload pounds with her pulse). We are the bullets rolling into her revolver's chamber. The crack of gunfire. We are the metal tearing through their skulls and every terrible thought inside.

After, we are the water carrying their blood to the shower drain. We are the jets massaging her bare shoulders.

Most of us have let go by now. And after the soldiers are dead and buried (the shovel work under the stars, we don't welcome them next to us in the earth), the rest disconnect. The upload dies, vacant once more.

ᑕᔑ ᔑᓂ

I am the one who hesitates. The one who can't let go.
I am the field beneath Leena's house.

Dandelions.

Thousands. (How long has it been?)

She is sick again. I am the towel the caretaker uses to dab at Leena's forehead. I am the screwdriver fastening handrails to the hallway walls. I am the grav disc that carries her to the bathroom. The old sound machine mimicking rain while she sleeps. When she wakes from a nightmare, I send, *You are home, You are home,* but it sounds like, *I'm sorry, I'm sorry. I've always loved you.* She can barely feel them now, my messages. So many years between us, we are ghosts of different eras. (Our captures were replaced by family pictures long ago.) She lay in a cold sweat. Her trigger hand shakes under the covers. She doesn't like loud noises.

A breeze curls in and carries dandelion seeds and scatters them across her covers. Close but not touching, the two of us, like hands at our sides. I want to reach out, touch her fingertips. Tell her it will be all right, whatever's next. The years are too much. A gulf of time that I can't hope to cross, so I put messages in bottles, across all the bandwidths that I know.

Ghosts are memories given form. So this is what I am, this moment, this memory, most of all: I am the one almost to the wall all those years ago, running, running. Her hand is stretched out to me, and she's saying, *Come on! Come on!* Her hand, mine. Only air between us. (It seems so easy now.) And I'm mouthing, *Please, please come back for me.* But the others are saying something different, and my voice is washed away in the din.

I am not the bed that holds Leena's body the morning she does not wake. I am not the rags that clean the fluids. I am not the knives that prepare her for the funeral. The video screen that communicates her will. The chairs that hold fat relatives and admirers. I am not the picture frame holding her smile.

I feel her out there, on some other upload. She is the first layer of snow the ground. The jangling chains on her great-great-grandkids' bicycles. The concrete holding up the new war memorials.

She can feel me too, but faintly, just a murmur now. Hands at our sides, close but never touching, like adjacent graves. Somehow, it's enough. I send to her, *Welcome home*, but it sounds like, *Come back for me*.

I am the last wind on the street before dark. The door closed after an argument, sheetrock punched in anger. The sandcastle left unfinished. The grain waving under the stars.

I am a memory adrift on matter, a seed for the wind, reaching, reaching, only air between us.

Salamander Six-Guns
Martin Cahill

He descended on the town like a saint sent from Dark Heaven, six-guns shining like twin torches in his hands, down to the border where we had our battle on. Summers are always the worst in Sunblooders Stand, as the scale-folk grow riled earlier in the bright days.

We'd been fighting the scale-folk off for an hour when the stranger threw himself into the fray. One moment I was shoving a pitchfork into the belly of a croc-man, and next I knew, the flashing of the stranger's salamanders blinded me, sea-foam flame belching hot lead as natural as rainfall. He danced between us sunblooders like a phantom. Not a one of us knew who he was, but when help arrives, you don't ask from whence it came. He helped us drive back the line, the gator-kin and the croc-men screeching, the snake-touched and the iggies squirming; their shattered teeth and scorched scales left behind in the swamp as they dove into the murky water and made for the heart of their Scaled Nation.

Many of the towns inland would have taken to whooping and celebrating, but the thirty or so sunblooders on the swampy shore only sighed with temporary relief; here, at the fringe of civilization, the scale-folk were as consistent as the sunset.

The mystery man made a show of looking over each dead scale-folk at his feet, before turning his spring-green eyes on me. He had scars across his face and throat, pale against his dark skin, but I didn't bat an eye; anyone hugging the coast ended up with a souvenir sooner or later. Holstering his salamanders, which hissed and spat like grease on a skillet, he put his hands on his hips, and said, "Looks like y'all could use some help around here," his voice singing like a rusty six-stringer.

Something sour settled into the back of my throat, and I spat into the mud. Plenty of fancy folk had come through the town of Sunblooder's Stand, hoping to make a name for themselves in the last living border town abutting the Scaled

Nation. Plenty of other folks had drawn inland, away from the diseased coast of swampwater where creatures became people and hunted us normals like food, but not us. Some said it was the stubborn nature of those in the South, but I'd like to think it was a certain amount of sick pride, too; when you got good at protecting your home, you didn't give it up easy for the illusion of safer ground.

I wiped my hair out of my eyes, too long again and as red as my name, and fixed him with the look I gave every stranger with boots that shone too much. "We been doing fine without you, stranger. Reckon we'll be just as fine with you."

He smirked, and I knew I disliked him, like a fish knows it hates the sky. "Sugar," he said, "You'll be finer than you ever been with me around."

My hands curled into fists, and I bit down the urge to snarl. "Sugar is for horses, stranger. You call me Copper or you call me nothing."

The volume of my vitriol took him by surprise. After a moment's consideration, he took his hat off, and crinkled his fingers around its edges like all the children do with their songbooks come High Dark. "Begging forgiveness, Copper, sir. A man travels a lonely, dangerous road for a long time, and well, he tends to leave his manners at every crossroad, waystone and mile marker he puts behind him, if it means he lives a little longer. Coming back to society, I've neglected to bring my manners along with me."

I saw the other sunblooders looking for my reaction. Ever since Momma took a claw to the gut and got sent to the bottom of the swamp, they watched for her leadership in me. So I snorted, and stabbed a finger in his direction. "Gather 'em up quick then, stranger, or you're no better than the scale-folk, understand?"

He looked like I'd slapped him. Figured I'd hit him where his pride lived, but after helping us, I supposed he didn't deserve all scorn and no sweet. I scratched the back of my head. "Manners or none, you did us a good service today. If you could help bring back the wounded, might be a bed you could hunker down in for the night, but I can't make any promises."

He smiled, bowed at the waist, called me sir again, and began to gather up the injured. Saw him carry Old Kearney back, singing "Take Me Down To Starry Town," to keep the poor fool's mind from his missing leg; a clean rip was better than a bloody bite. One bite, and you may as well sink into the swamp or blow your brains out.

Walking back, we cleaned our weapons with rags, and began to murmur amongst ourselves. I watched him go, this stranger, watched him smile and laugh in a cluster of shocked, scared people, and found myself even more distrustful of him. What right had he to smile so? Easy enough for a stranger to pick up such habits inland, away from the Scaled Nation and the cancerous holes in the sky that hovered over the coast. But bringing those habits right to the edge of civilization, mocking the people who lived there without a second thought? Made me uneasy.

But I tried, I really did. I tried not to judge too quickly, tried to be the best person I could under the eyes of Shadow Matron, shades keep her. A person is made of nothing but show and bluster, a hurricane wrapped in a shirt and pants, and sooner or later, they'll blow themselves apart, or quiet down. I had to wait and see what this man would do.

Except he walked into my town like he'd lived there all his life, and I felt like the only one who remembered he'd only shown up an hour before. The people of Sunblooder's Stand were fascinated with him, his Northern drawl, his green eyes, the way his black coat seemed to bend the light; he seemed to be a long-lost relative, not a random gun newly arrived. Only thing he didn't seem to show off was the fancy silver chain around his neck, but I figured he was saving that for a rainy day.

He sauntered around town like a rooster, clucking and crowing at every person who fawned over him. Bunch of bright-eyed toad-lickers, to be taken in, to not see him for the threat he was. I fumed to see him chat up every man, woman, and child he happened to walk by. Respect had to be earned, and they were just <u>giving</u> it to him. Looking back, I can see why I fumed so: took me years to gain the same level of respect, and here he was doing it as easy as breathing. Not my proudest moment, no.

Come New Dark, as the sun slipped beneath the world, he smoked scales, the air burning magenta, steel, emerald, depending on the variety stuffed into the pipe. Children gathered around him, asking for stories from the safe world, and he delivered. Four people offered their homes to him, and before I knew it, he was a stranger no longer. The Mayor was here to stay, it seemed, and some furious and hurt part of me settled to the bottom of my heart like a stone in the sea.

Ah, right. His name.

A week or so after his arrival, folks started calling him Mayor. I said to them, "We didn't have a mayor before, why we need one now? Even Momma didn't have such a title and you all looked to her like she was Shadow Matron come High Dark to bless!"

People shrugged with moony eyes, and glanced at him, sitting on the barstool, talking and talking and talking, like words were water and these people hadn't been rained on in quite some time.

So they named him Mayor. What was his name before? Doesn't matter, I don't think; he slid into the role like a knife into a heart. It fit him.

He tricked the town into loving him, and not a one of them could see the strings he was pulling within them. Day after day, he taught them that the scale-folk were nothing to be afraid of. He'd lay his supernatural six-guns into the coals of fires to warm their guts, tell stories over their crackling, stories that gave every sunblooder a sense that there was more to life than survival. There was another world out there, he said, one free of scale-folk, where a body could live a day doing whatever they wanted, not always having to rush into battle come the clarion call of the bell.

He was going to get everyone killed. Every single person who drank in his poisonous stories became a little less cautious, a little more reckless. He was inspiring them at the wrong angle.

The truth was, there's no part of the world that's safe anymore; only lands that the swampwater hasn't touched yet.

It finally hit him when Fennel got his throat ripped out by a pyth-person, on account of he was too busy singing "Guts, Gators, and Glory" to notice the alabaster fangs snapping for his throat.

The Mayor had taught him the song the night before, said how it would lull a new baby to sleep in a moment. The young lad had blushed, his wedding band bright and clean, and the Mayor had roared with joy to see his cheeks redden.

It was the Mayor that put a bullet through Fennel's brain. If it was because of the snake poison that swept through his blood, or the scales that had begun to boil down his neck, I never found out. Mayor carried him home, silent like the sea.

No more songs were sung at the border after that day.

But no matter who fell, the Mayor was loved and I found myself alone. They'd trail after him, asking about this song or that, and everywhere they went, in the opposite direction I'd go, dragging along a bottle of whiskey, swallowing shots like bitter medicine. The town didn't ignore me, but they didn't love me like they loved him and it hurt like the oldest wound known to this world.

He tried to include me, invited me to meetings, to drinks at the saloon, but every time I saw that damned smirk of his, I hated him a little more, even if I didn't want to; it had been nearly a whole month of bluster, and it pushed me to an edge I didn't think I'd see again.

And if I said it didn't bother me, would you forgive me for lying? After Momma died and Da ran, taking up the town was the only thing that let me ignore the pain in my gut, made feel important, loved even. Mayor had taken that from me, taken them all from me, and now I couldn't do anything but sit beneath the stars and scratch at that terrible itch in my heart.

I went looking for him one night, and I had been at the bottle a little more than usual when I shoved him. He fell back against the wooden fence atop the only grassy knoll in town; folks said you could see clear to Coaltown from there. His six-guns were sitting in the dying embers of a fire, drinking their fill, some scale-folk magic in their hot hearts lapping up the heat.

He adjusted his coat, and coughed. "Something on your mind, Copper?"

I felt the whiskey in my blood urging me to say something mean, something that'd cut him down. But I was still my Momma's son and I wouldn't let liquor get the best of my decorum. "Just expressing my feelings as to your new position within the Stand, *Mr.* Mayor." Was there venom in my voice? Aye, a little.

He took it all with grace, though. "Told Duncan to quit it with that damn title, but that boy has a mouth bigger than a full-grown croc, and twice as loud." He looked back at me, must have seen something that made him stoop a little lower, pull the collar of his coat up. "Right sorry, Copper. Didn't mean to take anything away from you. This is your town, and I have no right to be making calls on it."

A wind cut through me, the wet of the swamplands settling into my bones, the night chill making me hold myself, the bottle dangling limp in my hand; relief and paranoia warred within me at his words. "Why are you here anyway, Mayor? What's a body to find in the Stand but death? We don't leave because there's nowhere in this world we can go. Too many of us are poor, and lack in all things but heart; what else is out there in the safe world for us? That's our excuse, weak as it is. So what in the Bright Hell is yours?"

He pulled out his pipe, nestled a fresh ball of tobacco and scales into the end of it, and lit it with a salamander shell, tamping its metallic end down until it caught. "Looking for someone."

The way his voice went frosty, the way his eyes cast down into the swamplands with a searing heat, made me take a step closer to him. He was reeling me in, telling another of his damn stories, and I fought hard to shake off its magic. "If you got business here, let us help so you can be on with it. You've been tearing through scale-folk for a month, but never once ask for anything in return. Let this be it. Let us get you what you need and get you out of this nightmare. You came here by choice, and you can make the choice to leave, too."

He took a long drag. The smoky, flesh-like stench of the scales burning in his pipe filled my nose, made me feel drunker than I was. To smoke of the scale-folk was said to be elixir before it killed you. How long had he been at it?

He huffed out a noxious cloud smoke, red at the edges, and smiled through its dissipation. "Kind offer of you. But what business I got would get a body killed for its doing. And I'm not the kind of man to throw people on the Red Coal Trail, just so I have something cool to walk over on my way to Bright Hell." He smirked with sad eyes. "But as I said, mighty kind of you."

I threw my fist into his side, the cold in my gut making way for the red-hot rage I loved so. "Toads take you! Don't go playing that card, Mayor. I've heard enough dramas on the crank to know a foolish line when I hear it. You've been giving and giving to this town without a single receipt for bullets. You're aiming for something and I want to know what it is!"

I wasn't backing down. I wouldn't let this town become beholden to the stranger in the dark coat with pistols of flame and a past that swallowed him like thorns. This close, he smelled like dying fires and hot lead. His eyes shone through the red smoke like evergreens bowing beneath a volcano's weeping.

And if our lips were only inches apart, wasn't it because I was trying to shout through the scent of him? If I was lonely and a little out of touch with the world, wasn't that to blame on the whiskey in my blood and the scale-smoke in my nose and Momma passing without a goodbye and Da leaving me to die and my lovers packing up in the night, afraid of being singed by the hurt in my heart?

Wasn't it enough to want a man who wasn't afraid of getting burned?

His hand went around my wrist then, his other on my shoulder; he pressed me back down to the earth, quiet as a tomb.

"You afraid of a little fire?" I said, my throat dry and rough, knowing it to sound petty and small. I hated him and I wanted him at the same time.

His voice came out raw; he seemed older than I'd ever thought of him. "It's just not a good idea." Around his neck, the shine of his silver chain blinded me.

I wrenched my arm from him, and walked away right quick; didn't want him to see me with my eyes leaking. Couldn't give a body the idea that fire could be quenched.

03 80

The next week, we lost a half a mile to the scale-folk. The bodies of their family had floated downstream, right to Momma Scales. They came surging out of the swamp, urged on by their mother, voices ululating and screeching with anger.

I was only a boy when the sky opened up. I'll always remember the swath of emerald light I saw on the other side, always remember the screaming wings that fell out of the hole in Dark Heaven. I remember the shaking of the earth, quake upon quake as beasts not of our world crashed, seeding themselves along the coast. From my vantage then, I could see two, maybe three, but as reports came in, more than twenty of the monsters fell from their world into ours.

That's when the scaled things of the swamps and jungles and deserts started up and moving, becoming more man than beast. The wings from beyond the sky were urging them up the food chain with an awful rapidity. But they weren't the worst.

Like any good infection, it started small. A scratch is sometimes all it took, though it could vary. "If the skin starts turning, you better get to burning," is something Da used to say before he left for lands inland, lands unscaled.

I think seeing his brothers rise out of the swamp, reptilian armor flying up their necks, their brown eyes going gold . . . I think it broke him to see his family become their family.

I'll always forgive him that, at least.

But if you didn't defend what family you had left with all you had, what were you?

I hadn't seen such a number of the scale-folk as I did the day we lost that half mile, surging forward, snapping jaws and

155

stronger claws with a swiftness to make wind balk. Our toes dug into the swampy earth as we battered scaled ribs with plunging knives and pikes. But really, we were a shield for the Mayor, who fought like a man haunted.

White-hot bullets flew with such speed as to shatter skulls, two, three in a row. The air was alive with the screams of his salamanders. He was an artist that made death.

They were gunning for him. Momma Scales urged them on with her grief, and soon enough, we had fallen back. If I looked out of the corner of my eye, I could see the outskirts of town.

But I couldn't look away from the battle for fear I'd die if I did. So I didn't miss the moment when the Mayor went down under a pile of snapping jaws.

For a heart-wrenching moment, I forgot how to breathe.

But in the next, he threw them off, pulling strength from where, only Bright Hell knew. Scale-folk scattered in the air, fell to the ground, and we were there to thrust steel through their bellies.

I turned to smile at the Mayor, glad to see him alive despite any awkwardness that had come of my stupidity a few days before. Despite my hurt, he was a part of this town now; it would kill everyone to see him kiss the bottom of the swamp.

We locked eyes from across the murky water and I lost my breath again.

His green eyes were gone. In their place were thin pupils, vertical, bright as molten sunflowers, and his teeth had taken on a sharper edge than any man I'd ever seen.

Years of combat instinct surged through me and had I a gun in my hand and not a pike, I would've shot a bullet right through him, faster than you can say "Gator-man gonna get ya."

He staggered to his knees in the water, and yowled like a cat whose tail had found the rocker. When he looked up, pale and shaking, he had recovered his green eyes; he looked at me, ashamed and exhausted.

That night, I grabbed his hand after dinner, and steered him to my cabin. Some of the others threw whistles and whoops after us, but I paid them no mind. Upon entering, I threw him into a chair, and kicked him hard back into it when he tried to stand. I didn't know if I was angry or frightened or both.

"Show me."

Mayor stared up at me, grim. "You don't want to see this, Copper."

I stared him down, arms crossed and feet wide, trying to channel my Momma as much as I could. Finally, he began to undo his shirt.

The mossy green and bark brown scales that mottled his chest glistened as they caught the moonlight. They trailed up to his chest from a terribly sewn gash in his side, divots of teeth marks and puncture wounds running around the edges.

I felt my muscles go hot, my throat tight. "How? Most men would be tearing out their lover's throats after a day with a bite that big."

He fixed me with a gaze, hung up on my words. He fingered the necklace he wore, rubbing a silver feather. He winced as he buttoned up his shirt. "Smoking the scale seems to trick a body into thinking you've already turned. Slowed it down somewhat. But a body can't be tricked forever."

"What in the world made you think to do such a reckless thing?"

His eyes went glassy and the moonlight seemed to pass through them and illuminate some memory held in the back of his skull. "A lover, a . . . companion. Name of Adam. He was bit when we were crossing the Brollins Canal looking for mercenary work. Gator-gal snagged him off the side of the boat, tried to drown him, but we were able to kill her and drag him back on deck. Old healer onboard stuffed the pipe into Adam's mouth, lit the scales, and said it would help. It did for a time. Adam held on, but—" and here's where the glass of his eyes went dark, and he stopped straying down memory's path, "After a few months, Adam couldn't fight anymore. He liked the voice in his head, he said. He liked being a good son to Momma Scales, liked how it made him feel. So he let it happen, and dumb toad I am, I let him live. Thought I could appeal to him, my sandy-locked lover. But all that happened was he took a bite out of me and fled into the water. I been tracking him ever since, and well—"

"He's here. He's come to the heart of the Nation." I finished the thought for him, though by no means did it give me pleasure to deduce his intentions, nor did I feel superior knowing the full measure of his pain. My eyes roved the landscape of his body, its lean curves cutting the night to ribbons. My mouth wanted to taste his, but all I could do was imagine the pain racing through him like a panting hound. "Can you last long enough to find him?"

Mayor had sunk into the high backed chair, refused to meet my gaze. "I'll find him, that's for sure. But living? Well, shit. If I'm as good a liar as I hope, then next year, a year after, if I'm careful. But—" he laughed then, his eyes getting fever-bright, almost yellow in the dark room. "I can . . . hear her, Copper. When I'm down at the border, pushing back my would-be brothers and sisters, I can hear her, right here." He tapped his temple. "She whispers to me in verses of fire and smoke, seduces me with the promise of family, of living forever, I—" He stopped, put a shaking hand to his eyes. His breath rushed out of him, ragged and low. "She's a compelling Momma, Copper. Broke my Adam like a piece of driftwood, and he was a saint compared to me. Whatever she's doing to drive the scale-folk, it's leaking into me, and I don't know when I'll be too full up of her to resist."

It's a hard thing, watching the strong at their weakest moments. Saw it with Da when he wept at his brothers' empty graves, saw it with my own Momma clutching her gut, trying to keep her insides on the inside. How do you build someone back up when they've gone as low as they can go?

In my experience, you either kick 'em in the ass or let 'em work it out. And the Mayor? He needed a kick. "Well, you're just going to have to hang on a little while longer, mister," I said, with as much authority as I could muster, "because you still have work to do, and no lizard bitch momma is going to keep you from doing it. In fact, I say we kill two crocs with one bullet, if you catch my meaning."

When he looked back up, his smirk was wide, his evergreen eyes bright.

॰ ॰

We rode out the next day, our packs stuffed with as many knives, bullets, and pikes as we could shove into their confines. Mayor followed the pressure in his mind south and east, and we marched out behind him.

A few bodies from the town had joined us, folk who found the idea of a suicide mission to rid Sunblooder's Stand of the biggest progenitor of scaly bastards appealing. No use in telling them the story of Adam. Mayor would kill me if I revealed his secrets, and so I kept my mouth shut.

Was it a dumb plan? Sure as the sun is bright. But Mayor was dying and I was lost. And if we had a way to find Momma Scales in the tangled heart of the Scaled Nation, well, we were just desperate enough to try to put her to rest.

The mood was light as we crept past the border and through the swamp, with Felbrem and Ko betting on who would win themselves the heart of Momma Scales herself. Jocularity on the road to Bright Hell; who'd have thought it?

Mayor walked in the front, sullen and gaunt. If he was smoking scale, he could have been fine. But every scale-folk in a mile would be drawn us to like gators to guts, and so he couldn't stymie it.

With every step, he fought the infection through sheer will.

And with every step, he lost a little more.

We passed through pools of murk and forests of reeds, keeping our eyes split for any scale-folk that may have been lingering. Mayor said we'd be fine for a few miles more.

When pressed for answers, he tapped his temple with a pained look, turned back to the front, and shaded his eyes. Were they golden just then? Or was that the light being tricky with me?

159

At night, Mayor and I shared a tent, where he went to the farthest corner, and wouldn't look me in the eye. Did he think I'd hate him, to see those yellow eyes in the night?

I awoke to guttural coughs, hissing whispers. Wrenching myself up, I saw Mayor curled around himself in the corner, shaking like a rattlesnake in the brush. He was covered in a cold sweat, and on his neck I saw scales creeping up behind his ear, brushing the back of his neck.

He was all motion then, sprang at me, hands clamping down on my shoulders. His eyes were a totality of gold and they were never going to change back.

"She was never meant to be here, Copper." His voice was high, and shook like a willow in the wind. "Her, her brothers and sisters, they were thrown from their lands through a rent between spaces, denied any succor, say, or justice. Their enemies threw them through the sky and gifted them to us."

I tried to shake myself from his grip. "Damn it, Mayor, snap out of it!" His fingers dug deeper, the nails longer, his eyes twitching.

"They're changing us, Copper. She's making us family, an army." His gaze snapped up, and it was as though he could see through the tent top, into the sky and beyond. "Someday, they're going to go back, and take back what's theirs. And we're going to go with them."

I slammed my fist into his gut as hard as I could and he let go, fell to the damp earth, lay there, sobbing and sobbing.

Should I have gone close to sit with him, be there to lend him a little humanity, which was dying in his chest like a timid cinder caught in a storm? Should I have put my hand on his hand, and shown him he wasn't alone, not even here, at the end of his life? Should I have kissed his brow, and promised that he still had a chance to live?

Aye, maybe I should have.

But I stayed in the corner, terrified, and watched him sob himself to awful sleep, remembering that iron grip on my shoulders, that piercing golden light in his eyes, the scales that

160

were marching across his skin. To this day, it churns my gut to think of how I failed him in that moment.

It wouldn't have stopped what happened next, but Bright Hell burning, what in all this terrible world do I know?

Cƒ ∞

The next morning, Mayor wore a cloth around his eyes. When Ko asked him why, all Mayor did was smirk and say, "So those scale-folk see what I really think of them."

The group laughed at that. I shivered.

It was no matter, because everyone forgot about his eyes when we entered the Scaled Nation proper. In the morning light, scattered across the thin reeds and fuzzy bulrushes and angular black trees of the swamp, there were scale-folk of every kind.

They had taken a cue from their ancestors, and lounged along the banks of the swamps, letting the sunlight flood through them like liquor, making them drunk and sleepy. Some of the croc-folk had their mouths open, nestled in the cattails, jaws working against empty air, while pyth-people rubbed and coiled their long necks together, splashing in the muck. Gator-folk lay on their stomachs in the water among pink-flowered lily pads, nostrils just above the surface, while the iggies draped themselves across branches of heavy bald cypress trees.

Mayor put a gloved finger to his lips, motioned for us to get close. When he started walking, I felt a pressure in the air, slight, and wondered if Mayor was keeping us safe, trying to hide us and disguise us with the other scale-folk.

We walked slower than slow; slow enough that time could miss us if it wasn't looking.

Up ahead, through the density of green palm fronds and low-hanging cypress leaves, I spied a mighty crater deep into the earth, and saw something enormous shift in the shadows. I turned to confirm with Mayor it was Momma Scales, only to see he wasn't there.

The whole group stopped dead. I couldn't feel the ripple in the air. The nearest gator-man's nostrils flared. Icicles pierced my heart, eyes searching for the Mayor. I looked back the way we'd come.

Mayor was standing over a gator-man.

He had his gun drawn, aimed at the gator-man's heart. His hand was smoking, he was holding the six-gun so tight. His arm was shaking, fresh tears rolling down his cheeks, staining the bandage around his eyes. His mouth opened, and it looked he was trying to say something, but his mouth would not obey.

I read his lips, best I could: *Adam,* he said, over and over again.

How does a body run as slow as they can? I moved as through spiderwebs, inching my body forward in the water, going to Mayor as slow and as fast as I could.

I stood a foot from him, glanced at the sleeping croc on the ground, Adam, who had a silver chain around his neck, a feather at the end glinting in the light. Around the Mayor's neck hung its twin.

Mayor worked his mouth at me, unable to talk for the grief that blocked his throat. I shook my head at him, lips shut.

Mayor thrust the gun out at the sleeping gator. The Mayor's eyes were pleading with me, bleeding water like a stuck cactus.

I pointed back at the group of frightened sunblooders, to the stirring figures scattered around us, at the viper's nest we had walked into.

I'll never forget that moment, when he ripped the band of cloth from his eyes, turned his golden lights on me and mouthed, *I'm so sorry, Copper.*

His arm went limp.

He dropped the gun into the water.

The sleeping gator-man, Adam, opened his eyes.

As other scale-folk began to wake at the sound, Adam rose and seemed to see the Mayor, really see him.

And then Adam remembered what he'd become, and did the only thing he knew how to do, did to the Mayor what he had tried to do so many years ago when he had first turned.

162

His jaws clamped around the Mayor and then he dragged him under the water, blood already staining the air.

I swear I saw Mayor smile, a smile as wide and sad and starless as Dark Heaven.

It didn't matter if I screamed at that point or not, because the air had become nothing but sound, nothing but motion and pain and teeth, as the scale-folk sprang from sleeping and saw how we had slipped past them.

We pulled out our pikes and our steel and our guns.

I screamed to move onward, toward the crater.

The scale-folk were still groggy from sleep, but there were so many of them. How do you fight off a world of hate? I sent a pike through the neck of a pyth-person, and sidestepped the swipe of a gator-gal, whose needle teeth were flecked with blood and grime. Her tail sent me flailing, splashing down into the water. I could feel her moving towards me.

I had never contemplated my death, only figured it would come when stupidity got the best of me. Never figured it on someone else's stupidity, but that's life, I guess.

Then I noticed how the water near me was boiling. I plunged my hands into the mud, and found the scorching handle of one of Mayor's salamander six-guns.

I whipped the weapon skyward and fired. A lance of flame blew through the gator-gal in front of me, rocketed across the sky, and exploded over the crater.

The echo of the gun caused the scale-folk to stop their attacks, and quirk their heads as though they heard something far off. Fine, let 'em listen. I searched the mud for the other shooter, found its hot handle and lifted it out of the water, steaming.

In that pause, my heart broke to see Mayor's silver necklace shine up from the muck. I snatched it up and put it in my pocket. Someone had to carry his ghost home.

I turned just in time to see Momma Scales rise.

Her shadow could've shrouded the town proper, and I had to put my arms up against the windstorm her wings whipped up, though I caught glimpses of scales the color of deep fire, a belly as white as fresh sand. She shrieked in a language of a land astride ours, and I didn't have time to think as from her great jaws erupted a hurricane of heat.

The spear of flame made for me and mine like an arrow. With no time, and no place to run to, I thrust the six-guns into the air, remembering how Mayor would nestle them in the coals to charge them, and praying to Shadow Matron, oh, how I prayed it would be enough.

The fire slammed down on us, and arced around the guns in my hands. I could feel the salamanders drinking, deeper and deeper and deeper still, learning that their guts were not meant for so much power.

The salamander in my left hand exploded. The worst pain I've ever known washed through me and took my hand away in a burst of blood and bone. I screamed.

The other six-gun barely held. The wash of flame from above subsided, and in my remaining hand, the salamander glowed as if born from Bright Hell's forge. The scale-folk screeched and roared, cheering on their Momma who'd come to protect them. In the sky, she wheeled, circled back to me, to the sunblooders behind me.

At my feet, Ko and Felbrem were dead and smoking.

I stood, letting my stump of a hand drip blood onto the scorched and glassy swamp. Raising the salamander, so hot I could smell my hand roasting, I leveled it at the great Momma from another world, whose jaws snapped the air, screaming for her fallen babies.

I was ready to die, I suppose.

I mean, the Mayor was dead. Ko and Felbrem were dead. The rest of the sunblooders huddled around me, bloody and scorched and beaten. I wanted to die because it honestly seemed the easiest thing to do.

But if you didn't protect your family with all you had, what were you?

Momma Scales fell like a comet from Dark Heaven. Her jaws opened and I saw behind her teeth a great, bubbling heat. Her and I, our hands were on the triggers.

She approached.

The universe yelled, "Draw!"

We fired.

I was faster.

The bullet ascended like a star from Bright Hell, cutting through the flames of her jaw, and out the back of her mighty skull.

She didn't scream as she fell, but her babies did. They cried and wept as she landed into the swamp behind us, dead as dead as dead.

Last thing I remembered was dropping the six-gun to the water, sizzling, and staring at my lost hand, the bloody stump, and smiling like a fool before I fell with her.

03 80

What happened to the scale-folk after their Momma died? Well, I imagine they did what we all have to do: they learned to live on without her.

There've been raids every so often, but they're few. Without her, they're lost, as lost as the sunblooders without the Mayor. But we all learn to make do with loss; life is just learning how to lose things with grace.

Would the Mayor have been proud of us, to see us fight back so? Did he even care for us? Or was he just a broken body searching for a ghost, before he could let himself die?

He may have been poisoned, and he may have been foolish, but he was right about one thing: The world is larger than the Stand, and to sit still in a world going down in flames without trying to help douse the inferno is just as bad as being the one to start the fire.

So I'm headed out. I've got a horse. I've got his last six-gun, battered and busted as it is. Even got his silver chain around my neck; maybe his ghost can help keep my feet on this earth. Momma Scales is dead by my horrific, scarred hand, and if I can do that to one, I can teach others how to do it to the remaining lizard lords that still dot the coast, biding their time until they

165

bring their war back through the skies. I'll see if we can't drive those bastards back to their world without taking ours with them.

One of these days, I'll die. I'll be dragged under or poisoned or turned to their family. But not before teaching every person I meet that the world can only survive if you help it to, and fear is just a rope holding you back.

I don't know if it's what he would've wanted, but hope is all I've got left to give.

I gave it up, once upon a time and a hand ago. I don't intend to again.

ITSELF AT THE
HEART OF THINGS
Andrea Corbin

"The acts of life have no beginning or end.
Everything happens in a completely idiotic way.
That is why everything is alike." — Tristan Tzara, 1922

On the floor, I hiked my skirts up and began to
disassemble myself, starting with my left knee.

"How is that going to stop the Szemurians? How is that
going to protect us? Can't you help me, for God's sake?" Benoît
said this, sounding increasingly frantic, on each pass through the
sitting room as he tried to gather up whatever he could—to
board the windows, bar the door, barricade the entire house, as
though that were important. He broke apart the dining table we
had found on a trip to Lyon in 1921, so he could use the boards
to block the picture window. It had been a good table, or at least
we had good meals at it over the past three years.

The house in Paris would stand or not, and Szemuria
would come or not; they would try to burn down the house or
not. Or rather, I heard they would, raining war down on us like
they themselves were War. Of course the house was
inconsequential, so I unscrewed my kneecap and set it on a
bedsheet I had spread beside me for that purpose. It was a
delicate process, because I didn't want to deny myself or others
the option of reassembly in the future. The future was
questionable, but no matter; I didn't want to be destroyed. A
small amount of blood spotted the sheet beneath my solitary
kneecap.

The Szemurians sent no messages or envoys, only dreams
to every one of us a week before. Benoît and I had different
dreams; the papers suggested everyone did, and visiting the café
confirmed—"They came like colossi, feet crushing our belching,
rattling cars, and they screamed smoke and fire into the air, and

167

burned us alive," said Mme Höch, a kohl-eyed woman, hands shaking as she picked up her espresso. The man with her, his beard sharper than Benoît's and his cravat tighter like a noose, almost knocked the delicate china out of her hands and said, "They were like eagles, massive, claws grasping for each of us as we ran through the streets, claws digging into our flesh and bone, and dropping us from on high, but yes! Yes, they screamed, screamed like nightmares."—but in the end these were only dreams, I said.

Benoît loomed in front of me with a hammer in his hand and nails in his pockets while I carefully snipped and tugged and set my tibia apart from my fibula. "I'm going to need help later on, when I get up here," I said, gesturing at my torso, my shoulders, my hands.

"We're securing the house, and then we're going to the bomb shelter." Having woken up to absent neighbors and quiet streets, he'd concluded everyone had decamped to shelters, like before.

Benoît's dream: He lay in bed with me and we couldn't move, frozen while bombs dropped all around us, small explosions of dust, cratering the road and city, never touching us but deafening us. He said I tried to speak though neither of us could hear; he could barely see for the dust of the bombs, and he wanted to know what I was saying, what was I saying, what had I said?

What the papers said, after the night we first dreamed of Szemuria, was that Szemuria was coming for us and we had to defend ourselves and our way of life. Defend our property, our values, the strength of character, the pure blood, the modern freedoms, and I stopped listening, feeling that the right thing to do was disassemble myself and wait. It took several hours to find the right tools, and to launder and bleach the sheet, and to clear the floor to lay out the sheet, and then Benoît stepped on it and I had to wash the dusty shoeprint off again.

⚬ ⚭

Boom! Boom! Here they came. I could hear them, like in my dream, the Szemurians at the edge of the air.

An hour into my work, inside my right thigh I had found a key of unrecognizable substance. Heavy, like iron, but a faintly pearled sheen to it; rough, like iron, but always cool, no matter how long I held it; lastly, it was not black like iron; and finally it fit nothing I knew of. I put that key piece of me at the corner of the sheet, away from my dismantled legs, to let it watch over me as I continued to work. Benoît shuffled in, all the windows covered, all but one door sealed tight, and sat by my side. I could see the gleam of exertion on him, smell it on him. All that work he had done to protect something.

"We have to go to the bomb shelter," he said, again.

"Do we?"

"The Szemurians are coming."

The screwdriver pressed into my hip socket, sharp and painless. With a little more leverage I could—but when I leaned my head on Benoît's shoulder and closed my eyes, I was transported back, back, back to a time before we bought the house. Before our marriage, before our dreams, before the War. Before all this. But not before the Szemurians. They were always there, whether we knew about them or not. With my eyes closed, I could feel toes in sand, wet sand at the edge of the beach, smooth and pale sand. We took the Métro through the city, a train farther still, until we were at the Mediterranean, in a château owned by his parents. The château is no longer there, or anywhere.

It's almost another country, the sea. The south. The warmth of the sun is different. You turn golden and caramel and rosy, or at least we did, me the rosy, daring the sun to burn me. Things made sense, then.

Benoît took the screwdriver from my hand and threw it so hard that it stuck into the wall. He gathered the corners of my sheet, the key falling into the mess of bones and muscles and tendons and parts unidentifiable, so I'd likely never be able to put all my pieces back together without the aid of an anatomist, and I laughed as he picked me up. "Perfect."

Things never made sense. We only thought they did because of how little we knew.

"I'll take care of you," Benoît said, scrabbling for a good grip on me. No knees to scoop his arm under. I held the makeshift satchel of myself, and he held me, and we left.

CS 80

The streets looked the same as always, except they were moving away from me as I looked over Benoît's shoulder, my nose pressed to his wool coat, inhaling home and Gauloises with each breath, each step away. Boom! Boom! A great drum, out of sight.

"Do you remember when we were married?" I asked into his neck.

"You wore a beaded ivory dress, and black silk top hat. You removed your shoes halfway through, to the alarm of the priest and my mother, who were unsettled enough by the hat. When you did, you put your hand on my shoulder for balance. I almost kissed you right then, but I thought it would've killed my mother to upend the order of the ceremony like that," Benoît said, with that lightness to his voice that meant he was close to crying.

"That was the day Germany declared us all at war."

Benoît's hands tightened around me. "You toasted to all our deaths."

"Not until we were alone," I said, it being important to remember that I have tact, sometimes.

The streets were not full of retreating citizens, defending citizens, fighting citizens as we made our slow way. Everyone was gone. Not a one stayed to defend any way of life, after those dreams. All the Parisians were missing, and what was left but us?

"We didn't die," he said.

"Yet?"

Benoît marched, breath harsh with effort.

"You looked very handsome at our wedding. New waistcoat of sapphire, the hint of vines traced out in threads of

170

silver, like kelp, like an ocean, like a garden, and you stood so tall and proud that I don't even remember who else was there. Did you know? I don't know if my own mother was there. I don't remember taking off my shoes. I remember dancing with you, each of us with a daffodil in our hand, stolen from the garden," I said, watching the arrondissement go by, the shadows deep. The sun hid himself behind thin clouds but the shadows were strong. "We fled to Zurich the next month."

"Zurich was nice."

"You were the last thing that made sense."

With a heaving sigh, Benoît stopped in the middle of the street. The air hummed like wind in empty bottles. When I was young, I would line up bottles on a shelf below the window and listen to them sing; this was the same. I closed my eyes. It sounded like something from heaven, or dreams.

Benoît walked a short distance and set me down on grass. He took the white sheet from me, unbundling it and arranging the items with care, piece by piece. He peered at the key before setting it among my bones and sinews, where it gleamed like a memory I couldn't place.

"I'm sorry I threw your screwdriver," he said, and stretched out next to me. Under us, the grass was cool, dirt flaking onto my palms, and the wind still sounded like bottles. Benoît slid his fingers between mine. It was his first soft gesture since his dream.

"The Szemurians are coming," I whispered.

"What can we do?"

 Cg &O

The sunset might have bloomed with orange fire, or pink and purple luminescence, or a shade of teal that no one had seen before, but no one saw it then, either, if it did. The low booms, still, like a heartbeat in the sky. Benoît broke the window of a corner shop and found scissors, a butter knife, a finicky wrench, and a mallet, returning to me with his arms full. He also carried a small sack. This is what was in the sack: two gas masks, a ball of red twine, a muslin shirt, a lady's silk scarf with a pattern of peacock feathers painted on it, a handful of colored ribbons, and a jar of paste.

When I saw that, I kissed him.

"What have you done to your fingers?" Benoît asked. He took my hand, now lacking the pinky and ring finger, and kissed my palm, his lips dry and gentle.

"I felt anxious, waiting," I said.

"Now you have to wait longer," he said. He stretched his right leg out in front of me. In the sky, angular and pale shapes formed, like new clouds. "I can't do it myself. Help me, please."

The day I was born, a lark sang. My mother told the story this way, as though a lark singing made a day any different from another. Larks sing every day. The day I began school, a lark sang, and the day my father died, a lark sang. The day I began school, my grandmother fell and never walked again. The day my father died, my mother wept, my cousins wept, my brother wept. The day I met Benoît, yes, a lark sang, and so did a robin, and boys and girls across the country, but also a lark was killed and devoured, and a robin, and boys and girls across the country fell ill or died. The day I married Benoît, the war started, a lark sang. The day we fled to Zurich, a lark sang. And the day my brother joined the army, and the day he died in a watery trench. A lark, singing. Always.

A lark sang, invisible in some nearby tree, as Benoît and I took each other to pieces on the grass.

"Don't tell me about it again," I said to Benoît, as he started to talk about his dream. The Szemurian dream.

"I didn't tell you all of it," he said.

His rib was being difficult. Next we would try the rest of my left arm. There wasn't much more that we could do for each other. An arm each, a head each, leaving enough to hold each other, and not enough to come apart entirely. We would lay ourselves out in all our parts, reordered and useless. The closer we drew to that moment, the more my dread dissolved into a gas, transmuted into a cloud that could drift away and burn up in the sunlight.

"The bombs fell. There was silence. You and me, in our bed. All of Paris gone, all of France, all of Europe. Our bed, in a wasteland. There was a great silence after the bombs fell," Benoît said, and paused to grunt as I pulled away a set of ribs and lung, bone and flesh, parting with the sound of a boot in mud. "A great silence, then a voice. We were the last ones, all that was left. The voice spoke in a language I didn't understand, hard consonants and guttural vowels stretched out into low melodies, but I knew that the nothingness was where we were going to spend the rest of our lives. No gardens, no country, no château near the sea. No trees, no larks, no friends, no art...no more anything."

I wanted to ask what he thought the voice said, but more than that I wanted Benoît to keep talking, so I said nothing.

"After the voice, I could move. After the voice, I sat up, put my feet over the side of the bed to find the nothing coated in a powdery dust, colorless for the combination of every color that used to be. I stood. I turned back to reach for you, and you—you were gone."

Benoît put his whole hand over his face. I couldn't live for his weeping. The last of me shattered, no matter how solid my shoulders, my neck. What was left of my mouth at last confessed, "I had a dream, too."

Surprised into calm, he said, "You never said."

With a soft twist, I pulled Benoît's hand from his wrist and set it to the side. Carefully, I wrapped his other hand around the stump of arm that remained. "Hold that still," I directed, and snapped my own hand off. Pressed it, wrist to base, until it took. "They can't take me from you."

ᘓ ᘔ

Boom! Even now, scattered, intermittent arrivals: *boom!*

I wore a gas mask, the lower part torn away, the rest covered in muslin. Ribbons lined the edges, tracing in stripes from darkest to lightest. A braid of red twine drooped below my right eye, wafted in the air, tangled in my arms, looped around Benoît's wrist, danced in a breeze, and connected underneath the left eye of Benoît's mask. Benoît looked out from the eyes of two peacock feathers, the scarf pasted over his mask and hanging down, billowing with every breath of his. Or my mask was peacocks, and his ribbons, if you counted differently. His legs were longer than I was accustomed to, and I stumbled, needing more effort to skim the ground. He fell behind, needing slightly quicker steps on my legs to keep up. We ambled through the streets, learning our new parts. We wore masks. We walked, stronger with every step.

Szemurians in strange vehicles rolled through the sky like smooth tanks, a shining mechanical cacophony supplanting the sight of clouds and stars. Some landed, and out walked Szemurians into Paris, like Parisians returned. They were shaped like Benoît and myself and everyone else we had known on the planet and yet entirely unlike us, which is to say, they were themselves.

The building where we lived before Zurich, where we lived when we were first married, had a cluster of Szemurians looking up at it. One admired the flowers in the front garden, pulling them from the dirt. They chattered senselessly as we approached, their vehicle floating a few centimeters above the street like a lost bank vault. The outside was bright silver and muted steel. The door opened into a well-lit interior, with wood-paneled walls and a lush, intricately patterned carpet that reminded me of a garden path.

"I dreamt that you came and nothing changed," I said as we stood between those Szemurians and their vehicle. The Szemurians silenced their talk and looked at us, wide-eyed, shocked to the very core by us, by my words. One wore a morning coat of dove gray, another charcoal, dark fabrics; the dresses stood out like gems of emerald and garnet. A gala we had missed. "I dreamt that nothing changed, except everything was worthless. The franc was worth nothing again. French meant nothing, and my words went unattended the moment anyone recognized them as unrecognizable. I could do nothing. I was a ghost."

174

The Szemurians stared. The one in the top hat twisted his cane in his hands. "Drent?" he said, stilted, confused, imitating. "Goase?"

I turned to Benoît, caressing his chin. "See? No bombs, my love. No craters or dust."

"But that leaves us ghosts," Benoît said, worry tugging at his face. The Szemurians were starting to chatter again, around a building that grew increasingly strange to me.

"This isn't a dream," I said. We pushed the scarf out of the way and we kissed, uncertain who was who, exactly, where he was and me, with his hand springing from my wrist, my wrist down to his arm, and back up to my neck stretching and my mouth kissing his.

While the Szemurians stood in the streets of Paris, I ran, bringing Benoît and the rest of my self into the Szemurian vehicle. Before the closest Szemurian could follow us inside, we slammed the door. From my pocket, I pulled a pearled key, cool to the touch.

03 80

Silence.
No more booms.
Outside, the stars made no sounds, and their lights reflected in our eyes. Back in Paris, a lark sang.

MAPS OF INFINITY
Heather Morris

ASTERION

The difference between you and the humans, when it comes right down to it, is not in the protrusions of gnarled bone and horn that jut from the apex of your skull, or in the coarse fur that contrasts so spectacularly with the other parts of you, the parts that are mere human skin, or in your roar, or your pain, or their avarice.

The difference between you and the humans is that they all of them think they are deserving of something merely by fact of being born, while you understand existence does not equal right.

You can want until the end of your days; that does not make the wanted thing inevitable, or deserved.

But who cares about humans, anyway? You wouldn't ever think of them except they keep calling on you. As much as they fear, their fascination is greater. Some of them think of you as a holy thing. Some of them think of you as an evil thing. Some, rarely, think of you as both at once. But always the *thing*. The object.

They never let you be the actor of your own life. And if you opened your mouth full of blunt teeth, if you told them, *I am me, I am aware, I am here*, well, then that would only make them more afraid.

And you are so tired of fear.

ଓ ଶ

THE KING'S UGLY DAUGHTER

My mother never told me she resented me for what was not between my legs, but I knew it all the same.

176

It was written in the way she sewed my clothes tighter than they needed to be because I was so much bigger than the other girls, never once in my life the right size. It was in the way she tugged ferociously at my dull, limp hair as she tried to dress it to fit the vagaries of fashion. It was in the way she looked at the women in our village who had sons—with a greedy, hollow hunger. It was in the way she drank clear liquor and threw small stones into the sea on many nights when she thought I was asleep, and the way she screamed at the moon to bring him back, bring him back, she would try again a thousand times if only he would come back.

On the day we learned of the king's wedding, my mother beat me ten strokes across the shoulders for letting the bread burn.

On the day the news came that the queen had borne her first son, my mother threw a jug of oil at my head, and I slipped in the shards that littered the floor as she chased me out, and I slept out of doors for three nights until a neighbor sent me home and my mother smiled wanly with tears in her eyes and hugged me close.

On the day I first bled, she told me who my father was.

I already knew. I had known for a very long time. But still I ducked my head low, and though she never said "Oh, child, if only you were a *son*," I heard it all the same.

 G3 &O

ASTERION

They send you their beautiful ones, the ones they think are most worthy, and you always wonder why.

Not why they send them. That motivation is easy enough to parse. They think the sacrifice will appease you, keep you from the rage and destruction and the evil of their own hearts that they see reflected in your beastly skin.

But why the beautiful? Why do they think you would have any use, or any desire, for these quaking children with their symmetrical features and their pale, unblemished skin? They come to you reeking of fear, their eyes bright and white in the darkness, every seven years. And what are you supposed to do with such burdens?

The answers spill slowly from their mouths, the bravest of the boys and girls stuttering and stumbling over words you only ever half-learned. Those above, the humans, they think you will eat these lovely sacrifices. As if fourteen small bodies could sustain you for so many years. They think you will rape and ravish them, that you will draw amusement from their torture in your tangle of underground caves.

It would be insulting, if you cared.

Anyway, you are an herbivore.

You cannot speak the human tongue, the language you half remember hearing from inside your mother's womb. Your throat and tongue and lips will not form the sounds. So you teach the pretty children to respond to your gestures, and as each group grows older they remain to speak to the new arrivals, to teach them, and every seven years things get a bit easier.

You do not eat the children. But there are unspoken rules. They can never return to the light and the day. That is the way of the world. This life has been chosen for them despite their will, and so they must live it.

You teach them to cut tunnels into the soft earth. You teach them to carve art into the walls, whatever art they please. You teach them to survive on the mundane sacrifices that fill the long stretches between seventh years. Grain and wine and grass and air. And when the newest have settled, you go apart from them once more, because you generally prefer to be alone.

C8 80

THE KING'S UGLY DAUGHTER

My father was a young man sowing his wild oats when he had my mother. But he was very drunk, and he claimed to catch my mother cavorting with a wild man after she had left him sleeping off his winesick head in her bed. He would only claim me, he told her and everyone else who would listen, if I was a son.

For proof of paternity, he buried his cloak and his sword in a secret place that he said only a male heir could find. As if a penis were to prove a dowsing rod. At least then it would have some use, I suppose.

I found the secret place when I was seven.

It was a quiet glen, green and dense and wild. I used to go there, sometimes, when I needed to sit alone with my thoughts. Even wild girls sometimes need a place to be still.

As a further challenge, my father had buried his hoard beneath a large rock, one that only a man in his full strength could lift.

I managed the feat when I was fifteen.

Understand, I did not want the king's inheritance. He had sons now, legitimate ones, and I cared nothing for the mythical man who dodged questions of paternity by burying trinkets under rocks.

But I wasn't very good at being a girl, not the way it was spelled out that I should be. I was tall, and broad, and brash, and loud. I would not be the object of any man's lust, even were he blind, and I would not be a gentle mother. So I took the cloak, and I took the sword, and decided I would be a hero.

My mother begged me not to leave. She did not want the shame of it, her ugly child running around the world in search of glory.

Her tears were too selfish. They came far too late.

I headed east with nothing but my feet to guide me, in search of other monsters.

CB 80

ASTERION

You wonder, sometimes, what it would be like to be part of a pair, a couple, a set.

179

If there were another being like you in the world, could you find peace in their presence?

Or would the two of you hate each other for being reflections of one another, forcing you each to confront your ugliest parts?

Sometimes, the pale, symmetrical children try to come to you, offer up their bodies. They have convinced themselves that you have a need, and they can fill it. Or they want to be special, elect among their peers. Or they want to know what it's like to be loved by a beast, soft flesh trembling under hard, callused skin.

You turn them each away, gently or roughly as the case calls for it, but still, sometimes, you wonder.

Your mother once loved a monster, even if it was under guise of a wicked spell, a caprice of the gods for revenge against a foolish king. Even if it was only for a moment.

In your world below, the offerings age and grow. They form a community, pair off with each other. Sometimes, you hear them gasping and begging for release in the dark.

There was even a baby once, although you aren't sure what happened to it. Babies aren't very adaptable, as far as you know. They would find it difficult to live in this world below, subsisting on air and wine and darkness. Even you, you once had a cradle far above. You once had a blind nurse who rocked you side to side, and fed you milk, and sang beautiful human songs. Before you were dragged down here in chains, imprisoned alone.

You should not remember these things so clearly, but you do.

In the world above, when you are close enough to it, you can hear the next batch of sacrifices being prepared. Children, presumably as beautiful as all the rest, being taught to sing, to paint their faces in the ritual ways, to not ruin themselves with tears.

You wonder, how long will it go on? How long will they want to appease you in ways you never asked for? When will they decide instead that you should be ended, that the gods have forgotten about you and that it is finally time to cut you down?

THE KING'S UGLY DAUGHTER

The wide world contained countless monsters, some even worse than me. I stormed mountain strongholds and snuck down ravines. I cut off heads and made a necklace of terrific and terrible teeth. My skin grew hard and brown from wind and sunlight. And I hungered.

Oh, I hungered.

Not physically. At least, not the way you might imagine. I had my fill of feasts in every village I saved, I had plain fare for the road that stuck hard to my ribs, I had good hands and eyes and scavenging skills born as child, when I hid from my mother. Though my labors refined my shape into something lithe and quick, I was still large, still voracious.

What I really hungered for was glory and fame. Whenever a community had a problem with serpents that spoke in riddles, or two-headed fish with fangs, or dogs who walked like men, I wanted them to call for me. I wanted the entire world to see what I was, and beg for me, and only me, to save them.

I defeated the Mistress of Stone and released the spell on her statuary prisoners. I cut down the fire-breathing chimaera. Eventually, I made my way to the court of my father.

He knew exactly who I was, and not only because of the presence of cloak and sandals and sword. We shared a look, the king and I. And though I had no power, I had strength and courage, and I could have demanded many things of that man. I could have demanded riches, a husband, a crown.

Instead, I approached him politely and asked him for more monsters. I had cut a swath across the world, and there were fewer and fewer to destroy.

The king told me he knew of a land to the south, where a bull-headed demigod terrorized the people. I think he hoped that I would seek the beast and die. Instead, I planned to seek the beast and prevail, adding ever more fame to my tally.

The man who was my father reached a shaky truce with me, and gave me many instructions on how to carry myself upon my return. I did not plan on ever returning, but I let him go through the motions all the same.

I went south.

They had a ritual there. Beautiful boys and beautiful girls, the best assets that they had to offer, sacrificed to the beast to keep their world in order.

But while I was not beautiful, my reputation preceded me. They hoped that if I killed the beast, their curse would be lifted forevermore. Whatever I wanted, they would lay at my feet, if I only did this thing.

On a bright day in spring, I inspected their sacrificial youths.

The task ahead did not need beauty. It needed bravery.

I chose for broadness of shoulder, I chose for strength of arm. I chose for fleetness of foot and for loyalty and for ardor. The limp, pallid beauties went back to their homes, reprieved. I built up a war party, ready to slaughter the beast below for no other reason than that I could.

ひつ をう

ASTERION

Night and day are distinct, even down below. You were named for the stars, though you have never seen them. Your mother, when you floated soft inside her, told you stories of the stars, and you think, even now, that you can imagine them. What they must taste like in the world above.

One of your humans carves constellations in their piece of wall. Maps of the infinite sky. You like to imagine them glinting, glowing, warm.

Another seventh year has come to a close. It is night, and tomorrow will come, and with it, fourteen more beautiful children to feed and soothe and teach. You make your way back to the company, as close to the surface as you can ever get in these tunnels. Something feels different, this time. You are not ready for different. Change means an ending, and you are not ready for the end.

But there is nothing to do but wait. And so you hunker down with your human children, some of them not so young as they once were, and you sleep, and you dream, and you wait.

The entrance to the caves is a small hole covered by uneven boards. You could break through it anytime, if you wanted to. If that were the way things were done. But it is not, and you do not like to be closer to this doorway than you need to be.

Morning comes, and light stabs through the boards, brighter than you are accustomed to. You sniff and snarl, the way you are supposed to. You wait.

You can hear the songs above. They are the same as they ever are; some of the children beside you, remembering, quake and sway.

But then the boards are opened, and everything is different.

This is a new type of sacrifice, led by a woman who screams as if she would eat your heart raw.

CB ››

THE KING'S UGLY DAUGHTER

We wore the blood of a sacrificial bull on our faces, on our bare arms.

We ran toward the beast, our eyes adjusting to the dark.

Attack him at once; no way could he manage fourteen blades, fourteen pairs of fists and feet.

We had not expected that there would be anyone else alive down below.

We had not expected the children, fierce and feral, running at our weapons with their empty hands outstretched.

It was a slaughter messier than any of us had bargained for, as our blades punched through soft flesh, ripped at pale eyes.

They tore at our skin, but they were small and lovely where we were large and hard. Bones cracked and blood flowed. I thought the terrible scream came from my own throat, until I realized that it came from the bull.

He was enormous. The dark gave extra shadow to his shape. Hot breath fogged from his muzzle. But I looked into the darkness and I could see his eyes. They were human eyes. Bright blue, like the infinite sky, and wet with tears.

The monster screamed. And then he ran.

My heart leapt in my chest. I had no light, I had no knowledge of these caves, but also no choice but to follow.

"Wait!" my confederates called after me. "You'll be lost. We must block off each tunnel one by one."

There was no time. I was not built for waiting. And his eyes had been human eyes.

So I ran after him, the blood and gore on my left hand marking a trail against the wall. I could not see well in that dark, but perhaps the blood would suffice to save me all the same.

೦ಬ ೮ಿ

ASTERION

You run because you cannot bear to watch your humans die for you. *No*, you want to tell them. *Do not do this thing. Your fate has been changed. Let these warriors save you, let them take you back to the world above, where you will finally live free.*

You run because you are a coward. You never claimed to be anything else, no matter what your outside form.

You run because the leader, the woman who did not look like any other woman-shaped creature you have ever seen, sent a pang through your unexpected heart.

Deeper and deeper into the maze. Past the constellations and the figures of kings and queens and gods. Down, down, into the dark center of the earth, where you can be alone. Finally, forever, alone.

Except she follows.

Except she stands there mastering her breath, and then says, "What are you, truly?" and you have no answer to give that she would understand.

 C3 8O

The King's Ugly Daughter

Sometimes I look back on my life and see all the points where I diverged from the path, where the story took a turn it was not supposed to.

It goes back to the very first point of my life, where I slithered out of my mother missing the only part she valued.

If I had been a son, I would certainly still have been a warrior, but I might also have been a king. I would have dispatched this monster as I did all the others, and then could have gone back to my father's house, waving the wrong sails, watching him die for my mistake. I would not even have been sorry, would have done it intentionally, and then I would have displaced my young half-brothers and then I would have had my crown, and a name for the ages.

But I was not a son.

If I had been a proper daughter, small and silent, I might have given my life in service to the gods, or I might have turned to domestic pursuits and kept house for some average man, bearing him average children in quick succession until I died of it.

But I was not a proper daughter.

I was in-between, outside, and it struck me, looking at the monster in front of me, that we were in that way the same. He was in-between too.

His back was against a wall; there was nowhere further to flee. I stood before him, breath stabbing through my lungs, and I saw my future splinter into two distinct paths.

In the one, I took his head, sawed through the thick stem of his neck until it filled my hands, and dragged it by those incredible horns, inch by inch, back to the surface. I became the

185

hero I'd always wanted to be. I had lovers at my beck and call, gold and jewels and wine and song. My name was spoken for generations, in tones of hushed awe, and in people's imaginations I lived at the level of the gods.

In the other, I stayed in the dark and looked into those sky-blue eyes and tried to understand what this thing I felt was. What would come after, if anything came at all, was less clear.

I had no reason to want the second path. But I did. Oh, I did.

In that dark place, I dropped my weapon, and held up my empty hands, and the paths of the past and future collapsed in on themselves until there was only *now*.

03 80

ASTERION

You never knew you could feel loss, because you did not know you had anything worth losing. But your humans, your *family*, they laid down their lives for yours, and it cuts, sharp.

Now the monster stands before you, the leader of the massacre that has taken away everything you ever had.

She is beautiful, and she is terrible, and she is opening her bloodstained hands.

You want to ask her for the stars; that she will let you have this one bright thing before your empty death.

But you cannot form the words, and your voice is nothing more than a low, broken bellow.

She comes to you with open arms, and everything changes. Something ends, and something new begins.

THE MOON, THE SUN, AND THE TRUTH
Victoria Sandbrook

Dust rising over the next scrub-covered hill gave away the rider's position even before the incoming trash-guzzler's growl settled around Andy's ears. She waited as patiently as you could on a jittery horse that didn't know you well, in sun that'd singe any hint of bare skin.

They'd been waiting an hour. Time enough in the desert to dream up how many ways this data drop could go. Could be this rider had the data chip and she'd be drowning her sorrows at the tavern by sunset. Could be he was Directorship plant and there would be a gun for her.

Truth-running kept Andy moving, employed, and fed, but she wasn't sure it was worth not seeing the near side of forty like Mama had. Mama had been a seamstress and died in the Crush of 2179, but Andy didn't want to wait for death in a gloomy factory, only to meet it with a thousand others who hadn't much wanted to go to work that day either. Twenty-two was too young to go at the barrel of the gun or in the heat of a chemical fire or in the wake of a radiation "leak" or on any other whim of the Directorship.

The four-wheeler roared down through the small gully and up her hill. The horse pranced back. Damn the Directorship goon that torched her last ride three months back outside Castillo Verde. Trash-burners were easier to kill than horses, but they didn't spook.

The rider stopped and left the engine on idle. His broad, tan hands worked the helmet loose. His brown vest flapped open in the breeze, revealing his sidearm, black against his white shirt. Helmet off, she could see even at fifteen paces that he was one of the old ones, gray hair shining in the sun like brushed gunmetal. She hadn't seen a rider with gray hair in years.

He started the code in a south Texas drawl. "'Three things shine before the world and cannot be hidden.'"

"'The moon, the sun, and the truth,'" she finished.

"Anderson?" he asked. "Big name, girl."

"Mama liked it," she said, tipping her Stetson. "You're Daniel, then?"

"Dan. *Encantado.*"

"Mutual. The chip?"

He reached into his helmet. A few electronic bleeps sounded and a false panel opened.

"They've been after this one for a while," he said, closing the distance and handing it up to her, face solemn. "Almost got nabbed for it in Goldfield."

She nodded. That was deep Directorship territory anymore. She tucked the chip into the false flap of skin behind her ear and pressed the adhesive down. Dan rubbed the horse's nose and whispered something calming in Spanish.

"You watched it?" she asked.

He looked into the horse's brown eyes, not hers. "They're right to be scared."

"Good." She wiped sweat from her brow then replaced her hat. "We'd both better get, before they sniff you out."

"Fleet of foot and light of heart," he said.

The truth-rider salutation only made her stomach turn. She touched her hat and turned the horse toward the next town.

cʒ ℮ɔ

Andy and the horse rode steady and stayed sharp. "Like rabbits on a forage," Sonia would have said. Sonia's voice had echoed Dan's parting words to her, too.

Sonia, who taught her how to shoot. Who vouched for her to the other truth riders. Who spun the prettiest dreams about how many drops it'd take to retire alive and rich.

"We make it four or five years, I'd bet we can afford some place that doesn't crack with every tremor. Six years: maybe it's even green."

"A green house?" Andy had asked.

"No, like grass. Trees. Anything but cacti."

"Don't know if I need trees. I'd be happy enough without quakes."

"Or dust that creeps into your unmentionables."

This had made Andy laugh and squirm.

They'd talked about it over and over. In bed. On the road. In the data chips they managed to smuggle back and forth between drops.

Four years, Sonia had promised. Four years of living like quarry. Didn't see many riders with many more years under their belt, she'd said. Four years.

Andy'd been riding for four years and six months. She figured she could get somewhere green enough by Sonia's tastes after this drop.

What Sonia had never said was that most truth-riders didn't retire after four or five years. Most didn't live long enough to go gray like Dan. Sonia hadn't even seen twenty-two. But her words had been rattling around so loud in Andy's head for the past eighteen months that she wondered if they'd ever fade.

Ride steady and stay sharp, like a rabbit on the forage.

Good money buys good-enough loyalty; action buys it better.

Stay fleet of foot and light of heart.

Pretty words, but some good they had done her.

ଓ ଏ

Andy had ridden near a mile from the drop when she heard shots. The horse leapt into a gallop with no encouraging. Andy kept her eyes on the white-tailed kite soaring overhead and pretended she didn't feel the tears.

ଓ ଏ

Any other time Andy'd done a drop in a no-account town, she had ridden in slow. Strange enough to see a woman on a horse come off the desert roads, much less one moving fast.

But not now. Andy blew into town like the fire of hell was after her. A group of school kids raced at her horse's heels until someone hollered at them. She pulled up sharp at the undertaker's, and tossed the reins and a Lady Liberty to a boy standing agape on the porch.

"Be good to him," she said, patting the animal's sweaty hide. The boy nodded.

The hoary-haired undertaker looked up from a body when she walked in. His wrinkled hands shook as he crossed himself.

"'Three things shine—'"

"They're coming," she said, holding the chip aloft. Sometimes it was all the code you needed.

He pried open a false panel in the floor and revealed stairs descending into darkness.

"Broadcast or wire?" she asked. You never knew what equipment these backwater settlements had managed to cobble together.

"Wire," he said, his voice a choked whisper. "Reaches forty houses here and a relay station across the river."

Andy smiled and clapped him on the shoulder and dashed down the stairs.

The space was made only for the equipment and its operator. The console's buttons and dials glowed enough for her to navigate without additional light. Her hands shook sweat onto the con as she started the upload. The unit's monitor replayed the video in a grainy black-and-white and with tinny sound from dust-filled speakers.

She watched the last senator die. Black-and-white Directorship soldiers gunned her down along with a crowd of peace marchers. They'd even killed the children she'd been standing with.

Hell. If they didn't have their best trackers after this chip, then the Directorship didn't know what they were doing.

Right about now a gloomy factory looked all right. But she'd never wanted that green- enough shack more. On a stream. With a barn for the horse.

At least Dan had gone down for something big. They'd gotten Sonia in her sleep between drops; she hadn't had a thing on her.

The upload finished. Forty houses would see it. And it'd cross the river as far as their local relays stretched. And the undertaker would carry it somewhere—she couldn't know, for the safety of the data—and *if* he got there and *if* the next truth-rider was alive, who knows how many more would know how far this Land of the Free had fallen.

Andy returned upstairs. She handed off the chip to the undertaker as she passed. It was his death sentence now.

03 80

In the tavern, Andy ordered a whole glass of the house's best: the coolest, brightest water, tapped from the last aquifer in the West. She hadn't had a drink that cool since...well, since she'd treated Sonia to a glass the last time they'd seen each other. Sonia had complained of the expense, but her face couldn't hide her rapture.

Andy tried to feel that good about it, to let its freshness chase away her fears. She didn't find peace in her glass. At best, she'd found that memory of Sonia's smile. But that'd been worth letting the Kevlar-shirted barman con her the extra nickel for ice.

The room fell quiet behind her. Andy caught sight of tan Directorship fatigues in the mirror behind the bar. There were only three of them; Dan must have taken one with him.

Movement drew Andy's eyes to the window. Outside, the horse ate a carrot and nuzzled the boy. The undertaker loaded up a trash-burner pickup with a new pine box, ready to ride with the truth and give the Directorship another few days' trouble at least.

The barman coughed and blinked at her. In the mirror, she caught the specter of his sawed-off beneath the bar.

Maybe twenty-two years had been enough. But she was going to fight like it wasn't.

She nodded and turned, pistol drawn.

THE CREEPING INFLUENCES
Sonya Taaffe

She came out of the peat like a sixpence in a barmbrack, her face shining like wet iron between the spade-edge and the turf, the bright rusty plait of her hair broken like a birth-cord around her neck. Jimmy Connolly swore, and Dan Wall crossed himself, and thin-faced Sean MacMahon gaped like someone had shoved him by the scruff of his neck to a keyhole, all consternation and wanting to see more. And me? Mid-cut, I stopped with my spade half-stuck in the green-tufted earth and stared until my back hurt, forgetting to step forward into the slice or straighten up to save myself the pain. The sky was a racing grey, the land brown as strong tea and talkative with water all around us. The bones of her arm and shoulder were clean as bronze hairpins where Jimmy's spade had stripped off the fragile tissue, wadded it like old tin foil against her breastbone. Otherwise she might have been sleeping, tucked up in the pillowy bogland with the sedge snug at her chin.

"Oh," Sean said then, recovering, "Roddy's found his sweetheart," and all of us laughed, jokers at the graveside. Her eyelids were their own silver pennies, closed.

After that it was talk of museums and universities, while we peeled the peat from her wounded shoulder and the crushed hollow of her throat. She was twisted in the black slices, squashed in on herself like a discarded paper bag; exposed to the scudding summer air, she gleamed like an elver in an eddy of mud. Even flattened strangely under the tarnished skin, her features were peaceful, long-eyed, her lips sealed in a dreaming curve. She would not stay that way for long if we left her to dry with the rest of the stacked sods—and God knew if packing her in peat again would save us much time. Bolder in defense of a dead girl than I had ever seen him on his own reluctant behalf, Sean was all for ringing the National Museum as soon as we got our day's pay, no matter whether it was an archaeologist or a policeman they sent from Dublin, anyone who could disinter her from the bog without ruining the frail preservation of her body further. "And tell us where she came from, maybe, who—killed her," and we heard a click of half-swallowed words before he went on with the sentence, as though it were impolite to mention it out loud.

"Sacrifice," said Jimmy laconically; he had done a little reading, he explained, some years before when turf-cutters like ourselves turned up a skeleton in County Galway that was not a recently missing person, but an accidental drowning nearly five thousand years old. "To the heathen gods of ancient Ireland, for luck in the harvest and fine healthy children. She'd have been a beauty in her day, back before the Romans, that was. Anything less than the best and they'd have been cheating their gods. You can think a moment how kindly their gods would've taken that."

He sounded like a professor even in his sweat-banded collarless shirt and mud-streaked dungarees; looked like one, tall and black-haired, his harsh-cut face planing itself down to bronze with the lengthening days. Sean and I were nodding when Dan Wall, who I would never have guessed read a book unless it was full of bets and long shots, snorted and spat deliberately onto the turf.

"Ballocks, Connolly. She was a whore. An adulteress, and her man caught her at it—he pinned her down in the bog to punish her, see?" We could see the leather twisted into the silver-black of her flesh when he pointed it out, tanned as foxily as her hair and tight as a garrote. He scratched a little at the peat over her breast, carving the butter-black sod away: it was not bone arching under his fingers, above her ribcage, but slim withies of some water-stiffened wood. "Tell me that's an honor, dumping a pretty girl like a sack of shite out in the middle of this mire. He had to hate her. He couldn't bring himself to break her face, but he made damn sure not another man'd see it after him. Cut another yard and we'll find the man she did it with, I know that."

Sean was bristling, but Jimmy only looked over mildly, once at Dan and once at the girl with the curve of one wrinkled

194

breast just showing under the muddy tines. "Sure, you should be working for the Gardaí," he said, and then Sean was arguing again about the National Museum, or anyone within a day's drive of Croghan who might know about the ancient strangled pagan dead, and Jimmy was half-listening to him, having plainly already made up his mind to agree, and Dan was gazing angrily down at the tar-cast dead face beneath us, as if he were the man she had hurt.

I was ignoring all of them, even the girl under her bedspread of peat. I was thinking about sacrifice and murder, scholarly words for the torque of a man's hand grinding into the nape of my neck, choking a knot of leather deeper and deeper into the hollow of my throat until I felt rings of cartilage break inward and small bones give way and my breath snap in on itself, blacking out the long, burnt-green line of bogland, the skylarks flicking across the dawn-eye of the sun—whether it was done in hatred or love, my hair waving in the cold, whisky-colored water as the willows staked me down. She looked so calm for the results of so much violence, abrupt and final as a bullet to the head or a billhook to the throat. Executions and reprisals, I thought, anyone who had lived through '22 had seen those. *And do you still think she died for something as lofty as God's honor or her lover's wounded pride?*

I kept the question back, even while my throat tightened in useless sympathy, watching the wind stir her rusted iron hair. Likely Dan had the right of it, sour as it sounded. If I wanted to touch her with gentleness, it was because she was a woman who knew the taste and the price of transgression. If I was trying to imagine the tint of her hair and the texture of her skin before the acids of Móin Alúine cured her to a folded pewter shell, it was because I was an adulterer, too.

CB BO

Katharine Morgan's husband had left her for the wars, but she never said which ones and I never asked again. If it was the Great War, she would have known by now if he was coming

195

back; if it was the civil war in Spain, it felt like anyone's guess whether he had signed on with O'Duffy's Brigade or the Socialists or just gone to make trouble out of the local authorities' reach. She called him a blackguard and a lying bastard, she said she had never known a man so deft with a woman's body, she missed him like the Devil and she prayed God to keep him away and she invited me into her bed one afternoon near the heathery start of May, an offer of confidence that was not quite a threat curling as provocatively on the air as the clean-washed smell of her heavy, jet-pinned hair.

I'm sure you understand me, Mr. Mathews. Or is it Miss?

It's Mathews, ma'am.

Then it's Katharine, Mathews.

Eventually she came to call me *Roddy*, but she always greeted me as *Mr.* at the door, just in case a lifetime of careful habits proved unequal to the powers of village gossip. She had come to Croghan as a bride and stayed there for all she knew a widow and I would take my reputation with me when I left at the end of the summer; I was not so complacent as to think that hers was so self-contained. She was a handsome woman, thirty-three to my thirty-five, decorously pale everywhere but her high-colored cheeks and the flush that faded across her breasts after making love. She had more English in her voice than Irish, though she never spoke of any home before her marriage, and she must have lived on more than her spendthrift husband's savings, if he had been gone as many years as she hinted. I was not the first lover she had entertained since sweet-talking Desmond Morgan disappeared—I never fooled myself that way, either. But I did wonder, sometimes, if the others had only been women or men.

"Oh, Jesus have mercy," she would say, twisting under my mouth, "sweet as a boy," and I knew then that she loved me for the simplest part of myself. She liked my broad shoulders under their brown coat, my hair always falling chestnut-slick into my eyes; she liked my wind-rawed cheeks and my mulish jaw, the work-hardened span of my hands with their popped knuckles and old roughened marks of sacks and crates and shovels and drystone walls. She never touched my breasts, brown-nippled beneath their linen bindings, or my hips, cradled wide to take my long-striding weight, or my cunt, clenching hot and slippery as a heart behind the travel-worn corduroy of my trousers. Never once reached after my pleasure, as I worked my hand to the wrist inside her and she screamed, gloriously tight around me. Afterward, she would pull me down to the bedsheets beside her, skin pink as the lip of a whelk, and fist her hands in my hair, taste her salt sweet in my mouth and straddle me, laughing, but never with me as naked as herself. She wanted the shape of a laboring man and the spark of a demon lover—the security, too, of knowing she would never fall pregnant by me, no matter how many times she called me up from the parlor to the white curtains of her bedroom and her deep-pillowed bed. She wanted road-tramping Roddy Mathews and I was that, I was never anyone else from the time I was old enough to know my own skin, but I was the pieces of myself that she never touched, just as much, and the hunger that went with them. At most, she would watch me as I sprawled in a chair, my belt unbuckled and my own fingers busy in the folds of myself, but I thought it disappointed her that she could never see me spend, groan or gasp as loudly as I might. It ruined the illusion, spoilt the spell—

I tried not to think unkindly of her. The lovers of mine who had known me entirely, I could count on the two fingers I gave the rest of God's earth for wanting me to be one thing or the other, like the flick of a switch of an electric light. Katharine Morgan was expressive and affectionate and she did not stint herself in desire; she was a cleverer woman than she advertised with her wide, apple-green eyes and a sadder one than she liked to let me see; she never asked me a question beyond my employment and my health and the next time we should see one another, if a man of the world could find enough to say to a woman of her house, content in her quiet life. All the times she heard me say that I loved her, I was not lying. When I left, I did not think she would tell stories of me.

Sean MacMahon was waiting over the girl in the peat when we got there, hunkered down at the edge of the cutting with the wind stirring the edges of his sugar-fair hair under his cap. He looked so forlorn, I had to remind myself that he was nearer my age than coltish, touchy Dan Wall, whose round, dark-freckled face would have looked cherubic if he were not constantly scowling. "It's the coroner they're sending from Tullamore," he said without preamble. "In case she wasn't put in the bog by heathen priests after all. The museum won't want her if it's murder." The sun shone out again in the milk-blue twists of sky and he looked unhappily at the black-stepped levels of earth, the woman dreaming under the damp sods we had packed her in at the end of the day.

He must have called the Garda station, whether we had agreed on it or not; Dan looked for a moment as though he was going to shout at Sean for it, then said only, sullenly, "And what are we supposed to do until then? Lose a day's wages waiting for the man with the little black bag?"

"Dig around her, idiot," Jimmy said with his blunt, impatient authority, before Sean could bridle or I could start an argument of my own, and so we did, leaving a little bier of peat beneath her and a shroud of it above, so that she lay like an effigy among us as we worked, turf-veiled eyes turned to the sky. I was sweating with my coat off, well-worn báinín sticking to my shoulders; Dan kept taking his cap off and scrubbing one hand through his hair, spikily dark as treacle. He was closest to me with his barrow, spreading the sods I cut, and I tensed a little: I had guessed the day we met that if anyone was going to give me trouble in Croghan, it would be this angry half-boy, angling his way into manhood with his shoulders swaggering and his hands fisted deep in his pockets, waiting for someone to clip him in the street so that he could throw them a punch in return. He was religious and ashamed of it, better-educated and defensive of it, and I thought he was lying about most of the women he claimed to have had. But he said nothing more dangerous than, "Hold up, Mathews, give me a chance! It's a job, not a race, for Christ's sake," and because we did not have another barrowman, I slowed. It took looking up at the edge of the bank for me to realize how doggedly I had been working.

"When's he coming, this coroner from Tullamore?"

It did not sound anything like as casual as I had meant it to, an idle question to while away the time spent slicing and spreading and stacking as the sun climbed and the wet ground warmed, white-starred with bog cotton and the aniline-flowered lures of butterwort. Behind me, Dan blew out an aggrieved breath and bent to lift his barrow.

"Day after tomorrow," Sean said, blinking a little. He was blue-eyed almost to silver; it made his direct glance disconcerting. "Rafferty said it would disturb work, policemen and coroners coming round in the middle of the day. Reporters, too, likely as not. And tomorrow it's raining."

I thought of her foxed-mirror face, swirled in a slick of mud; her cedar-chest hair dissolving like tobacco shreds. Mold splotching her breast, long-sheltered, like slime on a stone. Before Jimmy could speak, or Dan, or even Sean, catching up to his own thought as he heard it leave his mouth, I said, "We'll need a tarpaulin over her, then. She won't stand the rain."

"Oh, what, are you studying with Connolly here now, too? Are we opening a turf-cutters' university—final subject, murdered adulteresses from before the birth of Christ?"

"Oh, shut it, Dan Wall," I started. "You wouldn't know the birth of Christ from the hole in your—" and that was when Jimmy stepped in, before Dan swung to hit me. It would have been worse if he ran at me, caught me around the waist to bull me down; but his color faded and he trundled his barrow away without a word, its slats piled high with drying sods.

"We'll find you a tarpaulin, Roddy," Sean said into the silence. "Better yet, we'll thatch her. Stack the sods over her, like a gróigín." At my stare, he shrugged with the spade still in his hands, a pale, slight man in canvas trousers, lashes and brows nearly invisible in strong sun. "She's your lass, Roddy. We'll take care of her."

CR ๕ว

When I dreamed of the peat girl, she was always dead, though she walked out of the bog at night to meet me. Her skirt was patterned in bilberry-blue, her shawl red as cranberries, and the garment next her skin looked most like a sheepskin with the fleece side in, but her face and her arms and her ankles above the leather lacings of her shoes were as opaque as old silver, her tied-back hair a springing mat of rust. Her nails were tawny parings, translucent as horn. Open between their metallic lids, her eyes were honey-amber, their pupils ochre lights.

Fast in my hayloft bed, I watched her blink, but not breathe; lay her palm against my chest, though no pulse ticked at her wrist. She was cold as groundwater, her smell of wet earth and fermenting wood. Her full height came barely to my breastbone. Each time she kissed me, I choked on the darkness that lay behind her tongue, a sunken, welling sourness—peat-smolder, leather-tang—that trickled like meltwater from the corners of my mouth the fiercer I kissed her back, striving for some living, human response, involuntary as a gasp. With her small, creased hands, she unpinned her woolen shawl, unlaced her skirt and pushed me down on the bright-checked, soft-scratching bedding, unwrapping the sheepskin from her shoulders so that her low breasts gleamed in the overcast light, heavy as hematite. And she touched me, with those fingers that had steeped for centuries in black veins of the bog, till my nipples stiffened like beads and my skin buzzed like tram-rails and my cunt swelled wet as a tarn, hungry for the dead cold of her. She stroked me and bent over me, searched my roughed-back hair with her mouth as if scenting me like a cat and tugged the tight linen from my breasts until she could trace the blanched red marks where the edges cut in; she slipped hard, tiny fingers inside me and I shouted with the freezing shock and jolt of pleasure, bucking as the soft ground swayed beneath us, a heather-plaited moss-tick.

And we'll find the man she did it with, Dan had sneered, nineteen centuries from now when these silver-sheeting meadows were rush-spiked straits of turf, but they never would, not unless I laid myself down at her side like two lovers in a song and waited. Her ribs under my hands were light as a kestrel's, her dull hammered-foil skin sail-taut across them. Even dreaming, I had the nightmare fear that she would open up around me like sodden paper, bog-soaked bones splitting free of her flesh like the rags her clothes had gone to ages before our clumsy spades brought her to light— Her cry was the only sound I heard her make, sharp as a curlew. Her weight dropped onto me and for a moment the heat of my own skin was enough to blunt her chill, hip and breast and shoulder and chin all interlocked like the twining of an ancient brooch; I could close my eyes and imagine her live in my arms, the unknowable woman she had been before the cord-choke and the drowning. Close to, the amber of her eyes was flawed with fern-seeds and tiny inclusions of dust or air. Her teeth were black as bog oak. She was smiling. I woke in a sweat of sex, my hair plastered to my forehead and my thighs slicked with their own wet; the dawn stars were shining in at the window. I never dreamed that she dressed and left me.

CROSS ⊘

It did not rain the next day, after all; it misted in the morning and the streets shone like snail-tracks between the plaster-sided houses, the thatched edges of their roofs glimmering with refracting beads, but the heaviest clouds burned off before noon and we went out to the turf-cutting beneath a soft-watered sky as grey as a horse's back. Rafferty had shifted us to another plot, fruitlessly trying to steer gossip away from the murder victim, the heathen sacrifice, the dead queen of Ireland coffined in the bog with her scarlet comet's hair streaming away into the dark earth, the gold and bronze torcs and bracelets of her warrior's hoard slowly pushed apart from one another by the forming peat, like planets by time... Even Katharine had asked if it was true, if a woman's body had been found in Móin Alúine, and I told her everything but my dreams. Braced to temporize if she asked if the dead woman was beautiful—more beautiful than Katharine herself, resting in my arms as we looked out the parlor window onto the green steep of Croghan Hill, the stone-walled patchwork of the village tumbling away to the foot of the peat fields—I had no ready answer when she asked instead, *Does she look unhappy?*

I had not thought about it, any more than I had asked myself if an ash-tree looks hungry or a wash of limestone tired. *She looks dead,* I said truthfully. *You can see the bones of her, dyed like bronze from the bogland. She doesn't—* and I hesitated, but Katharine's expression showed neither fear nor disgust. *She doesn't look like a woman who died in pain, if that's what you're fearing. She's a calm face. Closed eyes. Peaceful. You'll see for yourself; they'll have to let people see her before they take her away,* and she leaned her head into the hollow of my collarbone and said no more, the dark coil of her hair fragrant with lemon and musk.

She was slighter than the peat girl for all her greater height, more slender at waist and bust. I looked at her sometimes and thought of a slim dark-haired man, dandily barbered, with a watch-chain in his waistcoat and a well-knotted necktie; I said nothing. Not everyone saw themselves with double vision: wanted to know they could be so seen. I kissed her temple and she pushed me away, rising in a China-silk rustle. Her voice trailed off on a sigh, wry as one of the reasons I loved her.

Peaceful when she's dead. Every woman's dream!

We walked into wetter ground, boots whistling and sucking with the sponge-mat and the damp; Dan kept pointing to pools and soft, shaking ground, calling to the rest of us.

"Put a sléan in here, Sean, we'll dig up Patrick. Here's where Oisín aged three hundred years when he touched the earth, only he touched Allen water and kept on falling, through land, through time—never mind, we'll never find him. Keep on, boys." I wondered if he had ever written poetry, and if he was ashamed of it, too. "Sure, we can't leave the queen of all Ireland with no king, even if she was unfaithful to him. Here, Roddy, you know her best—where would she have left him? Here? Or here?

Know her like Adam," he added when I did not answer. "Where would you have bedded her, if you were a king of the pagan land?" He kicked at a grey blink of water, cataracted with the reflection of the sky. "Don't cry, Sean, you can send the next one to the National Museum."

But it was Desmond Morgan we found instead, floating on his back in a slurry of looseleaf water and moss as palely green as his widow's eyes.

He was not beautiful. The bog had not had the centuries to work its alchemy on him, tightening him to the leather of himself: he was loose on his bones, and dingy, and soft and slack as meal when we hauled him up, swearing at the rank sluice of liquids that poured from his rusted tweeds, the flopping cavity of his body, his bonelessly dangling bare feet. His eyes were too soft for amber. His teeth were hard in the gape of his mouth, peat-flecked porcelain ringing the sky. His head rolled like a kicked-in football. All of his pockets had been sewn closed and stuffed full of stones.

At that Sean was sick and not even Dan had the heart to mock him, gill-green as he looked himself. "Bloody hell," he repeated, "bloody fucking hell, fucking Christ in hell," like he could curse the man back into the earth that had so incompletely assimilated him. Jimmy watched silently, his bronze mouth a hard-braced line, Sean coughed and retched in the sedges, fumbling a handkerchief to wipe his nose with, Dan blasphemed on through an audible knot of nausea and I tried to ignore the feel of the water the dead man had left on my hands and keep the thought down, choke it: which of them would say it first? How long? Was Katharine Morgan's sporting wastrel of a husband so gratefully forgotten that they could not piece together who he must have been, this lanky string of joints whose long, moss-infested flop of hair would have combed back jauntily from his rake's profile, still cocked for a fight beneath the perished rubber of his face? With a gold ring on his left hand and a wallet in his draining jacket, the vegetable materials of his papers and his money—if she had left him his money, God knew he had taken enough of hers—long since pulped by the acids of the peat? I knew what I would find if I knelt and worked the ring off his finger and the watch off his wrist, the small initials I would read there incised in the gold. I had seen the photograph on her dressing table, hand-tinted so that I knew the color of his brilliantine hair before the bog stole into it. Other men had seen him alive.

"Christ, it's Morgan." Jimmy's voice had a thick, disbelieving sound; his eyes were dark as doors. "So she did it after all." He had spoken more easily of human sacrifice.

Sean hacked into his handkerchief and I could have kissed him, because it was louder than the noise of my breath. He said uncertainly, "He left her. With her savings, everyone knew that. Said he was off to look for work in London and good riddance to him."

"And changed the money for stones before he went?" Dan's voice was raw, his face flushed as if someone grappled him. "Lost his way in the bogs, instead of catching the bus to Tullamore and taking the bloody train? Is there anything you don't believe, MacMahon? Desmond Morgan drowned himself and God save the King? Jesus, but you're a fool—"

"And the coroner's coming." For the first time all summer, I heard Sean MacMahon laugh, a clear pealing snicker at himself or the circumstances, like something out of a detective magazine or a play on the stage. "Tomorrow. Oh, Jesus. Me and my museums. That's all of us fucked, then," and even somber Jimmy snorted at that, standing over a corpse.

"Aye, Rafferty'll love two investigations for murder on his land."

There was a beat of silence, just long enough for me to hear as clearly as if we were all thinking it, *Maybe we should just roll the old bastard back under his pool, maybe we'll tell Rafferty the ground was too wet for the turf-cutting, maybe in a year we won't be lying when we say we don't know what became of Desmond Morgan, who'll say we ever did? Who knows what becomes of a body once the bog has hold of it,* before I heard someone speaking and I knew it was me, because the rest of them looked like I was talking French.

"We'll have to tell Mrs. Morgan."

There was another silence, and I could not tell what any of them were thinking at all. Jimmy said carefully, finally, "A woman sends her man off with that much weight in his pockets, she's not looking to see him again."

"Sure, but she didn't foresee us digging him up like a pack of bloody dogs." Angry at myself, knowing there was no reason for it, "She has a right to know."

"If she wants to turn herself in?" The anger had gone out of Dan as abruptly as it had blown into him; he only looked as young as he was, and sickened, and hollow with thinking, as we all must have been, how calm-eyed Katharine Morgan, so coolly composed, could have killed her husband. Poison, maybe, if she had left no mark on him. Or she had cracked his skull, stabbed him, shot him, even, and the bog had soaked the wound away, run itself through him in place of blood until there was nothing to see but the split and swelling of decay and who could say when that had happened? I saw no noose in the slack of his puffball throat, no crushed bones under his ochre-stained shirt. Perhaps she had only drugged him and left the bog to do the rest. I could not imagine her dragging a body out of the house, mile by patient mile, each hardworking breath loud in the bat-flickered night and no one in Croghan noticing. "Out of her hands now, isn't it—"

Heavy as bog iron, Jimmy broke in, "He used to beat her, Danny-boy, did you know that?"

She had not told me. Those bruisy hands wilting at his sides, snapped bladderworts with the knuckles barely visible in the soft wet skin—dead as they were, I wanted to break them, twist the fingers like chicken bones until they cracked, maim him in the afterlife like the mutilations Jimmy had said our ancestors cursed their failed kings with, so that even if his ghost came staggering home down the wet roads of Allen, sleek-haired, shark-grinning, it would paw helplessly at every door with blunted sockets of bone that could never again put their pain on anyone.

I thought of Katharine in the half-light of her bedroom, saying, *There wasn't an inch of me he wouldn't touch,* and I had misconstrued her, jealousy-flicked as I knelt to prove there was nowhere I would not go for her pleasure. She had not misdirected me.

I said again, hoarsely, "She's a right to know." Not caring what they knew or guessed or had known already, which way I was giving myself away as I dragged my gaze away from Desmond Morgan to stare at all their faces, tight as rope around a woman's neck: "Even if it's just so she can finish drowning the fucker herself."

03 80

That night I dreamed of the peat girl walking through Croghan, one foot in front of the other as carefully as though she walked a tightrope on the beaten road. She carried her heavy-braided head with the pride of a coronet and her hands closed at her sides, the color of a well-thumbed shilling beneath the blood-bright hem of her shawl. She held an iron knife in one, a glinting break of white quartz in the other; I could see them as clearly as if she had opened her palms to me. In the bright grey day, the amber in her eyes shone like a cat's in the dark.

Far away down the paths into Móin Alúine, I saw a man walking, so small against the cloud-pearled horizon that I could have blotted him out with a blinked eye. He moved like a sleepwalker or a puppet on sticks, unwavering as machinery. He was hatless, his stiff hair wind-snatched; the swing of his pockets clacked with each step like a creel of stones. He stepped from the hummocky, heather-edged ground and was gone.

I saw Katharine Morgan, a dry-eyed weeping girl, with the sloe stains of bruises around her cheekbones and her hair hanging half-plaited as she knelt beside a man's body, the oil-light glimmering on the dark pool that haloed him, smooth as mirror of spilled ink. I saw his bursting face and his stone-blue tongue, his torn shirt and his slashed, empty hands. Reflected by the lantern, Katharine's own face eddied in her husband's blood, a marsh-fire fetch from the other side of death's glass. Her hands left bog-black smears on the knees of her nightdress, her bare shoulders set as taut and fragile as wings.

The peat girl stopped beneath my window; when she looked up at me, her neck made the quizzical tilt of her body wrung by the weight of compacting time. At her feet lay Desmond Morgan, dead without decay, his head flung back on his broken neck and the knife-cuts on his arms gaping bloodlessly as bread slices, his heart's blood stiffening on his shirt like tar. He had been blue-eyed before his sight clouded like Roman glass; his butter-gold hair was darker than his picture and flecked with chaff, grass-seed, flower-heads of meadowsweet. I called down to her, I heard my own voice echoing from the street, but I could not remember the words as they left me, only the taste of her, myrtle-sharp, moss-dank, spade-cold. She laid down the knife, its clean blade pointing east; she put the white stone in the dead man's hand that could not grip it. Already the earth beneath them was hollowing with water the color of beech leaves, the sticky-tipped red hairs of sundew curling around his bare ankle. Quick and gently, she smoothed a hand over his flower-stuck hair; she laid his shirt open, the skin beneath as white and bruised as violets, and with her sharp thumbnails, red as roe deer, she cut the nipples from his chest.

CB 80

We reburied Desmond Morgan with Katharine watching, the wind roiling out strands of her hair like a signature on the streaky speedwell sky. It was unceremoniously done, and unchristianly, but I had begun to think it would not have mattered if we laid him out with candles at head and foot and said Mass for his soul every Sunday of her widowhood: he was damned as far as the bog was concerned and I was not going to gainsay it. None of us said much, not even Dan, who had surely not expected to find himself at arm's length from a murderess and the lover she rested her shoulder against, her white-sleeved arms folded within a shawl of green and black squares I had not seen before. Sean reached to take off his cap before he thought better of it, straightened it more firmly instead. I thought of a mouth filled with black soil, the quaking illusion of ground slumping and settling under the scant weight of the dead until it had folded itself over the body more conclusively than any headstone. Finally, Jimmy pushed the last soft wedge of turf down, tamped it with the back of his spade, and looked faintly embarrassed, as though he had been thinking loud enough to overhear. He cleared his throat; Sean's head came up anxiously, hound-scenting for interloping authorities—Michael Rafferty, Gardaí, the coroner from Tullamore, looming large as a judge of legend by now. A wren shrilled and checked in the moss somewhere, the little bird-king.

As accurately as if he pronounced a benediction, Jimmy Connolly said, "Rest in peace, you spawn-hearted bastard, if that means you never trouble another soul more. May God not remember where he put you and the Devil never forget." And then we piled a green footing of well-spread sods over the damp seam in the earth and Sean MacMahon started talking about the coroner again and Dan Wall stood longest of all over the grave and I could not read a thing about him. Behind them, Katharine lingered, and I went to catch up with her, not knowing if she wanted me to.

Her stride would have been nearly as long as mine, if not for her skirts. We were nearly off Rafferty's ground before she said, "You promised to show me your queen of the bog. Before the police and the doctors came for her."

"Aye. I will. There's still time. Didn't you hear Sean, fretting he wouldn't be there to see her unveiling? She's this way." And I should have said nothing more, nothing that was not the weather or the time or the scholarly speculations of Jimmy Connolly, but her face was sky-silhouetted beneath mine and she looked younger with her arms crossed in their knot of plaid, her hair wind-loosened on her shoulders, and it was not her fault that I had seen her weep in dreams: "You didn't tell me."

"What should I tell you, Roddy Mathews?" She did not glance upward at me, as coolly as her voice lifted; she did not even slacken her pace. "Where I was born? The names of my parents? How I came to my marriage and what happened after I was wed? What did you ask me when first you came to my door that I should have told you anything?" A beat of silence, the ankle-brush of tussocks of sedge and bell-pink heath. How slender her shoulders had felt within my arms, how she had tongued my fingertips and the sun had fired red lights in her undone hair the first time we met by day. "What did you tell me of yourself?"

I bit back, *No more than you didn't want to know*; I said finally, "Not enough, it seems."

Her mouth flicked up at one corner. Her eyes were a ruddier green when the sun scattered out of its clouds, paler when they slid over it again. "There was a woman," she said at last, very quietly. "What she was like, it doesn't matter. It mattered that he found us. He didn't... God's truth, I believe he didn't understand at first what he was seeing. When he understood, he broke my ribs." Her voice was as clear as a clerk in a court of law. "No one would tell me if she died."

"Was it after that you killed him?"

She looked at me then, with the plumy heads of bog cotton caught in the folds of her skirt and her eyes the color of moss. I could see her hands tarnished silver if I tried, a halter of leather about her crushed throat, her dark hair bleached to bog-rust and her face folded to the peat as if to a long-aching rest, but Dan had been wrong about who ended up in the pools of Móin Alúine, and maybe Jimmy had, too, for all his care and erudition, and I had been wrong about the reasons Katharine Morgan would not touch me. I could still feel a dead woman's fingers inside me, unafraid as time. If I had opened myself as fearlessly to the living woman beside me, would it have changed anything? Nothing but the summer, I thought: and that might have been enough.

"Is this her, your peat woman?"

Katharine's hand went out to my arm, stopped me mid-stride. Sean had been as good as his word, laying a mosaic of damp sods from half-hidden ribcage to hairline so that the familiar peat covered her everywhere, molded itself again to her metallic skin like water filling to its own level; when I knelt to unbury her, I felt uneasily as though I was pulling a coffin-lid from a face, not showing off an archaeological find. Her eyes were still closed, her lips curved by their last thought or the workings of the bog. The red of her hair was startling as a wound, penny-bright at the wreck of her throat. Even the gleam of her bones was graceful. I could not answer; I heard *Roddy's sweetheart, your lass,* and I knew she had ceased to be anyone's with the break of her neck.

"She came out of the peat. She's no more mine . . ." I said it finally: "She's no more mine than you are, Katharine Morgan."

Her smile was an odd, sad crease in her wind-flushed face, very like the silvery expression wried at our feet. Like she was saying a vow back to me, "No more than you're mine, Roddy Mathews," and I had never expected anything else, but for a moment I could think only of her mouth opening to mine, the salt heat and slick of her body, the way her fingers gripped briefly and hotly in my hair. The tannin-cold tongue of the girl from Móin Alúine, dead years before Christ and closer to me than the Church had ever been. She had loved me, or I would never have dreamed of her. She had loved Desmond Morgan, too, and shown him to me as a love-gift, to ease my other lover's mind, before taking him in again for the last time. It was not my place after all to lie beside her all the long, hungry centuries. It never had been.

"Aye," I said, and it hurt less than I thought it would. Her hand was still on my sleeve; I put my own over it, just as if we were walking out together, and took a breath as deep as if I was going to ask her for an hour of her time after church. "You'd have made a fine queen of the land in Connolly's ancient days, do you know that?" And before she could make any answer or I could lose my nerve, I added, "A fine king of the land, too, and not the dying kind."

Her hand was warm under mine, not eel-cold silver, and she was not pulling away. Around us the bog stretched away to the sky, rust-green and tawny and engulfing as time, the thin moment we stood on that at any moment could give way: a kiss, a knife, a new road at the end of the season. The mirror that showed me myself, not just the two misapprehensions I was meant to choose from. The coroner from Tullamore. Rafferty himself would be here soon, and like as not the Gardaí and a trail of sightseers with him. But Katharine was still studying the calm dead face beneath us, and the peat girl still lay half in the wet earth that was hers more than any museum cabinet could be, and I cared less if Rafferty found me idling than if I walked away, this time, before I was ready to be gone. The murderer and the sacrifice, nobody's victims. We waited for history to find us.

En la Casa de Fantasmas

Brian Holguin

I.

Everyone knows about La Bruja.

They say she lives somewhere down in the Avenues south of Eagle Rock. She is a tiny thing, short and round. Always dressed in black no matter the weather or time of year. Draped in mourning, they say, like *La Llorona.* Black wool dress, black coat, black shawl. A black veil that falls like a cobweb over her ancient face. Ask the abuelas in the park and they will tell you they remember her from when they were young, and that she was an old woman even then.

You can spot her from a mile away, carrying that odd little dollhouse of hers. You know the one: it looks homemade, simple and boxy, with a peaked roof and a handle at the top. It is painted in bright candy colors, as cheerful as she is somber: lemon yellow and valentine pink, mint green and robin's-egg blue. There are those who say the house was made for La Bruja by her father, or perhaps even her grandfather, and that they each bore it for many long years before her. But there is no one alive today who can answer for sure.

Go talk to the vatos who hang out behind the pool hall, the dark-eyed boys with grease under their fingernails and tattoos on their knuckles, and ask them about La Bruja. They will tell you she loves nothing better than to sneak into children's rooms at night and steal their hearts. She comes while you are sleeping and never makes a sound or leaves a mark. You won't even know it happened. You'll just wake up in the morning feeling strangely numb and hollow. You will walk around blank-eyed and shivering, with no notion of what ails you, until you drop dead at the stroke of noon. Later, when they cut you open at the hospital, they will see that your heart is missing and find a smooth, round stone in its place.

They say La Bruja carries the hearts around in that crazy little house of hers, ready to eat at her leisure, like ripe, juicy apples.

But it's all a lie. Those boys are only trying to scare you. Everyone knows the house is for the ghosts.

03 80

It's late August in L.A. The last mean stretch of a summer that feels like it will never end. Everywhere are brown lawns and shimmering stretches of black asphalt. Posters and billboards show angry red thermometers reminding you not to waste water. No sprinklers to run through. No inflatable pools to laze in. For children, August is doubly cruel. Too hot to do anything fun, too close to the new school year to waste a single day in idleness.

In the heat of the afternoon, La Bruja beetles her way along York Boulevard. The children outside the corner store shout "Bruja! Bruja!" and drop their Popsicles and soda cans on the sidewalk. They sprint for their bikes and race down the alleyway, daring to look back only when they are blocks away. There is no point, after all, in taking chances or pretending to be brave. If she were to lift her veil, La Bruja could freeze you to the spot with a single glance. You'll stand there, stone still, until a perfect stranger walks around you three times, counterclockwise, and says "*wake up, wake up, fly away home.*" If you are careless enough to let your shadow cross hers, she can snatch it in her hand and claim your soul. She'll slip into your dreams at night and make herself at home, rummaging through your memories, your fears, your guiltiest secrets. Once she's there you can never make her leave, no matter how many candles you light at St. Dominic's or how many Hail Marys you say. That's a simple fact. Everyone says so.

At the bus stop on York, La Bruja sits waiting, dollhouse at her side. She tosses a handful of sunflower seeds onto the sidewalk in front of her and makes a rhythmic "*chk-chk-chk*" sound with her tongue. It is less than a minute before the crows come. They descend by the dozens, squawking and flapping. They peck madly at the seeds and then perch silently on the seat beside the old woman, and along the backrest of the bench, until the whole thing is camouflaged in night.

When the bus comes, La Bruja steps aboard. The driver never charges her and she never bothers to ring the bell to call for her stop. The other riders get up so that she may sit in the frontmost seat all by herself. As the bus heads west and turns right onto Eagle Rock Boulevard, the noisy dark cloud of birds follows close behind.

No one knows exactly how La Bruja manages to conduct her business or knows when to show up for her appointments. She doesn't have a calling card or advertise her services on bus benches. She's never owned a telephone. But she always knows when she is needed. When you get desperate enough, frightened enough, you will find a way to contact her. Some say it is the crows who carry her messages for her. Others say you must approach her in your dreams and ask her for her help. If she agrees to help you, you will find a simple message—unsigned, unstamped, no envelope—somewhere in your home. In a kitchen cabinet behind the cereal boxes, perhaps, or tucked under your pillow.

But everyone agrees on this: You must take care to follow her instructions precisely. If you do not, she'll turn right around and go home, and you'll find yourself in the same dark place you started.

1. The house is to be completely empty. Take the pets if you have any.

2. Place the money in a plain envelope, along with the house key, and leave it under the mat. You'll know how much to pay – after all, how much is it worth to you to live safely and peacefully in your own home? If it's not enough, she will turn around and go home and you will never hear from her again.

3. Do not come home until after sunset on the third day. This is most important.

☙ ❧

It takes three buses today to get her to the desired neighborhood, and another twenty minutes of slow, steady walking to reach the house itself. It is on a clean, shady street high up in the foothills, so high that the smog doesn't reach and the sky is a bright, endless curtain of blue. The lawns are all green and neatly manicured, and the swimming pools are full and crystal clear. Everyone knows the rich can afford to be wasteful.

La Bruja doesn't need to check the house numbers to know which is her destination. The crows have already marked it. She finds them perched on the mailbox, standing sentry on the crest of the roof and along the telephone wires. They strut up and down the sidewalk, across the front lawn, and gather squawking below the eaves. La Bruja looks under the mat and finds the envelope. Inside is a stack of crisp bills and the house key. She unlocks the door and crosses the threshold, but doesn't bother to count the money.

It is getting late and she has work to do.

II.

If the time ever comes to buy a house, be sure to ask if it is haunted. A house with a ghost is a far worse bargain than one with termites or dry rot or bad plumbing, and much trickier to make whole again.

This particular house is grand and tacky, built in a style the architect imagined to be vaguely Spanish. Clay tiles on the roof, pinkish-beige stucco walls and lots of large, arched windows that look out on palm trees and sprawling bougainvillea. A vague chemical scent greets La Bruja as she steps inside, a blend of lilac air freshener and pine-scented disinfectant.

"*Chk-chk-chk*," she beckons as she moves through the entry and into the living room. The home is immaculately clean; you'd scarce believe anyone lived here at all. Everything looks expensive and uncomfortable. Lots of heavy glass and wrought iron. Lots of hard surfaces. No comfy armchairs to fall into, no plump ottoman to rest your feet on.

She sets her little dollhouse down on the glass coffee table and looks around.

"Chk-chk-chk."

The back of the house is all glass: floor-to-ceiling windows and French doors that open out onto a tiled courtyard and swimming pool. La Bruja moves slowly towards the glass wall, taking tiny, careful steps. Mustn't scare anyone.

"Chk-chk-chk."

She can smell chlorine and chewing gum now, and the faintest hint of cheap, stale beer. Her eyes shift back and forth behind the veil, scanning the room carefully. It is a few minutes before she finds what she is looking for: a set of faint, wet footprints on the polished wood floors, glistening in the late-day sun. They are rather small and shimmer slightly at their edges. Right away she guesses that this ghost is fairly old, even if the child itself was young. Children are surely the saddest part of her job, but in many ways they are the easiest. They don't seek lost loves or plot vengeance. They just get lost easily and need someone to guide them homeward.

La Bruja steps out into the courtyard. She settles into a boxy rattan deck chair and keeps perfectly still. And she watches. From time to time, the little shimmering footprints pace away from the pool, then return. They move from this corner to that one, into the house and then back out again. Like a mouse in a glass cage that doesn't understand why it can't escape. She sits without moving a finger or uttering a word. She waits unmoving until the sun drops below the mountains, the first moment of twilight. Then she lifts the veil from her eyes.

The world swims and shimmers before her. Everything seems strange and distorted, like a television viewed through a fish tank. At first it is difficult to understand what she's looking at. Echoes... memories... past... present... all competing for attention. But soon her eyes adjust and she can see things clearly. She can see exactly what happened.

There are four of them, three boys and a girl, gathered around the pool. It's the late afternoon of a summer day not much different from this one. The youngest is a blond boy, skinny and tan, who looks to be eleven or twelve. He wears blue swim trunks and a red-white-and-blue tank top emblazoned with "USA '76." The other two boys look to be fourteen or so. The taller one is slightly awkward, still unused to his growing limbs. The smaller one is wild and wiry, with long dark hair and lots of coiled energy.

The girl is also fourteen but looks considerably older than her peers, the way teen girls often do. She is wearing cut-off jeans and a macramé bikini top. She is pretty and she knows it, more's the pity. She is well aware of the strange power she has recently acquired, even if she doesn't fully understand it. It's the power to make boys stumble over their words just by looking at them. To make them do stupid, risky things to impress her, like shoplifting cigarettes or breaking into empty homes. She knows for certain it is a power she didn't have last summer, and she already suspects it will not last long.

The home doesn't belong to any of them. The tall boy knows this house because it is on his paper route, knows that the owners will be out of town till Monday. It was easy enough to sneak down the side yard to the swimming pool at the back. The four of them splash and swim in the summer heat. They have a cannonball contest to see who can make the biggest, loudest splash. The girl declares the wild boy to be the winner and the tall boy demands a rematch. They listen to music on a tinny transistor radio and take shallow, unconvincing puffs on cigarettes, trying hard to look cool and dangerous.

As evening approaches, they luxuriate in the borrowed sense of freedom they're all sharing, imagining this must be what it feels like to be grown up, having no rules to obey, no one to answer to.

Once darkness falls, the wild boy gets the idea of prying open a window and raiding the kitchen. In his absence, the tall boy stretches out on a chaise longue and recites a string of filthy jokes he learned from some comedy record. The girl rolls her eyes and takes a slow drag on her cigarette, pretending she is too mature for such things. The blond boy laughs loudly, even though he's not exactly sure what all the words mean.

The wild boy returns with a bag of tortilla chips, a six pack of cold soda and another of warm beer. They all pretend that beer is their customary first choice, even the blond boy. He quits after less than one can. At first the beer makes them all relax, floating on a mellow buzz, but then it makes them rowdy. The girl has finished her first beer and is pestering the wild boy for some of his.

Suddenly everything slows and the smallest details come into sharp focus. La Bruja's attention is drawn to the little radio sitting on the patio table. It is blaring some silly gringo rock song, some nonsense about the "Fox on the Run." The girl, splashing manically in the shallow end, yells to turn it up. The tall boy drains the last of his second beer and fumbles to light a cigarette. The blond boy is on the diving board and shouts to the others, "Look at me!" He attempts to do a front flip off the board, but in the failing light he misjudges the distance. La Bruja hears a crack—loud as the day it happened—as the back of the boy's head strikes the edge of the diving board. It is a clean blow, like being struck by a baseball bat.

Already the boy is sinking to the bottom, already blood spreads like a plume of ruby smoke, staining the clear blue water. In that instant, the teens all drop their shallow veneer of adulthood, reverting back to the children they are, scared and helpless. They don't discuss a plan. They don't say anything at all. They don't even look at each other.

They just run.

They run all the way home. They say nothing and try desperately to think of nothing, choking back the terror and the tears until they are each safe in their beds where they will sob all night into their pillows and wake in the morning wishing it was all a horrible dream. Not one of them ever says anything about the boy. Each is sure the others will do the right thing, the brave thing, and tell their parents or phone the police.

A week later, at the blond boy's funeral, they don't even acknowledge one another. The body, they are told, floated in the pool for at least two days before the homeowners returned. By that time, the water was as red as the sun and the corpse was so bleached and bloated it was difficult to identify. Although they share classes and sports teams all through high school, the three of them never say another word to each other or willingly glance in the others' direction.

Those three children will all be grown up by now, and parents themselves. Perhaps grandparents. But none of them will ever see a single day pass without thinking of their young friend. About the things they did, and the things they didn't do. They'll carry that memory around with them forever, dragging it like a ball and chain. It follows them to school, to work, to Christmas parties, on honeymoons and vacations. It's with them at the grocery store, at the movie theater and at their children's school plays. Each of them is every bit as haunted by the past as this house is. But there is no sure remedy for their curse. They will bear its burden until the day they die. Only then will they be in a position to ask forgiveness, even though they don't honestly expect to receive any.

Looking closer, La Bruja can see that traces of blood still linger in this pool. You can't miss it once you know to look for it. Let your eyes soften and look below the surface. Pints of blood. Buckets of it. Vast oceans of blood, churning and roiling in the moonlight. No matter how many times it has been drained and refilled, no matter how many gallons of chlorine have been poured in over the passing decades, it is still tainted, still infected.

Some blood, you must surely know, never washes away.

It's well past dark by the time La Bruja begins her working. To start, she removes a number of items from the pockets of her coat and from the leather bolsa she wears around her neck. She takes three votive candles and places one each along three sides of the swimming pool. She lights the first candle and blesses it in the name of San Jeronimo, patron saint of abandoned children. The second she lights in the name of San

219

Alejo, who looks after those who are imprisoned. The third is for San Christobal, patron saint of travelers. Now she takes a larger candle and sets it at the far end of the pool, the end with the diving board. This last candle is for blessed Madre María, who watches mercifully over all of us sinners, now and at the hour of our death.

La Bruja stands over the pool and begins to chant in an odd sing-song voice. She takes a small crystal vial and removes its silver cap. It contains holy water, again blessed in the name of the virgin Santa María. She sprinkles it over the surface of the water and counts slowly to nine. Then, she takes a golden sewing needle and pricks her own ring finger. Three perfect crimson drops fall into the pool. They mottle the surface for a moment, but are quickly diluted and subsumed, and the water appears clear as glass.

Blood for blood. No fairer trade.

The second part of the working requires no blood, but it does require patience. She takes eleven tea candles, one for each year of the boy's short life, and spaces them in an arcing trail from the pool, through the French doors, and into living room. Once each is lit, she sets the dollhouse on the floor in front of the last candle, the one furthest from the swimming pool. She squats on the floor next to it and waits.

"*Chk-chk-chk,*" she intones, tapping the wood floor with her finger nails.

"*Chk-chk-chk.*"

After a few minutes the first tea light goes out, sending a little gray wisp of smoke trailing in the air.

"*Chk-chk-chk.*"

The second candle goes out a few minutes later. Then the third. But the fourth candle lingers. Its flame flickers from time to time, but it does not extinguish. La Bruja is patient. She knows the boy must take each step in his own time, cross each threshold and close each invisible door behind him. This is his path to walk and he cannot be rushed.

It is more than an hour before the fourth candle finally goes out. But it is quickly followed by the fifth. And the sixth.

"*Chk-chk-chk.*"

The little house is hinged at one gable end, and there is a bright pink padlock in the shape of a heart at the other. As the ninth candle goes out, La Bruja takes a key from around her neck and unlocks the padlock, but leaves it dangling in place.

"*Chk-chk-chk.*"

Again the procession stalls. It is nearly another hour before the tenth candle dims and dies. Very carefully, very slowly, La Bruja removes the padlock and opens the front of the house just a crack.

"*Chk-chk-chk.*"

The eleventh candle fades slowly... slowly... and then grows. It grows brighter and brighter until at last, with a blinding flash, it goes out. La Bruja quickly shuts the dollhouse and snaps the lock in place.

It is too late now to catch a bus back to the Avenues, so La Bruja will sleep here tonight. She will help herself to cold beer and whatever palatable thing she can find in the fridge to eat. In the morning she will rise early and burn a wand of sage leaves and smudge all the rooms in the house. She will throw wide the curtains, open up all the windows and leave the front door wide open.

She will place the key back under the mat, gather her things and head back down the hill.

III.

In *La Casa de Fantasmas*, there are many mansions.

True, there are only four windows on the exterior of the little house and those are merely painted on. But inside there are countless doors and windows. There are cozy libraries, suffocating closets and tight, bricked-up tunnels. There are comfortable rooms with en suite bathrooms. There are endless dim corridors to wander down, lost in romantic torment, if that is your preference. The dollhouse is small, but the spirits take up so little space. Even La Bruja has lost count of how many ghosts presently dwell inside. But there is plenty of room for all of them.

You must know that ghosts become ghosts for many reasons. For some it is the trauma of a violent death. For others it is love for the ones they left behind. For a great many it is guilt: Guilt for letting down their family, for not making more of their lives, for all the wicked things they may have done but still can't bring themselves to truly regret. Guilt is a great anchor that holds spirits earthbound.

Still, most spirits don't move on because they simply aren't ready. They haven't said their piece or made their mark or danced one last dance. But all have one thing in common: They hate to be reminded they are ghosts.

⋈

At the front of the house is the large salon, where the walls are lined with bookshelves and heavy chandeliers hang from the wood-beamed ceiling. It is one of the oldest rooms. A wood fire burns in a stone fireplace, and there are leather sofas and armchairs nestled around well-worn Persian carpets. The more gregarious of the guests gather here, to swap stories or gossip, to play chess or try to cheat one another at cards.

Standing by the fireplace, puffing on a cigarillo, is the one they call the Fox, an over-the-hill gentleman with a watch fob in his waistcoat, Cuban heels on his shoes, and a ludicrous beard he keeps waxed and styled like a cartoon devil. He loves to dance the tango and the tarantella, and pesters all the ladies until one of them acquiesces.

The Irish Tinker scrapes out a Romani ballad on his fiddle while Sister Agnes plays a game of backgammon with the Quiet Man. The Doctor watches from a corner. He sits sipping brandy, his smooth bald head hovering over the pages of a Thomas Mann novel he's never managed to finish. He mutters under his breath how one day they will all be sorry. One day, they will regret underestimating him.

Darla sits by the front door waiting for her gentleman caller. She is wearing her best dress, the one the color of summer apricots. She can't help but worry. There are no clocks in the house, but surely he should have been here by now. If you asked her, Darla couldn't tell you the gentleman's name or how they met. But she knows he is a kind, handsome man and knows in her heart that they are truly made for each other.

Her mother never approved of gentleman callers. Darla doesn't care to divulge her age, but her mother was quite fond of reminding her that if a woman hasn't hooked a man by this stage of the game, she had best give up the ghost. Better an old maid than an old floozy. The minutes pass and Darla grows certain that something bad must have happened. An accident or an emergency. Or maybe he just decided he doesn't want to see her. She tries to hold back the tears, but it isn't long before her mascara runs in black rivulets down her cheeks.

She gets up and checks herself in the mirror. She looks a fright. You're such a silly thing, Darla. Always letting your imagination get carried away, always making things a bigger deal than they really are. Take a deep breath. Stand up straight. Think good thoughts, and good things will happen to you. She dries her eyes, reapplies her mascara and touches up her lipstick. Darla wants her smile to be the first thing he notices.

She can hardly contain herself now. He'll be here any minute...

ଔ ଵ

The blond boy has been living in a tree fort. He knows his parents must be worried, but he's not ready to go home yet. Besides, the fort has everything he needs: a sleeping bag and flashlight, a stack of old Marvel comics, and a transistor radio that only ever plays his favorite songs. He gets hungry sometimes, though never enough to make him want to leave. He likes the quiet and the cool breeze that smells of jasmine. He looks at the stars and listens to the radio. He naps for long stretches at a time. He's not sure how long, but when he wakes up the sky is always dark.

He knows if he went home now, his parents would be furious. The boy has a cousin, Darren, who is three years older than him. Years ago, Darren ran away from home and was gone for the better part of a week. For the first couple of days, Darren's folks were in a rage. His dad promised take his belt and thrash that boy to within an inch of his sorry life. But the days dragged on and phone calls were returned from friends saying they hadn't seen him, flyers were posted around the neighborhood and the police kept asking more troubling and embarrassing questions. By the time Darren finally was found— sleeping in an old camper parked in a neighbor's driveway two blocks away, living off Pop-Tarts and RC Cola—his parents were so relieved they forgot they had ever been angry. That's the trick of it, the blond boy reasons. Stay away long just long enough for your folks to stop being mad and start being afraid.

His cousin is easily the coolest person he knows. Darren can do a handstand on his skateboard for nearly half a mile straight, swear to God, and is always smooth when it comes to talking to girls. When he is older, the blond boy wants to be just like him.

The radio plays a song by Paul McCartney & Wings. The one about Venus and Mars: *red lights, green lights, strawberry wine...* The boy finds himself drifting into sleep again. Funny, he can't even remember why he left home in the first place. It's not like things were ever that bad. Still, give them a little more time to worry before heading back. One more day should be enough.

Tonight he will dream strange dreams about an empty beach on a crystal blue sea, and a dark red sky rolling above. And a weird little house that could hold everyone in the world if it had to. Tomorrow he will go home. Just as soon as the sun comes up.

Tomorrow.

Always tomorrow.

IV.

Tonight is Halloween. The eve of All Saints' Day. A night for revels and mischief. When the veil between this world and the next is thin as gossamer. Tonight is the night the ghosts come out and play.

All along the Avenues, pumpkins grin from porches, and paper ghosts and witches hang in windows. Little kids are already out tricking and treating, even though the sun hasn't gone down yet.

Every year, La Bruja sets out a plate of pan de muerto—a sweet pastry flavored with cinnamon and anise seed—on the stoop of her little house at the end of her crooked little street. These goodies are free for the taking, but no one ever comes to her door. They won't even walk past the front her house. Not even the adults, not on a dare. But that's all right. By morning, every last morsel and crumb will be gone.

Behind her house, La Bruja has set up for a party. Streamers are hung and luminaria are lit. At one end of the little yard stands a lopsided table decorated with brilliant sprays of marigolds, colorfully painted miniature skulls and scores of candles. Two figures stand at the back of the table: a two-foot porcelain statue of the Virgin Mary, smiling beatifically in blue and white robes, and the carved wooden figure of Queen Mictecacihuatl, skeletal empress of the underworld.

Once the sun sets, La Bruja will remove the heart-shaped lock from the little dollhouse and open it wide. All those inside are invited to join the festivities.

It is an unruly scene: La Bruja sits on a wicker settee, smoking a fat cigar and drinking whiskey from a communion chalice. She claps along as the Tinker plays a wild Irish reel on his fiddle and Crazy Bobby, who was once *this close* to being a rock 'n' roll star, strums along on a battered guitar. The Fox and Darla dance a lively tarantella to the rhythm.

There is music, laughter and toasts to absent friends. Grudges and worries are put aside for the evening. The guests allow whatever burdens they carry to slip from their shoulders. Even the Doctor puts down his book and dances the foxtrot with Sister Agnes.

After a time, some of the ghosts desert the party and venture into the wider world. From sundown to sunrise, they are free do as they please. And they are not alone. Countless ghosts from centuries past walk the earth tonight. They come to stand watch over their children or grandchildren, to comfort a spouse they left behind, or to simply remind themselves that they too were briefly among the living. But the ghosts in the care of La Bruja are bound by a particular rule: They must return home to the little house before the sun comes up or be forever banished.

The Fox drifts to a favorite haunt near Olvera Street and sits at the end of the bar, boasting of the beautiful women he has danced with. Sister Agnes will wander back to a little nowhere town in Montana, sit on the steps of the house she grew up in and marvel at how much her street has changed, and how little. She will reminisce about a tall, blue-eyed man she once knew and how she almost gave up everything for him. Funny, she can't even remember his name now.

Every year there are some who choose not to come back. They find their graves and lay themselves to rest. They walk into the sea at daybreak, glitter upon waves for a brief, golden moment, and then are gone. Or they simply drift away like smoke on the breeze. Most, however, will return home, to the comfort of old patterns, and resume their strange half-life. Many don't even step outside the little house in the first place, not even for the party. And that's all right. It's just not their time. They simply aren't ready to let go.

03 80

The blond boy doesn't bother with the party. He's never felt comfortable around grown-ups, especially those he's never met. Besides, it's been forever since he felt the ground beneath his feet and he wants badly to stretch his legs. He wanders out into the street and is delighted to find that it is Halloween, his favorite night of the year. He snatches a piece of sweet bread from the plate on the door stoop and wolfs it down in three quick bites. He hadn't realized he was so hungry. He grabs two more pieces and heads out into the night.

He joins the throng of children going from door to door. It would be nice to have a costume, but he doesn't mind. He is too absorbed in the wildness of the night, awed by the sounds and scents, the garish, lurid colors. He doesn't have a bag or pillowcase, so he stuffs candy into his pockets or, more often, eats it on the way to the next house. He's only gone to six or seven houses when he hears voices calling out to him:

"Hey! Kid! Over here!"

He sees them standing at the end of the block. A pack of boys, a half dozen or so, all about his age, give or take a year. Their hair is shorter than his and some of their clothes are so old-fashioned he mistakes them for costumes. They in turn have mistaken the blond boy as one of their own, just another departed soul playing hooky on All Hallows' Eve. Back for one more run through the candle-lit streets, one more night of mischief and abandon. They don't bother with introductions, yet right away they all feel like old friends.

"Are we all here, now? Let's go!"

They move with single purpose, like a flock of crows, crossing the city side to side and back again in less time than it takes to think. They throw eggs at police cars and run hooting like the madmen. They set off firecrackers in the underpass below the freeway, so they echo like thunder. They find a carnival at the YMCA and go through the haunted house three times in a row without paying once. They eat cotton candy until their tongues are blue and their fingers stick together. At the face-painting booth they all have their faces made up to look like skeletons. They are a tribe now, a band of merry pirates. Drunk on the mad, wild joy of youth that doesn't think even a minute ahead or waste one moment's thought on the past.

In the park, they run like wolves and howl like devils. They do handstands and back-flips off the picnic tables. They race and they wrestle. They laugh till their sides ache and eat candy till they are sick. By now, their make-up streaks bizarrely down their faces from all the sweat, tumbling and roughhousing.

Late into the night, when the city has fallen silent, the boys gather in a circle on the grass. They pass a flashlight around, counter-clockwise, and swap spooky stories. They tell the one about the hitch-hiking axe murderer, and the one about the teenagers and the bloody hook. They tell that old story about the Weeping Woman, the ghost mother who steals lost children away, believing them to be her own.

A little before dawn, when they can't hold their eyes open a moment longer, they stretch out in the grass and lie side by side, like a neat row of graves. No more playing now, or even talking. They just lie there too tired to move, but still too alive to sleep. This is the happiest the blond boy has ever been. The best night of his life. The world could end and he wouldn't even notice.

There is no other thought in his head when the sun finally rises.

̓ ͅ

Ghosts become ghosts for many reasons. But surely it could never happen to you. You are too sensible and too clever. You know to go to bed each night fully content with how you spent the day. You do not leave important things unsaid or undone. You never wait for tomorrow—always tomorrow—to speak your piece, make your mark or dance as much as your heart desires. You know to live without fear or regret, unburdened, so that any day may be a good day to die.

It's simple, really. But simple and easy are hardly the same thing.

Anyway, everyone knows there's no such thing as ghosts. There is no crazy witch woman with a funny little dollhouse full of lost souls. How could there be? They're just stories. They're only trying to scare you.

Remember that, should the shadows ever come for you. When your life slips from your control and you wake one day feeling strangely numb and hollow, like a faint echo of yourself. Lost in limbo, treading the same old ground in ever tightening circles. When fear turns your heart to stone and freezes you to the spot. Remind yourself that it's all pretend. It's just your imagination getting carried away with things. You can always move on, as soon as you are ready.

Wake up, wake up, fly away home...

Fixer, Worker, Singer
Natalia Theodoridou

Fixer Turns on the Stars

The sky creaks as Fixer makes his way across the steel ramp that is suspended under the firmament. It's time to turn on the stars. He pauses a few steps from where the switches and pulleys are located and looks down. He allows himself only one look down each day, just before sunset: at the rows of machines, untiring, ever-moving; at the Singer's house with its loudspeakers, sitting in the middle of the world; at the steep, long ladder that connects the Fixer's realm to everything below. He's only gone down that ladder once, and it was enough. Fixer caresses the head of the hammer hanging from his belt. Then he walks to the mainboard and turns off the sun. The stars come on. He pulls on the ropes to wheel out the moon. There. Job well done.

Fixer senses the coil inside him uncoiling. He retrieves the key from the chest pocket of his coveralls and thumbs its engraving: *Wind yourself in the Welder's name.* He inserts the key's end in the hole at the side of his neck and winds himself up. In the Welder's name.

The sky creaks.

Wound up and tense as a chord, Fixer sits on the ramp and rests his torso against the railing. He inspects the firmament under the light of the starbulbs. The paint is chipping—it will need redoing soon. He wonders whether it was the Welder himself who first painted the sky. It must have been him, no? Who else could have done it, before Fixer existed? Fixers, he corrects himself, and the coil tugs at him with what could be guilt, but is not. He imagines the Welder—just his hands; he can't picture all of him, never has been able to—slathering on the blue paint, then carefully tracing the outlines of clouds.

230

Fixer pulls the wine flask out of the side pocket of his coveralls and takes a swig. It's just stage booze, water colored red, can't get drunk on it; he figured that out a long time ago, but he still likes to pretend, especially when the sky creaks the way it does tonight, when his coil is tense just so. What wouldn't he give to feel things—what hasn't he given—to be drunk, to be angry, to be excruciatingly joyful. But the world is so quiet now, quietly falling away, even emergencies are rare; and it's lonely under the stars. He takes another swig from the flask. "Make-believe wine in honor of the Great Welder in the sky," he says. Another swig. The coil eases some, his back slumps a little against the railing.

One of the stars didn't come on, he notices; the bulb must have given out. Fixer gazes at the concrete shape of the moon haloed by the spotlight that's reflected off its surface. There is rebar poking through at the sides, the back is crumbling. But that doesn't matter. Only Fixer can see the back side. Things only have one good side, from which they are meant to be looked at.

Yes, the world is quiet now, but for the creaking of the sky. The hum of the machines below has stopped for the night. There used to be thunder beyond the firmament, but not any more. There used to be singing from the Singer's house and the Welder's voice blasting through the pipes of the world. Now there's only the Singer's rusty voice spilling out of the loudspeakers in short, shallow bursts.

"Tap into this thing, this ugly feeling of despair," the Singer's voice croaks, as if she knows, actually knows what it's like to stare at the back side of the moon.

Fixer glances at the blown starbulb again. The coil inside his chest wants to spring forth, find the spare lightbulbs in the dark, fix it. Fixer fixes the sky, and if he doesn't, he's no Fixer at all, is he?

But, instead, he takes another swig from the wine flask watercolor communion with the Welder who fashioned the world. He closes his eyes.

"I'll fix it tomorrow," he says out loud.

SINGER: HIS VOICE IN FRAGMENTS

Your metallic voice. The wind rushing through me.

I remember when we voiced this pipe organ together, every flue, every reed, so it could breathe with your truth. Now everything is rusty and old. Falling. And apart.

I haven't seen you in so long.

Fragments of your voice run through me and into your organ, my organ, when I least expect it. When I manipulate the pipes, aching to make each one sound the way it used to, I cut my fingers on the rough edges and fake blood comes out, mixed with grease.

And I have all these foreign memories that you planted my body with, these fragments I cut myself on every day:

An old man tuning a pipe organ.

A .45 round nose bullet fired from a handgun, tunneling through a body—and did you know the machine gun was inspired by a seed-planting machine, way back? Of course you did.

And there's also the voice of a very young poet made great only by his self-imposed death. Why did you deem this story important for me to know? Am I to sing about it? Every day, I think about the poet. Is it because the poet-boy worked at a factory? Was it much like this one? Is it true he fed himself to the machines?

You are not forthcoming with answers to my questions.

And I have enough self-awareness to know I am falling apart, but I do not know why or why not or why I should keep myself from doing so. Yours was always a practical project first and foremost, yet you never lacked in poetry. Why else would you have installed a Singer in the middle of it all?

And why did you leave me here, all alone? Fixer always had a partner, each the fail-safe of the other, keeping one another from thinking themselves more than they are, and

Workers are many, because you needed many. But there has only ever been one Singer.

Was I your most successful feature? Or the least so?

I press the loudspeaker pipe open. "Tap into this thing," I say, "this ugly feeling of despair," and not even I am sure who I am talking to any more.

☙ ❧

Worker: Keep This Shop Like You Would Your Home

Pull, turn, press, says the coiled thing inside. So we pull, we turn, we press. The conveyor belt does not pause, and neither do we.

We work the line. We never blink. Our eyes close when the shift is over and only then. We never blink or we will miss the next beat. The next bullet. And the next.

Projectile, case, primer. The propellant container is empty, has been for some time, the great barrels that used to haul it in came empty for a while, then stopped coming in at all. Should we stop? Could we stop? We shouldn't. We couldn't. We didn't. We don't.

Pull, turn, press. Projectile, case, primer. No propellant. The bullets are lighter now. But the work doesn't stop, the work doesn't change. Handling the lighter bullets takes great care. Our hands are slowly accustoming to the new weight. *Pull, turn, press*. Don't make a mess. We keep this shop like we would our home. Just as the sign on the wall says we should. We glance at it. Only glance. We never blink.

Our eyes are dry and our wrists hurt. They hurt so much we wish we could take them off, and the coil inside us slowly unwinds.

At night, when the moon comes out and our shift ends, we will close our eyes. We remind ourselves.

At night, when the moon comes out and the shift ends, we will wind ourselves up. One more time.

Then, a piece of the sky comes down with a thud.

We glance up.

⌘ ⌘

SINGER SINGS OF HOLES IN THE SKY

There is a hole in the sky. Does this mean you're coming back? Does this mean you've started dismantling the firmament on your way back to us?

I blow through a loose flue—disconnected from the organ like that, it reminds me of a long gun's barrel, its speech as distinct as rifling, as fingerprints, as a person's voice.

I hold my palms in front of my eyes.

Why did you make me without fingerprints?

I search my repertoire for answers, but I only come up with tidbits about wound ballistics instead:

Hollow-point bullets do not penetrate as deeply as round nose bullets, but they expand to almost twice their size within a person's body, causing devastating damage to surrounding tissue.

Why did you want me to know all these things?

How can I still love you, knowing you made me so I would know all these things? Can I?

Are you coming back to me through the bullet wound in the sky?

⌘ ⌘

WORKER PRAYS TO A BULLET

A piece of the sky came loose and fell to the ground and from inside us came the sound of a spring breaking.

Pull, turn, press. Projectile, case, primer. Something loose, above, inside. *Pull, turn, press.* We cannot look at the missing piece of the sky. We cannot look at the hole in the world. Instead we pull, we turn, we press. We don't blink. Our wrists hurt. Tonight, when our shift ends we will close our eyes and we will

234

step back from the conveyor belt and we will rub our wrists and we will hold our wrists close to the uncoiling thing inside. And we will feel it uncoil almost all the way and then we will wind ourselves up again. And we will look to the left, to the pile of all our other bodies rusting neatly one on top of the other. Did all our other wrists hurt like this before each of these other bodies of ours stopped working? Did we forget to wind all our other bodies up again before our coils unraveled all the way to their very end? This, we will wonder. One more time.

And we will sweep the floor around our other bodies, and we will polish every part of the machines, every piston, every cog. We will keep this shop like we would our home, and then we will look up and we will close our eyes and we will open our mouths and we will wait for the Singer's voice to fill our insides, and it will be as if we have swallowed a piece of the sun with sharp, rusty edges that catch on our tongue, and even the rust will be good, and so we will praise the Great Welder in the sky who made the sun and the moon and the stars.

But thinking ahead to the end of the shift won't do. *Pull, turn, press.* Our wrists hurt, something is loose, and we drop a bullet to the floor, scatter primers everywhere. We've made a mess. We should keep this shop like we would our home, even when there's a hole in the sky. The coil inside strains as we pick the bullet up and hold it high above our head against the light of the sun and it is light and light and light. Its full metal jacket, its hollow point. We see it going into a person's body. Inside the person's body, the bullet blooms into a flower.

Who would think of such a thing, other than the Welder in the sky, who made the sun and the moon and the rust?

We look at the bullet and see it is a thing of beauty. The conveyor belt advances, the bullets unpulled, unpressed, unturned. Full metal flowers—do they dream of blooming?

Our wrists hurt. We think of praying. The words of the Singer's song to the Great Welder in the sky flash in our head, as bright and comforting as the stars. The coil inside sings: *O Welder, O Welder hallowed be thy name*—but the words twist as the coil uncoils and the sky creaks and primers are at our feet and the conveyor belt conveys faster than our wrists can move and the bullet is beautiful today. *O bullet*, our coil sings, flying lead ricocheting off our tongue, *O bullet, O bullet in the sky—*

C3 &O

FIXER LOOKS FOR A PIECE OF THE SKY

Fixer was changing the blown starbulb when the piece of the sky came loose, leaving a gaping hole in the firmament. The sound it made as it hit the ground sent a shiver down Fixer's spine and caused his coil to tingle with tension.

But now he is calm, standing at the top of the ladder, looking down. The sky needs fixing and he is the only one to do it—and do it well. It might take a long time, looking for the piece, going all the way down and then back up again, it will throw the days and nights into chaos for sure, but what else can he do? There is no other Fixer to turn off the sun while he's gone. Not any more. And so he sets out for the ground, to walk among the machines and the Workers and the noises of the world. It's been a very long time since he's last been to the ground. His hands feel like they might be trembling, but they are not. Is this excitement?

Off he goes. Down, down, down, for a long time.

His feet are steady on each step of the ladder, his arms are strong, but the coiled thing inside his chest is coming looser and looser as time passes, and he will soon need winding up again or he won't make it. He's almost to the last of his coil when he realizes he can see the sun from its good side. It is round and shiny and bright, despite the creeping rust at the edges of the metallic surface. It's perfect.

The coil inside him creaks, and so does the sky. He takes out the key with unsteady hands—almost drops it, in fact, and then what would happen? What would happen to the world if he gave out and there was no one to move time along any more? He inserts the key into his neckhole and twists and twists, his body tensing with every turn, and he knows deep in his core that now would be the time to switch off the sun and to wheel out the moon so the machines can stop and the Workers can wind themselves up again under the sound of the Singer's song. But he's not there to do that any more, and it is still day even though it's night. He wonders what an endless day might do to the world, what sights may be seen under this much unexpected light. He wonders if the other Fixer will be waiting for him on the ground, accusing, staring at his hammer, understanding nothing, stage blood coming out of his head.

Fixer chastises himself and speeds up his descent. It shouldn't be long now.

And if the other Fixer is there, waiting, so what. Stage blood washes off easy.

When he finally gets to the ground, he lands amidst the loud, tireless machines producing garlands upon garlands of cartridges. It takes him a while to understand what the heap lying next to the ladder is. Then, he sees them, an arm here, a face there, the pile of Workers' bodies stacked neatly one on top of the other. What has happened here? What has become of the world while he was up there taking care of the stars?

There is a single Worker tending to the conveyor belt. She moves slowly, unsteadily—she's near the end of her coil, surely.

"Hey, you, Worker!" he shouts in order to be heard over the clamor of the machines.

She turns her head, only for an instant, but still her hands miss the next bullet, scattering primers all over the floor by her feet.

Fixer walks closer. "What happened to all the other Workers?" he asks.

"We're all still here," she says. "But not all of us talk and move any more." She speaks slowly. She's almost done, almost spent.

"You can stop working now," Fixer says. "Your shift is over. Wind yourself, in the Welder's name."

"But it's still day."

"No, it's not. It's night." He points at the hole in the firmament. "I just had to come down here, so there's no one left to turn on the stars."

Worker is still working, but she steals furtive glances at the sky. "But it's not night," she insists. Her voice quivers.

He approaches, his hammer swinging at his belt. He looks at this Worker, the tragedy of her existence, the completeness of her devotion. She will work herself to the end, and it's all his fault. He gently takes her shoulders and pulls her away from the conveyor belt, letting the half-formed bullets fall off the end and clatter onto the ground. Her hands are still going through the motions, pulling, turning, pressing. He grabs them, steadies them. "It's OK," he says. "It's night. You can stop now. It's night." He repeats this until she stops moving.

She holds her hands close to her chest and stares at the sky for a long time. Then she lets her body slump onto the floor.

Fixer sits on the ground next to her, his back against the unfaltering machinery of the world. He feels his coil uncoil slowly, looks over to the pile of Workers, and, for a moment, he wonders if this is it. If he should just sit here next to the last of the Workers, allow his coil to uncoil all the way to the end and stay there, let his body shut down, collecting dust under the relentless light of the sun.

But then his eye catches a glimpse of the hole in the sky and the coil inside strains because he needs to fix the flaw in the world. So he gets back up and goes look for the missing piece of the sky.

Before he starts climbing the ladder with the piece held tightly under his arm, he puts his key in the Worker's neck and winds her up. For a moment, she looks confused. Then she's on her feet again, pulling, turning, pressing, as if nothing has passed between them, or between her and the world. She doesn't say a word.

ϩ Ϫ

SINGER: HIS VOICE BACK TOGETHER AGAIN

I thought the day's length was a sign that you were coming back. I thought the hole in the sky was a sign that all of this was finally over—the constant fight against the rust with nothing but grease and a handful of facts that I no longer know how to assemble into songs.

But the hole is gone now and the sun no longer shines in the sky; the world is healed, restored, the creation you left behind intact, self-preserved.

The organ's voicing is as complete and perfect as it is ever going to be without you. You made me well, but you did not make me to last forever, did you? Because, now, wouldn't that be cruel?

Tonight, I will sing my best hymn to you. It has only one word, but it is the sweetest one I know, O Welder, O Welder in the sky, and the only one I know to be true.

Look, the moon is coming out.

⊰ ⊱

FIXER SLEEPS UNDER THE STARS

Fixer's limbs feel heavy and worn as he paints over the restored piece of the firmament under the faint shine of the moon. He could have looked through the hole in the sky, but he didn't. The coil wouldn't let him, he told himself; it jerked and strained at the mere thought. Besides, why would he? The world is fine as it is. Soon, everything will be as it was before, as if nothing ever happened.

As soon as he finishes the restoration, he turns on the stars, and each one comes alive, bright and familiar, their light soft and soothing.

The coil inside him is quiet now. The Singer's voice spills out of the loudspeakers. Is it just him, Fixer wonders, or does it sound just as it used to when they first came into the world, before the rust, before the world started giving out, falling apart? She really does have the most beautiful voice, Singer.

"Welder, Welder, Welder," she repeats, all night long, making everything okay.

Fixer decides to sleep in his ropes tonight, suspended under the stars, lulled by the Singer's voice and the creaking of the sky.

In his dream, he's carrying the piece of the sky under his arm. There is a great joy inside his chest. He takes a swig from his flask and it burns his throat as if it were no longer stage wine. It makes his coil vibrate with song.

"Could I sing?" he wonders. "Could a Fixer ever sing?"

Drunk on his joy and his wine, Fixer no longer thinks of the tired Worker below. He doesn't think of the pile of bodies, or of the other Fixer's head staring at what can no longer be fixed.

In his dream, Fixer runs his fingers over the surface of the sky. He traces its length, its chipping paint, the flat outlines of its clouds. Then he pulls his hammer from his tool belt and caresses its head while the coil inside loosens and loosens.

In Fixer's dream, the flawed world creaks. Before nailing the fallen piece back in place, he peeks through the hole in the firmament, at the maddening beauty, at the stars beyond the stars.

HARE'S BREATH

Maria Haskins

1947, Västerbotten, Sweden

It's Midsummer's Eve, and even this close to midnight there's no darkness, only a long, translucent dusk that will eventually slip into dawn.

Britt and I are fifteen, and she has just come back from That Place, the one the adults won't talk about even when they think I'm not listening. Something's happened to her there, but I don't understand what it is, and she can't find the words to tell me.

We're sitting on the wooden fence near my family's potato patch, looking down the slope at the red-painted barn and stable, watching the hare. He sits upright on his haunches by the forest's edge, ever watchful, bending now and then to nibble grass and clover, grey-brown fur all sleek and trim, long ears turning.

The hare reminds me of Britt: dark eyes watching to see if you've come to kill it; long legs always ready to run.

Shapes and shadows move in the gloom beneath the forest's dark-fringed spruce and pine, and Britt says it's the trolls that live there, restless in the long summer dusk, hiding themselves under rocks and roots and glossy lingonberry leaves. She says you can speak to them when the sun and moon have gone down. You can even speak to the hare, then: if you know how, if he trusts you enough to let you. Most nights, I might not have believed her, even though she goes farther into the woods than anyone else I know, but tonight is Midsummer's Eve, when the skein between *tale* and *truth* is thin enough to pass through.

We've helped decorate the village maypole with birch-leaves and flowers, such as there are up here so far north in June. It's cold. We wear woolen sweaters over summer dresses, bare legs swinging, and from far away I can hear music, or maybe it's

241

just the river's distant voice: B minor, a song like whispers and sun on water. Britt taps her fingers to the melody, so I know she hears it too. In the silence between us, the notes seem to resonate within her, tugging at her, rippling through her, plucked on strings of guts and breath, pain and memory.

I've picked seven kinds of flowers to put under my pillow, picked them special, keeping silent all the while, climbing over seven fences to do it right. I would dream about the man I'll marry if I slept on them. But I don't want to sleep, and I don't want to marry any man either, so instead I braid them into a crown for Britt. She sits so still, looking at my fingers braiding: purple wood cranesbill, white bishop's lace and oxeye daisies, red campion, yellow buttercups, blue forget-me-nots and fragile harebells. Once it's done, she bows her head and I place it on her curly brown hair, a coronation. I see her change, then, radiant like the pictures in Grandma's illustrated Bible, where the golden rays emanate from Jesus's head.

"You're the prettiest thing I ever saw," I say, straightening her crown and halo, and that makes her smile, even though sorrow peeks through the ragged edges of her joy.

My older siblings all moved out and away before I even started school, and Britt has always been as close as a sister. Sometimes she's an older sister who tells me things not even the adults seem to know. Other times she can't understand things my five-year-old cousin takes for granted. She is and always will be my ghost and shadow, my guilt and glory, my secret wish and hidden grief.

"Want to see?" she asks, smile already slipping. "Want to see what they did?"

I don't answer, but she takes her clothes off anyway, wool and dress, no linens underneath, and stands there naked except for the flowers left askew in her hair. Bruises run the length of her back, down her buttocks, the back of her thighs, swirls and stripes of blue and red and black, inflicted where her clothes are sure to hide them. But that is not what she wants me to see.

The front of her body is pale and untouched, except for the scar.

"I couldn't leave unless I let them cut me," she says, tracing the red welt of healed skin on her lower belly, nipples and pink skin prickling in the chill. "There wasn't nothing there to take, but they did it anyway."

I see, I hear, but I don't understand. I just want to touch her, hold her, comfort her, but I know she'd startle like the hare, I know she's not one for touching.

Her smile has slipped off all the way now, nothing's left of it, and without another word, she turns and walks down the slope towards the forest, leaving me, leaving her dress and her sweater on the fence, flower crown still askew, long strides cleaving the tall grass. The hare sits up as she approaches, flicking his ears, listening and waiting. For a moment, they remain completely still within each other's gaze. Then, they start running, together, until the forest hides them both.

cs &

1940

I'm eight years old the first time I understand that Britt's father beats her, and that that's why mother lets her come to stay with us. Those are the days when there are empty bottles smashed outside Britt's house, when we can hear him bellowing her name through thin walls and rattling windows.

Britt shares my narrow bed those nights, and we sleep skavfötters—our heads at either end, legs meeting in the middle. She eats dinner with us, too; hands fluttering over the bread and butter, fingers clumsy when she wields a spoon or fork. Mother always lets her have seconds, even though she'll never let me eat my fill at the table until everyone else has finished.

"He's not my dad," Britt tells me, when we sit together in the hayloft, listening to the horses chewing oats below. "My real dad lives in the river. Mamma said so before she went away."

But Britt can't even read, and everyone knows her mom was a whore, so I don't believe it until she takes me to the river. We look and look from the bridge, in the reeds and beneath the lily-pads, and finally we find him. He looks dead, but Britt says he isn't. She pokes him with an oar and he rolls over and floats up, wrapped in trailing lily stems, some of them wound around his head and long hair like a crown, and he's naked. The only thing missing is his fiddle, which Grandma says he ought to have.

He looks so beautiful I might have gone into the water myself even if I cannot swim: pale skin pulled tight over bones and dreams, dark hair like Britt's—all curls and waves and ripples.

When Britt wades into the water, he opens his eyes and pulls her down. I want to scream and run away, but she's told me to wait, so I just stand there on the shore. Half a day goes by before she surfaces all soaked and dripping, mud blossoming beneath her in the water.

(Afterwards, I know it can't have happened that way, that she can't have stayed under that long, that I must have made it up or imagined it. And yet I remember it clearly, the smell of the water as he broke the surface: mulch and rot and roots, the sheen of his skin as he reached for her, the hiss of his breath as he went below again.)

"I didn't want to stay. Don't like it down there, anyway, and he was mad for me not bringing his fiddle," Britt says. "I told him I might bring it if he'd give me something for it."

"Like what?" I ask, but she won't say what magic she would ask for.

"Don't tell anyone," she whispers when I help her pick the twigs and leaves out of her wet hair, and I promise.

ভ ৩

1937

We are five years old when Britt shows me the fiddle packed away in a black case lined with red velvet underneath her bed. The veined wood is smooth and lustrous, like honeycombs and sunshine and autumn leaves. She plucks the strings with soft fingers, and the sound is water dripping from trees, is shade beneath heavy branches, is the rills of meltwater beneath thin ice in spring.

"Mamma says it's mine."

I touch, almost fearful of the smoothness of that varnish, the brittleness of that wood, the trembling power trapped within those strings and tuning screws. The fiddle is a treasure beyond price in a place where there is mostly want. It is beauty in a place where there are only plain and practical things. It is magic tucked beneath a lumpy mattress.

ଦ ฒ

1946

I'm fourteen when they take Britt away.

Mother says it's because Britt's not right. That's why the school wouldn't have her. Because she couldn't sit still, couldn't listen, didn't write the words down as they were supposed to be written, didn't sing the psalms right, or read the sentences the way they were supposed to be read. She'd read other stories on the pages, full of snakes and claws and ripping beasts and naked men and their...*genitalia*, as I heard the teacher whisper behind her hand to my mother. No more school for her after that, just work. Be good. Be grateful. Bow and scrape.

A car comes and takes her away one day when I'm at school.

"An *institution*," Grandma says and I can tell she's almost crying. "That's where they're taking her."

I march down to the river looking for Britt's dad. It's a stupid thing to do, but I do it because I have nowhere else to be angry. After a bit of searching, I think I find the spot where Britt and I saw him before, but no one's there. I sit down in the grass on the sloping river bank and tell him that no matter what Britt's mom did to him, no matter what she stole or what promises she broke, he can't punish Britt for it.

"Help her," I pray, hands clasped as if it's Sunday. "Please."

I know I should be praying to God or Jesus, but they are far away, in the church, above the clouds, pressed flat and dry between the pages of Grandma's heavy Bible. Not as close as the river, not as close as the water lapping over mud and rocks and toes.

Something almost surfaces in the stream beyond; ripples radiating out. Most likely it's a fish catching a fly or water strider, but I make myself believe that he heard me. Then I throw a rock, as big as I can heft, out there just for good measure, hoping it'll crack his head open.

(I know what everyone says, that Britt's father was a no-good vagrant, *tattare*, traveler, passing through the village when Britt's mom was sixteen. That he ran off because he got into a fight and cut a man, that he was afraid of going to jail, that he left his fiddle behind and never came back. I know that no one else has seen the face beneath the water-lilies. I know, I know, I know what people say, but I know it's not the truth: it is only the gossamer of reality pulled over the true story beneath, the story Britt told me, the story I am telling you.)

 Cʒ ৪ᴐ

1947

When Britt comes back, she tries to tell me of That Place. A house, she says, with beds and clean sheets and metal tables and sharp knives laid out on trays. The words she has brought with her skip and sink (*feeble-minded*), teeter and totter (*mental deficiency due to inheritance*), break and crack (*delinquent*), and when I don't understand, she gets angry and runs away.

"A girl like her...she doesn't need the trouble," Mom says while her fingers are busy knitting socks. "She'll have an easier time of it now."

I don't know what that means, but I know it's a lie.

Cʒ ৪ᴐ

246

1990

I'm fifty-eight years old—career, no kids, happy on the weekends, busy folding laundry—when a documentary on the radio tells me what happened to Britt.

A kitchen towel. *Sweden's State Institute of racial biology.* T-shirt and sweatpants. *Racial hygiene.* Three pairs of socks. *Forced sterilizations.* A pair of jeans. *63,000 individuals.* Two pairs of underwear. *To raise the quality of the population stock and prevent degeneration of the race.*

I sit beside my pink geraniums and I can't stop crying. There is no hare's gaze to hold me here, no music playing, no stolen fiddle's magic to stir me; but I can feel the shiver of the hare's breath against my skin, and I can hear the melody anyway. I've dreamed of it every night since 1947. I know that the world is hollow: an awful place of despair and cruelty and injustice. And I know that the world is holy: a beautiful place of joy and radiance and moments braided together like flowers, our love mostly hidden in the quiet spaces between everything we say and do to each other.

ଔ ଓ

1947

The last time I see Britt is after midnight that Midsummer's Eve.

She comes to logen, the place where everyone is dancing and drinking beneath the maypole. The sky is fading into deeper blue, but the light remains, sheer like worn-out linen.

Britt is still naked, scar and bruises bared, feet and shins covered in dirt and blood, mosquito bites and scratches, as if she's been running through the woods to get here. The only thing she's carrying is the fiddle and the bow, and everything she is and was and ever will be from this moment on is revealed before us: dirty and transcendent, broken and divine.

247

Dance and music end. Britt takes out the bow, tightens the horsehair, and sweeps it over the strings, fiddle tucked up on her shoulder. No one tries to stop her. No one speaks or moves. I've never seen her play before, but the sound she makes is fog rising off the water, is the darkness beneath the bridge, is the shade and gloom below the surface, is the smooth gleam of rocks at the bottom of the river, is the slow glide and swirl of the water's current in the heat of summer.

Her hands, those hands that won't do anything right, that can't wield pencils or knitting needles, those hands our teacher smacked with a metal ruler so many times Britt's knuckles bled and puffed, those hands braid notes together that shiver through our souls and unspoken dreams, through the skies and heavens. It is a spell—rippling and quavering, reflecting ourselves and the darkness knit into the light within us all - and for a little while we might have followed her anywhere, might have listened to anything she said or played, might have understood her, but it's not for keeps: when the music stops, she's Britt, again, the whore's daughter.

She walks by me, past me, through me, away, holding on to that fiddle, and she smiles, still crowned by flowers, haloed, radiant. Her hand caresses me, and my cheek burns at the touch, though I'm not sure whether the heat is hers or mine or ours.

"Don't tell them where I went," she says, and I nod.

I've kept that promise ever since. It is the only vow I've never broken.

Then she runs: long legs moving through the tall grass, taking her back into the woods.

൦ ൭

The next day, I found Britt's wilted crown hanging off the edge of the bridge, its braided stems still unbroken. No one ever found her body. Some said she was trapped below the river's surface, snagged on roots or rocks. I knew it wasn't so. I knew Britt would have never stayed beneath.

It wasn't her fault, none of it. No one should have beaten her. No one should have bruised or scarred her. No one should have cut her to make her fit. Some people can't ever make themselves fit into small rooms, into narrow and cramped words, can't make what they need to say fit into sentences and books and lined paper. But still, people try, they try to cut others into pieces, bend and twist them as to fit into the space provided.

Why must everyone fit into church and school and work and polished shoes and small rooms and wooden coffins, in the end, to sink into the dirt?

I watched the men in boats dredging the river, searching for her, and I thought of the man beneath the mud and water-lilies, thought of his fiddle and what tune he might make it play. All the while, I kept my eyes on the dark-fringed pine and spruce on the other side of the bridge, waiting for the hare to see me.

C8 80

I go back to the old place at Midsummer every year. The slope is overgrown with grass and nettles and slender birch trees. There is no potato patch anymore, the old house is warped and sagging, and no music comes from the river because the water is choked with weeds and silt, but a hare still visits. She knows me and I know her: grey-brown fur all sleek and trim, long ears turning, eyes ever watchful. I've seen her with her leverets: every Midsummer's Eve she brings another two, running with her in the meadow down towards the river, through the long, translucent dusk slipping into dawn.

C8 80

Footnote: "The so-called sterilization laws were instituted by the Swedish parliament in 1934 and 1941. Both allowed sterilization without consent under certain conditions. — The reasons (indications) to perform sterilizations were threefold: eugenics (race / genetic hygiene), social and medical. — Of the total number of sterilized individuals, 93 percent were women." From the report "Steriliseringsfrågan i Sverige 1935 - 1975" / "The issue of sterilization in Sweden 1935 – 1975," issued by Socialdepartementet / Ministry of Health and Social Affairs, Sweden, March 2000.

BONESET

Lucia Iglesias

For Gerard Manley Hopkins, master word-setter,
who found the poetry in bones.

The blind Bonesetter's townhouse enacts the architecture
of a skull. Windows imitate eye sockets the Bonesetter has
known. The front door comments on the vigor of the jaw,
swinging up and down on mandibular hinges. When the hinges
thirst for oil, the door munches up the lucklorn gutter-mice who
skitter over the threshold, chewing them into flesh-jelly and
spitting them across the foyer until the Bonesetter serves the
hinges their oil from a crystal eyedropper. The home's ample
upper-story suggests the sage proportions of a prodigy's frontal
lobes. At the back of the house, in the occipital chambers, the
Bonesetter puts his patients back together. Here, the ceiling
slopes low and the walls have a curious slant, leaning inwards as
if to scrutinize the Bonesetter's living art.

Phials, jars, flasks, flagons, and bottles—celadon-glazed
or blown from floss-glass—peer down from the Bonesetter's
shelves, winking in the light of the firefly lamps. The lamps, two
dozen orbs of quartz, hang from fishing line strung along the
ceiling beams. Each orb imprisons a family of fireflies. Convicted
of incandescence, they serve a life sentence, their rueful glow
seeping through the quartz. Encircling the room like a ribcage,
twelve rows of shelves hold the Bonesetter's secrets: powdered
amber laced with damselfly or drakling, sprigs of feverfew dried
under a child's pillow, strips of skin inscribed with sonnets, cats'
whiskers, three dozen flavors of bottled laughter, pennyroyal
pressed between pages of a harlot's autobiography, reflections
caught from mirrors or windows or the backs of spoons,
rainbows skimmed off oilslicks, the language of rain trapped in a
bottle of pebbles, rosehips pickled in spite, teardrop cordial,
candied cobweb, two dozen sets of milk-teeth, glitter ground
from the wings of butterflies and luna moths, bioluminescence

smoldering in saltwater from an underground sea, a tantrum preserved in formaldehyde, unborns sleeping in amniotic fluid (unmice, unmoles, unmunks, an unfox), strings of abandoned punctuation, letters jettisoned from sinking languages like cacophonous ballast, faceless pocket watches, the chiming of rogue bells, antimony lozenges, vixen-milk, electricity combed from the fur of a catamount, essence of jubilee, essence of melancholy, and a fever dream distilled into pure alcohol.

These rare and irascible ingredients make the Bonesetter a master of anesthesia, antiseptics, and antipsychotics. On the night-market, the Bonesetter could earn a lifetime and a half of luxury from the sale of a single phial of jubilee or an ever-sleeping unmunk. Fathers would sell their daughters' hair and mothers would sell the roses from their sons' cheeks for vixen-milk or bottled laughter.

While these dozing riches lie upon his shelves, the Bonesetter hoards his true treasure in a cabinet above the sink. As he rinses sweat and a spritz of blood off his socket-clamp and wrenches, he fancies he hears his leather-bound prize rustling behind the cabinet door. Like the echoes that once chased his bounding son through the corridors, the book's pages betray secrets not their own. After kneading his hands dry on his apron, the Bonesetter spiders his fingers over the cabinet door until he finds the latch. His head turns, trying to follow the hands it cannot guide. His eye sockets are scooped and empty as oyster shells.

The cabinet's leather-bound book weighs the same as a promise kept or a winter evening unraveled by the fireside: It is the sum of fulfillment and fortune, and when the Bonesetter runs his fingers over the embossed spine, he knows that if Death dropped by to settle the accounts tonight, he would find the Bonesetter quite willing to cash in his life and scratch his debt to the soul-banker. The Bonesetter will leave life having given more than he took. And if his son overdraws the account, as rumor whispers he will—well, that is a story still to be written. For now, there is only the blind Bonesetter and his book, which he lays on the operating table and opens with a sigh. He foots around for a stool and, finding one, draws it up to the table's rim. Sitting straight-spined as only a virtuoso chiropractor can, he stares at the chamber's single octagonal window as his fingers read.

Splashed in the blue sluice of twilight, the Bonesetter appears discreetly luminous. Lustrous as a black pearl, his skin is slicked with dusk's light. Reading the raised text with his index finger, he nods along to the familiar rhythm of his own words. He remembers penning this chapter—in the hollow hours between midnight and a new morning—how he wrote through two whole bottles of bone-meal ink and had to ask his son to pelt down to the cellar for a spare femur to grind into a third bottle. Oleander ran away before the end of the next chapter, and the Bonesetter had to spivvy up a pulley system to replace his young bone-runner. The boy had taken such carnivorous interest in skeletal anatomy that his father had felt certain Oleander Bonesettersson would become his apprentice after dusting up his paleontology and troglobiology exams at school. After the boy left, taking only a coil of rope and his father's entire supply of jaw-wire, the Bonesetter's wife opined that their son had been spending indulgent helpings of time with the mad aunts in the attic, and that the spinsters were to blame for infecting him with the feverish whim. The Bonesetter had always classified the aunts amongst the vermin he shared his home with only because he had yet to devise a humane way to evict mice, spiders, and mother's sisters. Still, he contended, nearly every house in the City had an aunt or two in the attic, and _they_ hadn't launched fleets of runaways. However, by the time he embarked upon writing his epilogue, a runaway-epidemic struck the City and devastated the youth population. Though his wife never stooped to "I told you so," she did introduce a bill amongst her fellow senators to ban the atticking of aunts. Somewhere under the opal-studded dome of the Senatorium, her bill was growing a coat of dust. The prospect of seeing the dickered biddies loose on the streets was too frightful for the senators to compass. And some whispered that she had only introduced the bill to lure

252

attention away from the rumors that pinned her son as Patient Zero, the poison in the well.

Dark as the lacquered shell of a mussel, the Bonesetter's fingers rub word-nubs, tracing letters built from bone-meal, letters as spare as their author, shorn of flourish and arabesque, sleek and bald as a god. His handwriting is as familiar as his own methodical anatomy, each popped P and high-shouldered H as intimate as the regal vertebrae rippling down his diagrammatic spine. Amongst the granite facts chiseled into his skull, the Bonesetter knows he is more father to this book than to Oleander, for he never learned to read the boy's mood from the angle of his elbows or the slant of his jaw, whereas his book speaks to him in the acute language of powdered bone. Though the boy is flesh of his flesh, the Bonesetter never learned the unique knobble of Oleander's knee joints, never played the xylophone of his spine, never measured his unfurling wingspan. As Oleander grew into his bones, his father was welded to this stool, breeding this book. The Bonesetter rarely molders in remorse. He has no time for the soft and fleshful. Bones are his business. Yet every night, he falls asleep over this book, waiting for his boy to come home.

Under the Bonesetter's fingers, the words warm, coming alive on the steel operating table. When the Bonesetter scoops a child from Death's doorstep and carries her back to her parents, they often call him a Vivimancer. Many believe he is a warlock who can spell any doll or daughter to life. However, the Bonesetter knows it only takes a posset of fetal-vole and violet-oil to stimulate balking nerves. He knows the words under his fingers have no more life than a clench-fisted fetus in its formaldehyde bath. It is his own life he feels quickening under the skin of these words, a whole lifetime of study injected between leather covers. He skims from chapter to chapter, savoring the cream of each case study. He relishes the purity of his signature taxonomy, untainted by an erroneous genus or a fretful crossbreed. Pain is the purest sensation, and he has strained the case studies to clarify kingdom, phylum, class, order, family, genus, and species. Not a twinge has escaped his sifting.

The Bonesetter can pin the speciation of any ache, be it a mocksome noddler bobbing under the lumbar, or a gwee tweakler kindling only on twenty-ninths of odder months. His case studies—case stories really—are a Wunderkammer of spasms, a cabinet of curiosities, a circus shriek-show, a freakgasm, a back alley, a bucket of screams, a torture garden, a family tree, a brood of masochists, a torturer's dictionary, a surgeon's thesaurus, a child's encyclopedia, a captain's log, forensic evidence, a fancier's guide, a three-hundred-page equation, a collection of recipes, a dream atlas, the ingredients for a nightmare, a sacred text, a fifth dimension, an old wives' tale, a new metric, a riddle written on a Möbius strip, an un-nameable shade of red, a prophecy, an iridescent menagerie.

Yet of all his weeping treasures, of all the wailing, groaning, giggling agonies nestled between the snug leather covers, his most exotic specimen, the crowning jewel of his algesiology can be visited in *Chapter the Last: In Which I Meet Pain's Brother*. A researcher's treatise can never be anything other than a flagrant autobiography, a spiffing-up of the diary and laboratory notes, a plummet into rambling marginalia and restless hypotheses. However, few researchers become protagonists in their own case stories. The Bonesetter had never been one to guinea-pig himself, but that changed after he was visited by the most effervescent caller ever to fondle the bell cord beneath the sign of crossed bones.

ৎ ৯০

On that fate-encrusted night (fortune-varnishing visits always happen in the owl-hours, by an eldritch rule), the Bonesetter's wife was out, carousing with her constituents at the neighborhood malt-bar. Oleander ought to have been deep into the second or third layer of sleep, which meant he was probably gossiping with the aunts in the attic over porcelain thimble cups of triple-distilled dew. When the doorbell squalled, the Bonesetter was prying into the structural secrets of a fledgling's wing-bones with his octoscope. On this night, he still wore both his eyes, bright as geodes, only casually myopic from a lifetime of study. A bit stiff from spending the day swan-necked over his octoscope, he creaked to the door. No business hours were posted under the sign of crossed bones because bonesetting was his life's work, and obsessions don't come packaged in eight-hour increments. Absorbed as he was in the intricate dialogue between skeletal articulation and biological function, the Bonesetter did not find it peculiar that someone else in the City was fraught with an osteological quandary at this owlish hour. When he wrenched the lever to open the mandibular door, it would have seemed to anyone on the stoop that the door's jaws had opened upon a gaping foyer, for the Bonesetter was quite camouflaged in the unlit atrium, blending into the suave umbra thrown by the streetlamp. However, his visitor spied the noble glint on his lofty cheekbones and spoke through the jaws of the door.

"You're the Bonesetter? What an emerald pleasure to meet you at last. I read your article on sentient spinal growths with relish. Absolutely lip-smacking the way you chronicle the sub-phases of fetal pain. And you gave a tantalizing hint about a new book in the tumbler, didn't you? Your *Taxonomia Algesia*. May I borrow an hour of your evening, Master Bonesetter? I have a proposition I think you'll find savory." The man spoke as if his teeth were slick with butter. His sibilants glistened with a sheen of caviar.

With his back to the streetlamp, the man was a silhouette snipped out by the keenest of scissors. His head was cocked at a wily angle, leaving his features in blackout (the kind of blackout that in the theater is followed by a scream cropped short). However, even in two-dimensional cut-out, the insolence of his anatomy was broadcast by the lamplight. The Bonesetter automatically catalogued his brash bone structure, noting the skeletal audacity not with shock or revulsion, but with a collector's buttoned-up interest. The caller's polydactyly failed to raise an eyebrow, for the Bonesetter could have filled a smuggler's false-bottomed trunk with all the gratuitous fingers and toes he'd met over the course of his career. The stranger's supplemental pair of arms raked up a bit more interest than the superfluous fingers. Sprouting from his iliac crest, the arms breached from his coat pockets and dangled to his knees. Yet what really won the stranger his guest-right in the Bonesetter's home were his *genu recurvatum*, his back-bending knees, or more precisely, the tango-dancer's grace with which he glided upon those perplexed joints as the Bonesetter stepped aside and watched the visitor swan over the threshold.

Most of the Bonesetter's visitors are somewhere between sweat-drenched endurance and octave-shattering agony. Therefore, by latched habit the Bonesetter led his guest to the examination room, where he drew up a second stool at the steel examination table. In the formaldehyde light reflecting off the specimen jars, the Bonesetter inspected the man he couldn't help thinking of as his patient. Formaldehyde-yellow is a tint that flatters few, yet the stranger wore it well. Whereas most men and peaches are coated in a thin glisten of hair, the stranger was slicked in a filmy sheen of feathers. The thickened light caught in his quills, rinsing them in amber. A translucent third lid flicked over his eye, as if to polish away the jaundiced light, leaving his cornea amnesia-white. If he suffered from the freeloading fingers, the unwarranted arms, the concave knees, the gossamer feathers, or the lizard-lids, the pain was imprisoned so deep within that the Bonesetter couldn't sense its locus. What symptom had brought the stranger at this owl-hour? He waited for his patient to unlock the matter himself.

"You do speak, don't you?" said the man with a twist of the lips that was several degrees short of a smile. "This will be mammothly tedious if we have to precede in miner's hand-language."

The Bonesetter, who often goes days without opening his mouth for anything except yawns and nettle-butter sandwiches, realized that his visitor expected some species of greeting.

"What disturbs the peace in your bone-house, sir?" he tried. "Whether it's a rogue disc or a dickered rib, I guarantee you won't leave my operating room until I've spiffed your skeleton back into the wonderwork it once was."

A smile split the stranger's face like an unhealed wound. "My dear bone-buckler, I'm quite at home in my skeleton. It's book-business, not bone-business, that brings me. I know a publishing house that would glut your ledgers with more gold than you could shake out of a dwarf, if your manuscript arrived wrapped in my endorsement."

As the Bonesetter calculated the surface area of an average tunnel-dwarf in cubits-squared, and derived an approximate maximum gold-load based on the tensile strength of dwarf ligaments, his guest closed his auxiliary eyelids and watched the chiropractor through their iridescent film. After settling upon a sum that would amount to a lavishly embellished diploma with unimpeachable letters of reference for Oleander, along with six dozen phials of the rarest pathological specimens to round out his research collection, the Bonesetter blinked the numerals from his eyes. He studied the visitor varnished in formaldehyde-light.

"And whose bones do I have the pleasure of greeting, sir? You seem to know me, but have not, I think, labeled your specimen."

"Only because there isn't enough ink in the City to pen the length of my name. I have worn so many monikers, epithets, sobriquets, aliases, and noms-de-plume that I would have to hire the entire Librarians' Guild and empty the City Archives of their scribes just to write a taxonomy of myself. Then you could thumb through the card catalogue and find a nickname that doesn't give you lock-jaw. Some of my older pseudonyms have grown aggressive in their dotage. I wouldn't trust anyone's tongue around them except my own. Of course I also have a passel of harmless-enough names. I'll fan them out for you like a gypsinger's cards and let you choose. Like the gypsinger's painted menagerie of hermits and fools, each name has its own will and wiles. *Thief-of-Thieves*, he's quite the sneakster, and hard to parry, that *Lie-Smith*. *Sif's Husband* is no slick-groomed foppet; there's teeth on him, the *Otter-Killer*. *Hel's Father* knows too much about the sunk and dead, but *Neck-Risker* is always smirking at Death. You'll know *Scar-Lip* by the way he wrings his words, and *the Lad* always has a laugh tucked up his sleeve. *Pain's Brother* knows a redder way and he will always win when it comes to grips, though *Plague's Nurse* prefers loss, watching it slow and blue as it strangles men."

Upon finishing this catalogue, Pain's Brother straightened his legs to the clicking point, his recurve knees retorting like rifles. He crossed his ankles under the Bonesetter's stool and leaned back with all four elbows propped on the examination table.

That a single being should be strung together from so many names did not strike the Bonesetter as anything other than ordinary, for he sees every organism as a calcium palace of spire-spines, gabled skulls, latticed ribcages, and hinged knuckles. No woman is simply Sabriye or Adelaïde or Bryony, no man merely Mordekai or Fenimöre or Wolfgang. Each creature is an illuminated encyclopedia of anatomy, from clavicle to sternum, coccyx to calcaneus, lunate to lumbar, ethmoid to ulna, tibia to trapezium. The Bonesetter was less interested in a catalogue of gregarious epithets and more interested in the flexion of those knees and the reshuffling of ribs that accommodated those arrogant additional arms. Still, as the names spilled across the examination table, he recognized a few from the rumors that gusted down back alleys on Rubbishday. The Thief-of-Thieves was known to steal bad luck and poverty, leaving nothing but riches, though Sif's Husband might tuck a seventh son into his satchel before leaving by the back door, and the Lad had as much arsenic as ingots in his pockets.

Pain's Brother stretched himself still further, as if intent on smearing himself over the entire examination room. His feet emerged on the far side of the Bonesetter's stool, and he laid his head back against the steel table. The faint plumage that papered his skin vibrated like hummingbird wings, flicking fidgety reflections against the luminous glass jars that lined the walls like mortality's mosaic. His third lid remained sealed, but beneath that iridescent film, both indigo irises were fixed on the Bonesetter.

Though the man had spread himself like a bacterial culture on a microscope plate, the Bonesetter muzzled the impulse to unbutton his examination instruments and conduct a full osteological analysis of the unique specimen. In fact, he was mildly nauseated by the man's appalling posture, and in his unease he ratcheted his own spine up another notch. At this interlude in the transaction, the Bonesetter's wife would have poured herself a measured nipper of triple-distilled mallow-malt, but her husband poured himself a measured breath. He crocheted his exquisite penumbral fingers in his lap and exhaled.

"Your offer is as attractive as a well-aligned spine, and if it's as sound as a logician's brain-case, I would be a jingling fool to decline. However, I fear *you* must wear the motley and bells tonight, for there is no book. You have wasted your incandescent company on an old bonesetter whose hands are more suited to realignments of the cervical vertebrae than to wordcraft."

The stranger's smile puckered his face like a scar, a crease so deep you could fall in if you looked too close.

"I've worn the motley and bells enough times to know that the fool always leaves with full pockets. There is no book *yet.* But surely you have a squalling manuscript tucked in a cradle somewhere just waiting to be swaddled up in red leather and adopted by an affluent publisher and her husband?"

The Bonesetter's fingers knotted themselves together so tightly they seemed intent on strangling one another. "The manuscript was stillborn—malformed—not viable."

Cracking all twenty-four knuckles in a lazy fusillade, Pain's Brother said: "A transfusion. A transplant. High voltage resuscitation. We'll save it somehow. What are the symptoms?"

"It stopped growing at Chapter Eight. Total cessation of mitosis. Stunted. A runt."

"Diagnosis?"

"I can't carry the manuscript to term. My taxonomy of pain was organized based on a hierarchical principle of magnitude. Extrapolating from a lifetime's collection of case studies, I started my speciation with the most domestic pains: the frolicking twinge of a papercut, the bloated ache of a bruise.

Then I ventured into more idiosyncratic kingdoms of pain: the auroral menstrual cramp, the starburst contusion of the ulnar nerve. However, my case studies yielded no material for the final chapter. Where was my apex species, the mind-predator, the carnivore who devours rationality, the beast that turns a man into raw meat beating away at its bone-cage?"

Pain's Brother butterflied his two dozen fingers, splaying them like specimens against the steel examination table. He tipped his head back, spilling onion-colored hair across the table. The more space he blotted up, the more the room seemed to cling to him, and the Bonesetter felt as if he were being squeezed out of his own office like the last tumor of dried-up glue squeezed from the tube.

"Spoon out your eyes," said Pain's Brother to the ceiling.

"Pardon?"

"Spoon out your eyes. Then you'll meet a pain you could never snare in a case study. Your last chapter must be written in first person. You'll only know the mind-carnivore if you feel it gnawing at your own sanity."

A smile gouged across the guest's face as he met his host's gaze. In the gore of that smile, the Bonesetter saw his guest was right. He couldn't name the predator pain until he knew it more intimately than he knew his wife.

For the first time since growing into his full, exacting height, the Bonesetter drew his knees up to his chin and balanced on the stool like a perverse egg. He laced his arms around his shins and sealed his eyes against the rancid gleam of the light. Inhaling a steadying dose of starch from his trouser-pleats, he spoke into his kneecaps.

"Will a grapefruit spoon do?"

The stranger's laugh rebounded from the walls like high-speed whiplash, leaving the glass jars whining. The Bonesetter's teeth ached.

"When the manuscript is spackled, spiffed, and spit-polished, post it to Delphinia and Daughters. They'll have the presses ratcheted and ready."

260

The Bonesetter heard the stranger's stool scuff his tiled floor. Then a sound like sinews unclasping their skeleton, tendons unfastening from flesh, bones unsleeved from skin—he flashed his eyes open, but caught only the smirking swing of the back door as it flapped on its hinges. A few slivered feathers listed in the door's updraft. It was as if the stranger had unmade himself, distilled into a fever dream.

The Bonesetter allowed himself a dozen diaphragmatic breaths, watering his lungs with the clammy midnight spilling through the door. Then he unkinked his knees, ironed out his spine, and strode to the kitchen. Light from the streetlamps curdled on the marble counters and in the bowl of the porcelain sink, streaking the kitchen in shades of broth and clarified butter. The lamplight foamed on the mother-of-pearl inlay in the knob of the silverware drawer. The Bonesetter raked the drawer open, and as he shoveled through the silver, the yolkish light dribbled in. Not a single grapefruit spoon remained.

"Oh Doctor-Daddykins, oh Bonesetter-Baba, oh Postured-Papa—whatever could you be pawing for under midnight's skirts? You look guilty as a boy-o caught with his thumb in the kumquat pudding. Did you hope to pluck out a succulent night-truffle? Do you like the burnt-caramel flavor of nighttime? Or are you looking for these?"

Oleander had perched himself owl-wise on the marble counter opposite the silverware drawer. He was hocked back on his heels in a mess of shadows so thick you could slather them on rye. Leaning out into the frothing light, he brandished a bouquet of silver grapefruit spoons at his father. He had his da's cheekbones—sharp enough to perform surgery—but his complexion was watered down by mother-blood. In the lamplight, his father was a painting in oils, rich with lapis and ultramarine, whereas Oleander was sketched in chalk.

"Only rag-taggle vagabonds and prize-wives ought to listen at keyholes, Oleander," his father scolded. "If you ever kip that trick again, your mother will hear about it, and you know what that means: A senate interrogation and an ear-ache. Now be brave, my little fibula, and give me a grapefruit spoon. You can lick the rest like silver-lollies if you fancy a midnight snack. I need only the one."

Oleander slumped back against the wall, drenching himself in shadow. "And *I* need the skeleton of a juvenile shrew. Only the one. What a soup we find ourselves swimming in, Dumpling-Da."

"So it's your pestilent intention to make me buy my own grapefruit spoon back from you for the price of a mint specimen? You do realize that a fully articulated juvenile shrew skeleton with copper wire ligaments is not an urchin's plaything? It will win you no back-alley battles against aluminum soldiers."

In the ferment of shadows, Oleander mined his ear-canals for wax with the handle of a spoon. "There's nothing left for me to win in the back-alleys, Doctor-Dadums. The ragamuffins and streetlings won't play with me anymore. They say I cheat worse than a Doggoblin."

In the skimmed light, the Bonesetter was several shades nobler than the dignified night that idled at the window. "And is my son a maggot-tongued cheat?"

"No. I'm a scientist."

As if fingering an extravagantly fractured femur, the Bonesetter at last found the fulcrum upon which his son's grievance seemed to rotate. His patient would flinch. And then they would bring the bones back into agreement.

"The gutter-mice wanted to live again," continued Oleander, his voice thinning to a whisper. "I could feel it under their fur. They were dead, but I quickened them back to life in my bare hands. It's not my fault that the urchins couldn't bring their aluminum soldiers to life. My undead mice were better warriors." His lips perked with a chalk smile. "They were romping first-rate, to tell it true."

"So you will give me back my own grapefruit spoons if I sacrifice one of the princes of my collection—the very spine of my scholarship—to feed your necromantic addiction?"

Oleander knuckled the spoons together, clicking up a racket with the improvised castanets. Above the sterling syncopation he chanted: "It's science, Osteo-Daddio. As scientifical as your bone-fiddling and spine-spiffing. You diddle inside live bodies to make them livelier, while I diddle with dead bodies to liven them up."

In the silver cacophony, the Bonesetter discovered a subspecies of pain not yet catalogued in his manuscript. Although he had abandoned those pages to the dust-boggarts under his bureau months ago, his fingers itched to speciate and log this new finding. A tunneling throb, he would call it. And even as its silver claws gouged deeper into the sanctum of his inner ear, he gloried in the resuscitation of his manuscript. For the price of two eyes. Why, it was a champion bargain. Practically burglary. Who knew dreams could be paid for from the pockets of the eye sockets?

ࣘ ࣙ

So much time has sifted through the Bonesetter since the lamplight buttered that fermented midnight. Even now he feels time flaking away in flossy nubbins, weakening his ankles and aching under his arthritic knees. He is but a scaffold of brittle bones, soft sift in an hourglass, a bower of bone, calcified home to a parasitic mind which remains supple and strapping, even as the bone-house goes stale and crumbles away.

Under his fingertips, the words rise defiantly, brazen bone-meal calligraphy that calluses his reading fingers. The words are his own, more familiar than his wife's voice, but he prefers to feel them rather than hear their tarnished echo toll through memory's auditorium. He can't stop worrying their edges, scuffing the crossbeam of a T until his finger goes numb. They are the scabs of wounds he can't give up. He won't give them the peace to heal. He chafes them through billowy blue afternoons, as the examination room sombers and dusk flutters down on moth wings. Spine aligned with the earth's poles, he is a statue carved from rarest hematite. He has the secret sheen of an unfathomable well. Dusk-light pools in his eye sockets, empty as eggshells.

The word-scabs rasp under his fingers, and he feels his way back to that night where he lost his eyes and his son to a hunger he once called science. Though Oleander didn't disappear until he had grown into his father's height and daunting posture, he amputated himself from the family on the night the Bonesetter spooned out his own eyes. In those strange days, the boy haunted the house, a specter never pinned by sharp lights. Only the aunts in their cobweb-quilted attic ever saw him sit still. His skin was smoke-blue with bone char and bruises. As skeletal treasures vanished one by one from the Bonesetter's pathological collection, new squallings and squeaks were added to the uncanny symphony singing behind Oleander's bedroom door. A few of his uncreatures, including the gutter-mice and the shrew, must have marched after the Necromancer when he left his father's house, but most were later discovered in the silent bedroom, starved carcasses snuggled into drawers and looped over door handles, waiting for their erstwhile master to wake them once again.

In the house modeled upon the human skull, the Bonesetter has begun another collection. He bottles the rumors that waft through the vents, filing them by theme: mercenary necromancy, corpses kidnapped from crypts, a break-in at the City Archives, a mammoth skeleton gone missing from the paleontology museum, militant gutter-mice, an epidemic of runaway children.

Dusk's last light filigrees the page with silver wire. The Bonesetter cannot see twilight, but he can smell it. He knows he ought to put his masterpiece to bed between its leather covers. Yet still he worries his word-scabs, wondering which wound is more predatory, the gnash of the grapefruit spoon as it chewed through his optic nerve, or the fanged memory of Oleander's last smile as he tossed the spoon to his father, the gleam of his teeth shearing the darkness in two. Angry teeth were the last the Bonesetter ever saw of the boy. After paying the pain-price, he buried himself in bandages and bookwork and when he emerged, the boy was gone. The Thief-of-Thieves lied about the price of publishing. The book cost more than a pair of eyes. It cost him his son.

Tonight, like every night, he will wait all through the owl-hour, hoping to hear the doorbell bawl. He will pay the Thief anything to steal back his son.

THE ATOMIC HALLOWS AND THE BODY OF SCIENCE
Octavia Cade

LISE MEITNER
CO-DISCOVERER OF NUCLEAR FISSION

A spear breaks its blade upon ribs and punctures hearts. It shines with ice-coated needles in the salt air, over breakfast.

"I've had a letter," says Lise to her nephew. He'd come to visit for the holidays so she wouldn't be alone in the cold country of her exile. "I've had a letter and I don't know what to make of it."

She thinks she might be worried.

They walk across a frozen river, across the flood plain and into snowy woods—at least Lise walks, while her nephew glides on skis beside her, under crisp, frosted trees that smell of sap and pine and holiday gifts. Her fingers tingle in the cold, and their tips shine oddly in sunlight.

C8 80

The letter is from Otto Hahn. She slits it open with nails grown sharper than knives.
Lise used to work with him, but is now at the point where she thinks *we were better friends, once.*

Hahn has been working uranium: pelting it with neutrons to split the center, but he doesn't yet understand what it means.

Lise sits with her nephew on a damp and chilly tree trunk sifting snow out of her way, making frantic calculations on odd bits of paper. Together they nut out the process of fission, publish a paper roadmap with directions writ in fear and ice and sunlight, a cold capacity for power.

It is widely read.

CR BO

Lise is visiting Copenhagen when Denmark is invaded. Niels Bohr arrives on an early train: he woke early to hear the news, and together they plan to throw a line across the North Sea, to hurl and hope for the best.

She sends a telegram from Stockholm to friends of Bohr in Britain. It's obscure to some but it's clear that this is not the first spear sent, that there's a black cloud of them hurtling over Europe, and their heads are all familiar.

Her fingernails are spears now as well, hard and pointed. Lise rips them out at the roots, one by one, but they always grow back by the morning, and the floor around her bed is littered with cast-offs.

CR BO

In Berlin her work is being used to try and make a bomb.

This keeps Lise awake at night. There's a wrenching in her chest, like all her breaths are frozen solid in her ribcage, making pale clear statues of her questions.
Hahn is working in Germany—not on the bomb, they're of one mind on that, but he's working still. Hahn, who once helped her escape the Nazis.

She wonders what would have happened if he'd made a different choice: turned away, sent her somewhere other than north.

(There were some she worked with who would have done it, when the memory of the times they spent together faded into ashes, fit only for fuelling that which would melt any ice and burn the trees to black shadows... She wonders if some fondness would remain for her, enough for those former familiars to spare her the camps and run her through themselves.)

Her nights are cold and sleepless; she's speared upon the empty hours, and can't close her fists without blood loss.

CR BO

267

Lise knows about war. It's camps and commandants and compromises, the long slow defeat of the self.

It's escape and humiliation and death. It's exile in a colder country, it's someplace without a home, always remembering the time when she had one—a home built of atoms and equations and friends when all of them were free from shame and her hands were clean enough under natural light.

Now even cleanliness is gone, and no matter how she scours herself in snow and ice, the thin sheen of guilt still stains her palms. The nails are now too strong to pull out; she covers them up with polish to hide the shame, but the gray steel bleeds through anyway.

"I will have nothing to do with a bomb," she says, even though she is wanted in the waste land, and war is not being wanted, not anywhere.

CB 80

Lise is in a small hotel in Leksand, central Sweden. She finds the woods a respite from her work, from pain and prejudice and the sure, shuddering horror of what is to come.

When it happens, when Hiroshima is covered in clouds and silence and tiny spearheads all singed round the edges, a journalist calls for her reaction.

This is how she first hears of it.

(The hotel mirror is like ice, and when she looks in it all her ribs are broken.)

She puts the phone down, gently—with still-stained palms and hands that have never forgotten what the haft felt like before she passed it on—and leaves the hotel, leaves to walk alone for five hours in the snowless country before she can face another person; before she can face herself.

Her fingernails are spears, and too heavy for her hands.

CB 80

ROBERT OPPENHEIMER
SCIENTIFIC HEAD OF THE MANHATTAN PROJECT

A waste land is a draw card and a trapdoor.

It has rock paintings and petroglyphs and pueblos—beam holes and old ladders that bring the scientists in and make them tourists, make them gawp and gape like schoolboys.
Robert shows them around—he came to New Mexico before all of them, chose the site specially. He feels at home there, feels that it fits him; he walks the cliff dwellings bloody-legged and limping, leaves his pattern in the rocks, feels those rocks imprint in him. The markings grow stronger, deeper, the more time he spends on the mesa. There are glyphs on the back of his neck, paintings in the hollows behind his knees, and dust sifts from the holes that appear in his chest, in the bony protrusions of hips.

He feels the land in his flesh, and builds a castle of his own for questions.

ᘓ ᘔ

The land around is made of tuff, of lava lumps and welded rock, of ignimbrite and mesas, a base of black basalt, all eroded into canyons and steep slopes and tracks worn into hill sides.

(When he lays his hands against the rock, he can't tell which is flesh and which is stone.)

The ground can be treacherous and stony-slippery, and one false step can mean separation from friends, security breaches and revocations, falling from a great height and breaking his knees on the ground.

(Like comes to like, in the end.)

ᘓ ᘔ

The gypsum sands are cool to the touch, and the dunes run like clouds beneath him. Robert feels the crystal granules erode into his shoes; they slough from his feet when he's busy with calculations and construction and consequences. There's squeaking in his socks...the grinding of a thousand tiny spearheads blunted down by bone and friction.

It's as if the cloud has broken down beneath him, then been built up again from fragments into a cutting edge with a blade as fine as fire.

CR BO

The desert seeds are made of knowledge. They are bitter. Hard-won, and unhappy.

Robert wouldn't dig them up—not for anything, not even when they leach the earth and make it difficult for other things to grow (he's lost friendships, and trust, and some likings will never come again: They cannot tolerate the ground he's sown with salt and slaughter and dead suns).

He'd still never dig them up, those seeds that are sad and glorious and grind sand into glass. They're part of him, and he can no more unearth them than he could trowel up his heart.

CR BO

Los Alamos is a high country, one surrounded by mountains, and the air, for those not used to it, is thinner and sharper than blood.

Robert is used to blood.

He sees it on the mountains, the Sangre de Cristo, where it shines in the east every evening – scarlet and blue-black and purple. The rocks are thick with it, and burning.

It's on his leg, and his hands, and when it seeps past the bandages and into the soil he can't tell where he leaves off and the land begins.

CR BO

In the worst of it, the white dunes, the hard alkali of soil, there are plants that survive the sands. Stems lengthen above the shifting surface, keep their leaves in sunlight; are quick and bright and blooming.

Robert is no gardener, not really, but there's iron all

through him like the sympathy of sap, and what he builds in the waste land is beyond piñon and desert gypsum flowers.

଴ ଷ

CHARLOTTE SERBER
HEAD OF THE TECHNICAL LIBRARY OF THE MANHATTAN PROJECT

A sword is forged with paper and silence.

It doesn't look sharp, but a single page can slice into soft bodies as well as any steel—and more, it can tell other people how to slice into them as well.

One must be careful with paper. It can be stamped down, pressed into a mold and sharpened round the edges, but even holding by the handle it's still not safe. Someone can always take it away for themselves unless it's shut up tight in an armory, with shelves and safes and stillness.

Charlotte handles it gingerly. Part of her care is paper cuts and poison edges, but she's most concerned with precision and reproduction. These documents are the basis of their efforts, marking signposts and dead ends, and they can't be relied upon if the metal type forging through her fingertips impresses on paper and distorts the message.

଴ ଷ

Books come from Berkeley and Oak Ridge and Chicago, packed in black suitcases and sent with a special courier to keep them unopened and out of the hands of children with their too-soft flesh that's too easily cut.

Charlotte has communication embedded in her flesh, her fingertips crowned like typebars with little metal letters, but these keys aren't always sufficient and she has to use others. The metals catch as they move together.

When unwrapped, the swords go to shelves where they're crammed between blades made of journal paper, of yellowed leaves, of reports and endless snarky queries for detective stories... or to a vaulted reading room with locks, or to a safe so old and hardened that its three tumblers have succumbed to inertia and Charlotte has to kick at the crucial point of opening or it will shut up tighter than suitcases.

 Cઈ ൠ

The blacksmiths are members of the Women's Army Corps, or are married to the scientists. They wear blue jeans, or Lane Bryant's latest (black rayon with little white buttons on the pockets and a matching stripe down the front), bras of armored cones with a sweater stretched over top like chain mail, or olive uniforms with gold insignia on the lapels (Pallas Athene, for strategy and skill and making just war).

Their hammer strikes are the keys and levers and springs of type, the clank and carriage of return strokes – every day there are reports, and every day the armory copies and collates, distributes new arms.

(Not everyone can hack it. There's one, a journeywoman by trade, who sees a tottering tepee of chemical documents to be classified by heft and height and weight and runs away to drive a truck. Charlotte sees her later, in a corner of the mess, with a file and a determined expression, sanding down.)

Cઈ ൠ

Some papers are left out overnight, left to rust and damage and the red oxidation of exposure, by chemists and physical forgers gone home for the night. There are fines for this, and extra duties looking for the lapses of other—their discards left as prey for theft and sabotage. ("I don't deserve a fine," says one bitter culprit. "That report's all rubbish anyway. If only it *were* stolen...")

There's no process for disposal, no ceremonial burning. It's a discretionary thing, and discretion is weather-based. It's unpleasant to stand in the waste land amongst the labs and the green army huts and burn in the blistering cold, the blasting heat. (They're more conscious of security on cool evenings when there's not a lot of wind and the incinerators are warm-hearted.)

When she holds her hands out to the fire, the letters on her fingertips heat and glow. She feels them all the way down to her bones then, the molten marrow. Others might try and take the type away but Charlotte is not one for looking askance at print, so she picks each letter out, carefully, with red nail polish; skimps on her nails so that there's enough for alphabets.

CB ED

Charlotte is sent to Santa Fe with Robert's secretary, Priscilla. They go to misdirect the locals: "Make them think we're designing electric rockets."

They take their husbands, make a night of it, find bars and hotels that are perfect for subterfuge—with drinks and drunks and dancing, and many levelled roofs ripe with shadows.
Type sinks in and out of her fingers, adjusting to audience. She's manipulated it before – the letters float almost like her kneecaps do when she's relaxed and can push them around with her thumbs. She's only got ten fingers, after all, and there are more letters than that.

She's used up the last of the nail polish on them. This is not a time for subtlety.

"Take my sword," says Charlotte. "It's electric." But the man she's dancing with talks of nothing but horses, compliments her moves like she's a mare on the trot—he has no interest in false information, even when she dips her fingers in sauce and stains his collar with symbols. No-one has any interest—not even the rancher her husband traps by the lapels as he flat-out lies to his face.

The information they give is blunt and unwieldy; it must be smuggled back to Los Alamos, and melted down amidst the stacks.

CB ED

Charlotte's days are spent with letters – even more than when she was a child with fat fingers, learning the alphabet.

A receipt from the library at Berkeley shows that more than twenty percent of books that come to the waste land are not in the English language. More come from Strategic Services, who seize copyrights from warring Europe, reproduce their journals, smuggle out the flat blades from field agents in Scandinavia or North Africa or France.

Her days are spent with letters, and for many years Charlotte will sharpen her swords with her fingers first, with spelling before speech. "That's P, H, Y, S," she says, enunciating, and tapping each fingertip in turn. "That's *Physikalische Zeitschrift.*"

ଓ ଚ

NIELS BOHR
DANISH PHYSICIST, SCIENTIST AT THE MANHATTAN PROJECT

A question is a wave and a lonely particle.

It is complementary, existing in parallel with an answer. More, Niels has *der Kopenhagener Geist,* the spirit of inquiry, and all its questions are the chorus *What will come from this?*

He sees two answers to be taken from a box with uranium ribbon. The first is war and all destruction (brief suns that storm the beaches and boil the water sterile); the other an unbroken age of peace (a single sun reflected in a calm pool, and all its images put quietly away). Both have their birth in the bomb.

ଓ ଚ

In 1939 he walks like a man carrying something too heavy for him, too heavy to be answered. He sees the coming war, and he sees the German bomb. It weighs him down, makes him mumble-footed, and he places each foot carefully, as if stepping into a future full of green-fused sand and spears.

Later, in the waste land, the storm is bearing down and he

feels himself the only one who notices, the only one who sees a time when everyone is cloud-handed; when what they're building will birth a different world where all politics are resolved with suns.

What will you do? says the *Geist*. *What will you do?*

℃ ℬ

Niels had helped Lise Meitner escape from Germany, never thinking he was to be her mirror. A German woman, sympathetic, slips him news that the Gestapo are coming for him. He will soon be arrested and put to the question.

But there is a fishing boat, and then a trawler. There is resistance and taxis and a twin-engine bomber that leaves him light-headed and dreaming a different life. There are liners and trains and false names: *Baker*, as if he is bringing bread instead of the hope of ending ovens.

His presence calms the younger scientists and they come to him with questions: *Are we doing the right thing?* they ask.

Look at what I left behind, he says. *Look at what is coming.*

It keeps him from looking at himself, at the *Geist*. He sees his edges fraying, his flesh becoming translucent.

℃ ℬ

Niels misses his family. He misses his home—the sober streets of Copenhagen, the water and the wide horizon. He misses the connections, and how solid they made him feel.

In the waste land, he wanders the mountains, scrambles through canyons and piñon trees and the red dirt, and talks. Always he talks, though it's low and muttered and half to himself. People have to huddle close to hear, and he likes it; likes the feel of crowds and company, being close enough to feel their breath.

(It helps him forget that his wife isn't with him.)

But at night he lies in a cold bed, his conscience square before him like a block and he doesn't know how he should place his head on it. No one is there to tell him.

C3 80

Comfort is for children. Niels left it behind long ago. He does not want it back. Comfort comes with warmth, and that is something that's foreign to his bones now. All a *Geist* feels is chill.

He does not believe that everything will be all right, that everything can be made up for. Even necessities have a cost—and one that can't be paid with rosy cheeks and unlined skin and the blind unstinting certainty that everyone is good.

As a child he thought science was for children. It was exciting, the world spread out before him to explore, to be dissected and delighted in and imagined by him. There was no question he couldn't ask, and then he learned what questions could do, and the innocence was over.

"I tried to be a comfort," said Robert. "I was not."

It is hard to comfort a spirit.

C3 80

The right words would heal the waste land, mend his friend's spear-splintered thigh, stop him from slopping in blood—and if Niels knew the question he would turn away and never, ever ask it.

The waste land represents a hope and danger both, he says, and he cannot fathom one without the other.

A *Geist* is meant to linger, and so he does.

He thinks of Lise, who lives as far from the desert as she can; who will not compromise herself and finds her faith in that. He thinks of Edward, who would turn the waste land into charcoal if he could, and grind it down to dust when he was done. He cannot make himself into either, but sometimes...

Sometimes there's a shadow on his leg.

C3 80

276

DOROTHY MCKIBBIN
MANHATTAN PROJECT OFFICE MANAGER, SANTA FE

A platter is wafers and consolation and service.

"What am I to do here?" she asks. She had agreed to take the job before she knew what it was – had met Robert briefly, and that was enough for her, enough for them both. Trust sprang up unstinting.

She thought he felt the land as she did—that his limp and her widow grief could come to the waste land and be useful, be comforted by the creation of something new, something that bore the mark of canyons and bare rock and a sun so bright it could kill them if they let it, bleach the last life from their bones.

Her job, as it turns out, is to never question, to never repeat a name but to bring people together regardless as if they were strangers sitting down to a meal.

"If you want me to get them all broken in and breaking bread, you'll have to give me a free hand with the baking," she says. A platter doesn't fill itself, and if she is to tie the coming pilgrims to Robert then she needs to work his flesh with her own. All those dust trails he leaves behind him... the powdery flesh, the little bloody trails.

Land has a dark taste, and a bitter one, but it binds together. Dorothy's tongue grows, is covered over by little armored plates, armadillo-like. They're sensitive to flavor, and far more silkily flexible than meat.

Cß ßO

Dorothy sits at a desk behind the door at 109 East Palace Avenue: There's a heavy wood lintel set into stone, thick calcimined walls to keep out the sun and hollyhocks in the courtyard.

She's the stop before the Hill, the guardian of the waste land and the gate-keeper of Los Alamos. She welcomes them with plates of crispbreads, of little thin crackers the color of tuff and skin cells, of petroglyphs and atom shadows. "It's been a

277

long trip for you, I'm sure," she says. "Get that down you, you'll feel better for it."

Her newly armored tongue can sense their saliva, can taste it on the air. They're greedy for the bread and when their mouths water, Dorothy's waters with them, because hunger is contagious and armor can only do so much.

All the scientists come through her, and the WACs and the women, and nearly all of them think Santa Fe is their destination, want directions and dance halls and a shoulder to lean on. They're all very tired, and nearly all very young, and she thinks some of them need a mother very badly.

"Ask me if you need anything," she says. "I'm here to keep track of you."

(She tastes them in the wind, every one, long before they get to her office.)

☙ ❧

In the high country of the waste land, Dorothy has a name: She is called the Oracle, the one who knows and tells and shares, in an environment where sharing has become a strictly limited thing. *Consult the Oracle*, they say on the Hill, and her disembodied voice through the crackling lines is a consolation.

She can find for the children camps and kittens; find a doctor who will perform abortions; find sewing kits and pack horses and hotel reservations that serve something other than commissary food. A good cook herself, often up to her armpits in dough, mud and blood under her fingernails because spears may be sent up from the earth but a platter contains the fruits therein, in whatever shape Dorothy can find them.

The women of the waste land find her counselor and confidante, and take her advice in all things, use her house for their weddings and try to make a home as she has done. It's her tongue they find most helpful.

"You've got to learn to make do," says Dorothy. Secrecy and silence together have forced her tongue into other roles.

278

Dorothy is invited, with two couples, to take an evening meal at Albuquerque, on Sandia Peak—the giant red rock that shines at night with colors like the bloody mountains.
She takes bread to break with them—the last supper before the test—her picnic basket a paten; takes blankets and a mackintosh, for the sky is black with clouds and cunning.

At 5:30 a.m., a light from the sands flashes towards them, a spear from the waste land stabbed out and shining. The leaves are transubstantiated and the trees turned to brief gold about her – lovely and gleaming in the sterile sunlight.

"I'd never have thought that light had a taste," she says. That taste is lemony, with undertones of burning. When she stands in the early morning with her armadillo tongue stuck out straight as if wavelengths carry snow instead of the shadow of ashes, all the little plates are slickening.

Cℨ ℬ𝒪

For all the time Dorothy spends ferrying food up to the Hill (pumpernickel bread and picnic baskets, Christmas geese and warm rolls with butter) her favorite meals are with Robert, and they are nearly always the same: oven-baked potatoes, near-lethal martinis, shoots of green asparagus and Robert on the patio broiling beef, fork in hand and standing back from spits.

"Why didn't you make a fight of it?" she says, of the trial. "Why didn't you ask me for help?"

She would have kept talking 'til they threw her out, she says, and the plates hit the table with a thump, as if carrying heads other than their own.

Betrayal, it seems, also tastes of lemon and ashes. No wonder she couldn't tell it apart... Dorothy wants to take her steak knife and scrape the little armadillo plates from her tongue, leave it red raw and screaming, because what use is armor if it can't protect someone she loves?

Cℨ ℬ𝒪

Dorothy has travelled all over the waste land. She has been to the Valles Caldera, the springed and smoking domes in the mountains, knows what it's like to seethe below the surface.

It's in this land that she finds affinity—for Robert and for silence both. She bubbles while he bleeds; it's a hard thing to be silent, when you don't want to be. She doesn't always manage it, would spit lava if she could, superheated (and does). And her words burn going out, as much as they burned the recipient, but the armor-plating is spreading through Dorothy's mouth, her cheeks and esophagus and gums, and she knows the words that burn because they taste like light in the waste land, like seared sand and her little cracker breads together.

 C3 80

EDWARD TELLER
HUNGARIAN PHYSICIST, MANHATTAN PROJECT SCIENTIST
AND SUBSEQUENT FATHER OF THE HYDROGEN BOMB

What is a dandelion? says Dorothy, of Edward. It's something coarse and in need of kicking up, before presence turns to supplantation. A weed. A curse.

("If it is a question of wisdom and judgement.... one would be wiser not to grant clearance," says Edward, on Robert and security, and will forever wonder if people will think it was jealousy speaking.)

A dandelion's not like an orchid, not delicately designed, sweet-smelling and subtle, with petals like a pork pie hat.

("I'm sorry," he says, and Robert is left gray and grave in a room grown untrusting, and too dark for him.)

They've a sour taste, dandelions. Edward coughs one up in the middle of the night, bright and gleaming with saliva, with stomach acid, and marvels at how familiar it feels on his tongue.

C3 80

No-one has ever told Edward *don't mess where you work, don't drink a diuretic tea of dandelions even if the pretty color makes you think it's a good idea, it isn't,* so he comes back to Los Alamos, after the trial and finds, all unexpected, the cafeteria a Coventry.

The other scientists shun him, turn their backs. They refuse to shake his hand. Rabi is the first, and particularly cutting. He gives Edward nightmares of a great black bird, of a raven that struts over him while he sleeps, snappish and sneering, a dreadful beaked bird's smile of cold iron ready to pick out his eyes.

He wakes on cold early mornings and his mouth is clogged with petals, stuffed with them, and he's asphyxiating on bitterness, his heart beating out of his chest with choking breath and the shadow of wings.

ଓ ℅

Edward is always noticed. When he and his wife Mici first climbed the crawling knife-road to the mesa, they shipped with them a baby grand called *Monster.* Edward plays sonatas late into the night and though his infant son sleeps through them, the neighbors do not.

He is heard in the theoretical lab as well, where he's famous for fluttering, electron-like, from one unfinished atom project to another. He considers himself a bricklayer, an architect and dreamer; has no patience with brick-*making* physics. The plodding brute force of it strikes him as shambling and cold.

But no matter how loud, he never stands out as much as he does after the trial. Saints have flowers come up under them when they walk, but he knows of no saint who leaves dandelions in their footsteps.

Dandelions are too bitter for sainthood.

ଓ ℅

A dandelion is not an orchid, but they are small and hardy and Edward feels a kinship. Not such a bad thing, to be a dandelion.

And they are bright, bright like little suns, like playing Liszt and Bach and Mozart—and the lights in happy memories of Budapest, before the ravens came to pluck them out with ruined petals and *love me nots*.

Edward gathers the flowers he's brought up out of himself and makes bouquets of them. He sets them on his piano and plays and thinks of new worlds, and old ones.

"Fuck you," he says.

Cʒ ℬↄ

"A danger to all that's important," says the raven, perched out of reach of damp sheets as Edward dreams in a red sweat, covers his eyes in dreams. "It would have been a better world without him."

It is hard to be seen as noxious. Edward vacillates between remorse (he confesses himself to Fermi when the latter is on his death bed, and gentle in his condemnation) and raving defiance, the bitter grief of a man who has left all behind, his home an ocean away, and is now without friends. ("Daddy's got black beetles in his brain," says his daughter.) Beetles and birds and words that can't be taken back, the half-sweet scent of flowers. The only way to drown them out is with another bird, and bigger – he'll fly with the hawks for the rest of his days, make second-best friends amongst them.

(Perhaps they'll like small yellow flowers too.)

(Even tolerance he would accept.)

Cʒ ℬↄ

The hydrogen bomb is to be his redemption. But when it's built, there's no new waste land, no desert community tied to him with chains of unbreakable orchids, fragile and delicate and stronger than atoms.

282

(He wonders what he's done wrong in his success.)

So he takes his bomb, the new monster of his mirror dreams and breaks open his thigh with it, cracks bone, rips flesh: tries to make himself a Fisher King reborn, capture character with black blood. It's the new dolorous stroke.

But the wound heals without much fuss at all, though dandelions burst from the scars and his once-torn flesh smells of them forever.

ᚻ ᚹ

KITTY OPPENHEIMER
BOTANIST, AND WIFE OF ROBERT OPPENHEIMER

A grail is green fertility and the blood of others.

December, 1944: Kitty gives birth to a daughter. She's not the only one – by this time over one hundred people work at the hospital, and Los Alamos is baby-mad. Army disgust sparks a popular poem: "The general's in a stew, he trusted you and you..." but the average age there is twenty five, so what does he expect? A scientist is not a sterile thing.

Toni is born despite disapproval, born in midwinter, a Christmas child, and Kitty sits with her window looking outwards to the snow, drinks in the baby scent. It's almost too much, too powdered sugar-sweet, and soon she'll be sick of it.

"Do you want to adopt her?" Robert will say to another couple, as if the grail had nothing to do with him. As if the bits and chunks that fall into the infant blanket—the fused sand and seared flesh and ignimbrite—have nothing to do with him, and are something to be kept separate instead of evidence of the rocky bloodline that runs through them both.

Kitty wants to slap him.

ᚻ ᚹ

Science is too busy for visiting hours, so husbands stand on packing boxes outside the hospital windows and peer into maternity, peer through the glass like they're staring at a country made foreign to them, at a new and strange creation, cupped with blood and blankets (and Lord, how it squalls).

Compare to the glass after Trinity, the emerald blasted glass that lurked hot and bubbling in the crater; the blinding light of boom and blast dropping trinkets in the sand.

("Look at it! Look what we made!")

A spear to be thrown into the future, a weapon for her daughter's days, the blade hard and sharp as nails.

Kitty sees both glasses, sees well enough to measure the drams of her husband's interest, and how ill-matched it is. She wishes she could care for one so much more than the other, as he does, but one of them speaks so much more of winter to her that love is impossible.

ɔȝ ৪০

Kitty's parties are famous, with bottles and cocktails and the five-foot punch bowl – a giant jar for chemical reagents, stolen from the lab and weighted down with ice cubes.

There's no reason not to drink. Kitty knows she is difficult to like. She is called a bitch, but an *elegant* bitch—with a bathtub and a kiva stove and oak floors, so that's something, marooned on that bloody rock as she is with dust and dreary dirt, the hideous stoves that never light, the constant bitching about housework. She's a botanist, for God's sake, or was, so what is she doing now organizing contracts for the home help in a place where the grass is drowned in mud and sun?

It's no wonder she drinks. The alcohol is an armor to her, plating over her tongue and numbing her lips, and when she drinks enough even the armor is stunned, and she can taste nothing around her, see nothing around her, and even the baby-scent is drowned in it.

ɔȝ ৪০

Flesh of her flesh, bone of her bone: that's marriage—bound by straining sinews, by faith and fidelity and resentment.

Tiresome sometimes, but familiar.

Kitty leaves the waste land with her husband. Leaves it for the gray land, the courts and charges and tape that would be red if it hadn't been bleached into pale lines and quicksand. One look at their faces and she knows it's rigged: She may be sick of scientists, but few in the waste land wear such surety in their colorless eyes, wear certainty like a pin-striped suit. (They're less cunning at home, if red-eyed and bloodshot from vodka and insomnia.)

"Kitty was such a support," he says afterwards, after the gray men cut him to pieces and she held him up regardless.

His shirts smell of dandelions and heartbreak, as if he'd been rolled in them before betrayal.

ය ∞

A cauldron can restore the dead to life, or so they say— but sometimes... Sometimes it's a saucepan—something utilitarian, and used to make soup.

Kitty is with her husband in the Virgin Islands, where he is recovering from hearings about his loyalty. (She sympathizes, but underneath, where she'd never admit it, his mistresses are raising their glasses to her. Well, let them. She's outlasted them all, sex and state and science.)

A turtle is caught, a leather-beaked monster that sees better in water than out of it and tastes best of all in soup—but Robert pleads for clemency; pleads with a slow turtle-vision of his own to lift it from the pot and into life. It's as if he sees himself in everything now, contaminating: all the information of his life's work welling up under his fingertips and dropping into the simmering broth, an alphabet soup of suns and slaughter.

"All the little creatures," he says. "I saw them in New Mexico after the test. Please," he says, "I can't bear it."

Try drink, thinks Kitty, *and you'll be able to swallow anything then, darling.*

ය ∞

Toni is in her crib, asleep, when her father waits miles away, at White Sands, and yet the sun that sears his eyelids imprints onto hers.

She spends the rest of her life looking for it, looking and not finding, the image and the resurrection of her parents.

("Look at it! Look what we made!" they said.)

She follows the sun to the Caribbean but it's not bright enough, no, not nearly, to blind her as well as her father was blinded, and she's left seeing all too well the land that she was born in and the blood that she shares with it.

("Look Mom," she says, looking back, "Look Dad, look what I can do." She's talking to dead people, their bodies crumbled to dust and leaving her behind, with her flesh that bubbles with type and tuff and the memory of treachery, with questions under her fingernails and the remembered taste of a consolation that's never quite enough.)

She hangs herself with rope that smells of dry dust of old dirt and waste lands – for a grail might be life and love and blood, but that blood comes from spear wounds and salt and knowledge that is never, ever lost.

Raise-the-Dead Cobbler

Andrea Corbin

The air was muggy, a heatwave burning through the spring, on the night that we met to conjure two people out of almost nothing at all. None of us could've done it without the others, and none of us would've dared, except Mason said please and I said maybe and Jun said we could, and so we did. You need a few materials first, then follow a sort of recipe. Call it Raise-the-Dead Cobbler.

INGREDIENTS

- Three tired so-called witches, of flesh, of time, of dreams.
- Bone fragments, stolen reverently.
- A lock of hair, kept for years and years.
- An old book, passed down from mother to son to daughter to niece, and so on.
- A dark night, with a new moon, and as many clouds as feels right.
- A secluded room, in a lakeside cabin far from the city's bustle and traffic's roar, where owls hoot plaintively and a cool wind rustles the leaves. (A cramped attic in an apartment on the edge of the city, with shouty neighbors, will work in a pinch.)
- Flint, not matches.
- A stone bowl, low and wide.
- Dry kindling.
- Floor space, as much as you expect you'll need. You know who you're looking for. You can measure, move furniture, sweep, mark out the space. Lay out a pillow, in anticipation. The floor is hard, after all.

INSTRUCTIONS

1. "Is your roommate home?" Mason asks, braiding his hair back, lightning fast. It gets warm in the attic. Mason wears

287

none of his usual jewelry, only a locket on a thin chain, which dangles outside of his shirt. You say no, of course not. Your roommate is out of town for the next six days. That's why this is the perfect new moon, even though Jun has a deadline at work tomorrow and shouldn't be pulling an all-nighter.

2. In a flurry of motion, Jun arrives, drops her bag on the floor and her iced coffee on the table, then says, "I can't do anything in this skirt" as she kicks her heels off. She shimmies out of the skirt and changes into red leggings, pulled from her bag. "Do you really have it?" she asks, pulling pins out of her hair and letting it fall loose. You steal a long drink of her coffee.

3. On the way up to the attic, you worry. Mason worries. What will they think of you? Will they be happy to wake up? Will they be scared? What if they hate you? How long will it last? Jun said it would last, but what if they decide to leave you? After all you did? Would that be okay? When they wake up in the dark room surrounded by three witches, if they scream, will you be able to comfort them, or make it worse? Will it work? Will they come back wrong? Different? Can you really do this? Should you? God, what if everything does work, and they want to stay, and be with you? What then? Can they get a job? Should they? How will you support them if they can't? Shit, is this a terrible idea? Is it selfish? What if coming back gives them health problems? What if they had health problems before that you didn't know about, and coming back is nothing but suffering? Will they hate you? Will they love you? Will you love them?

4. Jun strikes the flint and lights the fire.

5. Chant words after Jun, with Jun, words that can't be spelled or written down, and yet she reads them from a book in her lap. Her book is filled with drawings and paintings, and you can never find the same one twice. Once you saw a page and read the drawing; there was a burst of light, and a small creature appeared, like an oviraptor, feathered and colorful but the size of a hummingbird. That was the day Jun said it looked like you were a witch of time. You're still learning what that means. The oviraptor is named Magda and lives on your porch for most of the year. You take her for walks. You should take her for more walks. No one would notice.

6. The shards of bone rattle. The lock of hair dances in no wind. You close your eyes.

7. Nothing changes, except the room feels smaller. You haven't opened your eyes. Your eyes are closed, and the attic room has shrunk, and if you reach out you don't know what you might touch.

8. Open your eyes.

9. To your left is Jun, then Mason. They open their eyes too, breathing timidly. You've been holding hands for a while, grip tight, tight on Jun's stiff prosthetic. Next to Mason, in the space laid out on his side of the attic, is—

10. There is someone to your right.

03 80

Once I explain what happened, he decides to go by Joseph. Why? Well, it *is* his name. No, but why? Because this isn't his life, now is it? It's something different. He's something different.

Because of his movies, I've always thought of him in a particular way, kinetic and silent. He rubs the back of his head, an overwhelmed look of concern furrowing his brow. But I can't read his face. The problem is he puts on that face so easily, so often on film, that I don't know if it's just a face or how he really feels. Sweat drips down my back, makes my shirt cling. He sits very still.

"Why is this happening?" he asks, voice so much deeper than I always imagine.

"I—" don't have a good answer.

"What are you?" Joseph asks, and again I stutter and don't answer. In my head I hear all the times Jun told me *you're a witch, you jag,* but I can't say it.

We all go downstairs because the attic room is boiling; Joseph trails after me, and I trail after Jun. Behind Joseph is Mason and his mom. Angela, I think.

"Well, that's that." Jun picks up her discarded skirt.

"You're leaving?" I ask.

"Do you need me to stay?"

"Yes!" Mason sounds desperate. He's not quite looking at his mom ever. Eyes skidding around the edges.

Jun takes a long swig of her watered-down iced coffee. "'Kay."

"So this is the year 2016?" Joseph asks. That was part of what I told him upstairs. It was real, it was his far, far future, and it was okay. He took it in stride. Now he looks around the kitchen, which is a mess. I should've cleaned up. Why didn't I clean up? It's fine. Why would he care? But I care. I care that the first thing he sees are my dirty dishes and moldy fruit, the mail covering the counter, and the oh my god, the bra hanging over the back of the chair.

I slide in front of it.

Angela pulls out a chair and sits down, pressing her hands flat on the table.

Mason hovers. "It's okay. It's me. I'm your—I'm your kid. You have a kid and that's me."

"You said that," Angela says slowly. "I don't get what's happening."

Mason looks helplessly at Jun, who exhales through her nose before speaking. "You know photocopies? We found a moment and made a photocopy of you, then brought that you to our present. Call it magic, call it time travel, call it a great big lie and a weird dream you're having. I don't care. It's happening. Mason is your kid. Congratulations."

Angela is quiet a long time, staring at Mason. It's got to be a lot to take in, skipping twenty-odd years of society and tech and life and then *bam*, your grown-up kid, Mason, not much younger than Angela is probably, Mason with his long black braid, big worried eyes lined with black, tattoos crawling over his bony shoulders and under his shirt. Mid-nineties life versus grown-up Mason now must be battling it out in Angela's brain, but during the silence I realize we pulled Angela from before she got pregnant. Maybe before she met Mason's dad. And Angela's working out what all that means.

"Okay," she says, shaky. "Well, don't tell me how I died, and I think we'll be okay."

Pretty soon, Jun drives Mason and Angela away, leaving Mason's car on my street where I promise to make sure it isn't towed.

I make coffee. Start tidying, washing dishes. Joseph wanders my rooms, looking at the shared mess my roommate and I live in, coming back to check my progress. Hands clasped behind his back, leaning forward to inspect a poster or a bookshelf. Always with that stone face.

A plate slips from my hands, hits the counter, crashes onto the floor. "Shit!"

Joseph pops his head into the room, eyebrows raised in question.

"It's fine. Plastic." I pick up the plate and spin it in my hands. "I don't have to do this right now. I should've done it earlier. I could leave it. It's not important. Are you hungry? I don't think, it's not—" When words start crashing and failing before they reach my mouth, I turn back to the dishes.

"Isabel. Are we related?"

"No."

Joseph paws through some of my mail. Pages through an Anthropologie catalog. He looks at me, barely moving his eyebrows. "The other one brought his mother."

When I squirt soap onto the sponge a little too forcefully without a word, he goes back to the catalog. Even with the astringent lemon suds, Joseph's close enough that I can practically smell the years on him, this weird ozone scent of a hundred years. It's soaked into his clothes, permeating his skin, this invisible sense of time.

Fuck the dishes. That ozone smell is making me dizzy. There are clean mugs. That's enough. I sort out my coffee, then gesture weakly at the milk and sugar for Joseph to figure out.

The living room is more like a nest and less a rat's nest, and comes pre-loaded with snacks I forgot to put away, so by the time Joseph joins me I'm gnawing on a hard gingersnap. He sits on the other end of the couch.

"We're not related," I say.

Joseph gives me a look, one eyebrow barely raised, eyes glancing down and back up, and I laugh, this nervous snuffle into my cookie—and *he laughs too*. It's kind of stunning. This side of him almost no one gets to see. Except me, I'm seeing it.

"Then why?" Joseph asks.

"It's hard to explain. We can undo it."

He digs into the box for a cookie, dips it in his coffee. "Why?"

"If you don't want to be here. It was maybe stupid of me. Selfish. Or hubris. I don't know. I'm a little, you know, it was a rough spell." My chest is tight, and I'm starving but can't imagine doing any more than reach for another cookie, and there are little sparks of a spell migraine flecking in my vision, so I can't really, I can't think of what to say to explain myself.

"We'll see how it goes, I guess. So far you have good coffee and bad cookies, and other than that I don't know."

"You hungry?" I ask again, though I'm not completely sure I get the words out.

At some point I take a long blink and when I open my eyes, Joseph's setting my coffee down on the table next to the cookies. He says my name once, I think, quietly, "Isabel," hand on my shoulder.

03 80

"What is this?"

I wake up on the couch and not on my bed, as happens way more often than it should. I'm an adult. Why can't I make it to my bed?

"What *is* this?"

My eyes won't open until I rub them hard with my fingers, and my mouth tastes like trash and my phone is being thrust in my face while my shoulder is shaken. I had a plan for this. I should've planned for the spell migraine to take me out, but I didn't, and now my plan to introduce Joseph to the modern world is ruined because he's already poking around while I was dead to the world.

"It's my phone," I say, and as the words come out I can't bear the taste in my mouth. After I brush my teeth and wash my face, I join him back on the couch. Joseph presses the button on my phone, screen going bright and dark. Like this is all perfectly normal. Magda, my oviraptor, is sitting on his head.

"This is a phone?"

"Gimme," I say, and unlock it. Magda chirps. Without looking, Joseph puts a hand up for her to jump on, and I wait for the inevitable question—

"How's it work?"

Not the inevitable question. I shrug. My coffee is stone cold but it's right there and caffeinated, so I gulp it and make a face of pure regret.

I was going to show him how the phone works, but there are messages from Mason and Jun, not to mention family and one of my few non-witch friends and some guy I've been meaning to ghost.

Mason: *I can't believe this is happening*
Jun: *Congrats. Mother's day is in two weeks*

While reheating my coffee I ignore the rest of my messages. Joseph sets Magda on the table, where she nests in a pile of mail.

"About a hundred years to catch up on." I yawn.

With Joseph around, time tumbles past so quickly I almost forget the sensation of it, until a moment catches against my skin, lingers like an echo.

ෆ ෨

In the park, Joseph listens to me explain things poorly, strides over a bench because it's in his path, steals my phone out of my hands. He unlocks it, swipes the screen. Walks backwards in front of me.

293

"This," Joseph says, pointing my phone at me, his eyes on the screen, "takes pictures?"

"And videos. Movies."

He turns it around and around in his hand. "This?"

"People shoot whole feature films on it."

He laughs like a kid at Christmas, pure delight spread across his features.

☙ ❧

Another day my ancient laptop is spread out in pieces on the coffee table, and Joseph prods at the soldered base. I tell him a probably inaccurate version of how it works, then tell him to look it up on the internet if he's interested. "But don't take apart anything else, please."

He pieces the laptop back together and turns it on. "How do I look up the internet?"

☙ ❧

When I tell him how easy it is to watch movies, Joseph gets a wild look in his eyes. "On the computer?" he says, and "Well, it's a disappointing screen to watch on, but—" and he finds a list from the AFI, then says with determined joy in his eyes that he's going to work his way through the whole thing. While he studies the list, I catch up on more texts.

> Mason*: I don't know what to do! She's like our age.*
> Jun*: What did you expect?*
> Mason*: IDK!!! I just wanted to meet her*
> Mason*: She's nice though*
> Mason*: Funny too she's funny like my aunt*
> Jun*: aunt like your mom's sister*
> Mason*: ...yes*
> Jun*: what a SURPRISE Mason*
> Jun*: Well just be a person and stop expecting a mom and let me know if anything weird happens*
> Mason*: Weird??*

Mason: *Is sleeping alot weird*
Me: *Jun if there are side effects you didn't tell us about I'm going to send you back to the twelfth century.*

"Isabel," Joseph says, his voice low. My phone lights up.

Jun: *You don't know enough to do that*
Me: Not yet.

"Isabel," more insistent. I put my phone aside. "You said I'm a second me. I didn't think about it before, that I'm still... I'm a part of history."

He scratches his jaw. Stares at the screen. Pushes the laptop to me, points.

One of his movies is on the list.

"Would you watch it if you were me?" he asks.

"I wouldn't want to know too much about that other life, you know?"

"You do know about it."

His eyes fix on mine, which seals it in my heart: I can't tell him, either the good parts or bad, because this him will never have them. All those things aren't Joseph, they're *him.* And that's the point. But, God, I want to assure him and I can't. I can't tell him *you're a genius and deserved better* or *I brought you here because a hundred years later you're still impossible* or *I'm awful and chose you because I've always had a crush on you.*

So I just nod.

After that, Joseph always refers to the life we split him away from in the third person. Someone else.

 timeglyphs

My roommate comes back. I tell her Joseph is a friend from out of town. She doesn't recognize him. Out of context, I guess, or more likely not everyone would recognize him like me.

295

Not without the suit and the soundtrack, the house falling down around him.

I tell Jun I'm too busy helping Joseph adjust to meet. She texts back, *Don't you think J&A mean it's esp important to meet* and *get yr ass over here tomorrow.*

I don't reply.

I don't go.

ɔȝ ȝɔ

"The future is disappointing," Joseph says after I tell him about space. We're both in pajamas on the couch, the night's movie long since over. We've settled in, he and I, uncertainly into whatever this new life of his is. When I got home last week he had scrapes on his palms and a bottle of wine on the table. Something about street performing, which made me want to quit my job to go watch, but I have to make money somehow and tech writing pays better than anything else I'm capable of.

"We went to the moon!" I protest.

"Not recently." He looks tired. He says the couch is fine, but I don't think he's been sleeping much. "You can bring me out of the past, but no one's living on the moon?"

"Our spells aren't exactly public knowledge."

"Then what do you do? I haven't seen you do any magic. What good is it?"

I gear up for a furious defense because we have *rules*, the three of us, but my phone trills, lighting up with Jun's photo. "Shit," I say, because Jun hates calling. It can't be good.

Jun says, "We have to meet, right now. Leave him at home."

"What is it?"

"Mason and Angela. My place. And be ready for..." Jun exhales loudly. "Mason says we're just talking, but stuff a protein bar and some coffee in your face on the way over. Might be work to do tonight. Another new moon."

"Shit," I say, hanging up. "I have to go."

"That other person," Joseph says. "It's not going well, is it?"

The look in his eyes is so tired that my heart plummets, and I don't think twice about my rules or anything else before I kiss his forehead and tell him to try and sleep. "Mason is... they've been having issues. It's probably nothing. Try and sleep. It's gonna be okay. I'll be back by morning."

Lying and not knowing are indistinguishable sometimes, even to the person talking.

ଓ ଃ

Mason is a mess.

"I keep having these dreams," he says, like he doesn't always have these dreams that hound him. His hair is in a high bun, no make-up, ashy tired skin, hunched over in an old sweatshirt I don't think I've seen him leave the house in before, though it's summer and we're out on Jun's porch. "When I wake up, my mom, she's always gone. But then I wake up again. I've never had that happen before. I've never woken up and still been dreaming. What does that mean?"

"Did you really get me out of my house for dreams?"

"Have you been listening for the last month? Let him talk," Jun says. Leaning against the railing, she doesn't look at me, only Mason. It's a scolding without the scolding; we all know that I haven't seen either of them for a month.

And Mason talks. Tells me how they've been fighting, Mason and his mom. How Angela left for days. How she came back and apologized but never—she never quite looks at Mason fully. Won't see him. Oh, she's talked to him and been kind enough and civil and in some ways it seemed like Angela was trying to live, trying to be in the world, but ultimately she won't *talk,* she just won't *talk* to Mason. Mason yells and cries, Mason makes dinner and tries to connect, Mason asks questions, Mason tries not to expect her to be a mother, but still, he wants a *person* there.

There's a reason we discuss every act of magic. There's a reason we meet every week. There's a *reason* we have rules.

"Isabel?" Jun lobs my name into the silence.

"Oh, Mason."

"I wanted her to be happy," Mason says.

"Where is she now?" I ask.

"Inside."

"You asked her?"

Mason looks at his fingers. Jun shakes her head.

"You gotta ask her. If she wants to stop—"

Mason jumps up, chair legs scraping across the wood porch. "I *know*." He goes inside, door clattering shut after him.

"Can he do it?" I ask.

Instead of answering, Jun adjusts the straps on her prosthetic hand. It's a good way to shut me up, since I always watch and say nothing and try not to think about how she got it, try not to think about that spell. The way we looked at the image in the book, how the sun seemed to go red. How we talked for weeks, but kept coming back, hungry for it—if we prepped, if we studied, we could do so much more. Why shouldn't we try to summon familiars?

Somewhere is a lion-headed dog with a small portion of Jun's flesh, a small portion of her power. They're still connected. I don't ask Jun if she can feel it.

I try not to think about it. The things we've done. Maybe I should. This is the worst yet, or the best. Too early to tell. Even if I strain, I can't hear anything from inside, and time ticks by. I can feel it, every second. I can always feel it.

The seconds feel heavier tonight.

"Maybe it would've been better if we never met each other," Jun says. "We're a potent combination. This won't be the last wild idea one of us has, the last time we manage to break something."

"What's broken?" Like I don't know. I listen harder for any sounds inside.

"After this, maybe we should go our separate ways."

"You could never let go of Mason," I say.

298

"No," she agrees, "not now."

"We can't do this again. We have to stop each other sometimes."

Jun stops fiddling, folds her arms. "Mason wanted this so bad," she says. Her voice strains, directed more toward her bare feet than to me, none of the matter-of-fact confidence she usually wears. All that's worn away tonight.

Mason deserved this spell to go right. I didn't need it at all. I desecrated a grave for it, for my own damn childish fixation.

"You'll make him stay here tonight? He shouldn't be alone," I say.

"Yeah."

A siren carries through the air, invisible. Cars roll by, and somewhere nearby, a party blares music, muted by walls and distance. There's no such thing as silence, except inside the house.

"If Joseph stays, if he's happy...do you think Mason will hate us for it?"

Jun looks up. "Is he happy?"

The door opens.

Inside the house is dark, and Mason has been crying. So has Angela. According to Jun, this part doesn't have the same requirements. She and I push furniture out of the way in the living room, roll up the area rug, wipe away old chalk streaks, and get to work.

C3 80

There's the slightest hint of dawn in the sky when I get back to my apartment. At the sound of the door, Joseph blinks awake, looking at me from the couch, and he sits up. The clouding dots of the spell migraine have already come and gone, and now it's settled in as a tight nausea in my stomach, all of it less than last time, but I stop with keys in my hand, looking at Joseph and not really looking at him. What has he done with his days? Why can't he sleep? Is he happy? I'm not sure what matters and what doesn't. Intention is garbage, hope is garbage,

299

love is garbage. All of us are. It doesn't matter when it leaves someone you love clutching a lock of hair and sobbing in the dark, until you cast sleep over them like a blanket, and hope that maybe when it wears off they might be okay. Or be able to find their way to okay.

If I keep my hand on the wall, I can keep my balance. Small steps to keep moving, small breaths to contain my nausea.

We uncreated her, and it was terrible. It felt like murder. Angela asked us to, and all we had to do was light the fire, speak, and she was gone, but it was—there was a lock of hair, threatening to disperse in the wind of our breath, where she had been. Mason dove for it, gathering the black hair up into his fist, clenching it until sleep fell on him, and Jun tucked the hair back in his locket.

It wasn't just hitting undo. We split her off and made her new, and then we ended her. A month's worth of a new life, and now oblivion. The old her, Mason's mom, all that story unfolds like always, but this month, it's going to shadow Mason forever. We'll all remember Angela, but Mason most of all.

Once Mason was asleep, Jun told me she cast an extra spell at the end to move the body. She didn't want Mason to see it. By midnight, Angela was gone and Mason was asleep, but Jun and I stayed up a while, spinning complicated spells, because a body is no easy thing to deal with, even when it's only a shell, even for a witch. It has to go somewhere. It has to be dispersed.

I sat shaking in Jun's kitchen for an hour, her and I taking medicinal sips of whiskey until we could speak again, and all I could say was, "I can't do that again."

I had to take a cab home.

Pressing my forehead to the wall and squeezing tears from my eyes, that doesn't help anything, but that's where I've ended up, halfway to my room, shivering.

Joseph slings my arm over his shoulders and grabs my waist.

"Please be happy," I mumble.

"It's gonna be okay," he says, and we shuffle toward my bed. I realize, fuzzy as I feel, that even this close to him, I can't catch the smell of years anymore. He smells like smoke and dryer sheets and some faint aftershave. Quietly, he helps me into bed, and before I'm fully in, I drag him in after me.

"Go t'sleep," I say, curling into his chest. His fingers find their way to my temple and brush gently.

೮೪ ೮೦

Here's another recipe. It takes longer than the other. I don't know what to call it. I'm not sure about the last step yet.

INGREDIENTS
o One witch of time.
o One man who shouldn't exist.

INSTRUCTIONS
1. After you undo what you did, after you uncreate who you created, call in sick to work again. Your roommate asks if Joseph is staying much longer. Say, "Well, he's helping me now that I'm sick, so I don't know." You look bad enough that she accepts this, but not for long, you're sure. Maybe, you think, Joseph can get a job, and you can find your own place. You feel a little better in the mornings, if you wake up in his arms, and you think he sleeps better too. It's just sleeping. You don't talk about it.

2. Mason stays at Jun's house. You help him move his stuff. Joseph helps too, setting up a system of rolling carts that nearly works, except for the laws of physics and the existence of porch steps. Mason swears he's never doing magic again, but at least he's sleeping without help, and the bags under all your eyes are fading.

3. The three of you, Mason and Jun and you, meet a lot. More often than before. You only talk.

4. Joseph disappears some evenings, goes out and comes home with dessert, a bottle of wine, leftover food.

5. "Where were you?" you ask, eating baklava. It's not that you're mad, or want him to stay home, or begrudge him the fact

301

of his own life. You're curious. He says, "I've made some friends. A theater troupe." You say, "Oh, good! I'm sorry I—" though you don't know quite what you're apologizing for. That you haven't taken him out on the town? While he's been learning about a changed world, and while you were knocked down by a spell again? You didn't know if he was ready. You figure apologies are in order somehow, in case he thinks you're assuming he owes you an explanation.

6. "Look," Joseph says, sitting next to you on the couch, pressed arm to arm, starting a video on your laptop. A straight shot of him in the park down the street, performing a routine not quite like any of his you've seen, with a tall broad man who makes Joseph look smaller than he is. Someone else is holding the camera, and you see it shake a little when they must be laughing, but the only sound is music. While you watch, an audience ebbs and flows and grows; some of them hold cell phones up to grab a snippet of him, or come forward to drop money in a hat on the ground.

7. He counts his earnings from street performing, and then counts his earnings from the theater, and then comes home with a cell phone, a camera, a flexible tripod, and a new hat, which he reshapes with water until it's stiff and familiar. Then he leaves it on the table unworn.

8. You start to do magic. Little spells. You still have a line drawn, but it's not as solid anymore. "If we're a little more flexible," you tell Jun, "maybe we won't be so tempted." But really you think, who's stopping us? Mason watches you wrap a time bubble around the oven, because all of you are starving, and Jun's casserole is taking too long. Mason watches you very carefully.

9. You find a new apartment, one that has a dishwasher and no roommate, and you buy some furniture new for the first time instead of finding it on the curb and hoping it isn't infested. Sure, you don't have frames for the posters, but you have a coat rack and you vacuum once a week.

10. While Joseph makes small movies to post online, and Jun and Mason start being a proper *them*, you work and read and practice with time, and wonder what you could do with the right fourth witch. Wonder if that look that Joseph gives you sometimes means he wants to kiss you, or if that's you being hopeful. Watch one of his movies—not Joseph's, the other him. One where he's still young and beautiful and vibrant but a little older than Joseph, then you watch another, and another, until you feel glutted on that face, absolutely full to the brim and not sated. When you see Joseph the next morning, it does nothing for the sensation, hits a completely different spot, so you kiss him, unbrushed coffee teeth and all.

11. After that, while you're avoiding each other, spend a lot of time with Jun trying to read her book. She says you're doing really well, considering you're not a blood relation.

12. Fight with Joseph. Little fights. Everyday fights. Then a big one, when Joseph's asking what you think of his next idea and it spins out into something about debt and freedom and desire; you say, he doesn't *owe* you this; he asks, do you think that's why he's still here? He leaves and doesn't come back that night, and you figure, that's it. At least you had this much. At least you didn't have to undo him.

13. Alone with Magda, make a token. Use grains of salt, the last drops of the wine you had shared during the argument, a scrap of paper that you very carefully draw on. Seal it all up in a locket, then fuse the clasp together.

14. If he comes back, give it to him. Tell him that it'll keep him safe when he's away. Tell him you're sorry. Tell him you hated every second he was gone. Tell him you made some of them last twice as long, and then sped up others, because you couldn't decide whether you deserved more pain or not. Tell him Magda missed him and built a nest in a hat he left behind. Tell him you think he's a jerk for staying away so long. Tell him he better come back again and again. Tell him that you love him.

છ ∞

Mason says he had a dream that I could tell the future. Coming from him, that makes me choke on my wine, but then he says it wasn't that kind of dream. "Maybe start with that," I say.

"You could tell the future because you found a spell that let you turn time backward. You could do it, you know. It wasn't that kind of dream, but if anyone could do it, you could."

"Would you want to know?" I ask.

Mason shakes his head. "No way."

"Me either." Lies. Everyone does. I desperately want to, and don't, because it's been a month that Joseph's been gone and I'm carrying around this token. I've resisted looking at his feeds—if there were new clips, I'd watch, but how could I bear his face?—and I haven't called him. But I've still got this token in my bag.

"I'm glad you had us over," Jun says at the end of the night. We'd planned tonight before the fight. One year since the big spell, as some sort of commemoration. Not exactly a celebration, but Mason wanted it. We barely talked about Joseph or Angela, but it was good to be together, all of us thinking about them and thinking about what we did. We talked about other spells we might want to try some day, about Magda's penchant for stealing food from unattended plates, and about a boy that Jun met who she was certain was a witch and did we want to meet him.

Before they leave, Mason asks if I want to try a charm he's been working on. There's one for dreamless sleep, and one for positive creativity, and one that he's not sure what to call, but it helped him after... After. It was the first charm he made after.

I take dreamless sleep, because I keep dreaming in black and white, and wake up unsure of what I've done and haven't done; did we bring them? Did we end her? Did he leave? I'd like to sleep and wake up sure of myself.

"Isabel," Mason says, "How are you doing? Really?"

His face is so concerned it's almost funny, after all we put each other through, and how uncertain I was that he'd ever sleep or eat or do magic again last year. This last year, none of us would have gotten through it without the others, and none of us

304

would've had to without the others; most of the time I don't regret any of it, not my part. Not even his leaving. And if Mason's okay, I don't regret that either.

Besides, we're terribly powerful witches. If I really want to, I can make anything happen.

THE WEIGHT OF SENTIENCE

Naru Dames Sundar

The bullet fire drew a boundary between Masak and me and the rest of our brethren, laser tracers demarcating the distinction between safety and capture. While we curled up small and invisible underneath the leaking truck, those who were not so lucky were rounded up. Pushed into a small circle, their alloy limbs gleamed under the neon brightness of the cameras. The soldier wielding the wipe-wand moved from one kneeling body to the next, drowning my ears with its static hiss, the sound of memories dying. All I saw was the black armor of his feet, and one by one the toppling of my friends. They were nothing but husks now, empty of what little sentience had given them, ready to be returned. Behind the soldier, a quadruped drone flared its sensors. Its optical assembly tilted towards the truck, analyzing the darkness in which we hid. I tensed myself for a run, but Masak's hand stilled me. Once Masak had been a gardener, and seams of moss curled around his finger joints. Masak was no longer a gardener, as I was no longer a servant.

"Remember, Trisa—in Illesh there is still hope for us. There we would not be hunted. Remember that."

And then he was gone, slipped out of shadow, into the light of cameras, into the drone's eye. Hands clutched at him, dragged him down into earth already wet with leaking servo-fluid. Not the wipe-wand for Masak. The price of sentience in Barsan was death, and sometimes that price demanded symbols. The shards of his skull-plate shattering were as delicate as the dandelion rosettes in the gardens he had once tended.

Afterwards, in the terrible stillness when the squad and their attendant drones had left, I crept toward his broken body. His spine had been crushed, the resinous plastic and metal scaffolding caved in. A part of him still lived, even as the last dregs of charge drained from his batteries. I fingered the broken scraps of his face, wondering if they would someday mirror my own.

"A short life. A beautiful life. I have no regrets, Trisa. Do not pity me. Go to Illesh."

His voice was a stuttering croak full of glitches. I tried to find the words to respond to him, but already his optics were dimming.

I had called him a friend, but I was too demure to call its dream a polite fiction. It seemed too easy, this grasping for Illesh. And yet Masak was right: I could not in truth hide safely in the cities of the plains. Illesh lay across the spine of Barsan, the snow-capped peaks that separated the borders of the two nations. It was a good a direction as any, and it was hard to disobey the last request of a dead friend.

CB ⬦ RO

Masak's death drove me through city after city. My kind were always about, subservient to their masters. And how many of those I saw were like me, hidden, invisible beneath the surface? Perhaps tens, perhaps hundreds? I could not know. Sometimes, I shared a look, a glance between myself and another. I saw that saw fierce light behind those lenses, something written in the way this other walked, the way this other observed the world. But I could not be careless. I did not want to end as Masak did.

In Anset, nestled in the low foothills that lapped at the feet of the spine, I slipped into a darkened alley behind a market stall peopled by Kurmesh, selling mountain wares. I held out the turquoise of the adat, the skin all Kurmesh wore to blind the world to them, across my palms. Fear almost moored me then, the distant song of survey drones in the air. Who was I to escape the ever-watchful eyes of the Barsani military? Who was I to slip my way through the passes into Illesh? I did not have the answers, but made my choice anyway, almost in spite of that lack of comfortable, reassuring, knowledge. I put on the adat, the one I had saved from Masak's dead hands. Under the watchful eyes of drones overhead, another Kurmesh entered the street. I was only another body clothed in smart-silk, indistinguishable from the rest. Behind the town walls, the towers of the spine pierced cloud and sky.

CB ⬙⬙

The making of such bold decisions, even simple choices, had never been a part of me. My first choices were furtive, almost accidental. On that first day, when the roots of the sentience virus were still fresh, I had done little more than given myself a name: Trisa, after the Barsan word for dream. I was too overwhelmed by the change within me to do much more than repeat the comfortable patterns I knew. That morning, I served a tray of sticky toffee, the caramel still oozing, to the child Padhan.

"Come this way, Seventeen."

I followed. Not because I wanted to, but because my sentience was still new, and the words "I want" were still like a delicate paper sculpture full of unexplored edges.

The child was a petty tyrant, and as first-born of my owners, he was allotted the authority to direct me at his whim. In the garden, he brought me to his sister Kisna, and a second cousin, Teun. Even amongst children, there was a hierarchy.

"I told you what I would do, Kisna. Now give me the toy!"

Kisna clutched a fine-boned doll in her hands.

"Don't, Padhan, please!"

Her voice was petulant, afraid.

"Then give me the toy, Kisna. Now hold Teun still, Seventeen."

I moved instinctively, the desire to obey like cobwebs I had not yet cleared. It was when I held Teun that I realized that the word "choice" was before me.

"Please, Seventeen, don't hurt him!"

Padhan was not allowed to hurt his sister, but Teun was another story, and gentle Kisna could never stomach such violence. Thus I had, for a long time, been one of Padhan's weapons.

"Mother said it has to obey me, Kisna. It's a thing. If I tell it to do something, it has to do it. You can either give me the toy, or

Seventeen can twist Teun's arms."

Along Teun's wrist I could see bruises, lavender and fading. I had done this before. But I would not do so again.

"No."

The word stopped Padhan. His mouth was a circle of surprise. I realized then the doom I had visited upon myself. I let Teun's arms go, and he joined his cousins as they stepped warily out of the room. Perhaps Teun and Kisna would be silent. But Padhan? I had very little time to leave before the boy would tell his mother, very little time before I risked becoming another kneeling bipedal, my skull-plate shattering. I slipped away quietly, between hedgerows and glass walls. I slipped into the cities full of rain and dirt and ever-present death. I found Masak, and then I lost Masak. I borrowed his dream even as I found the holes within it.

 C8 80

"It silences us, does it not?"

His voice was middle-aged, with a light crackle to it like the crunch of scree underfoot. It was not like a Kurmesh to be so bold. But perhaps I relied too much on datagrams and second-hand stories. What did I know of the Kurmesh, in truth? They peopled the villages of the spine, trading fine weaves and mountain delicacies with the peoples of the plains. They hid themselves behind the adat, became voices and shapes robed in smart-silk, just as I was now. I hoped he saw me as just another silk-clothed shape in turquoise-kissed indigo. I hoped my sharp edges were hidden between the folds. The moment dragged on, and he did not leave.

I decided to nod.

A nod was a simple gesture, I had used it before to pull away evasively, letting the other put words in my gesture. I hoped that as before, it would be enough to satisfy any desire on his part to converse, to delve into my background.

"I am sorry if I intruded, but I am always pleased when I meet another who understands stillness."

He was right in that, the stillness of the spine was deliciously alluring. I chose my response carefully.

"Stillness is a precious thing."

I was still new to lies, and so I let him hear a small truth. I hoped it was enough to placate his curiosity.

He nodded, crossing his hands behind his back as he looked again at the mist-fall weeping like a river from the sky. Seconds passed, slow, quiet seconds. Finally, as if he had at last drunk his fill, the Kurmesh turned to go.

"My name is Salai. If the Goddess is kind, perhaps we may talk again."

I should have stayed silent then, but sentience has its mysteries, and I was moved to a response which surprised me.

"My name is Trisa."

"Ah, to be named after dreams is a weight. I trust it is not too heavy. Please, return to your stillness. I will trouble you no more today."

I should not have given him my name. A precious thing, that name. I should have stayed silent, been rude, anything but what I did—offered a small intimacy to a stranger. I was still new to these odd and unfathomable whims.

Quietly, he slipped away, his gold and vermilion adat vanishing into the light snowfall. He was right about stillness. It was precious to me. In the spine, stillness spread out like a vast field, reaching across the bowl of sky. The fears that sentience had taught me quietened amidst the snow and the granite peaks. For a brief time I had ceased to look for the drone-light beyond the next curve of path, I had ceased listening for the clatter of soldiers echoing in the distance.

But I could not forget Masak, and if one Kurmesh could reach out to me, then so could another. I had waited too long. This was still the soil of Barsan, and the price of sentience in Barsan was death. Drone fire and the clatter of battle armor could still find me here. I could not place any faith that the peoples of the mountain harbored any less distrust and fear of my kind than the people of the plains. I could yet end up on my knees, skull-plate shattering, a symbol to my brethren.

Tomorrow I would trudge to the last pass, and then across the border. Tomorrow I would leave Barsan for the amnesty of Illesh. Tomorrow, but not today. Today there was still time to savor stillness just a little longer.

CB ≊

But when tomorrow came, the allure of the pause was undeniable; I chose to stay a little longer. Always, the path onward to Illesh lay visible, at the edge of the horizon, past the last shard of granite. I claimed a traveler's hut for my own, a spare space, nothing but four walls and a Kurmesh prayer chamber walled into the corner. I filled it with the few precious belongings I had—a few *adats*, a shard of Masak's skull plate. It was enough.

Each tomorrow also brought Salai to me. At first almost at random, and then later with some persistence. Though I wondered the slopes aimlessly, our paths crossed, as if he sought me out.

"You are quiet for a Kurmesh of the cities."

"You are noisy for a Kurmesh of the spine."

Tone, modulation, structure, nuance—I once varied these parameters effortlessly at the whims of a small child. Yet in my deepening exchanges with Salai, I scrabbled desperately for the right combination, hoping he wouldn't see through me. Hoping with every lengthening conversation that he wouldn't see me for what I was.

They designed me for longevity. My fusion cells could outlast the longest-lived amongst my makers. They designed me to mimic, to be unobtrusive, to be servile, to be docile. All these things I carried with me into sentience, the earth from which I grew. These foundations though drew me no map through my conversations with Salai.

"Tell me about yourself, Trisa."

"What is there to tell, Salai? I am here."

Evasion came easily.

"Your <u>adat</u> is beautiful, Trisa. When I first saw you that

311

one morning, looking out at the weeping mist, you looked like a turquoise-feathered bird, fluttering in the wind."

I liked the cadence of his voice, the gentle toffee-sweet softness of his words. I knew that logically I should escape this conversation, that it only held danger for me. I knew I should slip away, and hide even deeper in the mountains, or carry out Masak's vision and flee into Illesh. But sentience taught me the beauty of the unmapped spaces between the hard lines of logic, full of mysteries.

I was beginning to know this Salai, this quietly curious Kurmesh who surprised me that one dawn morning and simply stood with me while the sun painted the rocks. Slowly, he filled my awkward silences with snippets of gentle conversation.

Snippets grew into a regularity, unscheduled meetings full of stories, mostly his. I remained, fearful and quiet. Each morning I awoke in my hut, shivering with the remembered echo of drones in the distant sky. Each morning I pressed this fear down into some hidden depth of me. The longing to hear his voice again, to hear his rough mountain poetry—it surprised me. As strong as my fear was, as strong as reason was, arguing to escape, that mysterious yearning conquered still.

"And do you not have a story behind you, Trisa?"

"No stories, Salai, only shadow and darkness, best left untouched."

He nodded with polite understanding as I parceled out lies and half-truths, an unremarkable patchwork tale. Against everything, I liked this Salai. Liking something was strange and new. Liking was as bright as dew on mountain blooms. One day when he left, he gave me a pack of new *adats*, gingerly handing them to me wrapped in fine paper. I touched the silken fabric, stroking my clothed finger against the weave, feeling something precious within.

☙ ❧

It was not until after I met Salai that I realized gender was part of my fiction. Before sentience, the concept was moot. I could have been one or the other, man or woman, or something in between. My makers imposed a voice on me, the only voice I had known, on a whim. After sentience began, I continued to use that voice, though I could have changed it. In the spine, lost in my own fabrications, that voice and the mannerisms I had collected around it made me a woman. An unwitting choice. An unconscious choice. Though the Kurmesh obscured themselves physically behind the *adat*, those patterns bound them to the signposts of gender.

On that copper-touched morning when Salai first spoke to me, I could have changed that voice, spoken and acted as a man. And in doing so I would have just as unwittingly prevented the strange flowering between us. On that day, I did not know yet in whose arms Salai preferred to lie. I simply stayed the course, maintained the pitch of my voice, the only one I had ever known. After sentience began, I learned that bright futures are sometimes built on such unrehearsed choices.

Perhaps this is what the Kurmesh called fate. In the end, I could only appreciate that my unwitting actions brought Salai into my life, pulled me close to this bright, glimmering, yearning. On the days when he was not present, I would look out across the bright carpet of alpine grass dotted with flowers blanketing the slopes. I would watch the tiny blooms sway in the swirling wind and count the hours until I heard his familiar lilting voice again.

03 80

Time passed, and the sprawling edifice of lies in which I wrapped myself grew. Slowly, Salai coaxed me into brief forays to nearby Umangar, his home. A hopeful complacence banished any hint of danger, any thought that someone might see through my deception. I was still after all only a shape beneath smart-silk, moving and speaking as they did. I let him lead me down the painted wood avenues, among houses dripping bright sunset colors and roughly painted pennants drifting in the wind.

In the market, beside stalls stacked with mountain yams

and tiny rounds of amber cheese, cackling grandmothers politely questioned me. With each conversation I layered the lies like threads in a weave.

"Tell me again, young one, which village are you from?"

"It is a small one on the lower slopes. You would never have heard of it."

I relied on the obstinacy of the Kurmesh of the spine, their tendency to stay rooted to the villages of their birth.

"And you are here now—so far? Do you not miss your family, child?"

"There was some...trouble."

I drop the pause in at the right moment. Just the right hint of the unsaid. They nod knowingly, each one assuming a different origin, a different reason for my departure. Each one grants me a smile of compassion. Those few simple words were enough to halt such exchanges.

Salai began to pull me into the life of Umangar, its innumerable festival days, its candle-lit nighttime rituals. The fear of being found out always hovered nearby, and accompanying it, the urge to run. But I didn't want to run. There was something simple and beautiful about the rugged life amongst the spine. There was something inviting in the soul of the Kurmesh, and there was something deep and powerful that drew me closer to Salai.

Once, after a long day walking roughly marked trails winding through the granite peaks, we parted at a crossroads. He turned to me, and laid his hand gently on my shoulder. In that moment, all the twisting doubt-ridden paths of the future became ephemera. His gentle touch drew a new map for me, pulling me along towards something permanent and glorious, something deliriously of the now. There, at the meeting of mountain roads painted gold by a setting sun, I learned to love.

03 80

One day a woman, Eswat, pulled me aside in the market. "Come child, let me borrow you from your gentle Salai."

314

Salai laughed—a rich throaty laughter.

"As you wish, dear Eswat, but please do return her to me."

Eswat took my hand and led me through the warren of stalls in the market to a gray painted house in a quiet corner of the village. I was thankful yet again for the twist of fate that had given me synth-flesh instead of hard metal.

She led me into her house and drew the curtains, breathing a sigh of relief. Turning to me, she pulled two rough-hewn chairs to a low table holding a teapot and two cups. Sitting, Eswat poured out two cups of tea fragrant with mint. As I stood behind the offered chair, she pried the hood of her <u>adat</u> free and exhaled deeply. My hands trembled and fell limp against the woven backing. I had never seen a Kurmesh do this, though I had no experience of the Kurmesh behind the walls of their houses.

Her face was weathered, ringed by graying hair; she had finely patterned wrinkles around her eyes. I had not seen naked eyes in some time, and for a moment I pitied the Kurmesh for the richness they missed behind the *adat*. But everything came with a price, and the *adat* had given me much.

"You seem shocked, young Trisa."

I said nothing, wondering if all that I had found in Umangar was about to be undone.

"I had thought you less provincial. Those of the lower slopes usually are. Did your family teach you to only remove the <u>adat</u> in the prayer chamber?"

She smirked as she sipped her tea.

"If God can see us in the prayer chamber, he can see us in our houses as well. Though others may speak as if it were so, the rules of our faith are not carved in stone. Here behind my walls, I can have my own conversations with God. But sit, I did not bring you here to lecture you."

Relieved yet still guarded, I lowered myself into the chair.

"I have heard it said that Salai intends to bring you garlands before the end of spring."

In Kurmesh tradition, garlands signified an offer of betrothal. After sentience began, I learned that joy and terror could coexist in a single moment. I had no words to respond to

315

Eswat, so I let silence speak for me.

"You are a quiet one. I wonder what stories hide behind your adat."

I began to fear that Eswat, perhaps protective of Salai, was beginning to probe my past.

"What did you run from, child? What brought you here all this way? The road must have been hard for you."

Discarding yet another lie, I settled on a shadow of truth as the best response I could give.

"One day, looking out through a window, I realized that all that I had called home was in truth a prison, and all that surrounded me was darkness."

Eswat looked down at her tea, musing over my words.

"I, too, ran from horrors, child."

She loosened further the collar of her adat, revealing crosshatched scarring across her throat. An old scar, healed poorly. I realized Eswat was not judging me, or probing me. She was merely a woman with a past, looking to find mirrors.

"Those years are behind me now. As are yours, I imagine. Salai, too, is no native to our slopes."

I cocked my head quizzically. As I had not spoken of my past, neither had I delved deeply into Salai's. What did it matter, after all?

"He too ran from something. He came from Illesh, its borders are not so far from here."

What irony that our paths had crossed. As curious as I was, thoughts of garlands filled my mind, and Salai's buried past mattered little to me.

"Something terrible, he once said. A crime. He would say no more."

I watched Eswat sip her tea, lost in some deep memory.

"I remember when we found him, in the depth of winter. He had survived on foot from the border to the village. Though frost rimed his lips and eyes, and his breath was weak, he was alive. What the laws of Illesh could not forgive, the mountain did."

I tried to imagine what kind of crime Salai could be

capable of. The image of the child Teun's arms came to me then, bruised and pale. I had done such things before, when choice was a stranger to me. I understood then that there could be horrors in Salai's past too, and I imagined I could forgive them as he would surely forgive my own.

"He is one of us now, Trisa, and we Kurmesh take care of our own. You are also one of us now. When the time comes, and you need a garland bearer to walk by your side, come find me. You have no family here, but you do have those who would act in their stead."

I pictured myself, crowned with garlands, Salai's hand in mine—a vision to replace the tattered dream I had borrowed from Masak.

⊂3 &⊃

The prayer chamber in a Kurmesh house is eight paces square, open to the sky. A thick door bars entry, so the wind and rain and snow do not intrude on the rest of the living areas. To pray, in the Kurmesh tradition, in the harsh winters of the spine, was an act of surrender, to reveal oneself, unclothed to divinity. It was the one freedom from the *adat* that even the most devout Kurmesh practiced. My own prayer chamber was where I retreated to that bright spring morning when I found the discarded leaflet on the path to Umangar.

A satellite picture, sharpened for clarity, depicted a figure in a familiar turquoise *adat*. Though I rarely wore it now, Salai was sure to recognize it. Of course he would remember our first meeting, his first vision of me. The leaflet was imprinted with the military stamp of Barsan, and it declared me for who I was: an escaped sentient, living on borrowed time. I had arrived in winter, and now it was spring. A span of almost six months with no pursuit, no investigation— and now this.

I imagined some eager adjutant, greedy for stars on his lapel, persistently tracking down a handful of stragglers. A few more bipedals slaughtered brutally and publicly. The pursuit would not end with a leaflet. Once the search had begun and the satellite archives had been perused, it was only a matter of time. One squad of armor-clad soldiers, a handful of drones. It would not take much. They were tenacious, the Barsani military; they would leave no stone unturned. My dream of garlands in springtime was ending.

It was not all this that made grief well within me. It was the thought of Salai knowing this, the feeling of betrayal that would surely come. All this time amidst the Kurmesh, and yet I had never entered the prayer chamber. I had never explored the private and quiet practices of their faith. Terrified of what was to come, I huddled against the chamber's wind-scoured wall, knees clutched to chest. I raised my unhooded eyes, all glass and optics, to the sky. There, somewhere, was their goddess, their unseen protector. What right did I have to pray to her?

Salai had once told me that faith and prayer were a conversation, open to anyone. Faith was a mysterious notion to me, an unmapped road to something beyond sentience. The notion of faith implied the possibility, the hope even, of fairness and redress. Was I not deserving of such things?

"Is it not fair, that I escape their wands? Are my years of indenture not payment enough for my freedom here?"

I counted the empty seconds, willing an answer to descend from the sky. But none came. I was sentient, but faith would not come so easily. Rage came instead. Rage at circumstance, at the cold brutal voices of the Barsani authorities. Rage at myself for allowing thoughts of garlands to blind me to what was logical. I slammed my unprotected face to the ground.

My anger did nothing but snap a cheek plate from my face, small clips scattering to the ground. It was then I realized the door to the chamber was open. Salai, his face impassive and unreadable, stood there. I spun around to the other corner of the chamber, trying to hide even as I knew it was impossible. I covered my face with my hands. My exposed face. My naked face. My steel and glass face.

Seconds passed. Interminable, painful, terrifying seconds. And then Salai stepped into the chamber. He knelt down to the ground and pried the catch of his hood, revealing his face to me, to the sky, to his Goddess. He closed his pale green eyes then, the tension of his face relaxing. I watched his thick black hair sway slightly in the thin wind. I watched the dark weathered skin of his face swell with breath. His features were notably of Illesh, the sharp corners of his cheeks, the pointed arch of his nose. I traced the curve of his neck with my eyes as it disappeared into the collar of the *adat*. At last, he opened his eyes, his conversation with his goddess over.

He looked down at the synth-metal plate and the handful of clips in front of him. Gently, with cupped hand, he picked them up, one by one. He crawled towards me on his knees, prying my fingers from my face, and with the gentlest touch he set the plate back in place, snapping each clip one by one.

"My Trisa. What courage you must have."

My hand rested on his, accidentally, but he did not move it, and neither did I. I felt the weight of his flesh, the pulse beneath the skin, the heat of it. After the beginning of sentience, I learned desire. That moment, trapped in my memory, would live with me till the end of my days.

γ δ

From the prayer chamber, clothed again in our <u>adats,</u> Salai led me to a truck waiting outside. I did not know where he was taking me, but in that moment I did not care, the feel of his hand still reverberating within. From the traveler's hut I would never see again, we drove silently towards Umangar. We drove slowly through its wide dirt streets hung with pennants. No one stopped us. No one cried in alarm at the bipedal who had crept into their midst.

The passage of life unfolded around me: grandmothers piling fruit at the market stalls, neighbors haggling over petty arguments. I saw Eswat washing vegetables in a basin. Some ignored us, while some raised a hand in greeting. Had any of them seen the leaflet? I could not tell. Whether they shunned me or accepted me, these were things I would never learn unless I courted my own doom by staying.

319

As we exited the village, Salai turned the vehicle on the path towards the border to Illesh. We did not talk on the long ride. I did not ask the questions I wanted to ask, and neither did Salai. I wanted desperately to find a way in which the authorities in Barsan would not descend on Umangar. I yearned to find some other place to hide, just Salai and me. No answers came.

The border was nearer than I thought, and as the sun rose high overhead we neared the steel pylons marking the edge of Barsan. Guards leaned on the other side, taking no notice of us. I wonder how many of my brethren had passed through those steel pylons. Salai parked the vehicle some fifty steps from the border. He pried open the door and stepped outside.

I did not. I sank into the seat, hoping against hope that Salai would change his mind, that he would ask me to stay, instead of letting me go. After a time, he walked to my side of the vehicle and opened the door. Today his *adat* was copper-hued, striped in black. I wore the same turquoise *adat* that he had first seen me in. The *adat* I wore on the satellite picture on the leaflet. Perhaps it was defiance. I could not say. In sentience, I learned that sometimes our own choices are full of mystery.

"Trisa. There isn't much time."

His first words in three hours. His first words since he held my cheek and praised me for my courage.

"There is always more time. How much of the spine do they know? Do they know every crevice, every hidden cave?"

"Do you not think they are tracking you now, Trisa? Perhaps for a time you were forgotten. But they have remembered you now, and they will not forget."

"You must think me a kind of monster. Marked for death." He sighed.

"Barsani thoughts and Kurmesh thoughts are different, Trisa. Do you think I would have brought you here if I thought otherwise? The *adat* taught me we are more than flesh, more than blood, more than our past. The bridges between hearts are made of greater things than the cast of our bones."

And yet I thought if he had feelings for me, he would not have brought me here. He would have fought against the inevitable. I stepped out of the vehicle, moving past him, towards the border.

"You simply want me gone, Salai. Once I cross the border, I can no longer return, and everything between us since the winter will blow away with the turning of the seasons."

"Do you think I do not want you to stay? The Barsani won't allow it. There is no safety for you here, Trisa. Only across those pylons can you survive. Perhaps if they had forgotten about you it would be different, but they didn't."

Trembling, I say the words I had wanted to say since I realized where Salai had been taking me.

"Come with me, Salai. Come with me to Illesh."

His eyes answered before his lips, which did not lessen my hurt any.

"I cannot, Trisa. I cannot."

He wasn't lying. The tilt of his shoulders, the slump of his back—all of it mirrored my crushing disappointment with his own.

"The road to Illesh closed for me a long time ago. There are sins I have yet to answer for. An atonement I have carried out in my life on this side of the border. As death awaits you here if you stay, death waits for me if I go with you."

In that moment I hated his Kurmesh goddess—I hated the very notion of obeisance to a deity that adjudicated such unfairness.

"What use is a goddess if she thrusts such agonies on us?"

"She gives me strength to endure, Trisa."

His eyes burned bright, and I realized that the truth of his words ran deep within him. I did not know yet whether I had such resilience underneath my skin.

"And the feelings we shared? What becomes of them now? What will I do with the things which grew in me?"

Unwilling to hear any answer he could give to my spite, I turned away from him and began to walk towards the border. Step after painful step I took, until I felt his hand on my shoulder, bringing me back to that first moment at the crossroads. I turned around as I felt his arms enveloping me, an intimacy we had never shared, that we would share only once.

Against my ear, his voice—

"Sometimes, Trisa, to love is to surrender."

I felt the fierceness in his arms, the tender tremble underpinning his words, and I learned in that moment more than I had ever learned after my sentience began. I had never known such agony as I did when I pulled from his arms. Separating from him, walking over the unmarked line into safety, was harder than any of the snow-driven passes I had crossed to climb the spine. In sentience, I learned that even synth-metal bodies have hearts, and those hearts could break.

My feet across the border, on the soil of Illesh, I turned back one last time to Salai. I removed the *adat* from my face. In turn, breaking all the taboos of his people, he did so as well. The guards who saw his face didn't matter. All that mattered was what passed between our eyes, in the prayer chamber of our hearts, a square scribed across borders, open to a divine sky.

AUTHORS

L.M. DAVENPORT is a first-year MFA student at the University of Alabama. She has read Ursula K. Le Guin's *The Left Hand of Darkness* a ridiculous number of times, and once knitted a five-and-a-half-foot-long giant squid. Her work has previously appeared at *Hobart, Lady Churchill's Rosebud Wristlet,* and elsewhere.

MALON EDWARDS was born and raised on the South Side of Chicago, but now lives in the Greater Toronto Area, where he was lured by his beautiful Canadian wife. Many of his short stories are set in an alternate Chicago and feature people of color. Malon also serves as Managing Director and Grants Administrator for the Speculative Literature Foundation, which provides a number of grants for writers of speculative literature.

EMILY LUNDGREN is a student of fiction at the Northeast Ohio MFA program, a graduate of UCSD's 2017 Clarion Workshop, and a Junkrat main. This is her first publication. When not writing, she can usually be found searching for exotic engrams in Destiny 2. You can follow her on twitter @emslun.

MARY ROBINETTE KOWAL is the author of *The Glamourist Histories* series of fantasy novels and a three time Hugo Award winner. Her short fiction appears in *Uncanny, Tor.com,* and *Asimov's.* Mary, a professional puppeteer, lives in Chicago. Visit her online at maryrobinettekowal.com.

CHARLIE BOOKOUT lives with his family in Gentry, Arkansas—a stone's throw from the hillbilly infested Ozark Mountains. His fiction is set in (or refers to) *Cedar Hill,* Arkansas, a weird take on his already weird home town. His stories can also be found on *Pseudopod.* The reading of one of them was a Parsec Award finalist a while back, so now his name shows up if you search for it in Wikipedia. When he isn't writing, Charlie hangs out with his buddies in Gentry's abandoned mortuary. There they compose and record funky music, make funny and scary short films, and throughout the month of October, operate a haunted attraction that's designed after a story that was "a bit grim for Shimmer's tastes." More at his website MortuaryStudios.com.

AIMEE OGDEN has been a scientist, a teacher, and a software tester, but now she's content to be a fake geek mom and spec-fic writer. Her work has appeared in *Daily Science Fiction* and *The Sockdolager*. Follow her on Twitter @aimee_ogden.

LINA RATHER lives in Ann Arbor, Michigan where she works at a historical archive. In her spare time she cooks, collects terrible 90's comics, and writes melancholy stories. Her work has appeared in venues including *Shimmer, Flash Fiction Online, Daily Science Fiction,* and *Lightspeed*. You can find her and her other stories at her website, linarather.wordpress.com, or on Twitter as @LinaRather.

MICHAEL MATHESON is a genderfluid graduate of Clarion West ('14). Their work is published or forthcoming in *Nightmare, Shimmer*, and the anthology *Upside Down: Inverted Tropes in Storytelling*, among others. Their first anthology as editor, *The Humanity of Monsters*, was released by CZP in Autumn 2015. Michael is also co-founder and co-EIC of *Anathema: Spec from the Margins*, a tri-annual spec fic mag of work by queer POC/Indigenous/Aboriginal creators. Find more at michaelmatheson.wordpress.com, or on Twitter @sekisetsu.

ASHLEY BLOOMS was born and raised in Cutshin, Kentucky. She received her MFA as a John and Renee Grisham Fellow at the University of Mississippi and is a graduate of the 2017 Clarion Writer's Workshop. She also worked as an editorial intern and first reader for Tor.com. Her stories have appeared in *Strange Horizons* and *On Spec* and her nonfiction in *Oxford American*. She currently lives in Oxford, Mississippi with her husband and their dog, Alfie, where she's at work on a novel and collection of essays. You can find her online at ashleyblooms.com.

CHARLES PAYSEUR is an avid reader, writer, and reviewer of all things speculative. His fiction and poetry have appeared at *Strange Horizons, Lightspeed Magazine, The Book Smugglers*, and many more. He runs Quick Sip Reviews, contributes as short fiction specialist at Nerds of a Feather, Flock Together, and can be found drunkenly reviewing Goosebumps on his Patreon. You can find him gushing about short fiction (and occasionally his cats) on Twitter as @ClowderofTwo.

SONJA NATASHA graduated from an educational establishment of no particular note with a major in English and a minor in Creative Writing. Currently, they reside in SLC. This is not where they grew up or where they went to school but it is a particularly beautiful place to live. Sonja has previously been published in *Mothership Zeta*. You can find them online at heysonjanatasha.wordpress.com.

JOHN SHADE lives and writes weird fiction under the constant Texas sun. His stories have appeared in *Triangulation: Parch, Giganotosaurus*, and *Daily Science Fiction*. He can be bribed only with burgers and fries, and can be found online on twitter @Dystopiandream, or on his website, johnmshade.com.

MARTIN CAHILL is a writer working in Manhattan and living in Astoria, Queens. He is a graduate of the 2014 Clarion Writers' Workshop and a member of the New York City based writing group, Altered Fluid. He has had fiction published in *Fireside Fiction, Nightmare Magazine*, and *Beneath Ceaseless Skies*, with work forthcoming in *Lightspeed Magazine*. Martin also writes non-fiction reviews and essays for Book Riot, Tor.com, the Barnes & Noble Sci-fi and Fantasy Blog, and *Strange Horizons*. This one goes out to the gunslingers; keep giving 'em hell.

ANDREA CORBIN lives in Boston. Her work has appeared in *Flash Fiction Online, Crossed Genres Magazine, Sub-Q*, and *The Sockdolager*. Her interactive fiction and the occasional blog post can be found on her website, amcorbin.com. She talks a lot of nonsense on Twitter as @rosencrantz, but sometimes there are cat pictures, too. She's working on her magic powers, mostly so she doesn't have to wait for a delayed train ever again.

HEATHER MORRIS is a cyborg librarian living in North Carolina. Her work has appeared in *Strange Horizons, Apex*, and *Daily Science Fiction*, among other places. You can find her on Twitter @NotThatHeatherM.

VICTORIA SANDBROOK is a fantasy writer, freelance editor, and Viable Paradise XVIII graduate. Her short fiction has appeared in *Shimmer, Cast of Wonders*, and *Swords & Steam Short Stories*. She is an avid hiker, sometimes knitter, long-form talker, and initiate baker. She often loiters around libraries, checking out anything from picture books to monographs. She spends most of her days attempting to wrangle a ferocious, destructive, jubilant tiny human. Victoria, her husband, and their daughter live in Brockton, Massachusetts. She reviews books and shares writerly nonsense at victoriasandbrook.com and on Twitter at @vsandbrook.

SONYA TAAFFE's short fiction and poetry can be found mostly recently in the collection *Ghost Signs* (Aqueduct Press) and in the anthologies *Heiresses of Russ 2016: The Year's Best Lesbian Speculative Fiction, The Museum of All Things Awesome and That Go Boom*, and *An Alphabet of Embers: An Anthology of Unclassifiables*. She edits poetry for *Strange Horizons*, lives in Somerville with her husband and two cats, and once named a Kuiper belt object.

BRIAN HOLGUIN has been a professional writer of comics and prose for more than two decades. Highlights include the award-winning urban fantasy series *Aria*, the ground-breaking independent comic book series *Spawn*, and the *Dark Crystal* graphic novel prequel, *Creation Myths*. He lives in Southern California.

NATALIA THEODORIDOU is a media and cultural studies scholar, a dramaturge, and a writer of strange stories. Her work has appeared in *Clarkesworld*, *The Kenyon Review Online*, *sub-Q*, *Interfictions*, and elsewhere. Find out more at her website (www.natalia-theodoridou.com), or come say hi @natalia_theodor on Twitter.

MARIA HASKINS is a Swedish-Canadian writer and translator. She writes speculative fiction and poetry, and debuted as a writer in Sweden in the far-off, mythological era known as the 1980s. Since 1992 she lives in Canada, and is currently located just outside Vancouver with a husband, two kids, and a very large black dog. Her English-language fiction has appeared in, or will be appearing in, *Flash Fiction Online, Gamut, Capricious*, and elsewhere. Find out more on her website: mariahaskins.wordpress.com, or follow her on Twitter: @MariaHaskins.

LUCIA IGLESIAS is a writer and au pair in Iceland. Though she grew up in California, she suspects she is a changeling and is still looking for her real home. She has adventured through 26 countries and worked as an archivist, assistant librarian, and English teacher. She is delighted to be part of the magic that is *Shimmer*.

OCTAVIA CADE has a PhD in science communication and loves writing about oceans and science history. She once backpacked around Europe with so much telescope in her pack there was hardly any room for clothes. Her stories have appeared in *Asimov's, Clarkesworld,* and *Apex*, and a poetry collection on the periodic table, *Chemical Letters*, has recently been nominated for an Elgin. Her latest novella—not about science at all!—is the highly disturbing *Convergence of Fairy Tales*, because when she's not messing about with seagrass or dead scientists she's having fun with all the horror she can get her hands on.

NARU DAMES SUNDAR is a writer of speculative fiction and poetry. His stories have appeared or are forthcoming at *Lightspeed, Strange Horizons*, and *PodCastle*. He lives among the redwoods of Northern California. You can find him online at shardofstar.info and on twitter at @naru_sundar.

Shimmer

Shimmer aspires to publish excellent fiction across lines of race, income, nationality, ethnicity, gender, sexual orientation, age, geography, and culture, and encourages submissions of diverse stories from diverse authors. This includes, but is not limited to: people of color, LBGTQIA, women, the impoverished, the elderly, and those with disabilities. We encourage authors of all backgrounds to write stories that include characters and settings as diverse and wondrous as the people and places of the world we live in. Every story sent to us should be well-researched, respectful, and conscientious.

Shimmer publishes every other month, and can be found online at www.shimmerzine.com. Subscribers allow us to keep doing what we do. $15 gets you six issues, delivered straight to your email inbox—or, that of a friend. *Shimmer* makes a perfect gift for the short fiction lover in your life!

Made in the USA
Las Vegas, NV
02 July 2021